A SINNERS SERIES BOOK

BRANDED

ABI KETNER & MISSY KALICICKI

Month9Books

BRANDED by Abi Ketner and Missy Kalicicki

Summary: A teenage girl is accused a crime she didn't commit, and is forced to live in the Hole, a place where all criminals are forced to endure inhuman horrors and all hope seems lost, until she falls in love with her captor, a crime punishable by death.

Published by Month9Books, LLC.
Cover and typography designed by Regina Wamba
Cover Copyright © 2014 Month9Books

Month9Books

Dedicated to

Abi: *My grandfather, Harold, my father, Keith, My husband, William*

Missy: *My father, Anthony, My husband, Kristofer, My sons, Brayden and Jacob*

Praise for BRANDED

"I haven't read a book this amazing in a long time. Better than Divergent and Hunger Games! This book has everything a dystopian series needs. Once I started reading, I couldn't put it down. I can't wait to see that happens next. I honestly think that this could be the next big movie series! If you loved Divergent and Hunger Games, you will love this even more."
– Stephanie Linden

"I've owned the book for many months now and I'm kicking myself for not reading it sooner it's that good." – Roberta

"Another great aspect of Branded was the world building. I've read a lot of dystopians over the last few years and I've never encountered one like this." – Lexie Reviews

"Branded is one of my favorite books I've read in 2014!"
– H.D.

"There were some tear-jerker moments. Some suspenseful moments and some swoon-worthy moments. Each and every one was essential to the story. It was such a great read and I had a very hard time putting it down." – Christy @ Captivating Reviews

A SINNERS SERIES BOOK

BRANDED

ABI KETNER & MISSY KALICICKI

CHAPTER 1

I'm buried six feet under, and no one hears my screams.

The rope chafes as I loop it around my neck. I pull down, making sure the knot is secure. It seems sturdy enough. My legs shake. My heart beats heavy in my throat. Sweat pours down my back.

Death and I glare at each other through my tears.

I take one last look at the crystal chandelier, the foyer outlined with mirrors, and the flawless decorations. No photographs adorn the walls. No happy memories here.

I'm ready to go. *On the count of three.*

I inhale, preparing myself for the finality of it all. Dropping my hands, a glimmer catches my eye. It's my ring, the last precious gift my father gave me. I twist it around to read the inscription. Picturing his face forces me to reconsider my choice. He'd be heartbroken if he could see me now.

A door slams in the hallway, almost causing me to lose my balance. My thoughts already muddled, I stand waiting with the rope hanging around my neck. Voices I don't recognize creep through the walls.

Curiosity overshadows my current thoughts. It's late at night, and this is a secure building in High Society. No one disturbs the peace here—ever. I tug on the noose and pull it back over my head.

Peering through the eyehole in our doorway, I see a large group of armed guards banging on my neighbors' door. A heated conversation ensues, and my neighbors point toward my family's home.

It hits me. I've been accused and they're here to arrest me.

My father would want me to run, and in that split second, I decide to listen to his voice within me. Flinging myself forward in fear, I scramble up the marble staircase and into my brother's old bedroom. The door is partially covered, but it exists. Pushing his dresser aside, my fingers claw at the opening. Breathing hard, I lodge myself against it. Nothing. I step back and kick it with all my strength. The wood splinters open, and my foot gets caught. I wrench it backward, scraping my calf, but adrenaline pushes me forward. The voices at the front door shout my name.

On hands and knees, I squeeze through the jagged opening. My brother left through this passage, and now it's my escape too. Cobwebs entangle my face, hands, and hair. At the end, I feel for the knob, twisting it clockwise. It swings open, creaking from disuse. I sprint into the hallway and smash through the large fire escape doors at the end. A burst of cool air strikes me in the face as I jump down the ladder.

Reaching the fifth floor, I knock on a friend's window. The lights flicker on, and I see the curtains move, but no one answers. I bang on the window harder.

"Let me in! Please!" I say, but the lights darken. They know I've been accused and refuse to help me. Fear and adrenaline rush through my veins as I keep running, knocking on more windows along the way. No one has mercy. They all know what happens to sinners.

Another flight of stairs passes in a blur when I hear the guards' heavy footfalls from above. I can't hide, but I don't want to go without trying.

Help me, Daddy. I need your strength now.

My previous desolation evolves into a will to survive. I have to keep running, but I tremble and gasp for air. I steel my nerves and force my body to keep moving. In a matter of minutes, my legs cramp and my chest burns. I plunge to the ground, scraping my knee and elbow. A moan escapes from my chest.

Gotta keep going.

"Stop!" Their voices bounce off the buildings. "Lexi Hamilton, surrender yourself," they command. They're gaining on me.

I resist the urge to glance back, running into what I assume is an alley. I'm far from our high-rise in High Society as I plunge into a poorer section of the city where the streets all look the same and the darkness prevents me from recognizing anything. I'm lost.

My first instinct is to leap into a dumpster, but I retain enough sense to stay still. I crouch and peek around it, watching them dash by. The abhorrent smell leaves me vomiting until nothing remains in my stomach. Desperation overtakes me, as I know my retching was anything but silent. My last few seconds tick away before they find me. Everyone knows about their special means of tracking sinners.

I push myself to my feet and look left, right, and left again. Their batons click against their black leather belts, and their boots stomp the cement on both sides of me. I shrink into myself. Their heavy steps mock my fear, growing closer and closer until I know I'm trapped.

Never did I imagine they'd come for me. Never did I imagine all those nights I heard them dragging someone else away that I'd join them.

"You're a sinner," they say. "Time to leave."

I stand defiant. I refuse to bend or break before them, even as I shiver with fear.

"There's no reason to make this difficult. The more you cooperate, the smoother this will be for everyone," a guard says.

I cringe into the blackness along the wall. I'm innocent, but they won't believe me or care.

The next instant, my face slams into the pavement as one guard plants a knee in my back and another handcuffs me. A warm liquid trails into my mouth. Blood. Their fingers grip my arms like steel traps as they peel me off the cement. The tops of my shoes scrape along the ground as I'm dragged behind them until they discard me into the back of a black vehicle. The doors slam in unison with one guard stationed on each side of me, my shoulders digging into their arms.

Swallowing hard, I stare ahead to avoid their eyes. My dignity is all I have left. The handcuffs dig into my wrists, so

I clasp them together hard behind me and press my back into the seat, unwilling to admit how much it hurts.

Did they need so many guards to capture me?

I'm not carrying any weapons, nor do I own any. I don't even know self-defense. High Society frowns on activities like that.

The driver jerks the vehicle around, and I try to keep my bearings, but it's dark and the scenery changes too fast. Hours pass, and the air grows warmer, more humid the farther we drive. The landscape mutates from city to rolling hills. They don't bother blindfolding me because they escort all the sinners to the same place—the Hole. Twenty-foot cement walls encase the chaos within. There's no way out and no way in unless they transport you. They say the Hole is a prison with no rules. We learned about it last year in twelfth grade.

To the outside, I'm filth now. I'll never be allowed to return to the life I knew. No one ever does.

"All sinners go through a transformation," one of the guards says to me. His smirk infuriates me. "I'm sure you've heard all kinds of stories." I don't respond. I don't want to think about the things I've been told.

"You won't last too long, though. Young girls like you get eaten alive." He pulls a strand of my hair up to his face.

Get your hands off me, you pig. I want to lash out, but resist. The punishment for disobeying authority is severe, and I'm not positioned to defy him.

They're the Guards of the Commander. They're chosen from a young age and trained in combat. They keep the order of society by using violent methods of intimidation. No one befriends a guard. Relationships with them are forbidden inside the Hole.

Few have seen the Commander. His identity remains hidden. His own paranoia and desire to stay pure drove him to live this way. He controls our depraved society and believes sinners make the human race unforgivable. His power is a crushing fist, rendering all beneath him helpless. So much so, even family members turn on each other when an accusation surfaces. Just an accusation. No trial, no evidence, nothing but an accusation.

I lose myself in thoughts of my father.

"Never show fear, Lexi," my father said to me before he was taken. "They'll use it against you." His compassionate eyes filled with warning as he commanded me to be strong. That was many years ago, but I remember it clearly. My father. My rock. The one person in my life who provided unconditional love.

"Get out," the guard says while pulling me to my feet. The vehicle stops, and I'm jerked back to reality. The doors slide open and the two guards lift me up and out into the night. A windowless cement building looms in front of us, looking barren in the darkness.

The coolness of the air sends a shiver up my spine. This is really happening. I've been labeled a sinner. My lip starts to quiver, but I bite it before anyone sees. They shove me in line, and I realize I'm not alone. Women and men stand with faces frozen white with fear. Some are hardened criminals; others, like me, are innocent. A guard grabs my finger, pricks it, and dabs my blood on a tiny microchip.

I follow the man in front of me into the next room where we're lined up facing the wall. Glancing right, I see one of the men crying.

"I didn't mean to hit the guard. I swear it!" he pleads.

I turn my head when I see a guard whip out his baton. The thumping sounds of his beating unnerve me.

"Spread your legs," one of the guards says icily.

They remove my outer layers and their hands roam up and down my body.

What do they think I can possibly be hiding? I press my head into the wall, trying to block out what they're doing to me.

"MOVE!" a guard commands. So I shuffle across the room, trying to cover up.

One.

Two.

Three.

Four.

Five of us sit in the holding room. A woman clings to a man sitting next to her. She grips his arm and I can see the whitening of her knuckles. Her eyes meet mine and then she quickly turns away. He's bent over his hands, defeated.

"I'm not the criminal they say I am," he whispers. His voice breaks.

One by one, they pull people into the next room, forcing the rest of us to wonder what torture we'll endure. I hear screaming from somewhere inside. An agonizing amount of time passes. I lean my head back and try to imagine a place far away. The door opens.

"Lexi Hamilton."

A guard escorts me out of the room, and I don't have time to look back. The first thing I see is a large photo of a regal-looking man on the wall. His frame is wide and he has cobalt blue eyes and a shock of black hair. He's handsome, middle-aged, and wears the uniform of the Commander. My jaw drops open. *It can't be...*

Then the door slams closed. Strong arms pick me up and place me on a table. It's cold and my skin sticks to it slightly, like wet fingers on an ice cube. They exit in procession, and I lie on the table with a doctor standing over me. His hands are busy as he speaks.

"Don't move. This will only take a few minutes. It's time for you to be branded."

A wet cloth that smells like rubbing alcohol is used to clean my skin. Then he places a metal collar around my neck. *Click. Click. Click.*

The collar locks into place, and I struggle to breathe. The doctor loosens it some as I focus on the painted black words above me.

THE SEVEN DEADLY SINS:

LUST — BLUE
GLUTTONY — ORANGE
GREED — YELLOW
SLOTH — BLACK
WRATH — RED
ENVY — GREEN
PRIDE — PURPLE

"Memorize it. Might keep you alive longer if you know who to stay away from." He opens my mouth, placing a bit inside. "Bite this."

Within seconds, the collar heats from hot to scorching. The smell of flesh sizzling makes my head spin. I bite down so hard a tooth cracks.

"GRRRRRRRRR," escapes from deep within my chest. Just when I'm about to pass out, the temperature drops, and the doctor loosens the collar.

He removes it and sits me up. Excruciating pain rips through me, and I'm on the verge of a mental and physical breakdown. *Focus. Don't pass out.*

Stainless steel counters and boring white walls press in on me. And that large, gilded photo stares at me like it's watching. A guard laughs at me from an observation room above and yells, "Blue. It's a great color for a pretty young thing like yourself." His eyes dance with suggestion. The others meander around like it's business as usual.

I finally find my voice and turn to the doctor.

"Are you going to give me clothes?" A burning pain spreads like fire up from my neck to my jaw, making me wince.

He shrugs and points to a set of folded grey scrubs on a chair. I cover myself as much as I can and scurry sideways. Grabbing my clothes and pulling the shirt over my head, I try to avoid the raw meat around my throat. I quickly knot the cord of my pants around my waist and slide my feet into the hospital-issue slippers as the doctor observes. He hands me a bag labeled with my name.

"Nothing is allowed through the door but what we've given you," he says.

I hide my right hand behind me, hoping no one notices. A guard scans my body and opens his fist.

"Give it to me." His eyes turn to slits. "Don't make me rip off your finger." He crouches down and I turn to stone. I don't know what to do, so I beg.

"My father gave this to me. Please, let me keep it." I smash my eyes shut and think of the moment my father handed the golden ring to me.

"It was my mother's ring," he'd said. "She's the strongest woman I ever knew." With tears in his eyes, he reached for my hand and said, "Lexi, you're exactly like her. She'd want you to wear this. No matter how this world changes, you can survive." I turned the gold band over in my palm and read the engraving.

YOU CAN OVERCOME ANYTHING...SHORT OF DEATH.

"You're going to take the one thing that matters the most to me?" I say, glaring into the guard's emotionless eyes. "Isn't it enough taking my life, dignity, and respect?"

A hard blow falls upon my back. As I fall, my hands shoot out to stop me from smashing into the wall in front of me. The guard bends down and grabs my chin with his meaty fist.

"Look at me," he commands. I look up and he smiles with arrogance.

"What the hell?" He staggers a step backward. "What's wrong with you? What's wrong with your eyes?"

"Nothing," I respond, confused.

"What color are they?"

"Turquoise." I glower at him.

"Interesting," he says, regaining his composure. "Now those'll get you in trouble."

Reality slaps me across the face. I have my father's eyes. They can't take them from me. I twist the ring off my finger and drop it in his hand.

"Take the damn ring," I say. I walk to the door. He swipes a card and the massive door slides open to the outside.

"You have to wear your hair back at all times, so everyone knows what you are." He hands me a tie, so I pull my frizzy hair away from my face and secure it into a ponytail. My neck burns and itches as my hand traces the scabs that have already begun to form. Squinting ahead in the darkness, I almost run into a guard standing on the sidewalk.

"Watch where you're going," he says, shoving me backward. His stiff figure stands tall, and I cringe at the sharpness of his voice.

"Cole, this is your new assignment, Lexi Hamilton. See to it she feels welcome in her new home." The guard departs with a salute.

"Let's move," Cole says.

I take two steps and collapse, my knees giving out. The unforgiving pavement reopens the scrapes from earlier and I struggle to stand. A powerful arm snatches me up, and I see his face for the first time.

CHAPTER 2

Our eyes meet. I get lost in a pool of darkness, unable to distinguish where his pupils begin and where they end. I notice a thin scar that runs through the right corner of his upper lip. I wonder how he got it. His brown hair, shaved close to his head, is faded at the top in a military-style cut. The angular shape of his face becomes more pronounced when he clenches his jaw. For a moment we're both still, looking at each other.

He gives me a pained look. "Get in the Jeep," he says with a flat tone.

Oh sure.

My hands are slick with sweat, unable to hold on to the handle, and I stumble backward, landing on a rock that sends shooting pains up my back. I grit my teeth and push up. I hear an irritated exhalation as Cole opens the door. He grabs my waist, and I lunge forward, smacking my head into the door.

He laughs, revealing his dimples, and says, "I would've thought you'd be used to being touched."

Jerk, you know nothing about me.

I don't entertain his remark as he lifts me inside the Jeep. He pushes my legs out of the way before slamming the door shut. I reach up, grab the seatbelt, pull it across my body, and click it into place. I tug hard to make sure it's secure. The thick fabric doesn't budge, but that doesn't alleviate my fears of falling out.

Cole doesn't buckle up; he slams his foot down on the gas, causing the Jeep to bolt forward. My head snaps back into the headrest, aggravating my neck even more. Turning onto the main road, the breeze whips my hair around and I let it carry my mind with it. My world has completely changed...

Back home, the upper class basks in wealth and their lifestyle is gluttonous with parties and all the trappings that come along with money. Snobbery abounds. You'd think since their lifestyle reeks of lavishness, they'd end up accused, but I've been told they pay off the guards to escape judgment—*the hypocrites*. I snort just thinking about it.

Outside of High Society, people scrape by. Our country isn't as wealthy as it was before the Commander, or so I've been told. The western portion of the country was bombed out during the last war. Between the epidemics of disease, the wiping out of major infrastructure, and the lack of jobs, most people left the west for the security of High Society. At the time, we lived in a small town in the Mid-West that somehow survived the years of violence, famine, and government transition. While we tasted some of the changes, we were largely left alone after the Commander came to power. The media always painted a rosy picture of what was happening, but in truth, the Commander wasn't how the people imagined him. Since the news, both television and paper, were so tightly controlled, my father was our only window of truth. He was the one who explained, in secret, about what the Hole really was. That there was only one Hole, for all sinners. He was the one who sat us children down and whispered some of the atrocities that the Commander and the guards were really committing. He retained connections that kept him updated, but one by one those people disappeared as well. He took a chance and lost. Most people wouldn't even do that. Only after he passed, did my mother meet my stepfather and move to High Society. I breathe deep and close my eyes. It was when we moved into the city that I witnessed the most amount of branded sinners that I've ever seen. I saw what my father tried to tell us, and it terrified me. Looking at me, you'd never know I lived in High Society. I'm thin, much too thin. *But not by choice. I was never given a choice, and it seems I may never have the opportunity to choose anything else in my life.*

Only sinners grind away doing the cleaning, bidding, and serving. They're transported out of the Hole by train to work each day, but High Society members are too afraid to associate with them, even if they once knew each other. Even commoners, those that aren't sinners or High Society, refuse to acknowledge them. Instantly, they become strangers.

The guards prove the exception and do whatever they please. They make the arrests, enforce their laws, and even dictate education. In High Society, most people were oblivious to the real gritty stuff. But right outside the perimeter, regular citizens lived in poverty. They keep to themselves mostly. Even being poor was better than being branded. I once heard my father whispering to a friend about it over a cup of coffee at the kitchen table. His hushed words come back like a nightmare now. If only I could remember everything I'd heard that day.

"There've been rumors of mass rapes and beatings," his friend said. "Keep your children inside. It's not safe out there anymore."

"I know, and I'm afraid it's only going to get worse. Yet somehow, they manage to cover up most of it. I'm not sure we'll ever know the full magnitude," my father replied. I remember peering around the corner from the staircase to listen and pinching my nose to hold back a sneeze.

"Have you heard anything about lab testing—?"

"Shhh, that's enough. We need to take this conversation somewhere else." Their chairs scraped on the tile floor, so I tiptoed up the staircase before they spotted me.

I always took for granted that my father would be there to protect me. Now, I'm seated in the Jeep with the enemy he tried so hard to shield me from.

Cole keeps his eyes on the road and rubs the back of his neck. He joins a procession of vehicles from the transformation center, escorting new prisoners to the Hole. Roadblocks occur every few miles and he flashes his identification each time. I'm scared to look at him, yet I find myself glancing in his direction more often than I'd like. His sharp jaw line and intense expression never falter as he grips the steering wheel. It's as if he's expecting trouble ahead. I don't know why, but his close proximity makes me self-conscious.

Part of me desires strength to deal with my present situation; the other half wants to collapse from mental overload and exhaustion. I give in to the latter.

I close my eyes and daydream. I bring myself back to my father, to the tall grass fields out west, to times of love and laughter, and in my dream I'm okay.

"Wake up!" my father says, but I realize it isn't his voice. A hand shakes me awake, and I open my eyes as Cole turns in his seat.

Holy crap. I did fall asleep.

"We're here," he says. "I must admit, I've never seen a sinner sleep during their transport before." He gives me a scowl.

"I wasn't actually sleeping, more like daydreaming with my eyes closed." I lie because I don't want him to know the truth. When I feel overwhelmed, I tend to fall asleep, as if my mind is trying to keep me from exploding.

"I don't recall asking you to respond," he says.

I shake my head and rub my bleary eyes. Before me looms a twenty-foot cement wall ominously rising from the earth. Barbed wire wraps around the top like a snake. There's no green, just a thick cloud of dust kicked up from the tires of passing vehicles. A colossal protrusion from the wall grabs my attention.

"What's that?" I ask, pointing to the immense structure.

"That…is none of your concern," he says, stopping the Jeep. We're at another checkpoint, and Cole flashes his ID. A young guard standing at the gate inspects it and then looks at me. He grins.

"She new?" he says with a smirk. "Damn, man. Why can't I have your job?"

"Yeah," Cole snaps. "Now, open the gate."

"I'll switch with you." He winks at Cole and then looks at me. "Good luck, sweetheart. You'll need it."

"Dammit, just open the gate."

He pushes some buttons that open the massive metal gate, and we follow the others through. It closes with a screech, thud, and a distinct locking sound.

Cole parks the jeep into an open space alongside other

vehicles carrying newly branded sinners.

"One more stop before you see your new home," he says. "Orientation."

I climb down and my joints crack, feeling achy from sitting so long. My hand unintentionally goes to my neck. *It's still there and it's not going away.* The brand radiates burning heat, permanently labeling me a whore. I drop my eyes to the dusty ground, feeling ashamed even though I know it's not true. *But they think it is.*

He gives me a quick shove in the direction of the door where I see others with bowed heads and new brands brightly singed into their skin. I imagine that we look like one sad convoy of losers filing into a small, dirty room. The fluorescent lighting flickers and there's standing room only. One large portrait hangs on the opposite wall. It's the same image from the Transformation Center. The eyes bore into me, and I turn my face away. Cole leans against the wall with the other guards, observing us carefully while we squeeze into the room like cattle.

A large screen mounted on the wall to my left flips on automatically as the lights go out. A female voice, powerful yet sweet, begins giving the history of the Hole.

"Fifty years ago, after World War V, society was downtrodden from years of fighting. Bombs destroyed highly populated areas leaving the former United States with high crime, unemployment, and depravity." Black and white images of the last war pop onto the screen—people running as explosions burst in the background. Children screaming. Bodies lying unattended in the streets of war torn neighborhoods that once flourished. "Then our Commander, our Savior, and Leader came to power." The screen flips to a photo of the Commander, wearing a black mask to protect his identity. "After witnessing decades of crime, he saved us from our sins—revamping our judicial system and creating jobs for all. Bringing peace and security to our country once again."

More like demolished our judicial system, I think. I barely remember my father talking about the war before the Commander. Most of my recollections are of my father cautioning me on being careful on what I say to others to avoid being accused.

Rough footage of the Hole being built by sinners pops onto the screen and breaks into my thoughts. "He created a system by which we would know, forevermore, who the criminals in society are, thereby protecting us from their crimes. By keeping all the criminals confined to the Hole, our society would remain pure and uncorrupted."

To my surprise, the video shows a state funeral with mourners dressed in dark clothing, parading through High Society. "After our dear Commander passed, his protégé, handpicked and trained, rose up to carry on our beloved traditions. We owe him our allegiance, our thanks, and our praise for saving us."

Once again, the image of the man with dark hair and blue eyes flashes on screen. He smiles, but it looks stretched. *Could this be the Commander? He looks so fake.* The propaganda video ends as static charges across the screen. Not a word is said among all of us while we wait. The guards straighten up as the lights come back on, dimly flickering as one guard stands in front of the room. He barely glances at us as he reads from a paper in his hands.

"You're all here because you've been accused of crimes and branded as criminals of the state. The Commander has ultimate power over all things. From here on, you have no rights. Each sinner will be assigned a job upon arriving to your quarters and you will report to your jobs daily as commanded. The siren is your warning to report immediately to your bus. Busses will transport you to the trains at the main gate. Do not miss your bus unless you're dead. You will obey all laws in the Hole. There is a hospital, but you may only seek treatment for your health if approved by a guard or if it is detrimental to the health of the guards. One guard will escort you to your new quarters and *most* of you," he says while glancing at me briefly, "will be on your own afterward. No questions allowed."

Fear catches in my throat. *I'm no longer considered human.*

My guard, Cole, pulls my elbow and leads me out of the dingy room into the hot bright light. He practically shoves me into my seat before sliding into his. I squint and bring my hand up over them as they adjust.

Nothing could've prepared me for what lies ahead. Along the main road, people sit in squalor, begging as each vehicle passes. Eyes mixed with hopelessness and despair meet mine. Children run in dirty, tattered clothing, chasing each other while women yell at them to go inside. Two men beat a woman in the shadows of a side street while guards stand watch with their hands in their pockets. *Why aren't they stopping it?*

The smell of sewage pierces my senses as dirt swirls in the air. The landscape never deviates the farther we travel. One block, two blocks, three blocks pass as the immensity of the Hole begins to choke me. Terror creeps into my chest, making it almost impossible to breathe.

"Hang on," Cole says, tapping the roll bar. "If you fall out, they'll kill you."

I give him a questioning look, but obey out of fear. The roads narrow, and gradually, crowds of people spill out from every crevice available. They rush the vehicles in the convoy, begging for food, water, and anything of worth to trade. Someone grabs my arm, screaming into my face.

"Slut!" Her fingers tear at my hair, my clothes, and my body. I grab her wrists and send her backward into the fray.

"I bet she didn't see that one coming," Cole says.

"I want you!" a man shouts. "Come here!" He clings to the back of the Jeep.

The crush of people suffocates me, and I franticly fight off their hands. "Don't touch me! Don't you dare touch me," I yell before shoving a scrawny man off my leg. The massive crowd slows our speed until we're almost at a complete stop. All the vehicles in front of us slow as they're swarmed with sinners. I feel my heart slamming in my chest, my blood rushing through my ears. *Oh my God, I'm going to die!*

"Grab her!" someone shouts.

"She's mine!" a dirty-faced man with multiple tattoos

bellows and clambers onto the bumper. I stand, holding on to the roll bar, and kick him in the chest, knocking him off the Jeep into the swarm of dingy colors surrounding us. They grab my ankles, scraping my skin, and start pulling me off. I begin to scream.

Cole slams the Jeep in park, stands up with his gun in hand, and indiscriminately fires at them to scare them off. Splashes of red explode across my vision, but everything within me fights to stay on the vehicle. I wipe off my face with my sleeve, look down, and see chunks of flesh hanging on my arm.

"Ahhhhhhh," I shriek. "Get it off me." I wave my arms wildly but can't dislodge them all.

I grab the bar again, but my hands and arms drip with sweat. I feel my hands slip. "I can't hold on much longer!"

He clenches his jaw and grabs onto my shirt. *Like that'll help.* Just then, all hell erupts as multiple guns open fire. Bullets ricochet off the walls to our left and right, chipping them and sending people for cover. The guards on the rooftops fire without restraint. Screams and shouts echo throughout the street, and bloodied bodies lie alongside our Jeep.

"Get down," Cole orders, shoving me to the floor. I cover my head with my arms, shaking uncontrollably with fright. All the while, Cole doesn't flinch. He sits back in his driver's seat and steps on the accelerator, rolling over the dead people in the street. The crunching of bones and constant thumping of the vehicle over their bodies turns my stomach and the acid burns my throat.

"Don't move," he says. "We're almost there."

In my shocked state, I follow his orders without question. My hands tremble from adrenaline and my throat stings from screaming. I feel their grimy handprints all over me. Their miserable, desperate faces encroach upon my thoughts as I relive the horror of their hatred.

They think I'm just a whore...not a real person.

Turning into a side garage, Cole turns off the engine, but I'm too traumatized to get out when he opens the door. Instead, I lean over and throw up. He steps back before I splatter his boots and waits for me to finish before dragging me out.

"Follow me. Don't run. Don't talk," he orders. The sour taste in my mouth and shear disgust paralyzes my vocal cords, so I nod in reply.

Then I puke again.

I move one foot in front of the other, slogging along. My feet feel like weights attached to my ankles. I just want to break down and cry, but now is obviously not the time, and there are too many things to cry about. I wouldn't know where to start.

Not too long ago I wanted to end my life…and now I'm fighting to survive. *Why?* Maybe it's pride. *Purple and blue would go well together.* Then it hits me.

"Because this wasn't my choice," I say out loud.

Cole whips his head around. "I told you not to talk."

"I didn't mean—"

"Shut up!"

So I do.

Graffiti marks the walls of the garage with words I wouldn't dare say at home. The bold colors stand out, stark against the muted gray everywhere else.

Clouds of dust follow each step and I hop to avoid the broken glass strewn along the street because with one misstep, the glass would go right through my shoe and pierce my foot. Tall, worn-down buildings made of cement blocks line every road. Cole checks on my progress, only to move faster. He shows no signs of pity or emotion about having to shoot those people earlier. And yet, he's not outright mean to me, either. I have no doubt what some other guards would've done in his situation. Just the thought makes me swallow hard around the lump in my throat.

We come to an intersection. I turn my head to the right, and men with no shirts lick me up and down with their eyes like I'm a fillet, ready to eat. To my left, brightly painted and scantily clad women summon Cole. They clap as I walk past.

"You got any diseases?" they ask me. I ignore them, keeping my eyes forward. "How many have you screwed?" The women sneer. They laugh at my obvious discomfort.

I trip over an empty bottle, but Cole grabs me before I fall. His touch refocuses me.

"Watch where you're going," he says while glancing at me. "Look straight ahead and don't pay attention to them."

I wish I could be so confident.

A massive building with a clean facade appears through the dusty cloud in front of us. It towers over the other buildings, making it an easy landmark. Vehicles pull through a checkpoint in the back. Small groups of people loiter outside, smoking and talking. It's almost normal, except for the armed men in black mounted on the rooftops.

"Over there's the hospital, where you'll be working." He points to the building ahead. "All sinners are mandated to work. I'll escort you there and back. This isn't the real world. You never miss a day of work unless you're on your deathbed, understood?" He glares at me.

"Yes. I understand," I whisper.

We walk for what feels like eternity and my feet throb. I'm not sure I can make it much farther. *Stupid slippers. What I'd give to have my sneakers back.* I gaze upward, and the bright azure sky makes a striking comparison to life below. I didn't know conditions like this existed.

"See the building over there?" he says as he runs his hand over his head to wipe away the sweat. "That's your new home."

He opens a door in a fence interlaced with barbed wire. People lounge around outside, staring as he leads me in. The citizens outside the building look fairly normal despite their brandings, but I'm still wary of looking at them too long. They banter with each other while negotiating over a bag of what looks like trash. *Maybe they're innocent like me—just normal people trying to survive.*

Cigarette smoke burns my eyes. Squinting, I follow Cole through the courtyard and into the building.

Yellow paint chips off the rough-textured wall. It smells like mold, mildew, and stinky feet. A dead body lies propped against the wall inside the doorway. The man's clothing hangs in tatters, and the bright red tattoo on his neck sags from years of malnutrition. My hand moves to cover my nose and mouth as I gurgle on bile. Before I can look away, a maggot squirms out of his nose.

"Oh my—"

"Get used to it." Cole shrugs his shoulder.

I'll never get used to that.

He cracks his knuckles and keeps walking. I'm pretty sure I hit my threshold for gore and my stomach lurches.

The walls, floors, and ceilings are black except for a few remaining yellow splotches. Cole flips on a flashlight and the dim light focuses briefly on a rat as it crawls across our path. I clench my jaw and feel ahead with my hands, guessing where to step next.

"Why is it dark?" I ask.

"Shhhh."

I hate the dark.

The doors are numbered, but completely out of order. My breaths echo in the hallway and I feel like a glass vase falling to the concrete floor about to shatter.

One.

Two.

Three flights.

One.

Two doors to the right #91116.

Cole unlocks the door, which creaks on its hinges, and gestures me to follow. The darkness prompts him to tug on the delicate chain in the center of the cell. The light intermittently reveals the stacked cinder-block walls that make up my small room. I lean against the door to catch my breath when a spider drops in front of my face, forcing a blood-curdling scream from my lungs.

He slaps his hand over my mouth. "Stop it! Just because you're behind a locked door doesn't mean you're safe." He pulls his hand away and lowers it to his side.

I nod, fearful of his touch, but more afraid of my new neighbors. He steps back, and smashes the spider between his hands.

Breathe, just breathe.

The musty smell makes me cough.

A thin mattress lies in the right corner, nearest to me, but no other furniture exists. A surveillance camera is mounted next to a metal doorway. Rodent droppings line the wall along the left side, and just the thought of their feet skittering over me at night gives me chills. Waves of heat roll over my body and I teeter, accidentally touching the filthy wall. I pull my hand away to discover a thick layer of grime. *What have you done to me, Mom?*

"That's your bathroom," he says, pointing at the curtain alongside the back right corner. I pull it aside and find a cracked porcelain toilet with a matching sink. The rusted showerhead dangles from the wall, framed in black mold.

Perfect, I can shower and use the restroom at the same time.

"Really, the Commander shouldn't have been so generous." Bitterness drips from my laugh. I know I shouldn't mock anything right now, especially in his company, but I feel so overwhelmed I've lost the ability to be rational. Cole remains quiet, but something like mischief plays in his eyes.

"Are you hungry?" He sounds concerned, but maybe my mind is beginning to play tricks on me.

"No, not at all."

"You eat when food's offered. The sinners out there have to scrounge for it. Consider yourself lucky," he says as he crosses the room.

"I'm far from lucky." I collapse on the scrawny mattress and let my hair explode out of my ponytail. My body aches. I pull my pant legs up to inspect the scrapes while kicking off the thin slippers. "You can leave now." My fingers scratch at the dry blood and then I lie back on my mattress.

"That's not gonna happen. For the next forty-eight hours you're on suicide watch."

He's too close to me, so I sit upright. "What?"

"You're not to be left alone," he says. He tugs at the collar on his shirt.

"As if coming here isn't bad enough. I'm already on the camera, so what difference does it make? Why do they care if I die?" I say directly into the camera.

He throws his bag into the corner of the room and takes off his boots.

"The hell if I know, nor do I care. But don't worry. I have no desire to touch a filthy girl like yourself." He stands across from me with his arms folded over his chest. I really wish I had something to throw at him.

"What I'd really like is a shower. Can you at least leave me alone for that?"

"No," he says. "Orders are orders."

Man, this guy is full of himself. They're purposely torturing me.

He opens the metal door on the right side of my quarters to an adjoining room. He flicks on two lights casting their brightness into my space. I lean forward from my mattress and attempt to peek inside, but he leaves the door cracked only a few inches. It looks very simple, but much cleaner than my quarters.

"Whose room is that?" I ask.

"Mine." He looks around the corner at me. My discomfort hits an all-time high.

You have got to be kidding me. Now, this crosses the line. Placing my head in my hands, I shake with disbelief.

"You got a problem with that?" he asks. His lips pinch together.

I give him a skeptical look. "No."

"Be thankful you aren't on the street where you belong," he says. His harsh tone sends prickles up my spine.

He thinks I'm a whore, too.

As I wallow in pity, I notice a stray ribbon of sunlight peeking through a window next to the bathroom in my room. Eager for natural light and wanting to see outside, I pull the dusty blinds away and use my forearm to clear a small circle in the filth. From here, I can see people loitering around the building and women standing on the corner two blocks down.

"Are the women on the corner prostitutes?" I read about it before, but never thought it existed until I arrived.

"Yeah, that's their job." He picks at a fingernail, standing in the doorway with the door cracked, like it's not a big deal.

"That's terrible. Do they get paid?"

"In a way. You're lucky you weren't chosen for that detail."

"I'm not sure luck exists here." I push away from the window. My body trembles from all the emotions of the today, and I need rest.

"Tomorrow we'll go over all the details and I'll show you around," he says. "You should clean up and try to rest."

I nod, unable to speak.

At his suggestion, I venture over to my metal sink. I pull the dirty curtain aside and turn on the faucet. After a high-pitched screeching noise that sounds like fingernails on a chalkboard, cold water spills out, and it's the best feeling I've had in days. I splash my face, my cuts, my neck and then furiously wash my arms.

I glance at the small, cracked mirror mounted above the sink and see a stranger. My hair flies around in an untamed mess, and the soot from the street makes my face unrecognizable except for the turquoise of my eyes. Blood and dirt form a thick paste on my skin, so I scrub it raw. When finished, I wipe my hands on my clothes. I turn and catch Cole watching.

I snap my head back around as fear pulses through me with the weight of his dark eyes on me. Any moment, he could try to take advantage of the situation, so I tread carefully.

"I'm not going to kill myself." I raise my hands, palms facing him, as if claiming innocence. Cole shakes his head, puts his hands in his pockets, and remains where he is.

"Don't you have a wife, girlfriend, or someone to go home to?" I ask, trying to make light conversation.

"That's none of your business." He raises his eyebrow. "Don't try to get to know me."

"I'm not. It was just a question," I say. I watch him for a response, but he says nothing. I should know the hardest and most proficient guards work in here. I can't imagine working here and not becoming desensitized to the violence.

I hope I never become like that.

A muffled whine escapes Cole's room and a bewildered expression crosses his face as we lock eyes.

"Who's in your room?"

"No one." He slams the door closed behind him. Sensing irritability on his part, I let the subject drop. I lie down on the mattress, curling into a ball. He fidgets in my room, fumbles for the door, and leaves it ajar. I'm pretending to be asleep when he leaves.

My eyes fill with tears as soon as he turns out the light. I can barely believe that just a day ago, I was free. I let out a small whimper. *Mom, did you know where you were sending me?* I can feel my chin trembling as the sobs build in my core. *She should be the one comforting me, yet she's the one who sent me here. What kind of mother does that to her own child?* I swallow hard, but can't force down the feelings of betrayal and hurt. Things were never the same after Dad passed away. Things will never be the same, ever again. I force my eyes shut, knowing I need rest. But I know I won't sleep tonight.

* * *

I must've passed out at some point because when I wake, I'm on my stomach and my neck cramps from the lack of a pillow. So I readjust, turning my face to the other side. A warm breath hits my face, tickling my nose.

I freeze.

Clinking of metal inches from my face, followed by the scraping of nails on the wall causes me to panic. Thinking it might be a rat, I sit up in a flash and try swatting it away. But it's bigger and doesn't move.

My heart pounds and I'm unsure what to do.

It can't be Cole.

I'm crawling in my skin as I reach around, feeling for anything I can use to protect myself. Nothing, of course...I have nothing.

"HELP!"

The very instant I scream, the beast starts to howl.

"Zeus, shut up," Cole yells as he crashes into my room. He flicks on the light, and that's when I completely lose it.

CHAPTER 3

Jumping back in the corner, I yank my legs in and squeeze them tight to my chest. I try to suck in air, but my lungs won't expand. My eyes blink rapidly. The monster stops howling and looks at me with his big brown eyes. His pointed ears stand at attention, and his sharp teeth shine in the dim moonlight.

"Zeus, what the hell's your problem?" Cole yells. "I told you not to leave my room, you—ah, whatever." He grabs the silver chain around Zeus's neck and pulls him off my mat. The creature's claws scrape along the floor as Cole drags him back. "Sit! And stay there before I kill you." Cole leans down and snaps his fingers before my frozen eyes, but it's no use. All I see are razor-sharp teeth protruding from its mouth and white foam dripping to the floor.

It's going to eat me. I'm sure of it.

"Meet Zeus, my crap-for-brains guard dog." He smacks the so-called dog across his head. Zeus snaps at his hand, but Cole's quick reflexes prevent him from biting anything but air. "He only obeys me, so I strongly suggest you don't try to pull anything stupid. Like make him attack me. It won't work."

Then why tell me?

I examine Zeus with cautious eyes, unsure what to think of him. "I've never seen a horse, I mean, a dog with—"

"He's Great Dane." He snaps at me, and then flicks the light on. "Stay seated."

Is he talking to the dog or me?

Zeus has a fawn coat with a black mask, eye rims, and eyebrows. He reminds me of a miniature horse. He turns toward me, licks my face, and looks down as he pushes his forehead to mine. I hold my breath. He tasted me and now I wait for him to eat me. He growls.

"Zeus, I think she gets the point. You're a badass. Now go

lay down," Cole says.

My filthy floor disgusts even the dog because he takes one glance, moves a foot, and slips. Then he slowly makes his way back toward Cole's room.

I need to get his slobber off my face... "I have to use the bathroom," I say.

"So go. I don't need a play-by-play," Cole says with a yawn.

I stumble to my bathroom. I see my ashen face in the mirror and know it's impossible to hide my terror. I wash it fast and attempt to use the restroom. No toilet paper hangs on the roll.

Good thing I only have to pee.

I pull up my pants, tie them in place, and yank open the curtain to find Cole leaning against the wall, almost asleep. His usual stern expression melts away as he nods forward and catches himself. Blinking back sleep, he looks around, eyes me, and retires back to his room, shutting the door completely this time.

I lie back down on my mattress, breathing deeply to calm myself and then curl up like a kitten. The heavy fingers of rest push my eyelids down only to be interrupted by an unfamiliar voice. Half asleep, I think the voice comes from within my dream, but when it repeats itself, I startle to consciousness.

"Skank! We know you're in there," says a screechy voice.

"Slut! Open the door," says a second voice. "We've been dreaming about touching you all night. We promise we'll we gentle." They laugh.

"Speak for yourself," another voice says.

I sit up, my heart pounding against my chest, and I press my back against the wall. Do I sit tight or call Cole? Their hands fiddle with the door, and I swallow hard, trying to decide what to do.

"I'm gonna ride you till the sun comes—"

"Leave!" Cole's voice demands from the other side of my door. "Now."

The men chuckle. "Oh, I almost forgot," the deep voice says with sarcasm. "The guards get first lay...damn, she must be number—"

"Get out of here! Before I smash in your skulls," Cole says. "Or maybe, I'll just shoot your asses."

"All right...chill...man. Just be sure to let us know when she's back on the market." Their laughter fades away. "That body of hers is making us crazy."

The door opens from the main hallway, and I shrink into the shadows, but instead of strangers, Cole walks in. He gives me a tired look of annoyance as he places a small paper bag onto my windowsill.

"Out of all the sins, you had to go and pick lust?"

His question irritates me. I have to swallow the dry lump in my throat before I can answer. "You don't know anything," I say.

"Well, then, enlighten me." He shoves his hands into his pockets and cocks his head. "If I'm supposed to keep these lunatics off you, then I deserve an answer."

"Why? No matter what I say you won't believe me. When you look at me...like everyone else, you see nothing but my brand. The Commander labeled me a whore, so that must make me one. Right?"

His eyes dart to the floor and he ignores my question. "So, what happened to you?" His question catches me off balance and the muscles in my neck tighten. I wrap my arms around myself, waiting for the darkness.

I'm in a closet. Waiting, waiting, waiting. What I'm waiting for is always the unknown. The sharp stab in the pit of my stomach causes me to double over. I feel his presence. I hear his breathing. I want to run, but there's nowhere to go. I want to scream, but no one can hear me.

And there's my mother, standing in her sequined dress, decorated in that gaudy jewelry he bought her. She's jealous of me for some warped reason. I'd give anything to change the past—to be free of this pain. I never wanted to be the focus of my stepfather's attention—his adoration. I've done nothing wrong, but my mother doesn't see it that way. She wants me dead. He wants me alive so he can control me.

"Snap out of it!" Cole's voice brings me back. My hands shake as I rub my eyes and crawl onto my mattress. "Geez, I only asked what happened to you. There's no need to go all psycho on me."

I clear my throat. "You wouldn't believe me if I told you," I say. "I'll never tell anyone, especially you."

Cole stares at me with a knowing look and raises his eyebrow. "Let me see if I can remember… My report says you were caught having premarital sex and your so-called partner jumped out of your window. And you refused to turn him in." His voice sounds inquisitive. "Leaving you the only one to brand."

"Believe what you want," I say with a shaky voice. I've never been good at masking my emotions, although I try really hard.

"What? You're not gonna defend yourself?"

"My bedroom was eight floors up in a High Society building. I think it's reasonable to conclude that a naked boy with broken legs would've been caught…but I bet your report didn't you give those details," I say, holding my voice steady for once.

He shakes his head, tucks in his T-shirt and fixes his belt. "There's no such thing as reasonable. Go to sleep," he says before leaving my room.

I've been trying!

In the darkness, my throat constricts and my muscles lock in place. I can't see a thing, but I hear everything—the *drip, drip, dripping* from the bathroom and the *tap, tap, tapping* as rain hits my window. Screams from outside bounce off my walls and then moaning from the hallway joins in. I shake my head, pry open my throat, and rub my face. Propelling myself off my mattress, I stand at Cole's door with my hands at my side. It seems weak, but I hate being in the dark. I give in and knock.

"Now what?" he asks.

"I can't sleep," I say.

"And that's my problem how?"

"It's not." I bite my lip. "Would it be all right if I kept my light on?"

"If you must," he says.

I draw my knees up to my chin, wrap my arms around my small frame, and start to count the cement blocks that make up my walls. My imagination runs wild with every noise in the building and the screams from outside. I hope this nightmare ends soon.

* * *

A blaring siren jolts me awake. *Did I fall asleep?* I leap to my feet and look outside, accidentally knocking over the paper bag on the windowsill. It clatters to the cold floor. I unfold the top and pull out a roll that's hard as cement.

Disgusting.

I throw it and begin to shake. Biting my tongue, I try to bury myself in the corner. I have nothing but these walls to protect me, and no one but myself to watch my back. I'll never be able to fight my way out because what lives outside is worse than what is in here.

A shower will help clear my mind.

I turn on the faucet for a long while only to discover ice-cold water rushing out. The water never warms and I begin to understand. The Commander thinks he can wash away my soul by freezing me to death. He thinks he can destroy me by stripping away my possessions. But he can't and I won't let him take my memories, my ambition, and my pride.

He thinks I'm so easily broken.

The Commander doesn't know anything about me, what I grew up with, what I endured—the father I lost, the mother I hate, the brother who walked out of my life, and the stepfather I was forced to accept. He thinks since I was rich, making me poor will cause me to give up. What he doesn't understand is that, after my father passed away, I grew up behind walls of hatred. I had nothing, but had everything at the same time. I owned expensive clothes, enjoyed good schooling, and lived in a nice home. But my body was just a shell protecting an empty, desperate heart. My life was a colorful façade.

I had so much time to sit and think. I spent the majority of my life between four walls. I was abandoned, neglected, starved, betrayed, and abused. I've already been treated like the scum of the earth, so the Hole is nothing new. He wants to erase every sign of my existence on this earth, but I won't let that happen. He can strip me naked, but he'll never reach my soul.

It's personal, completely personal.

I squeeze the excess water from my hair and slip back into my old scrubs. I tiptoe back to my mat only to find it occupied by Zeus.

Great! How did that happen?

I don't want him in my room, but I'm unsure of what to do. When he looks at me, his brown eyes widen, his tail whips back and forth, and his ears stand at attention. I wonder what he thinks of me. I don't know why I care, but I do.

He releases his gaze and drops his head. I comb my fingers through my hair and remain standing.

Cole steps inside my room through the open door from his bedroom. His eyes narrow at me as he shakes his head. He opens his mouth, then closes it, and scratches the back of his neck. Then he shrugs his shoulders and closes the door behind him again.

Weird.

I don't know what to expect, but it seemed as if he had something to say before he stepped outside. As I'm pondering his awkward facial expression, the door from the main hallway swings open, and Cole reappears, holding another paper bag.

"Here's your breakfast." He holds out the bag.

I shake my head, trying to be polite. "No, thank you."

"Eat it." He unrolls the bag and holds out crackers.

At least they haven't solidified like the roll. "Fine," I say. "But I could use some water first."

He crosses the room, hands me a bottle of clear water, and watches as I gulp it down. He places a hand on his hip, takes a step back, and starts rocking on both feet. I can't hold eye contact with him for more than a second. His stare makes me uncomfortable, and the way in which he enters and leaves through the two doors always reminds me that I have no privacy.

"Come this way," he demands.

"Where are we going?" I ask, feeling suddenly nervous.

"Don't question me." He glares at me. "When I tell you to do something, you do it." He points his finger in my face and he's close, too close. It's the first time I take notice of the stubble on his chin.

"Okay, I'm sorry."

I follow him into his room, breathing in the fresh smell of oranges. It's set up almost like a large studio with everything in one room except for the bathroom. To the left sits his bed, and to the right is the entrance to his small bathroom. His clothing is piled at the foot of his bed along with Zeus's metal food dish and black crate. His small kitchen area sits in the far right corner, with a doorway next to it; I'm guessing it leads to the main hall. Against the wall, near the kitchen, sits a wooden table with two identical chairs and a safe mounted above it, where I assume he keeps his weapons. A small laptop sits on his table. On the screen, I see a view of the main hallway and a view of my bedroom. The same picture of the Commander hangs above his dresser.

Do they all worship him? I hate it.

Outside the window, above his bed, the siren screams again. "When you hear that." He points to his window. "Your ass better be at work."

He sits at the table and points to the chair across from him. "Sit," he says as he packs up the computer for more space. "We have a lot to cover. There're certain rules you have to obey, and if you don't, you're toast."

"Do you have a pen and paper?" I ask. "So I can take notes."

He pulls on the collar of his shirt. "Don't move. I'll be back." He leaves through the doorway in his room and the door locks behind him. I check just to make sure.

Cole returns with a pen and a piece of paper. He sits back down and slides them across the table.

"Where'd you go?" I ask.

"The guards have a reporting station on each floor. Now can I start?" he asks, raising an eyebrow.

"Yes." I smile to myself because I actually got him to answer a question.

I try to steady my hand while I write, but the letters look like a third grader wrote them. I can't stop wondering why, out of all things, he chose to be a guard. I bet it's the control, but I'll never ask.

He tells me there's no public transportation within the Hole. He explains how the busses take the sinners to high-speed trains that transport them to their jobs if their jobs are up north in High Society or farther away. However, very few people are authorized to come and go freely—none of which are sinners, of course. The majority of the population is branded red, black, or yellow. He says the blue tend to die off quickly, either from suicide, disease, or murder. Orange keep to themselves and green hangs out with purple. Stay away from all reds—no matter what.

He tells me that the gangs are growing, violence is increasing, and everyone's starving. Some areas are safer than others, but pretty much everywhere is dangerous, especially for me.

I absorb every disturbing detail. Children born here are forced to live the remainder of their lives in the Hole. The Commander believes they carry the blood of sinners within them and, therefore, don't deserve to leave.

I drop my pen on the table.

He huffs a heavy sigh. "Now what?" I feel him shift in his chair.

"How could anyone be so cruel?"

"Forceful is putting it lightly," he says. "Then again, if he weren't, you'd think he was soft enough to try and escape, right?"

I shake my head. "I just don't understand. What's the point of having guards here if sinners can do whatever they please?" After the sentence slips out, I clench my teeth in expectation of his response.

Will he lash out and hit me or will he finally rip me to shreds?

He gives me a hard look and avoids my question. "In certain circumstances, the Commander orders us to intervene. Now, can I finish?"

"Yeah, go ahead." I lean back and cross my legs at my ankles. "But I have one more question."

"Seriously?" he asks.

"Are all sinners treated equally?"

"Yes."

"Then why are you protecting me?"

"That I can't answer."

"Can't or won't?" I ask.

"Both," he says. "My orders are to protect you. It's not my place to question it. Now please shut up and let me finish."

He tells me all the rules without any personality. His monotone voice flips through the pages. *No this. No that.* No one but the guards has rights here. Trudging through all the details of my new arrangement takes all of the morning, afternoon, and part of the evening. He shows me maps of the Hole and the hospital, which stands center of this monstrosity. He writes out my schedule for the week, which consists of my cell, work, and back to my cell. The Hole runs just like a prison, but without bars to hold everyone in place. He says the Commander believes the judicial system that used to exist was full of flaws and a waste of time.

"After all, it's easier, and cheaper to confine the sinners to one location," Cole says.

I totally disagree.

"You should just kill me," I tell him. "You have a gun, and no one would care."

"Lexi." I feel his eyes on me. "What's wrong with you? You think I want to kill you?"

"I'm a waste of your time."

"My job is to protect you, not kill you."

"And you're okay with that?"

"Without me you'd be dead, so yes, for whatever reason, I am."

I'm not sure what he means by that, but I'm done asking questions today.

I lower my eyes to the table, and crumble into my chair. I'll never get out of here. Either he'll be with me or some crazy person will do worse to me in the streets.

"I'm not going to hurt you." His voice is shaky with an edge of desperation. "I thought we already established that."

"Sorry, it's just…it doesn't make any sense." I stand and smooth out my shirt. "May I go back to my cell for a minute?" I ask. Tears sit on the rims of my eyes, and I pretend to rub them when I'm really trying to keep from crying.

"Sure," he says. He gives me a conflicted look and then rips his gaze away.

I head back to my empty room and cover my mouth with my shirt as the tears spill out. My circumstances seem so dismal.

Yet there's got to be hope, right? Cole said he didn't want to hurt me.

Zeus lies down next to me and nudges my elbow. I slide away from him, spying his silly sideways expression and smile.

Is he trying to comfort me?

Cole calls from his room. "As soon as I'm ready, we'll head over to the hospital. You have to be familiar with the building. Since I won't be with you while you're working, you need to know what to expect," he says from the doorway. "Would you come back so I don't have to yell?"

"Where will you be? When I'm working?" I grudgingly return to his room.

"Training." He opens the safe and straps two handguns onto his side. His dark-grey uniform emphasizes his muscular build and he catches me staring.

Trying to pass it off, I move forward, but nosedive to his floor. *Did I seriously just trip over the dog? Wow.* I roll onto my back. He offers his hand and pulls me upright with a smug look. I groan as embarrassment crawls up my face in the form of a deep, crimson flush.

"Now look. Whatever you do, stay on my inside. I need to know where you are at all times. Don't wander off. Follow me, walk, and breathe." He starts to move toward the door when he stops suddenly. He looks closely at me then rummages through his bag. He hands me a pair of sunglasses with large, reflective lenses that look like they will swallow half my face. "Take these and wear them outside." His voice is callous and indicative of his training. The tough-guy persona grates on my nerves. "Do you think you can handle that?"

"Sure, no problem," I say, remembering the last time we ventured out. After clarifying those details, we depart down the dark corridor.

Holding my shirt over my nose, I brace for the stench of the decomposing body, but it's been moved.

Thank God.

The courtyard's full of people. I get shoved from my left side, knocking me off balance. They smack, push, and yank while trying to get on the old dirty work buses that take them to their jobs each day. How on earth do those things still work? They look like wrecked sheet metal on wheels.

I walk beside Cole, and Zeus follows.

Turning toward the hospital, I feel the weight of multiple eyes resting on my back. People stare at me, or us—I'm not sure. Catcalls and whispers from citizens distract me. I duck my head and keep my eyes lowered to avoid attention.

"Nice disguise. Too bad you can't disguise she's a whore." A man emerges from the shadows in the alley with a knife in hand. He licks his lips, making my skin crawl. He reaches out to grab my arm when Zeus growls, low and menacing, at him. The man pulls back and raises his knife, but Zeus doesn't back down. He shows no fear. His hair stands up straight on his back and runs along his spine.

In one swift motion, the man cuts his knife through the air, narrowly missing the dog. Zeus jumps on him with a violent bark and shakes the knife out of his hand. His jagged canines dig in deep and force a cry out of the man lying on the ground. Cole picks up the knife and puts it at the man's neck.

"Come near her again and I'll slice your throat."

A mixture of fear and bitter resentment cross the man's bearded face. Cole removes the knife, leaving the man to crawl away. He turns toward Zeus and rubs between his ears.

"Now that's more like it. I can tell you've been practicing your scary face." Cole laughs.

Yes, thank you, Zeus.

Cole grabs my arm to push me forward. "Let's go!"

Sometimes I grab his shirt to keep from stumbling over trash or dead bodies. He jumps down into an alley, holds his arms up, and catches me while I take the leap. Zeus hops down behind without effort like a graceful gazelle. The walkway narrows between the buildings, and the only place I can go is behind Cole. So I walk blind.

Sewage pipes below emit an unpleasant aroma and the walls tower over us on each side, making me claustrophobic. After a rat skitters over my foot, I slam into Cole, knocking my glasses to the litter-ridden pavement. He turns and pushes me against the wall.

"What are you doing? We've been over this. You can't do that." He's angry. "I could seriously hurt you if you surprise me like that."

Here I am again, in the darkness. The walls surround me on all sides. I beg and claw the walls, but he slams the door closed again. My eyes squeeze shut as I try to hum a simple tune. Praying the sound will make it stop.

I open my eyes. Cole stares at me with sweat dripping off his forehead. His face is stern, as if waiting for me to answer his question.

"Sorry…"

"I bet." He bends down, picks up my glasses, and hands them to me.

Boxes and broken furniture block our path, and we climb over piles of trash. The alley opens up to another street. Across from me looms the entrance to the hospital. Guards stand watch from the surrounding buildings and people flood the street. They part for Cole as we cross. Their faces show mixed expressions, ranging from fear to hatred. There's older people and children without brands.

They must've been born here.

He opens the door and leads me into the lobby. It smells like crap mixed with flowers. The walls, made of cement blocks, are painted a dull gray that goes on endlessly. Drywall from the ceiling crumbles onto the cement floor, leaving a dusty powder that mixes with whatever else lies there. My feet stick to it. My slipper comes off and my foot touches something wet. I reach down to grab it when I realize I'm standing in a puddle of fresh vomit.

"Wow, that's disgusting," Cole says, pointing to my soaked foot.

"Tell me about it." I take off my sock and throw it in a trashcan.

A middle-aged woman with orange hair sits at a crooked table. She doesn't look up while we stand there for what seems like forever, and I observe the violet brand on her slender neck. Pride.

Cole clears his throat. She glances up as she shows me an ID tag with my name and picture on the left side.

"Make sure it's you," she says in a squeaky voice. It's labeled "8 West" on the right side with my photo and the name "Dr. Sutton" in the bottom left corner.

Cole reaches over and yanks my tag out of her hand. "She'll need to wear it, not stare at it." The woman snaps to attention and glares at him, but he doesn't seem to care.

I don't even have my tag on when he snaps, "You coming or you just going to stand there?"

I lean against the sheet metal wall in the elevator while

he pushes the number eight. From this angle, he looks more intimidating. I can't see around his broad shoulders, so I look at the back of his head and notice a small patch of hair he missed while buzzing it.

He taps his fingers on his thigh as we move upward, but doesn't speak. I wonder what he thinks about being my guard. I'm sure it's not something he wanted or chose to do. And then there's Zeus. It's perplexing why Cole loves such a colossal doofus of a dog.

We stand in front of a door with the name "Dr. Sutton" carved into the wood.

"Who is it?" asks a deep voice. It's low like a distant rumble.

"It's Cole, sir." A beep follows a click and then the door swings open, revealing a well-lit room with a desk at the opposite end. Two chairs sit in front of it. Pictures of the ocean hang on the walls, and a sign hangs opposite.

TREAT EVERYONE EQUAL. WE ARE ALL BORN THE SAME AND DIE THE SAME.

Hmmm. I didn't expect to see that.

"Lexi. Lexi Hamilton." The way he says my name would make you think he knows me.

My eyes snap to his face, but I don't recognize him. He walks around the desk and reaches out his hand, enveloping mine with roughness and strength.

"Yes, nice to meet you, sir."

He smiles and sits down at his desk, gesturing me to sit as well. He looks up at Cole. "You're free to go. I'll take it from here. Lexi's shift ends at seven so make sure you're here."

"If she's finished earlier, page me." Cole whistles at Zeus, who pops his head out of the trash. Zeus looks up, a piece of tape stuck between his eyes.

"Oh, dear God. Let's go. You know that scary face you made earlier? Totally down the drain." He talks to Zeus as if he understands every word that comes out of his mouth.

"She'll still be done at seven," Sutton says.

"All right, I'll be here," Cole says.

I shift my weight in the chair and glance up at Dr. Sutton. He looks about forty years old, salt-and-pepper hair, with some deep creases in his forehead and a crooked nose. The sea-green scrubs bring out his eyes. He reaches down into a drawer.

"Are you thirsty?"

"Yes, actually I am, thank you." I sit fiddling with my shirt.

He tosses me a bottle of water. Catching it with trembling hands, I twist the cap off and chug. The thin layer of soot I accumulated from the journey made my tongue swell. He catches me staring at the sign as he leans back and crosses his arms.

"Obviously, I'm Dr. Sutton, but please, just call me Sutton."

"Okay."

"I'm the only licensed doctor here, and what few supplies we have, I've paid for. So I expect you to treat them with respect, and if I catch you stealing anything, I'll cut off your arms."

"I would never…"

"Good, then we have nothing to worry about. I do things a little differently here. You work your way up and learn as you go. I'm willing to teach, if you're willing to learn. There are nurse's aides and nurses who will work with you and show you the ropes. Make sure you pay close attention to detail and ask them any questions you have. It might take years to get to a nursing level, but if you strive for it, you'll get there."

He has a serious look about him, a professionalism I imagine isn't found here often. "I don't judge. I don't care about your past. You have a new beginning with me. So as far as I'm concerned, you're just a fellow employee. It's up to you, though, what you make of yourself. Oh, and I don't give second chances. If you go behind my back in any way or break the rules, you'll be reported to the Commander. If you try to escape, I will catch you. Understood?"

"I understand and I won't let you down." I don't know why

I said the last part. Maybe it's because he seems compassionate, yet strong, and maybe he reminds me just a little of my own father by the way he looks at me. Either way, my muscles begin to relax, and I find myself meeting his eyes and enjoying the warmth in them.

The only warmth here.

"I need to warn you about a few things. Well, a lot of things, actually. Just because you're in a hospital doesn't mean you're safe. There's been a fair amount of murders, rapes, and thefts in the last couple of months. Don't go off the floor. Don't wander alone. If you're uncomfortable around a certain patient, don't go into their room without someone. If they ask you to do them favors—refuse. Don't accept gifts, money, or anything they offer. Just the other week, a nurse ate chocolate that was given to her by a patient she adored and died from rat poison." He pauses. "I've read a lot about you, and I know everything."

I jerk my head back. He clears his throat but tries to be discreet about it while closing the folder he's holding.

Does everyone know about me around here? I wonder what he read. No doubt, he read about my sin, but what other information is there?

"Please, come with me," he says.

As I follow Sutton down the hall, my stomach somersaults. I grip the front of my shirt as sweat drips down my back. I hate the unknown. New things intimidate me and the last few days have been nothing but new. It makes me feel devoid of any energy at all.

I hear nurses laugh and then immediately turn and whisper as I pass.

"Ignore them," Sutton tells me.

"I'll try," I say.

Men whistle from their rooms, and I keep my head locked in place.

"I love me a naughty nurse," one says. "Can you bathe me, sweetie?"

Again, the nurses laugh and Sutton shakes his head. I want

to curl into a ball and roll far away from here. Being called something you're not gets really old.

I put my fingers in my ears, trying to make it look like I'm rubbing them, and enjoy the muffled voices. Sutton takes me around the hospital floor, showing me where everything is and where not to go.

"Do you usually give tours?" I ask.

He chuckles. "No, today's actually my day off. I have to catch up on some charting," he says. "We got slammed last night, and I couldn't keep up. But it all worked out. Since I had to come back and finish my paperwork, I got to meet you and show you around. Something I never get the chance to do."

I try to suppress my surprise, but it's hard to do. *Why would a doctor want to do my orientation?*

"You actually keep records here?" I ask.

"In a way, yes," he says.

He leads me down the main hallway, and I count ten doors as we pass. He reads the expression on my face.

"One patient per room," he explains. "No such thing as having a roommate here. It's safer that way."

Luxury in the Hole. That's a first.

The rooms are identical with one mattress on a wooden frame that's supposed to resemble a bed and a simple bedside table. A chair sits in the opposite corner near a four-drawer chest made from corkboard and a bathroom you can almost stand in. White industrial-grade tiles with small specks of color line the floors with multiple cracks and warping. No light. Just a candle.

"This is the soiled linen closet that you'll get acquainted with. It's your new best friend." He opens the door and lets me look inside. "All new personnel start here."

Two guards, in their typical stiff uniforms, walk toward us. They nod at Sutton as they stroll by. As he turns to speak, one of them winks at me.

"There're always guards coming and going. You have to be on your toes at all times," he says as if he knows what happened behind his back. He swipes his badge, and we reenter his office. "The guards are cocky and will give you a hard time because they can. They have no boundaries, even in the hospital. Just watch your back."

He sits at his desk and leans back.

"Everything on this floor is under surveillance," he says. "The back staircase is the only exception. Years ago, the cameras were damaged and fixing them isn't within our budget. There's no way in or out of the building from those stairs. You can go to the basement or the morgue—both of which are dead ends." He pauses and says with a laugh, "Not a very upbeat orientation, is it?"

I smile. "No, not really."

Finally, someone with a sense of humor.

I can't remember the last time I smiled.

"Did you pick me or was I assigned to you?" I ask, remembering my earlier conversation with Cole.

"To tell you the truth, I don't know what their methods are," he says as he pulls something out of his desk. "Your keys." He throws them to me.

I catch them with both hands, losing my balance and falling off my chair.

"Well, that was graceful. Are you all right?" He offers me his hand, and I take it. "Do you have any questions for me?"

"Not that I can think of," I reply, even though I'm dying to know why he's been so nice to me. I dust myself off and try to pretend I didn't just make a fool out of myself again.

For rest of the day, I shadow a nurse's aide and get to know the basics of patient care. By the time seven rolls around, my feet throb. These slippers have no soles and no arch support. My shirt sticks to my skin, and my hair is plastered to my neck.

Cole and Zeus arrive at the nurse's station. Cole talks to one of the female nurses and smiles his crooked smile. His dark eyes catch mine for a quick moment, but that's the only acknowledgement he gives.

Nauseous much? I can totally see him being a man whore.

"Talk to you later," he says to the redhead.

"I'm looking forward to it." She grins and flips her hair.

Oh please.

He silently leads me out of the hospital. We're back in the alley with Zeus in front this time. The sun sets in brilliant hues across the sky, but the tall silhouettes of the buildings obscure my view. Now and then, we run into a beggar. Cole ignores them like he does the discarded furniture we step around, but one in particular haunts me. On his neck, he's branded red.

Wrath.

"Can you spare some change, ma'am?" he asks.

"I don't have any money," I say.

Cole yanks my arm, but not before I hear the beggar say, "I know you're innocent. Your eyes—"

I stop and turn back, about to question him, when a loud bang rattles my brain. Something warm splashes my face. I wipe it off with my hand, which is now streaked with red.

Blood.

CHAPTER 4

Cole shoves me to the ground, forcing a grunt out of my mouth as he lands on my back. My ribcage feels crushed under his weight. Bullets kick up dirt in patches around us and ricochet off the walls. Looking up, I see the beggar crumple. Blood pours from holes in his torso, and a vacant expression is plastered on his worn face. My stomach lurches at the violence. We lay there for a few minutes as more shots are fired and a troop of guards sprints past. We wait.

"Crap," Cole says under his breath. A group of sinners flood the entryway. Some carry crowbars and sunlight glints off the others' knives. Zeus charges toward them.

"You have to run!"

"What?"

"Run! Now!" Cole points in the direction we were heading. "Go!"

I turn and run.

The streets all look the same. I bolt down the alley and sprint past a series of dead bodies. Some of them are branded, some not. I have no idea what I'm doing, where to run, and why I think I can get there without getting killed first.

"Get her!"

Their words bounce off the walls and echo in my ears. I don't look back when I reach the end of the alley. Left looks like it takes me down more narrow alleys, but right looks like it takes me back to where Cole is.

"Now what?" I say aloud. I tangle my hands in my hair and look up at the sky, but only for a second. I wish I had Cole's map with me now. Just then, someone pushes me from behind. I should've sensed danger when the noise around me ceased. I turn, and a group of sinners encloses me.

I'm trapped.

I'm shaking uncontrollably.

I can't stop my head from spinning or the pain from my nails digging into my palm.

I'm looking all around, and especially behind me.

I see a red, a black, and maybe three green brands closing in on me. My heart pounds in my throat at the thought of them killing me. *Should I plead for them to make it quick or will that just make it worse?* I'm about to scream when one smiles. His eyes linger a little too long.

Oh please, no!

"Where do you think you're going?" asks the tallest man.

Laughter erupts behind him. "What are you waiting for, Sarge? Get her," another says.

I clench my fists, unsure whether I should fight to my last breath or give in to their demands. The ending seems inevitable either way. My eyes flood and the men become blurry. I squeeze them shut, rub, and pry them open.

"Hello, dear," Sarge says with a smile, stepping closer.

There's a gap where his two front teeth used to be, and his tongue protrudes, resting on his lower lip. He loosens his belt, yanks it off, and holds it like a whip.

He's going to publicly humiliate me.

As if I haven't already been branded.

My legs buckle and I plunge to the ground. Blood rushes through my veins like a rapid river, and I'm drowning in fear.

Beads of sweat drip from my lip.

"Leave me alone! Please. Leave me alone." I place my hands defensively in front of me, backing myself up as far as I can.

He pushes me to my back and leans over me. I kick at his chest.

"I wouldn't do that if I were you." Spit flies out of his mouth, landing on my cheek. "It will only make me angry. And trust me, you don't want me angry." He slaps his belt into his opposite hand and lets it unravel for the full effect. "It's time to pay your due."

I don't move.

I won't move.

I can't move.

But this is my only chance.

I kick my foot into his groin, causing him to fall over on his side.

I jump to my feet and at the same time, he grabs my ankle. "Help!" I scream, hoping someone will rescue me, but they stand there with blank faces. They look at one another, eyes wide. "Somebody help me!" I shake my leg as hard as I possibly can, but he never loosens his grip.

"You stupid twit." Sarge grabs my other leg from underneath me and pulls me slamming my body onto the ground and instantly knocking the wind from my lungs. "Now, I'm gonna cut your throat."

He sits on top of my chest and startles me to my senses.

I gasp for air.

His knees hold down my arms and he flips out his blade.

I'm pinned.

I'm staring at him, but at the same time, I can't see him and I'm frozen under his control. I close my eyes and hold my breath. *Make it quick... Make it quick.*

"Sarge, get up, man! *Now!*" someone screams.

My eyes snap open.

The crowd scatters.

Sarge looks up. "Oh my G—"

Out of nowhere, Zeus flies through the air, plowing him over while wrapping his mouth around his throat. Sarge swings his arms and kicks his legs to no avail. Zeus jolts his neck.

I hear a snap.

Instantly, Sarge's body hangs limp.

Just as I'm about to scream, Cole plants himself beside me. "Get your head down!"

Cole pushes me down just as bullets fly past my head. He grabs my arm, lifts me to my feet, and drags me along behind him. My ankle screams at me to stop, but I keep running forward. The sound of feet pounding the dirt gets louder, the chanting gets closer, and the firing of weapons in rapid succession makes my brain feel like it's hemorrhaging. I know this has to do with us.

"Why are they after us?" I shout between breaths.

Cole doesn't respond. He just keeps running. I look over my shoulder and see people bolting to shelter and screaming, leaping away from the men who rush toward us as they pistol whip the unfortunate ones who refuse to move.

Cole yanks me away from the main street and heads toward the hospital down another alleyway. Every building has boarded-up windows. The doors hang off their rusty hinges and glass crunches under our feet as we run. It screams death. It screams poverty.

Cole turns abruptly.

"They're after you!" He exhales.

"Then why are they trying to kill you?"

"I'm in their way."

"But you're a guard—"

He yanks my arms and we're running again.

I guess they aren't all as scared of the guards as I am.

We dart down all the alleys we come across, going up one, down the next, and across the other. I'm guessing Cole's trying to throw them off course or confuse them as much as he possibly can.

My ankle burns and I feel it pop. "Cole!" I yell.

He comes to a complete halt, turns to me, and meets me on the ground.

"What's wrong?" He looks behind me.

I gasp for air and Cole pulls me behind an overflowing dumpster. His breathing is unlabored, but he drips buckets of sweat.

"My ankle…" is all I can muster.

He puts his fingers under my chin and tilts my head back until we're eye to eye.

"I want you to trust me," he says. "Can you do that?"

"I already do," I say.

I can't believe I just said that. I don't trust anyone.

Cole grabs my waist and flips me into his arms, taking off

down the same alley we just traversed. His arms are strong, secure, and wrapped around my small frame, and I'm glued to his torso. I tuck my face into his neck, hiding from this sick world.

"Wrap your arms around my neck." And I do as he says. "Tighter."

I squeeze.

"Too tight." He chokes.

I relax. He boosts me higher, closer, and my forehead rests against his ear.

I clench my teeth.

He runs.

I hold on.

I'm shaking my head, because I'm overwhelmed by my thoughts.

I don't want them to hurt Cole—not because of me.

"Just leave me," I whisper into his ear. "I won't let you die trying to save me. I'm a sinner. Let them have me."

"Those aren't my orders," he says in a short gasp.

The gunshots come from behind, but I can tell they're far from us now. Cole seems to know this place by heart because he never second-guesses his next step. I wonder if he ever had to do this for anyone else.

Or am I his first?

"Hide here." He drops me to my feet in front of a cellar door. "I'll be right back." Before he leaves he says. "I promise."

And just like that, he disappears, sprinting farther and farther away. I creep into the cellar and close the door behind me. Zeus decides to stay with me, and I'm okay with that. He's proved his loyalty.

I listen for movement where Zeus and I hide, but hear nothing. I smell burned rubber and trash, then wipe the smeared dirt from my eyes. This must be the most impoverished area of the Hole where the real hardened criminals live. Normal, well-adjusted sinners don't all act this way. *Then again, who knows what a few months in the Hole can do to someone.*

Before I know it, the door swings open, but with the

lighting, I can't make out who it is. My breaths are bursting in and out.

"Lexi. It's me." Cole speaks low as he approaches. "I want you to keep breathing, just like I am." He grabs my hands and beckons me to inhale and exhale when he does. I hear the voices getting closer again. His sweaty hands drop mine, and I can tell his attention is directed toward the alley we just ran down. "We have to move." He throws me onto his back. "Wrap your legs and arms around me. It's the easiest way to hold you." I cling to his neck, locking my ankles together above his hips. "Now, hold on." He sprints down the alley.

He comes to a sudden halt and drops me to my feet. In front of us stands a chain-link fence. "Do you think you can climb this?"

"I'll try." I climb, ignoring the constant throbbing in my ankle as I make my way to the top. I swing my leg over at the bar and start my descent, letting myself drop the last foot to the ground, and land on one leg to spare my opposite ankle any more damage. I look up, but Cole's nowhere to be found. My lips are trembling.

"I'm right here." I turn and he stands parallel to me.

"Zeus?" I ask. "What about—?"

"Don't worry about him. He'll find his way back. He always does." Cole looks down at my feet and sighs. "They could've at least given you sneakers."

"Tell me about it."

We move slower now, but still at a brisk pace. I fight through the shooting pain in my ankle because I don't want Cole to carry me. Without warning, a loud gunshot penetrates the area behind us. The bullet must've found its target because fiery objects fly in our direction. Before Cole gets me to the ground, I feel the earth rumble with a violent concussion, and everything goes black.

* * *

My head pounds like a sledgehammer, making my thoughts

hazy and my body stiff. I try to sit up but can't seem to get my muscles to do what I'm commanding them to do. There's a distinct smell of blood in my hair, but I can't remember exactly how it got there.

Someone touches my hand. I pull it away and tuck it under my back.

"Are you all right?" Cole leans over me, his face coming into focus.

All of a sudden, memories circle in my brain, and the picture of Sarge's body lying next to Zeus pops in front of my eyes.

The running and the chase. The blast... the flames.

"I'm fine," I say as my entire body screams at me. "Was I the target?"

"I'm not sure, but our timing couldn't have been worse." He looks down at the ground between his legs. My hands shake as the adrenaline wears off. Ironically, it's not the blood that bothers me the most. It's the violence, or at least, my inability to protect myself, that bothers me.

Zeus licks my face and I'm not sure which is worse—dog slobber or blood.

"Dude, cut it out!" I wipe my face with my shirt. Cole reaches over and pushes Zeus's head away, but Zeus refuses to budge.

"Zeus. That's enough."

"Was that normal? What just happened? Is that normal?" I say.

"Not exactly. Fighting between citizens is normal, but lately, there's been more fighting with the guards," he says, brushing off his pants. "But you. Well, you're the prettiest girl they've ever seen, so instantly, you're their greatest reward. I bet there's countless bets going on that involve you... You're the talk of the Hole... And they all want you to themselves. Some just want to kill you because that's their passion. Others want to—"

"I get the point," I say, cutting him off before he talks about the color that's branded on my neck. "These people are crazy.

Let's get out of here."

We jog to our quarters. Well, Cole jogs. I hobble along behind him. My clothes are spattered with blood, dirt's plastered in every crevice of my body, and my head thunders. My heart hammers against my chest. My ankle throbs and Zeus keeps running into me. The damn dog doesn't watch where he's going half the time. He grins at me with his huge tongue hanging to the side of his mouth. I can't complain about him too much, though, since he saved my life once already.

He might be the most compassionate one here.

Everything looks abandoned. I glance warily around me while we make our way back. The faint echo of a skirmish occurring in the background terrorizes me, and I don't want to get caught in a situation like that again. As we turn into the courtyard of our building, a voice pierces the darkness.

"Skank. Skank! SKANK!" The voice yells louder each time. Cole grabs my arm roughly and speaks directly in my ear.

"Don't worry about him. It's just Bill. He's mentally disturbed, but harmless. He screams something about your brand the very first time he meets you. It won't happen again, at least not from him."

I'm branded for life. I'll always have lust tattooed on my neck in blue... It will happen again. I self-consciously pull some strands of my hair over my brand as we pass him. He sits on the cement pavement outside the entrance, inhaling a cigarette. His appearance is barbarous with wild, unkempt hair and missing teeth. His cackle disturbs me as I follow Cole into the building.

"Try not to take it personally," Cole says.

"Easier said than done."

At what point do they believe what's been branded on their skin instead of just knowing who they are inside?

My eyes focus on him ahead of me, his muscles flexed as he opens the door. Moonlight slips across my cell, and breathing finally becomes easier. Collapsing on my mat, I squint when Cole flicks on the light. I roll over, too tired to talk and too traumatized to eat. There's no way out of this place now. I'm going to live the rest of my life in this hell.

I toss and turn on my mat and can't stop the flood of memories from burning me up inside. I promised myself I'd never go through the pain of telling my story again. Nothing hurts more than the disbelief of people who are supposedly your friends.

"You're a damn liar, Lexi. All you're looking for is attention." They said to me. "How could you make such terrible accusations?"

Only heartless people don't believe a child. A part of me died when my father passed away. A slow withering took place in our family, and my mother deteriorated into a shell of her former self. When I needed my mother the most, she turned her back to me. Feeling nothing and caring about no one but herself. No protection existed for me. I prayed every night that my brother would return and take me away. He never came.

I was once full of life, happy, confident. My father loved me. He gave us protection and peace. I didn't know anything about the outside world except what they taught in school. How that's changed since he passed. Everything changed.

My family would've been forced to live on the streets if I hadn't obeyed the rules. My stepfather bought my silence with the threat of consequences. He promised retaliation and he followed through.

All these thoughts swirl through my head as I lie down, pretending to sleep. I jogged the whole way back without consciously knowing it. I braved a gunfight and witnessed the murder of a man in the street. I succumbed to the screaming of an insane person outside my own building, and still I'm alive.

Giving up on sleep, I walk to the bathroom and turn on the shower. Cole left his door open and I see him. He looks deep in thought. His eyes focus on something I can't see, or maybe they're not really focusing on anything at all. Zeus stands on his hind legs and drinks from the kitchen faucet in Cole's room. *Please don't tell me he turned that on himself.* He drinks so fast he starts to hack. *Must've gone down the wrong tube.* Cole doesn't even look when he does it, so I assume this is normal.

"Care if I shower?" I say.

"Yeah, no problem. I'm gonna update the chalkboard. It only takes me a few seconds, so I'll be back before you finish," he says. He averts his eyes.

I step backward, excitement blossoming on my face. "Chalk?"

"Yeah. Why?" His head snaps my direction.

"Any way you could bring me some?"

"I guess so, why?" He scrunches his face, scrutinizing me like I'm insane.

"To decorate my cell. It's starting to get to me."

"What do you mean decorate? How on earth can you decorate a—never mind. I don't care," he says with his hand on the door.

I fold my arms across my chest. "Do they ever come by and check the rooms?"

"No, there's no reason to. We follow orders or people die. Pretty straightforward, don't you think?" His voice comes out bitter. His laughter fades.

"Hey," I say. He sits on his bed and looks up. His facial expression softens and tired lines appear below his eyes. "I never got the chance to thank you."

"For what?" He pulls his shirt over his head and tosses it on the floor, distracting me with his broad chest. I stutter while staring.

Crap!

"Uh…for saving my life," I say while crossing my fingers and trying to stay focused on his face. "I know I don't show it, but I'm grateful…that I have you." I know, the words shock me as I say them.

"I'm just doing my job. There's no need to get all emotional and crap." His cheeks turn a shade of pale pink. "White or colored?" he asks while searching through his piles of laundry for a new shirt. His back stretches taut, his muscles hardening while sifting around and coming up with a black

T-shirt. He quickly puts it on, and I exhale, his shirtless image uncomfortably burned in my memory.

"Both would be great, if that's possible," I say.

"Both color shirts?" he asks. A playful smile crosses his face.

I shake my head, confused. "No, chalk."

He releases a heavy sigh when he realizes I don't get his joke.

I run back to the shower before he changes his mind. *Or before I say anything else stupid.* I close the curtain, take off my bloodstained clothes, and scrub them with my hands under the icy water. The thin material tears under the strain.

Dang it. Now what?

Unsure of what to do, I call for Cole. I turn off the freezing water and stand shivering behind the curtain.

"Now what?" he asks from the other side.

"Do you have a towel or another pair of scrubs by chance?"

"You're lucky. I just grabbed you another pair." His hand reaches past the curtain and holds out a folded pair of blue scrubs. I take them and put them on. The fabric sticks to my wet skin, but I know it could be worse.

"Thanks," I say, but he's already left the room.

I push the curtain aside and am surprised to see two containers of chalk sitting against the wall. One is colored and the other is white. *Sweet!* I open the colored container and grab the purple. Turning it over in my palm, I marvel at the small things that bring me so much joy.

A noise that sounds like a foghorn bellows from Cole's room. I almost drop the small piece of chalk. At the same time, Zeus storms into the hallway, looking over his shoulder. Cole's in his shower, singing some weird song I've never heard before.

"What was that?" I ask Zeus. It happens again but louder this time. Zeus runs into my room as a foul odor drifts by. "Was that a fart?" I laugh. "Oh my word, I can't believe you're afraid of your own fart." I'm laughing so hard I snort. It's a small reprieve from the violence and stress. I'm on the floor, doubled over, when Cole walks in with a towel wrapped around his hips. Everything else is bare, steaming flesh. And I pry my eyes away.

"What's so funny?" he asks.

Oh my God, does he have to keep doing that?

I tuck my face in my shirt.

"Zeus farted and he came running in here with his tail between his legs… It scared the crap out of him." I continue to laugh in hysterics. Cole laughs with me. "Is that why you chose him? Because he scares people with his ungodly odor?" I wipe the tears streaming from my eyes and gasp for breath.

I keep my head down and try not to look at him. But it's hard, really freaking hard. I've never seen a naked man before, so I guess my curiosity's getting the best of me. He has the most defined chest, arms, and abdomen I've ever seen. Until this moment, I thought of him only as my guard, but seeing him standing there half-naked makes me extremely uncomfortable. I stop laughing and squirm under the weight of his eyes.

"On that note, I'm getting dressed and hitting the sack," he says.

"Yeah, me too," I say, eager to get out from under his stare.

"I'll see you first thing," he says as he walks into his room.

"See ya." Confusion takes over. At first, he seemed stoic and cold. But now, he seems…human. Guards aren't supposed to be human. They're supposed to suck the life out of sinners and enforce the laws of the Commander. And yet he already saved my life twice. Even if it's his job, it seems hardly worth the trouble. I shake the thoughts from my head.

I just can't win. For one, I can never be alone. But the second reason, the one I don't want to admit, begins to torture me more…

Sleep eludes me. I need a release, so I pick up another piece of chalk.

CHAPTER 5

The screaming sound of the alarm wakes me. *How long have I been asleep?* The light filters through the window and I rub my eyes as they struggle to adjust. An instant burn shoots through my shoulders as I prop myself to a sitting position. I should've known I'd feel like this.

Two knocks bring me to my feet.

"Are you decent?" Cole peeks around the door.

"I guess so," I say while throwing my hair into a messy ponytail.

Good thing because he certainly didn't give me any time to get dressed.

I'm shoving my shirt into my pants when he struts in, staring at me. He gives me a sly smile that melts into complete shock when he focuses on the walls of my room.

"What the hell is that?" He points at my wall.

"What?" I play ignorant.

"You know exactly what." His face turns red.

"Oh, that. I could've sworn I told you I wanted to decorate."

He throws his hands in the air. "I didn't think you'd actually draw on your freaking walls."

"Do you have a better idea?" His face remains hard. "Don't worry. It washes right off."

Please don't make me.

He stands in the doorway, quiet for a minute, then crosses the room. His fingers stretch out, faintly tracing my picture. "So, you like the forest and the beach?"

I feel my shoulders relax. "Not just any forest or beach. That's the forest I grew up in before moving to High Society, and that's the beach I was named after—Lexington Bay." I avoid eye contact and point to the beach. "But this one's definitely my favorite. The turquoise water is crystal clear with bright, beautiful fish and soft, powder white sand that goes on for miles. It's breathtaking, don't you think?" I ask, getting lost in my memories.

Cole stares with his mouth slightly parted and his top lip curls up slightly at the corner. He probably thinks I'm a lunatic.

"You're telling me a place like that actually exists?" He cocks his head and puts his hands on his hips. "Where I come from, we have mountains stretching for miles, but never have I seen a beach like this."

I smile. "It's farther south somewhere. My parents went there for their honeymoon and it's all they talked about for years. So you can imagine why I have such a detailed picture tattooed in my head. My father used to tell me that when I was born, he looked into my eyes and was lost in Lexington Bay."

"Leave it...for now," he says. "Who taught you how to draw?"

"Myself."

"Huh?"

"You asked me how I learned to draw—I taught myself."

"Oh, right. Really? Damn, that's pretty impressive. You've got talent."

"No. Not really. Just a good memory, that's all." I fidget with my fingers. I don't take compliments well. I never have and especially not from a guard.

"We have to leave in about ten minutes. Think you can be ready by then?"

I spin around. "I am ready."

He rubs the back of his neck. "No. Mentally ready."

"That's impossible. Death waits for me everywhere I go. The only reason I'm still alive—if that's what I am—is because of you."

Looking a little uncomfortable, he clears his throat, quickly diverting my attention to the bag in his hand. "I brought bagels."

This time we eat facing each other, but there's little conversation, which is fine. I find myself enjoying the quiet, but appreciative of the company—weird, I know. The tendons in his jaw flex as he chews, and I watch a glob of butter land on his chin. I'm hoping Zeus will come and lick it off because I'm definitely not pointing it out. The last thing I want to do is embarrass him—if he even gets embarrassed. Whenever he glances up, I lower my eyes. Sometimes I think he's staring at me. Then I hear a sigh, and he continues eating.

"Why do you do it?" I'm afraid of his reaction, so I avoid eye contact. "Risk your life to protect a sinner? I don't get it. I don't get you... I know—you have orders and you follow them, but seriously. You could've died yesterday. And for what? Me? Don't you think that's an odd assignment for them to give you?"

"Stop asking me that." His fist slams down on the table, causing my glass to wobble off the edge and shatter. "It's starting to piss me off."

His words tear through me, and I cower away from him by pushing my chair back from the table. The sudden change in his demeanor horrifies me.

He bites his lower lip and closes his eyes. "We should go." He exhales.

"I lied. I'm not ready." After that outburst, the last of my reserves are gone. I clasp my hands together to stop them from shaking. "Out there scares the hell out of me."

"Well, we're going. So, you better get over it."

Arguing with him isn't an option, so I zip my lips. He stands and straps his guns on as I keep my head lowered. If this is a game, I just failed. Coming here has already taught me one thing—I'll never understand the mentality of a guard and I hate being vulnerable.

So I won't be.

We take the alley and trek to the hospital at a faster pace than the previous day. As we near the entrance, something seems different. A large crowd waits in front of a rough-hewn wooden stage. The guards in their black, spotless uniforms stand at attention in perfect rows like soldiers prepared for battle. Men, women, and children gather in front as a bulky guard saunters up the stairs to the platform. The body language of those around me tells me this guard is formidable. Some of their faces turn white, while others shed silent tears, and the children shake with fear.

This isn't going to be good.

The sheer dread on their faces makes me tense. I can practically smell their terror. Cole comes to an abrupt halt, flings his arm out to stop me, and stands rigid and alert.

"Stay here and don't move, whatever you do," he demands.

Before I can question him, he turns on his heel and pushes his way through the multitude. I stretch onto my toes to watch, but lose sight of him for a few minutes before he returns with a pained expression. I move directly into his path and try to get him to look at me, but he avoids my eyes.

Now he's playing my game.

"I'm sorry," Cole says.

"Wait. What? Sorry for what?"

"I never intended for you to see this." And that's all he says before another voice pierces the air.

"Thank you all for coming," a man with red, wire-rimmed glasses announces into the microphone.

"That's Wilson," the lady behind me whispers. "He's almost as bad as the Commander."

Wilson's heavyset face belies a pair of sparkly, mischievous eyes and thick lips that smack together as he enunciates each word. "It's come to our attention that some of you have obtained illegal arms and are using them against us. This is something we will not tolerate, so we thought a little reminder of what happens to those who violate our laws would be quite beneficial."

Of course there are laws when their safety's at risk. Freaking hypocrites.

As he speaks, guards parade four men up the stairs with pistols pressed to the back of their skulls. Their faces remain shrouded underneath blindfolds and their hands are tied securely behind them. Wilson commands them to kneel, so they do in a row across the platform. Even though the stage sits approximately fifty feet away, I see their bodies quivering.

My eyes widen as it dawns on me... *Holy crap, it's an execution.*

"By order of the great Commander, you are all charged with the possession of unauthorized weapons. The penalty is death." Wilson pauses for effect as an evil smile splits his pale face. The silence disconcerts me. Never have I heard the Hole so deliberately quiet.

Wilson stands in front of the accused and yanks off each blindfold, one after the other, tossing them off to the side of the platform. Starting from the right, he takes aim, pointing the barrel of his pistol at the first man's forehead. Without hesitation, he pulls the trigger, sending a bullet right between his eyes. Then he fires three more shots and finishes the others.

I gasp with each blast.

"Don't watch," Cole says.

But no matter how hard I try, I can't rip my eyes away. Wilson forces the spectators in the front row to carry the bodies off the stage. They struggle under the dead weight, so minutes pass before they pile the bodies in a heap. Their blood leaves a sickly, foul trail behind.

I feel a small raindrop hit my forehead and roll down my face, but I'm too afraid to wipe it away. It's as if someone hit a pause button, and Cole and I stand frozen in place.

Once the stage is cleared, Wilson announces with disgust, "The next punishment is reserved for the worst offenders."

"There's more?" I ask in a whisper. I know Cole stands next to me by the familiar sounds of his breathing, but he doesn't reply.

A young woman with long, golden hair and fair skin is shoved onto the stage.

"She used to be a model before she was accused," the same lady says behind me. "Being beautiful is never a good thing here."

Bruises mar the woman's neck on stage, making her purple brand barely distinguishable, and her right eye bulges, dark blue and swollen almost shut. She possesses no blindfold and wears only her torn underclothes, stained red and clinging to her body. Her eyes stay glued to the floor, but her terror is evident even from where I stand.

Then to my surprise, two guards drag another guard in full uniform up the stairs, casting him next to the woman. He reaches over, taking her face between his hands. Tears track down his cheeks as he stares only at her. His lips move, but I can't hear what he says. She nods her head and he kisses her.

"Guard Mac!" Wilson shouts. "Evidence has been set before us that proves you have been consorting with this sinner—this disgusting, worthless, prideful leach." He pauses for effect. "The penalty awarded those who proclaim to love the branded"—he licks his lips—"death!" he screams and points at her with his thick, sausage-like finger. "And you, my friend, will watch her die." The kneeling guard cries out, but a sharp blow lands upon his head, silencing him. "But first, you need to learn to keep your hands off these filthy sinners."

Wilson motions for others to come. They carry a small wooden table to the platform, set it down, and proceed to secure the concussed guard's right hand to the table with solemn faces. The once guard—now prisoner—struggles against the restraints.

"Stop! You're the lowest of the low. You bring shame to the guards," Wilson says. The pitch of his voice rises to a squeak and his eyes focus on Mac with unwavering intensity as a crude smile makes its way across his face. In another life, I might've laughed at him, but not here. Not now.

With all eyes riveted upon them, Wilson arches his back and swings a machete down to the table with all his might, attempting to slice off the man's right wrist. A terrible, bloodcurdling scream escapes the man's throat and splits the air. Thinking it's over, I cover my mouth to keep from screaming, but then he swings again and again, chopping roughly through the wrist bones. Vomit rises in my throat when I see the blood spurt from where his hand once was. Splinters of bone, broken and uneven, lie limp on the table. A collective groan flows swiftly through the crowd like a wave.

The guards lift up the man, who's almost unconscious, and

places him face-to-face with his lover. She cries and pulls him to her.

"I love him," she wails.

Don't they have any remorse? Any at all? I begin feeling woozy and sway slightly to the right, but Cole's arm steadies me for an instant. And then it's gone.

Mac looks at Wilson, who now stands at the woman's side with a red-hot iron as large as a bat. A sanguinary light forms in Wilson's eyes and froth bubbles at the creases of his mouth like a hungry beast waiting for the final slaughter. Then Wilson torches her skin with the heavy iron as another guard restrains Mac.

"Ahhhhhhhhhhhhhhhh!" She shrieks in agonizing pain. The sizzle of her skin and smell the burning flesh reaches even me. Her head flips back, the tendons tight, as her mouth opens to scream again.

The sound of her shrill vocals snaps Mac from his bloodied stupor, and the next part happens so fast I barely catch the blur of movement. Mac breaks free and uses his remaining hand to pull a dagger from his boot. He lunges forward and throws it straight into her heart with a sickening thump. Instantly, her chin flops to her chest.

"Oh my God!" escapes from my mouth.

Wilson shakes his head, aims his pistol, and blows Mac away. Bits of brain and blood spatter those closest to the stage and they frantically try to brush it off. I bend over and heave at the sickening sight.

"What a pity," Wilson says. "I wanted to torture him just a tad longer."

The people around us stand with grim faces. I feel their hatred, anger, and despair. The message is clear—the guards still own the Hole and no one, not even their own, is free from their judgment.

I look at Cole, but he shakes his head as if saying *don't speak*. I wonder if he knew the guard who was executed, but there's no chance to ask him as he pulls me along while shoving through the crowd, dispersing with heavy feet. I feel hopeless.

Cole leads me around the back of the hospital and past the stares of several groups of distraught guards. The eyes I want to avoid most are Wilson's, but he glares right at me. His uniform is slick with the blood of his victims—a picture of Satan himself.

"ID card and access code," the guard says at the post. Cole hands over his ID.

"Access code 0406."

"I need to see hers as well." The guard motions to me.

After checking the paperwork, he turns, eyes me with a hungry smile, and winks. "You may proceed," he says.

I wonder what the paper says, but there'll be time to ask later.

We enter a garage filled with tanks and other military vehicles. No graffiti lines the walls, no broken glass littering the cement floor. It's the cleanest place in the Hole. The incandescent lights of the training center brighten the garage, making it seem almost livable in comparison to everywhere else. Halfway in, I stop to throw up between two parked vehicles. I can't purge my mind of the images of the executions, and my stomach won't settle.

"Pull it together. I don't have time for this."

"I'm trying," I say, trying to catch my breath. But then I heave again, making a loud, retching noise.

Ugh, stop bringing attention to yourself.

"Is that it? Geez."

"You could try being sensitive, you know." I stand and wipe my face with my collar, attempting to make myself presentable.

"No, I won't." He gets in my face and squints at me. "You witnessed firsthand what happens to the sensitive and weak. I'm not a moron like Mac was."

"But that's different," I mumble back.

He jerks me aside. "Are you trying to get yourself killed? Me? Just shut up and move." He stands so close I can see the veins in his eyes.

"I didn't mean—"

"Is there a situation here?" A guard interrupts us.

Cole steps back and salutes. "No, sir."

"It sounds like your sinner has quite a mouth on her. Do you need me to set her straight?" His icy stare is unreadable, but his hand moves to the baton strapped at his side.

"No, that won't be necessary. I have it under control, sir," Cole says.

The tall guard glares at me with cold, blue eyes and steps forward until he stands in front of me. He twists his head toward Cole. "I know she's your first female prisoner, so I'm making this clear now... Weakness is *not* acceptable." Then he touches a lock of my hair, fiddling with it between his fingers. "She's delicious though, isn't she? Lust. How tempting. You should really watch that mouth of yours, darlin', or we'll find a better use for it." He hisses in my ear like a snake.

I pull my head away from him and step backward into Cole. His chest tightens the second I touch him, so I freeze.

"At ease." The guard spins, but shouts as he walks away, "Oh, Cole...don't forget we're watching your every move!"

For a moment, I'm frozen and Cole's face turns various shades of red. I can't tell if he's furious with me or with the guard, but he's definitely angry. Zeus whines at his side, startling me. With the intensity of the morning's events, I forgot he was even with us.

"Let's get out of here," Cole says. "And don't speak."

Fear overrules my humiliation. My fingers tremble and my heart flutters anxiously. I stay close behind him as we enter the training center. The last thing I want to do is enter a building teeming with more guards, but I have no other choice.

The training center looks like an indoor dome. Different stations take up sections of the massive room. On the walls, I glimpse an arsenal of weapons comprised of numerous makes and models of guns and knives of all sizes and even unsuspecting weapons such as sticks and batons. Everything gleams in the light as if polished daily. I don't have a name for most of the things I see, but know they're all lethal in the hands of a guard. At one particular station, men line in a row, shooting at a moving target. The noise is deafening without ear protection and I cringe at the echo of each discharge. Another group suit up in all of their combat gear to perform a simulated attack. Some turn to watch us, while others focus on the task at hand.

"Keep your head down and keep walking straight," Cole says to me. Zeus growls at the man nearest to us, so the man turns around and goes in another direction. The elevator door closes after we step in and Cole swipes his badge.

In the relative safety of the elevator, I can't hold it in any longer. "I can't believe he killed her. Why would he kill her? If he loved her—"

"Because he loved her." Cole cuts me off. Without any invitation, he keeps talking. "Mac's a former friend of mine. And everyone's known about Mac and Claire for a while now. I have no doubt he did it because he loved her. He knew they'd torture her just to break him. And they'd do it in front of him." Cole pauses and closes his eyes for a moment. "He killed her out of love. The very love that most of us will never feel because we aren't allowed."

"Wow. How did I not see that?" I ask.

"Because you don't know what it feels like…to be in love."

"And you do?"

"I'm not having this conversation with you."

I shake my head and quickly change the subject. "What was up with Zeus back there?"

Zeus cocks his head when I mention his name. Cole leans against the wall and puts his hands on top of his head.

"That's him being protective of you, I guess. Not sure why he didn't rip off the guy's head in the garage, but he didn't."

"He can do that?"

"Have you not seen his teeth?"

"Okay, stupid question." I look down at Zeus as he presses his wet nose into my thigh. I place both of my hands around his head and kiss him between his ears. "Thank you," I say to him.

Nothing more is said. One, because I'm trying to block

out what I just witnessed, and two, because I want to forget about the "him being in love" question. The elevator heaves to a stop. Getting off at the eighth floor is harder today than yesterday, but I pull my shoulders back and walk toward the desk, attempting to mentally compose myself.

Cole signs me in. "I'll be back at seven," he says in a brusque manner.

"Yes, sir," I reply. The trauma of the morning has me itching to go back to my dirty room and lie on my mattress.

Without any further instructions, Cole reenters the elevator with Zeus. Rage is written on his face as he punches the buttons. His eyes narrow to slits and his posture stiffens as if ready for a fight. I make eye contact with him just as the door closes with a squeal. *If anyone accused him of rage, he'd have a hard time proving them wrong.*

The monotony of work comforts me although it takes forever to fold the huge mounds of linens. I'd prefer to hide in a closet somewhere, alone in the dark, away from the eyes of the guards who pass in the hallways. Most of the nurses avoid me because of the attention the guards pay me. I don't blame them. No one wants to make herself anymore of a target than needed, and I seem to be a magnet for it.

The hours pass quickly, and at seven, Cole and Zeus show up right on time. Cole looks no less enraged than when he left. His fingers jab the buttons in the elevator and he says nothing as we jostle downward. Then, once outside, he walks briskly ahead, never acknowledging me or speaking.

Did I do something wrong? I'm too afraid to ask because of his outburst at the table this morning. *Maybe the execution made him afraid to talk to me.*

Once inside my quarters, he spins around and shoves me against the wall. I bite my lips in fear, shaking in his grip.

"Don't mistake my niceness for weakness, okay?" he asks.

I nod.

"Yesterday, I saved your life because it was my job. Nothing more." He releases me and I'm not sure what hurts more, my arms or my feelings.

"Okay," I say, unconvinced, but trembling.

Yet, this morning, he seemed to think my life was worth something.

He turns, drags Zeus with him, and slams his door.

I crumble to my mattress, unable to shake my fear and the memories.

The salacious look on the head guard's face as I passed. The icy blue eyes of the guard in the garage, how his fingers in my hair made me shiver under his control. The way my stepfather looked at me with greediness.

I wake up sweating and panic, bolting upright in the dark.

When I calm down, I hear someone knocking on a door nearby.

"Sure, man. Come in," Cole says.

A parade of feet shuffles into his room, followed by laughter and the sound of cans popping open. I press my back against the wall and pull in my knees. My chest heaves with the agony of the unknown.

What if they see I drew on my walls? What if they come into my room and beat me...or worse?

Then his door creaks open and a sliver of light trails across my room. I freeze.

"Lexi, get your ass in here and come serve these men," Cole says.

I stand cautiously, staring at his silhouette in the doorway, unsure of his demanding voice.

"Did you not hear me? Get in here. Now!"

I skitter nervously into his room. Four guards and Cole sit around the table, playing cards, drinking beer, and laughing. Their eyes all lift to mine in expectation and they smile in unison.

"Grab them another beer," Cole says.

I breathe deeply and retrieve four beers. Cracking them open, I set the drinks on the table. I look at Cole, waiting for him to say something. He raises his eyebrow.

"Did you forget something? Where's mine?" he asks.

The others roar with laughter.

"She's real smart, buddy," the dark-haired boy says. A part of his right ear is missing like something or someone bit it off. *Gross.*

"Aww, come on. If she was smart, she wouldn't be here now, would she?" Cole says.

"How'd she manage to escape red-light duty? What makes her so damn special?" one asks. "Sucks to be you, dude. If she were my assignment, I'd go nuts not thumping her."

Their comments make me dizzy. I give myself a mental slap, pull myself together, and pop open Cole's drink. I want to run from the room, but it would only make things worse.

"Why are we ordering our entertainment when we have her?" Cole asks while raising his beer. The others tap their cans against his and down their beers in thirsty, sloppy gulps. Setting down their drinks, they get back to their game.

I stand against the wall, heat rising up my neck from the humiliation. Every time they need a new beer, they motion for me, and I scramble to get one.

"Sit on my lap, sweetheart. I don't bite," one says.

"He might not, but I do," Cole says.

The one chokes, spewing beer all over Cole's shirt, and smacks his back like a good ol' boy.

I roll my eyes. *Drunk, dirty, and disgusting.*

"Naw, seriously, go back to your room. Our girls will be here in three, two, on—"

A knock on his door brings cheers from the others and barking from Zeus. Cole opens the door and prostitutes pour inside. They're tall, leggy, painted ladies wearing clothing that leaves almost nothing to the imagination. One of them immediately sits on a guard's lap. He runs his hands up her back and fondles her beneath her clothing.

Slinking away, I fumble for the doorknob. Cole steps in my path, blocking my exit. He's so close I can almost taste the beer on his breath. His eyes are glazed over but dark as ever. Unsure of what to do, I wait.

Please don't make me stay.

He turns the knob, opens the door, and follows me out. His hand catches my wrist, jerking me back.

"It's not what you think," he gruffly whispers.

Then he slams the door.

What?

Walking back to my bed, feeling defeated, I trip over my own feet and crash onto my knees. I don't have the strength to rise. All the goodness I so desperately clung to doesn't exist here. I bang my fists on the bed in anger, pain, and suffering.

I just don't understand anyone or anything.

With gaudy music playing in the background, I fall asleep, pleading with God to make tomorrow bearable.

CHAPTER 6

Dawn breaks through my window in one glorious streak of white light. My head aches from lack of sleep and the pounding music last night. I must've clenched my teeth while I was sleeping because it hurts to open my mouth.

I rub my eyes and drag myself out of bed. As I get dressed, Cole's statement—"It's not what you think"—keeps playing over and over in my head. I want to ask him about it, but I doubt I will…at least not now. But it frustrates me because he could be referring to so many different things. My thoughts swim laps in my head, trying to make sense of his words.

The hospital does nothing to dull the now-roaring scream in my mind, and the noise sets off a constant ringing in my ears. The smells are too putrid to block. So all around, I feel like a disaster.

And today of all days, they give me my first assignment—other than folding laundry. Lovely.

The charge nurse pulls me aside immediately upon Cole's departure to let me know she has work lined up for me.

"What do I do?" I ask.

She leads me to the patient's doorway and stops.

"Go in and see if she needs anything. Change her linens. Clean out her trashcan…if she has one. Otherwise, pick up the trash on the floor, and if you moan about it, I'll send you over to the Horney Hank's room. Which I'm pretty sure is the last place you want to go." Her round face scowls at me. Whenever she talks, the imposing mole on her chin speaks to me with its three straw-like hairs protruding. It's hard not to fixate on them.

Why doesn't she pluck them?

I enter my patient's room and take a moment to look around. There's no one here. The silence disturbs me. Perplexed, I stand and scrutinize the room.

Now what?

I gather the dirty sheets and drop them on the floor. I glance down and that's when I see the body. Her snow-white hair lies matted across her forehead. Her urine-soaked hospital gown is stained with feces and plastered to her body like saran wrap. Her chest doesn't move. I kneel and check her for a pulse, breathing, anything to indicate she's alive. No response.

Straightening up, I feel numb. This patient probably fell out of bed and no one heard or helped her. Maybe she would've died even with help, but either way she was alone, and I can't help but feel bad for her.

My mind wanders to my father. He abhorred situations like this and that's exactly why he spoke out. He risked everything by opposing the Commander, yet he did it regardless. I hope I possess his bravery, his compassion, and his belief in the dignity of others. Moments like this test my resolve to the core, though. I look at the lady lying before me, and the indecency of her plight makes my neck tighten and my nerves edgy. I turn in one swift motion and bolt back to the nurse's station.

"She's rotten, isn't she? Nasty old hag. What did she want this time?" the head nurse asks.

"She didn't say a word…" My voice trails off as I try to suppress my emotions.

"Well, did you at least change her linens?"

"No." I take a step forward and look her full in the face. "She's dead."

"Oh. Well, she's better off stiff." Her lips draw down in a look of dismay. "I guess you'll need a new patient, then." She flips through her charts like nothing happened. I wonder how she does it.

"Give her Alyssa," a quiet voice from behind her says. "I need a break." A nurse with silky black hair peers from behind the charge nurse. She pulls her hair back from her face, revealing an orange brand—gluttony—which distracts me, and I want to punch myself for judging her by the color of her brand.

"I'm not sure she can handle her."

"She needs someone to take care of her, and I'm not going to do it," the quiet girl says. "I can't."

"Okay, she's all yours." The charge nurse points toward a wooden door at the end of the hallway. "Room six."

"What's wrong with her?" I ask. I'm not thrilled about meeting another patient after the last one turned up dead.

"She's sick," the head nurse huffs.

I get the feeling I'm missing some crucial piece of information and she's not willing to give it to me. So I shake it off and stand straight before putting my hands on my hips. "I'm not going anywhere till you tell me. You can't expect me to just walk in there and pretend I know what's wrong." The head nurse gives me a stern look. "Please."

"There's nothing we can do for her except try to keep her comfortable. Her pain is difficult to manage. Sutton's trying everything he possibly can, but there isn't enough morphine here and the Commander won't allow us to have more medicines since it's all for sinners anyway. What she has now is all we have left. So we need to make it last until she—" The quiet nurse chokes on her words. "Until she dies."

I'm still as a statue, hardened like stone. *They want me to take care of someone who's dying?* My heart sinks into my stomach, churning with anxiety.

"She's too weak to get out of bed, so you'll need to give her a sponge bath, and please, whatever you do, make sure you don't drop her IV bag. If you do, the gravity will cause her blood to go back up into the IV line and possibly into the morphine bag, which will dilute it and make it harder to administer the correct dosage."

The charge nurse describes the IV, what it looks like, where it hangs, and how it enters her veins. And she says not to touch her blood no matter what. My head spins with the newly acquired information. I rub the back of my neck. I hope I can remember all of this.

"Whatever she has lives in her bloodstream and it's lethal." The dark-haired nurse hands me a paper. It reads like a tombstone, her name carved in black letters on the thin sheet of paper.

Alyssa Jenkins.

I can do this. Just go in, check her, and get out. Hopefully, she won't want a bath or her linens changed. I knock on the door three times, drop my hand to my side, and that's when I feel just how badly my body is shaking in anticipation.

"Go away," Alyssa croaks weakly. I ignore her request and walk in, closing the door behind me. There's a sheet hanging from the ceiling, which I assume is for her privacy, but it blocks my view of her and, for a moment, I'm thankful.

"Alyssa?" She doesn't answer me and the fear of the unknown seeps into my bones. My palms sweat and my heart thumps with anxiety, so I stay behind the curtain. "I'm Lexi." Still nothing. I bite my lip. "The nurses asked me to come check on you and see if there's anything I could do for you."

Please don't die on me. Please don't die. I clench my eyes shut, grab the sheet and move it to the side. I exhale, pushing out all the fear that's trapped in my chest, then open my eyes and look at her.

I gasp.

Alyssa's eyes snap open. She gives me a blank stare and makes no attempt to talk as she turns her head toward the window. Her skin's so thin it's almost transparent, and her dry, cracked lips are the faintest shade of pink. She has crystal-blue eyes that contrast the dark circles underneath them, and her dirty-blond hair lies in silky threads across her makeshift pillow. Enclosed around her neck is a yellow brand for greed.

By the time I'm done staring at her, she glares at me. Her body trembles as her fragile finger points toward the door. "Get out. Now. Leave me alone." She pulls the cover over her head.

I can't believe it. Alyssa's just a child.

She lies in a bed that swallows her whole and she curls up with a thin white blanket. Her head rests on a rolled-up towel, and judging from the lump under the covers, she's not very big. I'm unable to look away, but out of the corner of my eye, I spot the folding chair across from her bed. I tiptoe over to it, slide down, and as soon as I sit, the darn thing makes an awful squeaky sound. I jerk forward. I feel light-headed as reality settles in, and my insides squirm in panic. My eyes blur with heartbreak. I close them, and after a moment, the sensation fades, and I glance her way one last time.

I bolt from the room and close the door behind me before sliding down the wall, pulling my knees to my chest in exasperation. It's not the kind of patient you want to take care of—ever. What hell this girl must be going through, knowing she's going to die alone, just like the lady down the hall. Pain squeezes my chest tight.

The dark room envelopes me. When I look up, he stands at the foot of the bed. His face is hard and cold. I try to scream, but nothing comes out. Knowing I can't call for help, he sits next to me. His hot breath overpowers my sense of smell as I wait for him to talk. Sometimes he talks for hours, and sometimes, all he does is stare at me. I cringe under the intensity of his deep-green eyes. Occasionally, he brings me flowers and sets them on my bed stand while I sleep, and I find them in the morning. I tense up and wait—the unknown, always the unknown. I don't want to die, but at the same time, I wish I were dead.

"Lexi, can you hear me?"

I open my eyes and Sutton hovers over me. His eyebrows draw together in a worried expression. He reaches around my shoulders and helps me up. "You're drenched with sweat. Are you all right?" He glances around for a nurse. "Amber, please grab my stethoscope and blood pressure cuff. At the nurse's station." The auburn-haired nurse Cole often talks to grabs his things and hands them over with a sour face. "Did you eat anything today? It could be your blood sugar—"

"I'm fine. Trust me. I get these dizzy spells occasionally and sort of check out for a while, but I always come around." I wince with embarrassment. "Please just let it go."

His expression softens as he kneels in front of me. "I can't let it go. I'm a doctor, remember?" He pushes his hair off his forehead. "I'll find a way to make them stop."

I know he can't, but I'm not going to explain that to him, so I quickly change the subject. "Why can't you help her?" I ask, pointing to Alyssa's room.

He furrows his brow and releases a long, deep sigh as if reaching for an explanation. "She has an incurable virus. I have scientists working on finding the cure as we speak, but they're nowhere close to finding one. I've already allocated too much pain medication. There's not much else I can do." He pauses to wipe his forehead with his hand. "How do you tell a thirteen-year-old she's going to die? How do you tell her there's nothing you can do to save her life?" He balls his hands into fists and then relaxes them like he's releasing his pain. "I hate failing, and I'm failing her in every way possible."

My heart breaks for him. I see the pain in his eyes when he speaks about her and wish there was something I could do to make it all go away. I know what it feels like to be a failure. It haunts you constantly.

"Can I get it?" I ask.

"No," he says. He shakes his head and gives me a distant look.

"Then how'd she get it?"

"Look, you can't get it, all right? So try not to worry about it," he says.

"Okay. Doesn't she have family?"

"We're all she's got." He leans against the door.

"Tell me what I can do to help, and I'll do it."

"I need you to be there for her. Be her friend." He gives me a pained stare.

"Anything but that," I say. "I'm not the right person—"

"You're exactly the right person." He pats my arm.

"But she hates me. She told me to get out and leave her alone."

"Because she's scared. She came here without her family and she's afraid to let anyone in." His face softens. "Reminds me of someone else I know. Now, go say good-bye."

Is he referring to me? He doesn't know me.

I knock, but silence greets me as I nudge open her door. I stop behind the hanging sheet, unable to move any farther. "I'm leaving now, but I'll be back in the morning. Would it be all right if I brought something for you?"

"Whatever," she says.

I don't respond as I leave. *Sure, we'll be great friends.*

Cole sits on the nurse's desk with his back toward me. Zeus trots over, licking my hand and bringing a subtle smile to my face.

"Nice to see you too. How was your day?" I wipe the slobber on my pants.

Just as I near the desk, Amber reaches around Cole and covers his eyes.

"Guess who," she says in a high-pitched voice.

"I don't know," he replies with annoyance. He extracts her fingers from his eyes and pulls her around to his front.

"Heard you had a good night…hot stuff." Her haughty laugh is annoying.

How fake can she be?

He laughs. "Yeah, yeah. Who told you?"

"Your boys. Maybe next time you'll remember to invite me." She gives him a coy look while she plays with the large curl of her ponytail.

"Nah." He punches her arm playfully, and she wraps her arms around his neck.

"You wouldn't have to pay me," she says. "For you, I'll do anything."

Cole shoves her away and looks angry. "I don't mind kidding, but now you're crossing the line. Back off."

"Just messin' with you. Lighten up already," she says. Her eyes meet mine and her air of innocence doesn't fool me. "But seriously, if you want me to come over, let me know."

Can she scream "I want to die" any louder? Did she not see the execution?

Cole leads me to the stairway in silence since the elevators malfunctioned halfway through the day. Eight flights down and still nothing's said between us. Zeus's nails click on the concrete as we descend, and I'm grateful for the noise.

His hand touches the small of my back when he leads me to the door of the Jeep. I stiffen and he removes it.

"We're taking the Jeep?" I ask.

"For now. Just get in." His brusque voice reminds me of how mean he was last night, ordering me around like some lowly servant.

So I lift myself in, holding the door handle, then strap the seatbelt on tight while averting my eyes. All day, I pushed the thought of him, his buddies, and the prostitutes out of my mind, but now the memory comes up fresh and sharp. Anger flows through me like a bursting dam.

Why does he act all nice and then treat me like crap? Why does he bother saving my life if he's going to treat me like trash on the street? He doesn't make any sense.

He puts the Jeep in drive and we traverse back to our quarters. The entire time I stare at the bleak, colorless monotony that's become of my life. The humid breeze plays with my hair, but doesn't bring much relief. I feel Cole's eyes boring holes into the side of my face and try to ignore it, regardless of how many questions I want to ask.

I'm scared too. I saw the execution the same as he did, but there's no excuse for being hostile now.

I've only been here a week and I'm already exhausted with trying to read his signals and dance around his moods. At times, I want to explode like a bomb or give in to my animalistic instincts like the others.

But my father raised me better. He'd be disappointed if I became what I've been labeled. And I won't give the Commander the satisfaction of ruining me.

"There's something I don't understand," I say with hesitance.

He swings his head my direction and raises an eyebrow. "Go on."

"Prostitution is a sin. Why is that allowed, yet the others

were executed? Makes no sense to me." I swallow and wipe the sweat from my forehead.

He stares at the road as he turns. "It wasn't always that way."

"Explain to me. Please."

"The first Commander wouldn't have allowed it, but this one, well, he doesn't care if people sleep together in the Hole. In fact, he encourages it to keep his men loyal and happy." I feel my eyebrows pinch together with disgust. "As long as it's just sex and nothing more." He glances at me for a response. "It's their job. They're already branded, so what does it matter?"

Because he's a hypocrite, and so are you.

I don't give him a response.

After Cole retires to his room, I let my hair down, giving my scalp a rest from the ponytail. My long tendrils hang freely over my brand as I stand in front of the mirror. I try to mash out what he said in the Jeep, but still cannot make sense of it.

"Sorry about last night. If I don't treat you that way when they're around…they'll start asking questions. I can't have them doubting my ability to follow through with my orders."

His quiet voice startles me and I spin around to face him. His tired eyes meet mine. His shoulders slump and his face looks apologetic. "And when they're not?" I ask. "What about the camera in my room? Aren't you worried about them watching you talk to me right now?"

"I'm the one watching you on camera, not them. And from now on, in private, we'll be civil."

I nod my head and turn away still feeling uneasy.

"You should be thankful I'm apologizing at all," he says. His voice turns bitter.

My eyes snap to his in disgust. "I trusted you with my life."

"And I did my job."

"So that's how it's going to be?" I ask.

"That's all it can be."

Okay, then.

Days pass in the same manner. Cole escorts me in silence. I nurse Alyssa, fold linens, and keep a low profile. *God knows*

I have enough to think about. Alyssa loves the pillow I gave her, so she's been a little more receptive of my presence, but still only gives me one-word answers when I ask her how she's doing. Every night, Cole leaves me food to eat, but neither of us speaks. After our last exchange, I lost a lot of respect for him. It makes me uncomfortable so I don't ask him about the papers he had or if I'll ever be free from surveillance.

I know he can't enjoy watching me do nothing every night.

I lie on my mattress and run my hands through my long hair. The loneliness is driving me crazy, so I start talking to Zeus, which, to tell the truth, is kind of nice. He at least pretends to care, or seems to anyway.

Thursday. The day means nothing as usual. The head nurse, whose name I finally found out is Bertha, rushes around with the dark-haired nurse. The eighth floor seems particularly swamped today, so there's no time for questions. Left to my own devices, I'm determined to develop a deeper relationship with Alyssa.

Our interactions have been limited to her basic needs for the most part. I change her linens, give her baths, and attempt conversation with her while getting nowhere. She's like an armored battleship ready for war. I tiptoe around to keep from disturbing her whenever possible. However, her situation still pricks me. She must feel so alone and deserted.

How can I get her to let me in, to be her friend?

This time I don't knock. I pull open the curtain, go to the window, and open the blinds.

"What're you doing? I'm tired and want to be alone," she snaps. It's the longest string of words she's put together since I started taking care of her and I don't want the opportunity to pass. I drag the chair across the room and next to her bed.

"I know what it feels like to be alone and I wouldn't wish it on anyone. I've been trying to help you. Can't you see I want to be your friend?" I lean in, using a gentle tone.

"Why? What's the point?" The bitterness in her voice cracks with weakness, so I gingerly reach out and wrap my hand around hers. It's cold and lifeless.

"Because I need a friend." I squeeze her hand slightly, praying for an intervention.

Tears flow from her eyes as she leans her head back into the pillow.

"I don't want to be this way." Tears slip down her face. "I don't want to die. I don't want to be alone. I...just hate it here. I hate everything."

Tears pool on the rims of my eyes as I focus on her.

"I'll stay with you. I won't go anywhere. I promise."

"I think I've been here five years. Maybe longer? Sutton's the closest thing I have to family." She clenches and unclenches her fists. "I lost my family when they brought me here."

"Me too," I say. "Well, I lost mine over time...but I still lost them."

"It sucks, doesn't it?"

"Yea, it sure does." I take a deep breath and smile at her. "You know...we could be each other's family. If you want?"

"Really? You mean that?"

"Of course I do. I've always wanted a little sister."

She sits up and wraps her thin arms around me. She starts to shake as she sobs, so I hold her. I wish there was more I could do for her—anything. I want to make her remaining days as wonderful as possible, but how does a child enjoy her time when she knows Death parked himself just around the corner?

"What can I do?" I ask.

"Don't let me die."

Her words tear my insides to shreds. A hopeless feeling overcomes me and I want to scream at the top of my lungs "Take me! Take me instead!" I would, without a doubt, trade places with her if I could. I know it's impossible, and the loss of that control throws me into a frenzy. There's no way she deserves to be here. I don't even know where to go or who to blame, but there has to be someone.

"I'll be right back."

I run down the hallway and into the linen closet. I ball my fists and pound on the door. I grab the sheets and chuck them over the laundry bins and all the way to the trashcans on the other side. Burying my face into a blanket, I let out a scream that's been balled up in my chest for way too long. Towels fall off the shelf. I pick one up and throw it, then another and another until they form a disheveled pile. I push the bins out of my way and bolt to the supply closet.

I run my arm down the line of supplies, sending them to the floor. I pick up an IV pole and swing at the wall. I pound harder and harder until it breaks in half, sending one part into the mirror, shattering the glass into tiny fragments on the tile. I dig my nails into my palms.

"Why!" I scream. "Why her?"

"Stop." Sutton's calm voice breaks my tantrum.

Slowly sinking to the floor, I rest my head against the wall behind me and look around at the mess I created.

"I'm sorry." I pull the collar of my shirt up over my face, sniffling and wiping my tears away. "I'll clean it up." My arms throb and my muscles twitch from adrenaline. I push myself up, ashamed for losing all self-control, and start picking up gauze and tape.

"Stop," he says again. "Tell me what's wrong."

I watch as he makes his way toward me. My lip starts to tremble and I shake my head frantically. "It's not fair. She's so young."

"I know," he says.

"We have to do something. We can't just let her die."

"I'd give my life to save hers." He puts his hands on my shoulders.

"I thought the very same thing."

"Because you're a good person. If you didn't care about her, you wouldn't feel this way. Believe me, I've tried everything I possibly could for her, but the virus is…too complex. It might take years before a cure is found, and obviously, she doesn't even have weeks."

"I hate the virus," I say. "I hate this place!"

"Me too." He pulls me into his chest and wraps his arms around me like my father used to do. "Sweetheart, me too."

I can hear his heart beating. It's strong with a consistent rhythm. I know good hearts are hard to find, so for the first time in a long time, I feel comfortable around a man. Maybe it's because he could easily be my father, or maybe it's because he treats me like a human being. Either way, I almost trust him.

"What can I do?" I say.

"You know what I think?"

"What?"

"You should read to her. Not just any book, but a story where she can fly away and escape the world through her imagination." He releases me from our embrace and steps back, placing his hands on my shoulders. "Come with me. I have a collection in my office...and don't worry about the mess. I noticed some nurses sleeping on their shift earlier. I'll send them to clean up and restock." He laughs. "I hope you feel better now. I'd like to keep my office intact if you don't mind."

"Yeah, I'm okay."

He leads me into his office and then opens the closet door. The heaps of boxes and random items overwhelm me.

"How can you possibly find anything in this mess?" I ask.

"What mess?" he asks.

"Oh, dear heavens."

"Ha. I'm joking. I collect the belongings people leave behind and throw them in here. When you close the door, the mess is gone, so I don't see anything wrong with it. As long as I can't see it, I'm fine." He winks at me mischievously.

I nod my head and push past the shelves of bedclothes and sheets. Large boxes stacked on top of each other sit along the back wall. I pull down one box and cough as the dust particles float into my nose and mouth. My fingers slip off the edges, causing it to land on my right foot. *Dang it.* The top flops open, and I peer inside.

Jewelry, magazines, and old CDs rattle around as I sift through them. A baby rattle makes me pause. These were someone's prized possessions at one time, but I let the thought go as quickly as it arises, knowing I'm going to use them for a good purpose.

The next box contains more of the same, and I let out a long sigh of exasperation. Alyssa's probably wondering where I am, and I haven't found anything to read her yet. Then I see the stack of books at the bottom. I delay my excitement until I lift them out. Their tattered bindings make them fragile, and their browned pages curl at the edges, but I found them!

One by one, I read the titles and settle upon *The Last Silk Dress* by Ann Rinaldi. It's the only one that seems appropriate for a thirteen-year-old, and the cover even has an elegant young woman on it.

I put the rest of the belongings back in the boxes and stack them together. Then I skip-walk down the hall and back to her room with a huge smile on my face.

"What are you all happy about?" she asks.

"I got you something." Proudly, I pull the book out from behind my back and place it on her lap. "It's the only one I could find that was appropriate for your age."

"What? Are you kidding me? I'm dying and you're worried about corrupting me?"

I cock my head. "Do you want me to read it or not?"

She nods enthusiastically and then lays her head back on my flat, measly pillow. I sit in the chair and open the book to the first page. Ironically, it begins with a fourteen-year-old girl and her father at the beginning of the Civil War. I find myself and Alyssa drawn to her vivacious spirit and her close family connections. Will Susan side with the confederacy or with the abolitionists? I remember reading about the Civil War in school, but this book begins to bring it alive for me.

After thirty minutes, Alyssa falls asleep and I fold the page corner to keep our spot. This has been the best day in the Hole since I arrived. I tuck the book under her mattress and step into the hallway. Sutton slams into me while I walk, deep in thought.

"I'm sorry. I wasn't paying attention," Sutton says.

"It's okay, neither was I."

"Did she like the book?"

"Very much so. Thank you for everything."

He tucks his pen into his coat pocket and straightens his glasses. "Good. I'm glad," he says, his concentration fixed elsewhere.

"Okay, well, I have to meet Cole. It's almost seven."

Sutton glances at my face, nods, and rushes away without another word.

Of course Amber's talking and drooling over Cole.

How does she get out of work all the time?

Her fingernails newly painted, she brushes her hand against his and bats her eyelashes to gather his attention.

"Well, hello there. Seems like you've had a cakewalk day," she says to me.

I scrunch my forehead and retort, "Not as easy of a day as you've probably had."

"I'd watch my mouth if I were you." She sneers. She places her hands on her hips and raises her over-plucked eyebrows in a challenge. I don't know what I did to earn her nastiness, but she instantly hated me, even before I ever talked to her.

"That's enough, you two. Let's go." Cole shifts his posture and beckons me to follow him to the staircase.

"See ya," Amber calls to him.

He swings the door open and it almost smacks me in the face as I pass through behind him. My good feelings about reading to Alyssa are gone as I think about spending another night alone in my dark, damp room.

I'm sitting on my bed going through our family photos and the belongings my father left for me. I pick up my favorite picture, the one that was taken a few weeks before my father died. His turquoise eyes shine with joy as he smiles, his arms wrapped around Keegan and I. He looks happy...and so do I.

The dark mahogany frame is simple, just like he was. I clean off the dust, make my way to the wall across from my bed, and grab a pin and hammer when I hear my doorknob jiggle like someone's playing with it.

"Unlock this door at once, young lady!" My stepfather's

voice carries through my body like a tidal wave. His presence alone makes me uneasy, but when he talks to me, it's hard not to show my hatred for him.

"Be right there," I say. I place the picture frame on my dresser and unlock the door. He steps in and takes a look around. I can tell from the blood vessels pulsing around his green irises that he hasn't slept in a few days. I know that's never good. So, I stand in front of him frozen; I'm scared to even move a muscle.

"What have we got here?" He walks to my bed, his shoulders back, his head cocked to the side. "Oh, I see. Trying to bring back some memories, are we?" He picks up one of the photos.

"I'm only going to hang a few of them," I say with a shaky voice.

"You know, I don't recall you asking my permission." He puts the picture back down. The way he glances at it makes me scared he's going to rip it up.

"Was I supposed to?"

His eyes dart to mine, his mouth forming a thin tight line. "These walls belong to me, therefore, I decide what gets hung on them." He takes a few steps over to my dresser, lifts the frame with his large hands and smiles a devilish smile. "Aw, isn't this sweet."

"Would it be all right if I hang that one?" I say through gritted teeth. My body starts to twitch as I wait for his reply and I take a slow, deep breath.

"Now why would I allow that?" He walks back to my bed where the box sits and places my picture back inside. He grabs the others off my plaid comforter and tosses them in as well.

"Because it's my father, and I would like to have his picture in my room. You're rarely in here. Why would it bother you?" I can feel my fists tightening into balls.

"Seems you've forgotten something. He's dead." His words hammer at my heart and my nostrils flare.

"I haven't forgotten," I say. "Please, sir, it's just one picture. That's all."

My stepfather closes the box and picks it up, holding it close to his chest. He shakes his head no and frowns at me.

I narrow my eyes at him. "What are you going to do with that?"

"Your memories, like your father, will be locked away."

"Oh, please! Don't do that. I'll put them in my closet...I won't bring them out again. Just please don't take them from me. They're all I have." I'm begging now and tears start to fill my eyes. "Please, sir, let me keep them."

"Absolutely not," he says with a stern tone. "I'm your father now, and no other man will be hanging from my walls for you to see, for your mother to see. He's gone and you're my family now."

He leaves with my belongings, shutting the door behind him. I throw myself onto my bed and cry. How can anyone be so cruel?

I'm sweating and breathing hard when I bolt up in my bed. My hand goes to my face, and I realize I'm crying. This time, it wasn't just a dream. *It was just one of my many painful memories.* I slump back into my bed, knowing that work's going to come fast. But I'm not longer tired. I'm just heartbroken. And alone.

CHAPTER 7

Prostitutes, three of them, rush into the hospital, screaming about someone who's hurt. I can't turn my eyes away from them as the staff tries to herd them back to the front waiting area.

"Stay here." They're told. "Or you'll have to leave."

All three of them, dressed in promiscuous clothing that sticks to their slim figures and wearing chunky high heels, lean against the wall. Tears track down one of their faces. She looks familiar. *One of the girls from Cole's party the other night.* Her dirty blond hair hangs in tangles, matted against her back from the rain. The heavy, black charcoal lining her brown eyes drips down her cheekbones. Her nervous fingers fiddle with a small handbag. I try to ignore her brand to keep from judging her because I don't want to treat her the same way I've been treated. My hand moves to my neck self-consciously just thinking about it. Looking up, she locks eyes with me, and then nods like she remembers who I am.

I quickly nod back and walk upstairs with an overflowing container of ratty, washed blankets. The undependable elevator is stuck on floor three, so I huff my way up to my wing. My breathing comes heavy and labored under the weight, but I welcome the break from reading to Alyssa. I'm not used to reading so much and my eyes hurt. Guards pass, but I duck behind the height of the blankets, angling them in front of my face.

Just keep walking.

Fortunately, the stairs teem with people today. The eighth floor comes as a reprieve and I drop the basket into Alyssa's room to keep her company while folding it. Her solemn expression lifts and a smile crosses her face like she's bursting at the seams to tell me something.

"Well?" I ask, waiting.

"What?" She smiles.

"Spit it out," I say. I flip open the first blanket and begin matching the corners.

She pushes herself up and laughs. "Okay, so I read ahead a little..."

I cock my head sideways, giving her a knowing look. "And?"

"Her brother Lucien, well, he's against owning slaves, so the family shuns him. BUT, it just complicates things more because the Confederates surround Charleston and..."

"Whoa, slow down! How far ahead did you read?" I drop the blanket to my lap.

She grows quiet, and then mumbles, "The whole thing."

"You read all of it? That's a three-hundred-some-page book!" My jaw drops.

"Well, I liked it and felt good enough to finish... Hope you're not mad." Her hands clutch the book protectively as she pleads with her eyes.

"I'm not mad at all, just surprised. Well, glad actually." I finish folding the blanket and place it on top of another. "I'm not sure if Sutton has any more—"

"It's okay. It was really good and I'll probably read it again, anyway." She lays back, places the book on her chest with her hands over it, and closes her eyes. "The confusion and the violence remind me a lot of the Hole, except she has family..."

Her soft words cause me to pause and let my thoughts linger. She's so mature for a thirteen-year-old. I can't imagine drawing comparisons between a Civil War novel and the Hole at her age, but then again, my childhood aged me too.

Maybe the Hole ages everyone beyond their years.

"Why are you here?" I lower my voice when I ask.

Her eyelids flutter open. "I'm not a bad person, really, I swear," she says. "I was only trying to feed my family. They were starving to death and stealing was the only—"

"I never, not even for a minute, thought you were." I lean closer to her. "How old were you when this happened?"

"Eight," she says, dropping her eyes. She fiddles with her hands in her lap.

"And what? The guards took you away?"

"They came late the next night, didn't bother knocking. My family and I were getting ready for bed and they barged in like animals on a rampage. I knew they'd come for me, so I went because I didn't want them hurting my parents because they did nothing wrong. I did." She looks directly at me, her eyes glistening with the memories.

"I'm so sorry," I say, wrapping my arms around her.

"It's okay. Everyone here has a story," she says as she snuggles in closer. "On the bright side I got to meet you."

"I guess," I say. "That's one way of looking at it."

"Do you want to know what bothers me the most?" Another tear slides down. "I'm going to die a sinner. This is who I am. And there's not a thing I can do to change that." Her hands pull her hair away from her chest, revealing her sickly yellow brand. "They even took my dignity."

Her words stump me. Dignity—it's a word I never thought about until arriving at the Hole. It's an unusual word for such a young girl to use, but when she says it, I know exactly what she means.

"No you're not." I choke back my tears. "You're my friend and I'll do everything I can to help you go with dignity."

A plan begins brewing in my head. "I have to get something." She looks at me before clutching my hand. "I promised you I'd come back. I've never gone back on a promise and I'm sure not going to now." It's true. I don't. I've had so many broken promises in my life I could never do that to anyone.

"Okay, I'll just close my eyes for a little while," she says, sinking farther into her bed.

I half-walk, half-run down the hallway. My feet barely touch the steps as I glide eight floors down to the main entrance of the hospital. I look around, then casually walk across the lobby, careful to avoid any bodily fluids, and stop directly in front of the prostitutes.

The blonde raises her head, evaluating me with her angry,

tearful eyes. "What do you want?" Behind her accusing tone, I sense a vulnerable, weary, and sorrowful individual.

"I need a favor." I speak slowly and gently so as not to make her more wary of me.

"You're asking us for a favor?" The other girls narrow their eyes at me while crossing their arms in unison, but I continue on.

"I need makeup...well, not for me. There's a young girl—"

She raises her hand to silence me. Then she digs through her small handbag and pulls out a few items. "If I'm going to die in this godforsaken place, I might as well do something decent." Then she presses the containers into the palm of my hand, willing her eyes to mine. "Hell with the guards and the system. Take this, make your friend happy."

"Oh, thank you, thank you so much," I say.

As I make my way up to the floor, I turn the items over in my hand—lipstick, mascara, and blush.

I can do this, I think.

I lose track of time, and before I know it, an hour has passed. *Those worthless elevators.* Running up and down eight flights is exhausting. When I arrive back at her room and pull the curtain aside, Alyssa scoots into a sitting position to talk to me.

"Told you I'd be back." I hug her.

She gives me a partial smile. "What're you up to?"

"I got makeup!" I bounce to her bedside.

"What?"

"You heard me." I pull the chair to her bedside. The sunlight fades as the sun sets, so the room darkens with shadows from the candles. "How about lipstick, mascara, and blush?" I ask.

"What are you going to do to me?" she asks, nudging me. "Try to make me look pretty?"

"No, you're already beautiful. I'm just sprucing you up a little bit." I open the mascara and begin looping it through her eyelashes. Putting on makeup feels awkward. I'd never actually used it myself, but I remember watching my mother do it years ago. She'd sit in front of her mirror and curl her lashes before running the thick, bristled mascara wand through them. Her eyes looked sultry and mysterious when she'd finish. I always wanted to try, but never had the chance and my heart sinks a little just thinking about it.

"I hope you trust me," I say. I finish her eyes, and plug the mascara up again. Her lashes flutter as she gazes up at me. Their beauty astounds me.

"I do, silly," she says. "It's your beautician skills I'm a little worried about."

I snort at her reply. *If she only knew how beautiful she really is.* I finish with the blush and lipstick. "Now, do you want to take a look? Or would you rather save the screaming for later?"

"Very funny." She opens her eyes wide, almost as if testing her new lashes. She grimaces for a moment, breathing in and out in concentrated gasps.

"Wait. Are you all right?"

"I'm fine. It only hurts when I move, so I can't complain. Don't worry. I can suck it up."

"Do you want me to go get a nurse?"

"No. I said I'm fine." Then I remember she has the only morphine bag in the entire hospital and it shrinks daily. I take the tubing in my hands and examine it. "What's this?" I ask.

"That's the clamp. They use that to control the amount of morphine they're giving me. Make sure you don't touch it. If you roll the ball on the clamp toward the bag, the morphine will pour into my vein and I'd get too much too fast."

"Let me help you to the chair, then I'll push you to the bathroom so you can get a glimpse."

She struggles to move, so I help lift her off the bed and onto the seat. Her body weighs nothing, even for me. The legs of the chair scrape as I push her toward the doorway. "Close your eyes, and don't you dare open them until I count to three. One...two...keep them closed. No peeking!"

"I'm not!"

"Three!" Her face says it all, her eyes widen and her mouth forms into the biggest smile I've ever seen. Her eyes glaze over as her hands gently trace her cheekbones.

"I forgot what I looked like." She smiles. "This virus has been whooping my butt. And you just showed it who's boss! Where'd you learn how to put make up on?"

"I used to watch my mother years ago... Anyway, can't screw up too bad with three items. There are only so many things you can do with a tube of mascara." I shrug the tears off with a smile.

Then the shy, black-haired nurse peeks her head in, looking at me. She gasps at the sight of Alyssa. "My God, sweetie! You're so beautiful," she says.

Alyssa's smile stretches from ear to ear. "This is the nicest thing anyone has ever done for me. Am I allowed to keep it on, or are they going to make me wash it off?" Alyssa asks.

"I won't let that happen." I kneel at her bedside. "Hey, if I was a boy I'd date you in a heartbeat!" She doesn't answer, but I can tell she's pleased as she turns her face to view it from all angles.

Then with quiet humor she confesses. "I've never been on a date before and obviously I'll never get that chance."

I look at her and smile. "Me neither, so I guess that makes us equal." I laugh freely. Her hand moves to cover her brand as she glances in the mirror again.

"Hold on one second." I pull a sheet from the clean load. *No one will miss one sheet.* I rip it into a rough shape of what I want, throwing the shreds in the trash, all while she watches.

"Okay, now just work with me," I say. "Lift your head for a second." She raises her head, and I wrap the sheet around her neck to cover her brand like a scarf. I tie a small knot and look at her. "Now what do you think?" Tears creep out of her eyes and make small paths down her face.

"Thank you," is all she manages to say.

I drag the chair back to her bed, lift her, and tuck her in. She's frail, yet stronger than anyone I've ever met. Being with her opens my heart. Good people really do exist here. That brings me to Cole—I don't even know what to think of him. A knock on the door interrupts our conversation and Sutton steps in.

"It's after seven. Cole's waiting for you."

"For me?" Alyssa winks at him. "Just kidding."

"All right." I give her a hug. "I'll see you tomorrow."

"Okay," she says, still beaming.

When he shuts the door behind us, I realize I might not have time alone with Sutton again until tomorrow, if he's even around. "Can I ask you for a favor?"

"That depends," he says, "on what you're asking."

I tell him my plan. He seems hesitant at first but then agrees it'd be the best thing for Alyssa. Now, I have to talk to Cole and I'm more worried about his reaction. After the past few weeks, I don't want to push too much, but this situation calls for a particular kind of compassion.

I saunter up to the desk where Cole and Zeus wait. He continues talking to Amber, ignoring the fact that I stand behind him. I lean against the wall and watch until the flirting session ends. Amber gets out of her chair, stands behind him rubbing his shoulders and asks, "Do you want more to drink?"

Ugh. She might as well drool on his head while she's at it.

She doesn't even wait for a response. She walks to the fridge and bends over to grab his water. I swear he checks out her backside. *Gross.* Her pants slip down, showing a bright pink thong. I really didn't need to see her butt-floss but there's no way to avoid it. *I wonder how many favors she had to do to get those?* She returns with his water and he sips it casually. Her triumphant eyes meet mine.

"Oh, didn't see you there," she exclaims with a bubbly voice.

Cole turns around. "How long have you been standing there?"

"Long enough," I say.

His face and ears turn red. "I've been here since seven... waiting on you."

"I know," I say. "I'm sorry. I got caught up in something."

He gets up, grabs my arm, and pulls me down the hall. He stops. "What's wrong with you?" he asks while pointing his finger in my face. I have the slightest urge bite it. "When I give you an order, you obey it." He gives me a stern look, his eyebrows pulling together.

"I was finishing up with a patient, sorry. I'll pay closer attention to the time from now on," I say. His expression changes and he releases his grip.

The truth is that time doesn't matter to me when it comes to Alyssa. That girl has changed me in so many ways. *Who ever knew a thirteen-year-old could teach me so many things?* She's the only one who's accepted me for who I am. It's something I've never had, and I'm not willing to let go, but I have to change my approach if I have any chance of getting him to agree to my plan.

"I need to talk to you about something important, but not here, okay?" I ask.

"And you're telling me now…because?"

"I'm not sure really." His face remains stubborn, but he nods, giving me permission. *I think.*

After we arrive at our quarters, tension hangs in the air. This isn't how I wanted things to start. He changes his uniform, grabs a bottle of water, and stands stiffly in the doorway to my room. Zeus lies beside me as I sit on my mattress, fearful of setting Cole off.

"So what's your deal?" he asks in between gulps from his bottle.

"I need a huge favor. Just hear me out before you answer, and just so you know, I already asked Sutton and he gave us permission."

He folds his arms across his chest and takes a deep breath. "Go on…"

I tell him about Alyssa, her sickness, and what she wants the most before the inevitable. His head shakes "No" before I finish.

"No way, you're not staying there!" He squeezes the bottle so tight that it crumples in his fist. "We are not having this discussion. It's completely out of the question. Anything could happen if I'm not there. I won't—"

I stand and close the distance between us. "I don't mean

tonight! Please, put yourself in her shoes, even if it's just for a second. She's all alone in that God-awful place and she's petrified of dying. This is about her, not me. It's not about her brand or your orders. It's a gift we can give *her*. Damn it. She's only thirteen," I plead.

He shakes his head. "Any other guard would've beat or raped you by now, and you just keep pushing me when I'm trying to do the right thing." His face turns a purplish red, and a vein in his neck bulges. "It's bad enough that you're on the radar with my superiors. And you expect me to leave you there? You've lost your damn mind."

"Believe me, I'm thankful I have you, but please, try to understand… I promised her. I promised her she wouldn't die alone. I know you don't understand, and don't expect you to, but I don't break promises. Ever." I continue. "Look, if leaving me is the issue, then stay with us. There are cots we can bring into her room and you can sleep behind the curtain with Zeus and keep watch. That way I can be with her in case she needs me."

He's still shaking his head with his jaw clenched. I know he's right. I'm asking a lot of him, especially with the tension so high between us.

"How much time does she have?" he asks.

"Any day now, or maybe next week."

He closes his eyes for what seems like eternity.

"Please—" I start to say.

"I'll think about it, all right!" He exhales. "You have no idea what you're asking of me." Then his face softens. "You must really care about her."

I don't know what overcomes me—joy, I suppose. I step into him and wrap my arms around his waist. He stands motionless but his heartbeat thumps in my ear, moving faster and faster.

"I really do. She's like a sister I've never had," I say.

He squeezes my shoulders for an instant, and then pushes me away, carefully avoiding eye contact. I step back and exhale with relief. He'll allow me this favor because deep down there's a side of him that's decent and kind.

"Sorry, I didn't mean—"

He puts his hands on his hips and says, "Don't do that again."

The rest of the evening remains quiet. Cole keeps to himself after our conversation, almost like he needs time to digest it all. I watch him pack his bag, four shirts, four pants, four pairs of boxer briefs and his shaving kit. I feel all giddy inside although his solemn expression forces me to withhold my triumphant emotions. *I think I touched a nerve.*

He manages to say good night before he closes his door. And I begin to realize for the first time how much security Zeus brings me when he lies down beside me. I find it therapeutic to rub his head and receive his warmth in return. His presence seems to scare away my nightmares and I sleep in peace.

We drive through the checkpoint at the training center, and this time I keep my mouth glued shut. Our walk through the garage is uneventful. I perspire from the stress and twirl one of my locks nervously as we enter the hospital. The whooshing of the doors blows my hair back. His steps echo in the hallway and he looks engrossed while pressing the eighth floor button. *It's now or never.* I take a deep breath and ask him one more favor.

"I'm scared to ask you—"

"No more favors," he says. He spins around and the gleam in his eyes melts away.

"It's not for me. It's for her," I say.

His lips turn thin and he folds his arms over. "I'm already risking too much."

"It doesn't involve me. It involves you."

"No way, no more favors," he says, raising an eyebrow.

"She's never been on a date." I hurry on before he can protest. "It's something every girl dreams of. She needs to be swept off her feet."

Ding. The elevator doors open and Zeus bolts into the hallway.

"You're positively killing me. You know that right?"

Sarcasm boils over, but he gives in with his next breath. "I'm not very good at this sort of thing."

"I highly doubt that," I say, accidentally brushing his hand with mine. He pauses for a brief moment and his onyx eyes flash to his hand then jump to my eyes. Something bubbles up within me. It's weightless and yet foreboding. Whatever passes between us in that moment runs deep. I clear my throat and knock on Sutton's door. I feel a tug on my ponytail causing me to spin around. Cole is holding a white string in his right hand.

"It was stuck in your hair,"

"Oh," I say as I run my fingers through my curls. "Thanks."

"Come in," Sutton says. He speaks on the phone in a hushed tone. "Gotta go." He hangs up, swivels his chair, and raises his eyebrows. "Now what's wrong?"

"Nothing. I spoke to Cole and he's willing to stay." Sutton looks at Cole and pauses while evaluating his face. "Wonderful. Just make sure—"

"It's all right, sir. I already got the clearances from my superiors last night," Cole says.

"Well, then I guess you should go see Alyssa. I won't bother you unless I'm needed." He dismisses us with his hand and begins dialing a number on his phone. "Oh, and, Cole, thank you. This little girl means a lot to me too."

* * *

Alyssa musters as much excitement as she can. She falls in and out of sleep most of the day, but at eleven thirty p.m., she's perky.

"Are you up for a visitor?" I ask her.

"It's almost midnight, who'd visit me now?" She purses her lips together. Zeus's nails click from behind the curtain and she tries to peek underneath.

"Ready?" I ask.

She nods, scrunching her eyebrows, as she tries to peek around the curtain. "Are you sure?" I stand at the curtain with my hand on it, waiting to reveal her surprise. I laugh at her impatient expression.

"You're killing me... Just open it, would you?"

I slide open the curtain with painstaking slowness, giggling as she gives me a dirty look. The candlelight hits them and Zeus bounds into the room without his manners, peeking up at her, resting on his front two paws and swiping her small hand with a giant slurp. Alyssa erupts into laughter.

"Hey," Cole says as he follows behind Zeus.

I try to reply but his appearance renders me speechless. He wears a pair of carpenter jeans that sit on his waist and a white collared shirt. It's slightly wrinkled, but that doesn't detract from how handsome he looks. The wind is sucked out of my lungs. I'm drawn to him, and don't like it. His clean appearance, sweet demeanor, and the fact that he nods and smiles at Alyssa with respect make my walls crumble a little. I almost want him to be here for me, not her, but I quickly shove those thoughts away. Thinking about it will only get me into trouble since it's forbidden to even have these types of feelings.

What's wrong with me? It's too dangerous and he made it more than clear that I'm just part of his job.

He whispers, "Do I look all right? I wasn't sure what to wear." He puts his hands in his pockets and does a complete three-sixty.

His butt looks amazing in those jeans. I catch myself before my jaw hits the floor and arrange my face in what I hoped was a purely virginal appearance. *Ugh, there I go again.* "You look...nice," I lie. He looks so handsome, but I don't tell him.

"Then why are you blushing?"

"I'm not!"

"Okay, so when did you put a crap load of blush on?"

"I didn't. I don't wear makeup!"

His eyes linger for a moment and he smiles crookedly. "Exactly." He laughs and I swat him. His hands move up in a surrender position as he backs away.

Is he really joking around with me? A smile stays plastered on my face, thinking about how sweet it is he showed up despite his reservations.

Then Zeus comes to my side, breaking the trance, and I look into his big brown eyes. "I guess you're my date, boy. Hope you like my outfit." I laugh at myself.

Cole stares at me. "Take good care of her," he says to Zeus. My heart skips a beat, startling me.

He looks away and sits next to Alyssa's bed. "It's nice to meet you. I'm Cole." He reaches over and shakes her hand. "Lexi told me a lot about you, and I couldn't help but want to meet this special girl." He scoots closer to her and takes her hands into his. "I was wondering if you'd do me the honor… of going on a date with me?"

If a girl could light up, she just did. Alyssa grins as if she received the greatest gift in the universe. "I'd love to." She giggles as her face turns scarlet.

"Give us a few minutes. I want to freshen her up a bit." I close the curtain and brush her hair, pinning it up into an elegant hairstyle my mother used to wear. After I'm finished, Cole places one arm under her knees and the other secures her back as he lifts her fragile body. Alyssa wraps her arms around his neck with a look of pure rapture on her face.

"Oh, I'm sorry," Cole says. "I probably should've asked you if it would be all right to pick you up."

"Oh, that's all right," she says softly and then gives me a wink.

He carries her without effort down to a vacant room, and I wipe a tear away as I watch him fulfill a dying girl's dream.

It's dark except for the melted candles lit on the end of the table. The plastic ware, which I scrounged for after talking to Sutton, sits in all the correct spots. Cole carefully lowers Alyssa into her seat for the night. Even Sutton makes an appearance and places a soft kiss on her head.

"Enjoy, sweetie. You deserve it." Sutton offers me his arm and leads me out. Before the door closes, I glimpse one more time.

Cole sits across from Alyssa, the candlelight flickering across their faces as they laugh at something together. The ease with which he relates to her makes me smile.

Every day, I witness the ugliness of humanity and it diminishes my faith in the goodness of people. But watching Cole show kindness to Alyssa, reminds me of the kindness my father showed others. Whenever someone needed him, even if it was dangerous, he'd help. Instances like this give me the spark I need to keep going despite the horrific obstacles thrown in my way. *Unbelievable that I've found more depth here than I ever had before.* The emotional peaks and valleys exhaust me, but my heart feels content, and it doesn't make sense to me.

When I return to the room, Zeus snores in my cot. *I guess I'm sleeping somewhere else.* I take Cole's and slide under the warm covers. I fall asleep with the image of Alyssa looking alive and happy while sitting across from Cole.

* * *

"Hey, wake up." Startled, I fly up, smacking heads with Cole.

"Ouch," we both say at the same time.

He rubs his forehead, his face scrunching with the effort. "Sorry, I didn't mean to startle you. I just wasn't sure where I'm supposed to sleep since you're in my bed and all."

I rub my eyes and yawn. "The cot's yours. Zeus took mine, so I'll sleep on the floor." I swing my legs to the floor, and the cold tiles sting my feet.

"Um. No you're not!" a voice says beside me. "I don't take up even half this bed. Come in. I don't mind sharing." For the second time in less than thirty seconds, I jump at the sound of a voice I wasn't expecting. I stand, straighten my clothes, and climb in next to Alyssa.

"Thank you!" she says. "For the best day of my life." My heart drops as she wraps her weak arms around me.

"You don't have to thank me. He was the one who took all the risk here."

"But you had to ask him," she says. "That couldn't have been easy for you."

"No, it wasn't. But it was worth it." I kiss her cheek. "Plus, when it comes to you, convincing isn't even needed. It's impossible not to fall in love with you. You're a wonderful person and I want to thank you for sharing your life with me. I'm forever changed because of you."

She wipes her tears, rolls over to her other side, and I cover her with a blanket. "I love you, too," she says.

Before I can count to ten, she drifts off. I watch her, and then my eyes wonder over to Cole. He stares at the ceiling, looks at me, and holds my eyes for a minute as sadness, joy, and an unidentifiable emotion pass between us. He motions good night, and I nod, but I'm not ready to sleep. Not yet.

I watch him. The curves of his face are soft in the moonlight and his sculpted arms wrap around his bunched-up blankets. I picture those arms wrapped around Alyssa, the way he cradled her, the way he cared for her in a way I'm sure she's rarely felt in her short life. I close my eyes, and as I drift off, I think of how lonely Alyssa must have been, how lonely I've been. And I fall asleep, the vision of Cole carrying me accompanying me to the peace of my dreams.

The next two days pass this way. Cole and Zeus stay with me in the hospital while Alyssa slowly slips further away from us. Each morning, Cole takes Zeus to the training center for the majority of the day, and every night he returns at seven.

Alyssa's condition worsens. She sleeps most of the day and barely stays awake long enough to hold a conversation. Occasionally, she moans and shifts positions in her bed. The only gift I can give her is my presence. It seems like such a small gift, but it's what I'd want if fate switched our positions. My heart seizes when I see her grimace when she coughs or even turns her head, and I wish I could take her pain away. But it only grows worse each day. Sutton even gave me a pamphlet on the dying process, which at first I refused, horrified by the idea. Now I'm glad I read it because I'm more aware of what Alyssa might need from me through her journey.

At seven p.m., Cole brings Zeus back to our room. Zeus's eyelids droop and his legs wobble. He flops to the floor, and within a matter of seconds, he begins snoring.

"How's she doing?" Cole asks.

"Okay…I'm hoping I can wake her long enough to give her some ice chips. Her mouth is so dry and she says she's thirsty but chokes on water. She stopped eating today, which I know is normal at this stage, but it's really hard to watch. I'm afraid she's starving even though the book said she's not. Weird, right?"

He shrugs his shoulders. "You finally read the book Sutton gave you? That's good." He stands with his feet shoulder width apart and strokes his chin pensively. "I don't know how you do it, sit here with her knowing she's going to—"

I scoot the chair back fast enough that it screeches obnoxiously, and I pull him into the hall. "Shhhh. She can hear you. The book said hearing is the last thing that goes right before *it* happens…" My tongue gets stuck and I have to clear my throat. "So we have to be careful about what we say around her. All right?"

"Really? Wow. Okay, good to know." He looks down at me, worry lines creasing his brow. "How are you holding up?"

"I have my bad moments and my good moments. I just wish there was some way I could take her place." In the dim light I notice what I think is ketchup, stuck to his chin. "Did you just eat?"

"Yea, why?"

Without even thinking I reach up and wipe it away with my thumb. "I hope you weren't saving that for later."

All of a sudden, Zeus barrels out of Alyssa's room, growling with his hair sticking up on his back.

"Hey, calm down," Cole says.

"What's he growling about?" I ask, trembling. I steal a glance at Alyssa's door.

"Who knows, he probably hears something." He reaches down and rubs furiously between Zeus's ears. I can tell he's a bit worried too.

I peek into Alyssa's room, making sure she's still breathing. Her chest rises and falls with each shallow breath.

"Like what?" I ask, turning back to Cole.

"Dogs have incredible hearing. It could've been a noise he didn't like coming from the ground floor. He's capable of hearing things up to a mile away in the Hole. But, in the woods. A mile and a half."

"Wow, that's unreal." I tilt my head to the side. "Why can he hear farther in the woods?"

"Less distractions and not as much noise."

"Makes sense." I lean against the wall, feeling a little tired. "How was training?"

"Rough," he replies. "This whole situation makes my life pretty difficult."

"What situation? Being here in the hospital?" I perk up, and push off the wall to scrutinize his face.

"No, and yes—well, sleeping up here night after night with all the other guards knowing we're here. Just makes things edgy," he says. He doesn't usually share anything about his training so I pay attention.

"They all know you have clearance right? You told them I'm tending to someone who has a virus... So it's not like you're doing anything wrong." I shrug it off while clearing my throat. His eyes meet mine and his hand pauses on Zeus's head.

"It's not me. It's you. The fact that you're eight floors up from the training center has them itching to make trouble. I've been taking a beating for this, you know. I don't like the feeling I have—not at all. They're obsessed with you. I've heard some of them talking about what they'd do if they got you alone. We need to relocate soon...real soon." He stops and rethinks his last statement. "I'm sorry...I don't say it to be mean or insensitive, but your brand makes you a target for their games, and your face sure doesn't help matters."

"My face? Do I make weird faces?" I try to change where this is going. I know what the guards think. I've heard the catcalls, and I'll never forget the way his comrade touched me in the garage while giving Cole his warning.

"Yea. That's it." He shakes his head then looks at his feet.

"Lexi, you're beautiful, there's no denying that." He shuffles his feet and shifts his weight uncomfortably. "They can't stop looking at you." He glances up at me for a brief second before locking his gaze on something behind me. "And I understand why." The words come out so soft I can barely hear them.

Butterflies don't just flit through my stomach—they do cartwheels and somersaults. Feeling flustered I say, "For the same reason all the girls can't help but throw themselves at you." His eyes snap to mine and we hold our gaze for a minute.

"I won't leave her," I say. "Cole, I can't."

"I know, but you might not have a choice." His eyes, still locked on mine, harden.

"You can't do that to her. To me—"

"Lexi, you don't understand. I have orders, and I can't just throw my arms up in the air and leave you here, although there're times I want to. I'm trying to do the right thing, but you make it so damn hard sometimes. I respect what you're doing—really I do. But I'm telling you now, this can't go on much longer. It's starting to look suspicious," he says. The grimace on his face makes my insides freeze with flashbacks of the execution.

"They don't seriously think it's like that... Do they?" I ask.

"Lexi? Where are you?" Alyssa interrupts our quiet conversation.

"I'm right here." I run to her side. She lies under multiple blankets and no longer has the strength to sit up on her own. "What do you need?"

"Can I try some ice chips?" she rasps.

"Of course. I'll be right back."

I leave the room and rush down the hall. Amber isn't at her usual post, but that doesn't surprise me. I pass the linen closet on my way to the small kitchen area. Heavy breathing and the sound of scuffling feet force me to stop. It sounds like someone's messing around in the closet. I tip toe into the kitchen, fill a glass with ice chips, and scurry past the closet. This time I know I'm not imagining things.

Someone's definitely in there.

Curiosity wins over as I quietly set the glass down and turn the knob. It's dark inside, but there's enough light to see two figures. As I peek through the small viewing space, I decipher a male and female kissing passionately. My mouth falls open. I didn't know there was a male on the floor aside from Cole. Sutton went home an hour ago. I pull the door closed, pick up the glass, and hurry back to Alyssa's room, all while wondering whom it was.

"Thank you." Alyssa's been propped up with at least four pillows. "Cole helped me sit up while you were gone." She smiles at me. I glance at him, but he's already asleep.

"Can you wait one more minute? I'll be right back." I ask and she nods her head while attempting to suck on an ice chips. I peek into the hallway. Amber walks toward me, fixes her hair, and surveys her surroundings.

"Where were you?"

Her hands fly up to her face and she jumps at the sound of my voice. She composes herself and says, "I took a fifteen-minute break. Why do you care?"

A few yards behind her, a guard enters the hallway from the linen closet. Amber looks at him, at me, and then at him. *Disgusting.* He's tall like the others and wears a rigid, collared uniform. His relaxed stride proves that he's not worried about getting caught. We're all standing in the hallway now.

"What's the problem?" He directs his question to me.

"Umm, nothing," I stammer, putting my hand on the wall for support.

"She was just asking me for something, Zane. There's no problem." Her shoulders go tight as she replies.

"Then why are the both of you standing in the hallway looking stupid?" His question is more of a statement. He tugs at his collar and steps toward me with a smile on his face. It's cold and doesn't reach his eyes. "Would you like a turn with me? I can grant you special privileges around here if you make the right choice."

His bold offer knocks the wind of out of me, but I don't waste any time. My hand reaches for the doorway behind me.

He steps closer and Amber nervously fiddles with her hands. Just then, Zeus plows into the hallway, snarling, and stands in front of me. A low growl comes from deep within his chest and fur stands up on his back.

"Back off, Zane. She's not yours to toy with." Cole's voice cuts through the tension. Relief comes over me but quickly dissipates when I see his hand move toward the gun strapped on his leg. He unceremoniously sweeps me behind him into Alyssa's room and reaches to close the door all without ever taking his eyes off Zane. Zeus dashes inside behind me and whines while I stand against the wall. An altercation takes place, but their low voices make it hard to decipher. After a few minutes, Cole reappears.

"What happened?" I sweep my hand across my forehead, wiping away the sweat.

"Zane's been reaping victims tonight. You almost became one." He sits on his cot and attempts to unlace his boots. His fingers fumble with haste so he gives up with an exasperated sigh.

"You mean Amber didn't choose to do that?" I ask.

He swallows in frustration. "Oh no, she chose to go. She likes the attention and the privileges that come with it. It's hard to earn a living here if you don't have some means of doing it."

"She was scared though…"

"Because we all know what happens when sinners defy guards."

"So you're telling me that she slept with him for extra benefits?" I say. *Ugh. Sometimes people are exactly what you think they are.*

"People do all sorts of things in this place," he says. "It's not black and white like you think."

"Did you know she was doing that? Have you—?" I can't even finish the sentence.

"Yes, I've known for a while. And no, I haven't and wouldn't do that, ever." I let out a sigh of relief, willing my mind not to think of him doing something so disgusting. "Don't worry about it. That's why I'm here plus Zeus woke me up when he heard Zane outside. So there's no doubt you have the best team protecting you." He collapses on his cot, not even bothering to take off his guns. I'm starting to love that dog. I make my way over to Alyssa's bed.

"Is everything okay?" Alyssa's concern humbles me.

"I'm fine. Just a mix up... Nothing to worry about." I brush it off for her sake.

"I hate those guards," she whispers as if she is afraid they can hear her through the walls. She gives a small cough and tries to get comfortable again. "Are you sure you are okay? The way Zeus bolted out of here I thought something really bad happened."

"One of the guards decided to try and push me around, but it's okay, really. I'm fine. Plus, Zeus is quite the protector from evil." I stroke her head and help her settle down to sleep.

"You're lucky you have Cole. He seems to be the only good one around here."

"I guess." I make a face, and her laugh sounds like tinkling bells. "But he's still a guard."

"I heard that," Cole says. Alyssa laughs louder and I roll my eyes.

After a few minutes of playful bantering, Cole lies back down and falls asleep in one motion. I sit on Alyssa's bed and braid a few small strands of her hair as she stares at me.

"Doesn't it scare you...that you'll never be free?" Her playful expression turns serious, and her crystal blue eyes pierce me. "I can't imagine being as pretty as you, and having all those guards around. If it were me, I'd try to find a way to escape," she whispers. Her eyes dart to the door and her hands shake at just the thought.

"Lexi, can I ask you something?" She raises her searching eyes to mine.

"Sure, you can ask me anything. You know that."

"If you got out of here, where would you go?"

"Now, that's easy. I'd have to say Lexington Bay...if I could ever find it. Hey, what about you? Where would you go?"

"Anywhere would be better than here. But I don't know what's beyond the Hole anymore. It's been so long." She tilts her chin down.

"I'm afraid it's not much better, really."

"Anything has to be better than this." Alyssa's eyes snap to mine with the desire for knowledge.

"Well...after my father died, my mom remarried and we had to leave the countryside, so I spent the rest of my time in High Society—where what's left of the wealthy live. It's a northern city, the largest one left...which isn't saying much since only 1/18 of it remains after the war. Outside High Society, we're surrounded by poverty and beggars just like the Hole."

"Really?" Alyssa says.

"Yup, really. Anyway, pretty much everyone lives in terror, trying to survive without being accused—money doesn't always buy them freedom. It just happens to be the luck of the draw. If they're accused by someone who's got a vendetta against them, then they get arrested... It's so sick and twisted. I hate it there too. There are a lot of empty houses and abandoned buildings. Not much to see, nothing to enjoy, and really no life anymore. Mostly everyone stays in their homes, only going out for errands and things like that. Although there are some lucky ones who hold onto their jobs."

"Did you go to school? I used to love learning..."

"Yes I did, although it's pretty warped what they teach these days. I'm lucky my dad taught me a lot from home."

Alyssa's eyes drop to her hands, disappointed. "I wonder if my family's still alive."

"If they are, it's because of you." I take her hand in mine and give her a small smile.

"Lexi, I want to be cremated." Alyssa blurts out.

"Where did that come from?" I jerk my head back.

"I don't know...I guess from a dream I had," she says. "Please, promise me you won't let them put me in a box and bury me where bugs can eat my body."

"Of course, if that's what you want, I'll do it for you." I

clasp her hand harder and feel the tears well up in my eyes. "Anything for you."

"If you ever get out, take my ashes and spread them in the ocean, would you?" She's so mature for thirteen; I forget sometimes she's just a child. "I'm not afraid of dying anymore because I know you'll be with me." She smiles faintly while clutching my hand. "But you know what? I think dying is easier compared to living here."

When she finishes, tears obscure my vision. I hug her as tightly as I think I can without hurting her. I know exactly what she means. I was in that place not too long ago, where taking my life would've been easier than continuing to live. But now, it's different.

"I wish I had your strength. I don't think—" My voice cracks and I'm unable to finish my sentence.

Her eyes close as she fades out. "You're strong. You just haven't realized it yet, but you'll find your strength. I know you will."

A loud beeping sound coming from Cole's pocket causes me to jump.

"You've got to be kidding me. Now what?" He shoves his hand in his pocket, pulling out a beeper, and squints while trying to decipher the number. The light from the pager illuminates his face like an apparition. "Unbelievable." He sits up, rubs his bleary eyes, swings his jacket over his back, and glides his arms through the sleeves.

"Where are you going?" My voice shakes as I speak.

"I have to run across the street real fast. Something's going down and they called for backup. When I leave, put your chair under the door knob like this." He demonstrates exactly what he wants me to do. "Let me grab an extra one for you to sit on." Cole brings me a chair and puts it down right next to the window and across from Alyssa.

"Thanks."

"Yeah, no problem. Don't open the door for anyone until you hear Zeus bark, all right? Even if it sounds like me, don't do it. You got that?" He arches his eyebrows in expectation.

"I understand. Please hurry." I check on Alyssa, feeling the panic rise in my chest, but she remains peaceful. Thankfully, the alarm didn't disturb her.

"Will do. All of the guards within a mile radius of the call have to respond, so you're going to be guard-free for a little while."

"Is that a good or bad thing?"

"Good. I don't trust any of them when it comes to you. Okay, I gotta go."

After he leaves I place the chair under the doorknob. I sit down, lean back, and decide to count with the clock. The ticking doesn't calm my nerves though. It only reminds me of how slow time moves when you want it to go faster.

Within five minutes, I hear a male voice reverberating through the hall. The string of vulgarity that easily slips off his tongue puts me on edge. It sounds unfamiliar, but who knows. My eyes lock on the door, waiting for any motion, I can feel my hands getting clammy.

One knock.

"Open the door," the voice demands.

Out of the corner of my eye, I see Alyssa stir and open her eyes. I leap to her bed and fling my hand over her mouth. I whisper, "Don't say a word."

"I said open the door! Now!" he yells while pounding his fists against the frame.

Go away, go away, please, please go away and leave us alone.

"All right. I'll do this my way," he says, the menace of his words reaching me even through the door.

Alyssa grabs my hands with all of her strength and I realize I'm the only one here to protect her. I shove my fright back into the corner of my brain and answer him.

"If it's me you're after, you can have me, just don't hurt her."

"HA." The door bashes in and a man whom I've never seen before walks in wearing a hospital gown. The smell of his body odor causes me to scrunch my face. His bloodshot eyes match his red brand, but he doesn't look at either of us. "I don't want you." He points behind me and laughs mockingly at my face. "I want her morphine."

"No," I say, grabbing a fistful of my hair.

He doesn't like my answer, not one bit. His face turns scarlet like he's going to detonate. He smiles sadistically and cracks his neck. "It doesn't work that way. I get what I want, when I want it. So do yourself and the little girl a favor and move."

"There isn't anymore," I lie. Not convincing enough. I move in front of Alyssa's bed to block her view of his face.

"I know. I've checked all the other patients. She's the only one. Now move."

I can't focus or think straight, so I say something I regret the second it comes out. "Over my dead body!"

He cocks his head and sneers. "That's not a problem."

He comes toward us, so I grab the chair near the window, turn my head away, and swing it into the glass with everything I have. The jarring crash sends glass flying everywhere, and then I release the chair and let it fly out the window. Immediately, the crashing of the chair coupled with the sound of vehicles in the street and people bickering waft into the room.

"Now, that wasn't necessary, was it?" Then with unexpected speed, he darts forward. I lunge into him to try to block him from getting to Alyssa. He shoves me into the wall, smacking the back of my head, and I crumple to the floor. Darkness fills my vision for a moment, making it hard to focus. He turns his back to me, thinking I'm finished, but I have enough sense to latch onto his legs.

"Stupid girl," he curses. His fist hammers my back, jolting my shoulders with excruciating pain.

"Stop it!" Alyssa yells. "Don't hurt her. Here, just take it." I look up and she has the bag in her hands.

"Drop it!" I yell to Alyssa. *Can't hold on much longer...*

His brutish arms wrap around my waist and he pulls me up like a sack of flour, ripping my hands away from his legs. In one motion, he sends me crashing into the side of Alyssa's bed. The room spins as I attempt to gather myself.

She tosses the bag to me and it lands on the floor. I grab the clamp and slide the ball up leaving the tubing wide open.

"What the hell are you doing? Just give me the damn bag."

I watch anxiously as Alyssa's blood starts running down from her hand, creeping closer to the bag. I pick up the bag and lay it on my lap. *Hurry, hurry.* His eyes register deceit and he punches me in the face. My head whips back but I manage to hold onto the morphine. I look down just as her blood reaches the bag.

"Clamp it," I say. I stand up on wobbly legs and hand Alyssa the bag of morphine. Broken but victorious, I say, "You can have it now, but I wouldn't take any if I were you."

"A little bit of blood doesn't scare me. Now hand it over or I'll put you in a coffin."

"Well, it should."

"Oh really. Why's that?"

"Hers is lethal. That entire bag is now contaminated with the virus that's killing her. So do us all a favor. Take it. Go inject all your drug buddies and take bets on who will be the last to die."

"You're lying!" He grabs me with one hand, lifting me off my toes.

"She wouldn't be lying here if I was!" I scream at him. I've taken a beating and run out of ideas for holding him at bay.

"Then I'll kill you both." He jams his fist straight into my windpipe and I'm unable to scream. At the same time, he releases my shirt and I land flat on my back. He mounts me and wraps his hands around my neck.

"No stop! Get off of her!" Alyssa sits ramrod straight in bed, her tiny voice projecting louder than I thought possible. Her wild eyes plead with him.

"You. Shut up," he says.

I'm struggling to get him off my chest, but my head's spinning and I'm gasping for air. My throat is in a knot where his fist smashed me. It's no use. He overpowers me. His grimy smell and devilish eyes make me panic. His dirty fingers close around my windpipe like a vice. If I could just breathe. In a frenzy, I claw at him with my fingernails but his grip proves unbreakable. My legs flail at nothing but air. My chest feels like it's going to explode with the need for air. This is it. I hope he makes it quick.

Nothing can brace me for the slow deprivation of oxygen. Images around me blur, and darkness creeps up like shadows, but then something slams into him forcing him off me and onto the ground. He screams for mercy.

"Look away." Cole's steely voice fills my ears.

Alyssa pulls the sheet over her eyes. I roll over, clutching my neck, and I'm choking on the air I'm trying to get in my deflated lungs. *Thank God, thank you for air.* Out of the corner of my eye, I can see Cole's eyes squint in anger. The vein in his forehead pulses with fury.

"Hold him there," Cole says to Zeus. He turns to the man. "Were you going to kill her?"

"No. I just wanted the morphine and the stupid bi—"

Cole punches him in the jaw, making the addict flop like a rag doll. "Don't you dare call her that!" His hands wrap quickly around the man's head in a jerking motion and I hear a snap, followed by a thud. Then I see the man's lifeless face just a few feet from mine. His eyes remain open, and his neck bulges from where Cole broke it.

I gasp.

"Dammit, you all right?" Cole kneels beside me and touches my neck ever so gently. "I didn't think we'd make it in time."

I search for his hand, and when his fingers interlace with mine, I squeeze it as hard as I possibly can. "But you did." My limbs tingle as the feeling returns to them. My vision clears, and Cole's eyes catch mine. His forehead creases as he strokes my fingers with shaky hands. I don't think I've ever been so happy to be alive in the Hole.

"I was standing in the building across the street, dealing with the incident, when suddenly Zeus took off out the door, across the road, and darted into the hospital. I didn't even ask permission to leave, just turned and sprinted after him." He's shaking his head and staring at the floor. "If anything would've happened to you, I'd never be able to forgive myself."

"But you got here, and we're fine."

"Speak for yourself," Alyssa wheezes out.

"Crap, your morphine... We have to get it running again." Zeus licks my face as I push myself into a sitting position. After surviving that ordeal, the fog lifts and new worries come to mind. Alyssa looks like a ghost as a sheen of sweat glistens on her forehead and the circles under her eyes darken even more.

"I already paged Sutton. He's on his way," Cole says. "Who broke the window?"

"I did," I say, slightly defensive. "And it worked."

"What do you mean?" Cole and Alyssa ask in unison.

"I was hoping Zeus would hear it and figure out something wasn't right." Their mouths fall open. "What? You didn't realize you have the greatest dog ever to walk this earth?" I adjust the pillow behind Alyssa's head and kiss her forehead while imagining the danger she was in.

"He's the only dog you know." Alyssa attempts a chuckle.

"That's not the point," I say. "He saved our lives and that makes him the best." I sit next to her on the bed and take her hand in my own.

"Wow," Cole says while shaking his head and smiling.

"What?" I say.

"That was absolutely brilliant. And it explains the broken chair outside the entrance."

"I wouldn't say that." I look down at Alyssa, not wanting to meet his eyes.

"No, he's right. It was," Alyssa says. "I never would've known to do that."

The rest of the night was uneventful. Sutton fixed the morphine bag and then examined my injuries, which consist of a lot of deep bruises. Other sinners came in and patched up the window. Cole didn't leave the room, not even for a second, and Alyssa slept. When my adrenaline wore off, my legs were shaking and my knees started to buckle. So, I lay down and pulled the blanket over my head.

"Sweet dreams," Cole says.

"Let's hope. Good night." I snuggle into the cot as much as possible.

Darkness. My bed is large, fluffy, and envelopes me in its warmth. My fingernails dig into my palms, and my eyes are alert as he raises my blanket.

"Lexi," he says with a cruel tone as he shoves me into the wall. "I remember telling you to never mention any of this… to anyone!"

With a shaky voice I say, "But, I didn't." He picks me up holding me to his face. My legs dangle, unable to touch the floor.

"Don't lie to me!" His spit hits my face, and I can taste stale cigarettes.

"I'm not. I swear. I said nothing!" I'm squeezing my eyes shut and my chin won't stop trembling.

"Are you awake?" My eyes open to Cole's face peering over me. His full lips inches from mine.

"Well, I am now." I push upward and he steps back. He wears the stiff black uniform of the guards on patrol and has his guns strapped on.

"Are you leaving?" I ask.

"After you fell asleep, I received orders for a special op. I don't have a choice on this one." His voice hardens as he steps away. "I'm not sure when I'll be back. Maybe later today or tomorrow evening."

"What about Zeus?"

"Sorry, he has to come with me."

"I thought you—"

"Try not to worry. I've got it all worked out. Sutton's going to stay with you tonight and you should be safe during the day with all these people around. No matter what, try to stay here with Alyssa. If you need something, have another nurse or aid get it for you. If for any reason Sutton has to leave the floor, he's going to take you with him. Do you understand?"

"Yes, I do." I stand up and face him with my hair undone and clothes all rumpled. I can see the struggle he's having reflected on his face for a brief moment before he clenches his jaw.

"Take care of her," he says as he waves toward Alyssa and turns on his heels to go.

"Be careful," I blurt.

He doesn't turn around, just leashes Zeus. "I always am." His boots echo in the hallway on the way out.

Everything within me desires to run and hug him good-bye but my head spins like a turnstile. I worry for him. I worry for Alyssa. She worsened overnight. All of her energy was sapped from her body after the incident with the drug addict. *So much to think about.*

She moves under the sheets, so I step closer. Her eyes are glassy and sunken in, her mouth so dry she can't speak. I pour some water in her cup since I don't have any ice chips and reposition the straw so her mouth can reach it. I lift the straw to her lips, but she clamps her mouth, refusing to drink. Her lips are dry and cracking, so I put some Vaseline on my finger and gently rub it on and around her mouth.

Sutton joins me at her bedside. His eyes scan over her before checking her vitals. His mouth seals into a grim line and he gently pats Alyssa's head.

"It's going to be soon. She's starting to mottle." He lifts the sheet off her feet.

"You have to get her socks. Her feet are purple."

"That's the mottling. It's when the blood vessels start to shut off at the extremities to try to keep the blood circulating to the heart and lungs. It's a normal part of the dying process. Our bodies were made to fight hard, even till the very end."

I try to swallow the lump in my throat, but am unable to push it down. It comes out as a hiccup before the tears reach my eyes.

Sutton puts his hand on my back and rubs in circles. "She's

comfortable though. I can assure you of that." He sits next to me. I rest my head on his shoulder and he takes my hand. We hold hands, and celebrate the life of a girl so special that she changed our lives.

"Plus she has you, and you're giving her the greatest gift of all…just by being with her. Alyssa is very dear to my heart." Sutton's voice cracks a little. "I wish I could save her, and, Alyssa, if you can hear me, I am *so* sorry I failed you." I sniffle as he says those last words. "I remember one time I fell asleep in her chair and she threw a cup of water on me to wake me up." Sutton and I laugh, but then he grows serious again. "The virus beat her down and she withdrew for a while…until she met you. Lexi, she lights up when you're around her. I never saw her so happy. Honestly. Thank you."

I wipe the salty tear gliding over my lip and hiccup again. He laughs. "The truth is she helps me more than I help her. I truly love her." I have to stop to keep from blubbering more. He gives me another squeeze, wipes his eyes, and stands.

"We need to run down to the main supply closet. It's on the first floor," he says. "Just need to grab a few things."

"But—"

"It'll be quick. Come on let's go."

I whisper in Alyssa's ear that we'll be right back and then accompany Sutton to get the supplies. He fills my arms with gauze, a Foley catheter kit, staple removal kit, and some other items I've never heard of.

"All right, that should do it." His pager starts to beep. He puts his things down, reaches for his pager, and holds it closer to his eyes. The color of his face washes away.

"No!" I drop the items to the floor, turn, and sprint down the hall.

"Wait for me," Sutton calls out to me.

I keep running and don't look back. I swing open the door to the stairs and take two or three steps at a time. I push through a slow crowd, and ignore their indignant expressions. "Get out of my way!" I slip through them and around them like liquid in rocks. Two men block my way. "You have to move. I need to get to her!"

"Maybe you should learn some manners," a man with white hair says to me.

I have no idea what his problem is, but it causes me to erupt. "I'm tired of being polite. Now get out of my way!"

"Nope."

"Let her through!" Sutton yells from a few flights down.

He doesn't budge.

"Screw it." I throw a punch directly into his groin. He topples over groaning and I leap past him. My lungs burn and my legs feel gummy. When I reach the eighth floor, I have to take a second to catch my breath before I take off again.

When I look down, I see Bertha standing outside of her door crying. *No, please no!* Like lightening, I run. I turn to go in her room when Bertha grabs my arm.

"What are you doing? Let go of me."

"She's still with us," Bertha says.

"Oh, thank you God,"

Sutton joins us. "What's wrong?" He huffs the words out.

"Alyssa's talking…to her mother," Bertha says. "And she wants to go with her."

"Her mother's here?" I ask. "No, after all this time she decides to show up and see her daughter? No way she's leaving. I won't let her—"

"Lexi, her mother's dead," Sutton says.

Then I remember, the book said sometimes when the end is near, they can see people who've died before, and it's possible they might talk to them. You're not supposed to tell them they're wrong because it only makes the patient more anxious.

"Okay, I get it. Now can I see her?"

Sutton nods his head.

Nothing can hold back my tears. My chest aches and I have no idea how I move my legs, but eventually I get to her and she smiles.

"Don't be sad," she says softly. "My mommy came to take me home, and she said they're going to let her. I'm going to get out of here. Can you believe it? I won't die a sinner in the

Hole. I never thought this was possible."

I lean over and kiss her head before sitting on the side of her bed facing her. I take her hand in mine, feeling nothing but her cold skin against mine. "That's wonderful. I'm so happy for you," I say with a trembling chin. "Would you like me... to pack your things for you?" I run my other hand down her silky hair.

"Oh, that would be great because we have to leave soon."

I nod slightly and feel my shoulders slump. My body wants to convulse and my eyes are pools about to spill over. I do everything I can to hold it back but it doesn't work. Tears escape and she feels them trail down her arm. She looks up at me, her glassy eyes opening wide.

"Please, won't you come with us?" She takes a gasping breath and says, "I don't want to leave you."

"Alyssa, I really...wish I could," I say in a whisper because my voice is cracking with every word. "But, I have a few things... I need to take care of first."

"When you're done then, will you come?"

"Of course." I climb into bed with her, get under the covers and hold her in my arms. She rests her head on my shoulder, so I straighten my back as best I can.

"I'm so tired." Her voice softens.

"I know," I say. I rest my cheek on her head and smell her hair. It smells sweet, like roses.

"Lexi."

"Yes."

"You're my sister." She gasps another breath. "And I love you."

Like a waterfall, my tears spill over, drowning me. "And you're mine." I'm shaking and struggling to speak. "I love you too, so much."

"Thank you for saving me." I feel her body relaxing and her head starts falling down. I scoot deeper into the bed with her.

"You're welcome, and thank you for saving me," I say back to her because she did. Somehow, this girl found a way into my heart and taught me how to live, how to care, and most importantly, how to love someone.

"My mom's here now. Should I go with her?"

Every part of me wants to tell her no because I'm not ready—stay a little longer, tell your mom to come back tomorrow. But I know that's me being selfish because I'm not ready to say good-bye and lose her forever. I want to hold her tight and keep her from leaving although I know that won't keep her with me. I kiss her on the head, again and again.

"It's okay, you can go with her now," I say through my sobs and my convulsing body. "I'll see you soon."

"Promise?" she whispers.

"When it's time for me to go, I'll come find you. I promise."

"Did you hear my mom?"

"No, what did she say?"

"She said I was lucky to have such a wonderful friend and thank you for taking such good care of her daughter."

I press my head back into the pillow and say, "Tell her I was the lucky one. You're the best thing that's ever happened to me."

"She said, not for long."

"What?" I ask.

"We have to leave now or we'll miss the train."

"Go on. Go to her." I squeeze her tightly. "Alyssa, I love you... I'll see you soon."

I feel her go limp as she lets go and leaves her failing body. I'm holding her, rocking her, shaking and bawling. Sutton closes the door, leaving me to mourn my friend.

I cover her with a blanket, trying to warm her body even though I know she's gone. Darkness overtakes the room as the candle melts down low. She's been gone only a minute, and already her room feels colder, devoid of the brightness captured in her spirit. I long to read to her one more day or tell her what she means to me, but it's done. Instead, I just sit and stare at her, asking why...why...why her? That could've been me instead.

I feel an arm on my shoulder, and turn around hoping to see

Cole, but it's Sutton, standing behind me with an unfamiliar man. At first, my grief clouds my judgment and I think they're here for me. I cling to Alyssa's body, unwilling to move. *I won't let them take me away.* But when Sutton reaches out to stroke my hair, and his sad green eyes meet mine, my stomach drops. *I know who they're here for.*

CHAPTER 8

My intention wasn't to accompany Alyssa to the morgue on the fourth floor, but I can't seem to let go yet. The reality doesn't hit me even as her body lies in front of my eyes. Her chest doesn't rise and her lips are a pale white. The mortician ambles about the small room, performing various duties that seem to seal Alyssa's fate. He zips her tiny frame into a heavy black bag and I watch as every last inch of her skin disappears from the world, sealing her inside. It's like her light has been snuffed out by that bag and I want to rip it off. Then the mortician places the bag onto a gurney and begins to wheel her out of the room. I stand rocking in place. *I can't let her go alone!* I jump in front of the door and block his way out.

"I'm going with her!"

"No, you're not," Sutton says. "You're very much alive and I plan on keeping you that way." He grabs me around my waist, picks me up, and moves me out of the way.

Before he puts me on my feet, I wrap my arms around his neck and plead.

"I promised her I wouldn't leave. I have to go with her. She wanted to be cremated. I have to make sure it happens." His grip relaxes and he sets me on my feet. "I have to make sure she gets there safely."

Beep. Beep. Sutton glances at his beeper. "A guard's been injured and that takes priority. I have to go immediately." His eyes plead in apology. "Stay here." He disappears down the hallway, so I take off and catch the gurney.

"I thought he told you to stay," the boy says.

"What's it going to hurt? He won't even know I'm gone."

I glance up in time to see two guards walking toward us. I recognize the one from the incident in the garage. His skeptical eyes evaluate us as we pass, so I fix mine ahead, attempting to avoid provocation. The weight of their stares burn holes in my back, and I shudder. I feel vulnerable without Cole around and I doubt Mr. Mortician boy knows any fighting tactics. They pass without a word and I exhale with relief.

"I'm Benjamin by the way," he says. "Sorry about your friend."

I look over forcing a grin. "Thank you," I manage to say. "I'm Lexi."

He wears thin glasses and has shaggy red hair that partially hides his yellow brand. He pushes Alyssa's body into the elevator and I squeeze in beside him. Before I finish my deep breath, we reach our destination.

As the doors open, the air sends a shiver up my spine and goose bumps rise on my arms. I glance around and rub my arms, trying to ignore the fact more people like Alyssa lay hidden in this room. It's dark and cool with large refrigerators thrumming in the background. Three homemade wooden tables line the middle of the room. *Don't get sick. Don't pass out.*

Benjamin must sense my nervousness as he rolls the gurney to the back wall. "They're just refrigerators," he says.

"I figured. Just kind of freaks me out a bit," I say. "It's just… I don't want her sealed in a body bag and locked in a refrigerator—"

"It's not her anymore," he says. "It's just her shell, which she had to leave in order to go to heaven."

"And you believe all that?"

"I have to. It's the only way I make it through each day. Knowing there's a light at the end of the tunnel calms me."

"Oh, I've heard that saying before, about the light at the end of a tunnel."

"Lots of people used it before the Commander took over."

"Oh, that's right, my dad used to say it." Thinking about my dad and hearing his voice in my head make me choke on my words a little. "Once, when I was about six years old, I had an argument with a girlfriend of mine from school. At that age, it seemed like the end of the world. I remember crying when my dad picked me up in his small blue car. He wrapped his arms around me and said, 'Honey, I know you don't see it now, but there's always a light at the end of the tunnel.'" At the time, I didn't weigh his words carefully, but now they ring fresh and true in my ears. So many times he tried to prepare me for the future without ever knowing what I'd face. *God, I miss you, Daddy.*

"I'm going to roll her over there now." Benjamin smiles at me, then moves toward the refrigerators.

I can feel my heart in my throat. I never liked death and this is way beyond my comfort zone. He pushes the gurney toward the back of the room alongside a dozen, square rusty doors. Six line the top and six across the bottom. They're numbered one through twelve.

"They're all empty except for one, four, and five," he says. He unbuckles the straps holding Alyssa's body in place. "Pick one."

"Um, I don't know," I say.

"I can do it if you're not—"

"Let's go with nine," I say.

He turns the handle, opens the door, and pulls a large tray-looking thing out. He moves to the other side and rolls up his sleeves.

"Do you need a minute before I…?"

I don't wait for him to finish. My hand glides over the black bag as I move toward her head. Taking the zipper between my fingers, I slide it down just enough to reveal her face. She looks peaceful, content. The coloring is off but her features are relaxed. I sniff and wipe my nose with my sleeve before I push a wisp of her hair away from her cheek.

I lean over and whisper in her ear. "I promise I'll set you free. I don't know when, but I'll get you there." My hands are shaking and I struggle to pinch the zipper. "I hope I was the friend you needed me to be."

I know she isn't there and she can't hear me. Maybe those words are to remind myself that I always keep my promises. Either way, she changed my life for the better.

I close the bag, pat the top of her head, and put my arms under her back. Ben and I lift her small, fragile body placing it onto the table. He repositions her and I step back as he slides her body into place, closes the door, and locks the handle.

"Damn it. She was just thirteen years old!" I pound my fist into door three. I clench my teeth so hard my jaw immediately aches. A sob racks my body as I beat my forehead against the door.

Bang.

Bang.

Bang.

I've haven't endured this kind of pain since my father died. I forgot how intense the emotions are that flow through you when you lose a loved one.

Ben places his hand on my shoulder, giving it a quick squeeze. He hops onto a table resting his head in his hands. I can't take it anymore, plus I have to get back before Sutton knows I'm gone. Too much time has elapsed since we left. I stumble out of the room, trying to hold myself together. Ben jumps from the table and slowly follows me to the rackety box.

Once I'm in the elevator, I push number eight. Nothing happens. I slam the button with my fist and still nothing. Ben pushes the red emergency button and presses his ear to the panel.

"It must be jammed again. The cables aren't moving at all. Man, I hope it's not the motor." He shakes his head. "We just don't have money to keep fixing these damn elevators."

My patience runs thin, but I restrain myself from punching the buttons. Instead, I place my hands in my hair and release a loud sigh. I don't have time for this. I need to get back before Sutton realizes I'm missing.

"Is there another way out of here?" I breathe hard like I just ran a race and am having a hard time catching my breath. *I need to get out of this forsaken place.* I step out, round the corner, and see "STAIRS basement/8 West."

Ben follows on my heels, wiping sweat from his forehead and frowning with disapproval. "Please, just wait a few minutes. Let me see if I can get a hold of the repair guys." He tugs at my wrist in desperation.

I shrug him off despite his attempt to dissuade me. "No, I need to go now!" Ben raises his hand in opposition about to open his mouth but I cut him off. "Please don't make me kick you in the nuts," I threaten.

"At least let me lock up, and I'll go with you."

"No. Stay here. I'll run up." My voice rings with force.

He drops his arm to his side, letting me by.

The door closes behind me with a click, followed by a beep, locking me out of the morgue.

It takes a minute for my aching eyes to adjust to the dim lighting. The grated stairs make a light strumming noise as I begin my ascent and my palms stick to the tacky, crumbling paint of the railings. One floor, two floors pass before my slipper gets caught on an edge and I tumble forward onto the landing. *Crap. Where is it?* My fingers shake while feeling around for it. As I place the worn slipper back onto my foot, it starts.

Thud.

Thud.

Thud. Getting closer each time. A flashlight flicks on. I look upward. Instantly, I start sweating profusely and my muscles tense.

Through the grated stairs a few flights above me, two silhouettes tap their batons against their hands. My heart beats so rapidly that I can't hear their voices.

I inch backward until I'm up against the wall. I look for a door, a person, or anything that can help me. Nothing. Sickness washes over me, but there's no time to be weak. For the moment, I shake off my fear and take off to the basement. I'm leaping down the stairs when they start calling out.

"Hey, where do you think you're going?" Their raucous laughter bounces of the walls and exhilarates my fear. *Don't panic, don't panic...too late. I'm panicking.*

"Sutton's on his way!" My voice cracks. I'm not sure they heard me but I had to try something. "Leave me alone!"

"Oh, no!" More obnoxious laughter echoes down the staircase. "Isn't the elevator working?" they ask with sarcasm.

As they inch closer, I look over my shoulder and recognize one of them as the guard from the garage. Dread wraps its fingers around my heart. They're getting closer and I feel like I'm running through quicksand. I want to go faster, but my legs won't respond. I grab the railing with my right hand, swinging my legs over the bar, and down the next flight of stairs trying to gain some distance.

"Whore on the loose! Yes! I love this game," the other guard says. They hop over the railing with ease.

"Help! Someone *help me!*" I scream even though I know nobody can hear me.

"Who the hell would help you?"

I look up and one flight is all that separates us. As I get closer to the bottom, I notice there's only one door. *You have to be open!* Slamming into the door, I turn the handle, and bolt through. *The stairwell was well lit compared to this. Where to go? Where to hide?* At the other end, I spot a window where the sun seeps in. *If I can get there, someone might hear me. There's a light at the end of the tunnel, right?* I sprint toward it.

Tables, beds, and chairs litter my path to safety. Boxes piled upon boxes jam-pack the walls and floors in every crevice. I glance around trying to find a backup plan. The window is too far and too high for the amount of time I have left. Rushing, I smack into a folding chair and slam to the ground, making a loud, clanging noise.

"That was graceful," he says from behind me.

I didn't know they were that close. Out of options, I crawl under an empty cardboard box and await the inevitable. I'm trapped and they know it.

"Now it's a game of hide and seek. You're making this way too enjoyable."

Banging and crashing noises tell me they're digging for me. I'm shaking so hard I'm sure they can tell what box I'm hiding under. A guard kicks boxes and throws chairs out of his way. *Please don't kick me.* In the midst of the noise, I lose track of the other guard, but don't dare look. It becomes silent. *They are going to kill me. It's over.*

They rip the box off me and I lunge to get away. A blow lands on the back of my head with a sickening crack and searing pain makes me dizzy. I blink my eyes as my vision fogs up. Hot, sweaty hands grip my arms and I'm flung into a pile of chairs that clatter to the floor underneath me. They drag me to the other side of the room as the blood drenching my hair leaves a trail behind. My head is yanked up and I'm forced to look into the steel, cold eyes of the guard from the garage.

"Thought you could get away, didn't you?" he says. He orders the other guard, "Hold her down."

I kick with force, managing to free an arm, and rake my fingernails down his face, tearing his skin. Furious, he lands a blow across my cheek and sends me back to reality. I don't stand a chance.

"I said hold her down!"

He pins me, wraps a piece of cloth around my head and through my mouth to muffle my screams. Then he climbs on top of me.

At first, I glue my thighs shut as he tries to pry them apart, but then he punches me so hard I see flashes of light. He sends his fist into my gut, knocking the wind out of me. My body goes limp, and he spreads my legs as I struggle for breath. His hands explore me like clay being modeled, tracing every curve and inch of my skin.

I cringe with every touch. His hands are rough like sand paper. Everything that belonged to me has been taken away, and now my purity will be plundered as well.

I'm humiliated.

I'm violated.

I'm treated like the scum of the earth, and they're proud.

He slaps me across the face. "Look at me." He drools over his words.

No, please God.

His eyes are alight with ecstasy. He whips out a knife and

slices my shirt to shreds. I squirm and buck, but his solid form remains immovable. He turns to the other guard.

"You can have your turn when I'm finished…"

The other guard grins, sweat dripping down his face and staining the starch collar of his shirt. His hands squeeze my arms tighter but nothing compares to the splitting pain in my head.

I gain strength for one last push, but to no avail. I have nothing left.

He throws an elbow across my face, jarring my brain sideways, and the room goes pitch-black for a second. He unbuckles his belt and loosens his pants.

"That's it. Give in," he says. "Good girl."

He moves his mouth over my ear and neck as I thrash my head side to side. If I didn't have this gag on, I'd bite his nose off.

"Ah, damn you!" He grabs a fist full of my hair and yanks, provoking a horrific scream from the depths of my chest. The sound is muffled through the gag, but I'm desperate. A chill of pure sickness runs down my spine. He wraps his hands around my neck pretending to strangle me, and then smacks me across the face.

"How did you know?" He moves his hands down, eventually resting on my thighs, and grips them. "I love it when a girl's rough with me."

My head spins, my eyes burn with fear, my ears ring, and my heart is being torn to shreds. Heat crawls upward from my toes to my head.

Then everything turns black.

* * *

"Open your eyes. Damn it! Open them!" I recognize the voice but can't move. "I can't stop the bleeding. Zeus, go! Now go!" His voice sounds panicky.

Zeus? I know that name but can't conjure an image. *I'm so tired. Just let me sleep.* A soft material covers me and something is tied around my head before I'm lifted into the air. Blackness overtakes me again.

Dreams and images pass through me like a slideshow. My father hugs me securely with his strong arms directing me toward the light. My brother, with his wild smile, climbs trees in our backyard. My mother, before she remarried, when she was young and full of vitality. She sits at her bureau, brushing her long, dark hair. Alyssa smiles brightly with her makeup newly done. Cole, even he's there. The first time I met him, riding in his jeep then watching him sleep in his cot for the last few nights. Memorizing the contours of his strong face. Our shared quarters with the walls decorated. I haven't finished them yet. Zeus runs in his goofy way, making me laugh with his silly antics. Sunshine. Flowers. The guards, their ugly faces in the dim staircase, chasing me. My head. It hurts so much. My mother whispering to me while I feel a burning sensation in my arm. My stepfather forcing me to wear clothes I hated, forcing me to lie to everyone, manipulating every decision I made. Uglier images—people running on the filthy streets, screaming obscenities, brandings. Darkness. Hatred. I'm a cauldron of hate.

CHAPTER 9

A familiar smell wakes me but my eyes are crusted shut, and every move sends searing pain through my entire being. My lungs allow only shallow breaths as I pry my eyes open to take a look around. I'm alive. I'm in Cole's room on his thick mattress, covered in heavy blankets. It smells like vanilla and Old Spice. Zeus snores at my feet, and Cole rests on the floor beside me. *What's he doing here?* It's barely dawn it seems. My brain feels scrambled and I can't seem to remember how I got here. My tendons crack as I slowly push upward and the pain blurs my vision.

"Hey—" I jump and look at Cole whose eyes are open, staring at me. "It's just me. It's okay. You're safe now."

His warm hand grabs mine but I pull away. His face looks pained with his jaw clenched tight and his lips pursed. *I feel like I got hit by a train.* I strain myself, trying to remember how I got back to our quarters. And what condition I was in. It's too soon to speculate though, and I lay my throbbing head back down. He stands over me in an instant, scrutinizing my every bruise, looking troubled as he chews on his bottom lip. He grabs a phone and dials.

"Hello, it's Cole. Can I speak with Sutton, please?" He pauses, waiting for Sutton. "Hey, it's me. She's awake." Cole starts pacing. "Sure, come over." I meet his gaze with humiliation. Then I rip my eyes away, unable to vocalize how damaged I feel.

"I'm so sorry about this. I—"

"Stop please. I don't want to talk about it. Not now," I say. "When did you get a phone?" I bring my hand to my eyes and rub them.

"Sutton gave it to me, so I could call him when you woke up. He said he wanted to see you the second you were conscious… He's really worried about you, and frankly, so am I." His hand rests gently on my arm and I look at Zeus who sleeps at my feet. Blood mars his fur and he has a gash above his eye. My head pounds against my skull like a drum.

"Are you all right? What can I do?" Cole says. "Do you need a drink?"

His questions overwhelm me. My hand reaches up and feels a bandage wrapped around my entire head. My hair clumps together and dry blood flakes onto my shoulders. My tongue feels thick, and it hurts to widen my jaw. I lick my lips and feel two stitches on my right bottom lip. Three more stitches line the inside of my cheek. I can't remember what happened clearly. Closing my eyes, the memories resurface of taking Alyssa's body to the morgue and getting attacked by the guards. A whimper escapes me.

"Shhh, it's all right. They can't hurt you anymore," Cole says in a whisper. "I promise you."

"So, how—how did I get here?" I stammer and blink rapidly.

"I found you. Well, Zeus found you, and Sutton told me to bring you here." He stops, lowering his eyes. "He said you'd be safer here, with me."

"I see," I say. "What happened to the guards…that…were there—?"

"We took care of them," he says before I finish.

"Oh." I nod my head. My chest burns with each breath I take, causing me to groan. I don't bother asking what he saw or how I ended up in new clothes. I pull the covers up to my armpits and look away from his face.

"Lexi, they didn't—they didn't finish." Cole stares at the floor. His gentle voice forces me to raise my eyes to his and I see his Adam's apple move with his next swallow. "We got to you just in time. And I'm sorry, I know you don't want to talk about it, but thought you should know that. Damn, Lexi, I'll never forgive myself for what happened to you, and not being there for Alyssa. I wish I could go back and change everything. But, I can't," he says in a pleading tone, and I see his eyes soften.

"Cole, I don't blame you." I pick at my bottom sheet. "What happened wasn't your fault. It was mine. I never should've left the floor, but I had to go with her." I comfort him when I feel like a shipwreck, aimlessly navigating the waters. "You and Sutton both warned me. But, I'm the one who didn't listen." What an idiot I was for not listening to him and then ignoring Sutton and Ben.

"If you're trying to make me feel better, it's not working. When I got those orders, everything within me fought against leaving. And now look at you. They could've killed you, Lexi," he says. "Or worse." *Yeah, that makes me feel better.*

"But, they didn't," I say. I don't want him to grovel anymore so I change the subject quickly. "Will you get in trouble?"

"I don't think so. No one knows what happened except Sutton," he says with confidence. "He helped me take care of the bodies so I doubt anyone will find out." The tension runs out of his muscles as he sits on the edge of his bed.

"What about the other guards? Won't they notice they're gone?" I ask, scooting away.

"Sure, but I doubt anyone will care. Nobody really liked them. Plus, the back stairs aren't monitored, so they can only guess what happened...and with all the violence in the Hole, it's nothing new. Anyway, I'd be willing to bet, they'll just assume they took off," he says.

"Well, that's a relief." I mumble, staring toward the window.

"Forget about me. How are you feeling?" He leans closer, taking my limp hands into his strong grip. His hand warms mine. I stare at it, unsure whether to pull away.

"I'm hurting," is all I can say to describe my physical and emotional pain."

"God, I'm sorry—" he says, his eyes downcast. I cover his mouth with my hand to silence him.

"Cole, stop saying that! Seriously, I'm only here because of you and Zeus." I reach over and tilt his chin up until his eyes meet mine. "And don't worry, in time my wounds will heal.

You'll see." *My emotional wounds are a different story...*

Someone knocks softly on the door and Cole hurries to answer it. He opens the door and Sutton drops a chart. It clatters to the ground when he sees me. The noise rattles my brain and I close my eyes. I'm sure my injuries look worse than they feel which is pretty bad.

His hair reminds me of a bird's nest. His clothes are as wrinkled as a rippled potato chip and his glasses slip sideways off his nose. *Something is seriously wrong with this man.*

"My God," Sutton says as he sits down beside me. "I'm so relieved to see you're awake." His green eyes pierce mine.

"Oh, Sutton, I'm so sorry," I say. My chin quivers. "I should've listened to you."

Sutton grabs my hand and I blink back my tears. Without warning, Cole slams his chair back and leaves the room. I frown, but I take my eyes off the door and focus on Sutton. His face warms my heart.

"You're alive and that's all that matters. No one's to blame here, especially you. Cole's just, well, very angry with himself. And the sight of you tore him to shreds. Of course... he blames himself. That's who he is. Just give him time, he'll come around." He adjusts his glasses and clears his throat. "So, please. Don't worry about him. You only need to focus on your recovery now," Sutton says as if reading my mind. "You took quite the beating. You cracked your skull, and I had to remove the bone fragments. I shaved some of your hair, but there was no way around that." He takes a sip of water and continues. "After the wound was cleaned, I used a special glue to help hold the skin together. And just to be safe, I added a few staples. Now, you'll be on antibiotics for ten days. This will help to make sure no infection sets in. Other than that, you'll heal just fine, my dear." I've never seen him with stooped posture before, and his worry lines seem deeper somehow. He adjusts the pillow behind me and leans me forward to assess the rest of my injuries.

He pushes the chair away from Zeus and it dawns on me— Zeus didn't follow Cole. He stayed with me. This dog has officially won me over.

I reach my hand toward the end of the bed and feel Zeus's wet tongue meet my fingers. I take my arm away and pat the spot next to me. Zeus crawls up next to me and lies against my side. His body takes over half the space on the bed, but I don't mind. Sutton's eyes almost bug out of his head.

"Uhhh, I'm not sure that's a good idea," he says. I raise my eyebrows at him in a challenge and he lets it go without saying anything more. He leans over and squeezes my shoulders.

"Lexi, don't go anywhere without Cole or myself again! Is that clear, young lady?" His eyes squint at me. "When Cole trains, I'll arrange for another guard who I personally trust, to be with you."

"Okay. But what about work? How will you explain my absence?"

"Oh, that's not a big deal. I'll forge the paperwork. It's not the first time I've done something like this, and won't be the last. Trust me," he says.

"Yeah. Trust's a really hard thing for me," I say. A wave of guilt overrides my anger when I realize that Cole and Sutton are the *only* reason I'm still alive. "I'm sorry. I didn't mean it like that." I can hear him tapping his foot while he carefully pats my hand.

"Look, I can't imagine how hard this must be for you. But what happened to you, it really shook me up. And I need you to have some faith in me." He touches my chin, bringing my eyes to his level. "Lexi, this is some serious stuff. Cole's life and yours are at stake. He could be executed for his part in this." He lets go and rubs his neck. "The few guards that have protection orders have no room for error. On top of that, he killed two guards to save you. Do you understand what I'm telling you?" He pauses with raised eyebrows. "You think this is bad, and it is, but it can always get worse. Much worse." I can see the seriousness in his eyes over the rim of his glasses.

"All right," I say. "I'll try my best."

"That a girl." He smiles at me.

I don't really have a choice. Cole and I will spend a lot

of time together as usual, and I need to realize I'll never be independent again. I shift my weight to my other side, gritting my teeth against the twinges of pain that shoot through every muscle.

"Ugh. I feel helpless lying here." Staying in bed only exacerbates my anxieties. "Would you mind helping me get out of bed?"

"No. You're on strict bed rest. With help, you can use the bathroom, but otherwise, you must lie here and rest. It's more than likely you suffered from a severe concussion." He leans back into the chair and evaluates me carefully. "Oh, before I go, there's one more thing we need to discuss." He lowers his eyes, and folds his hands in his lap.

I seriously don't want to talk anymore. I just want to be alone. I'm scared what he's going to say next, but I'm about to hear it anyway.

"You already know I've read your reports." I nod yes because he's already told me this much. "With that being said, there's a particular detail that doesn't add up. It says— 'The prisoner was accused by her mother of having sexual intercourse with an unidentified male.'"

"Yes, it does." Every Monday the newspapers publish a list of new sinners and their crimes. But why are we going over this now? My muscle tense up with the reminder.

"Here's the part that confuses me. You were branded for having premarital sex," he says. "But this never happened, did it?"

I look at him and feel lost. What on earth could he possibly know?

"I don't understand," I say. "Why are you asking me this?"

"Because, Lexi. I performed a rape kit on you...only because Cole wasn't certain if you were raped of not. But, thank God it was negative." He takes a cleansing breath and says, "You see, not only will the test reveal a recent sexual encounter, it also reports any sexual intercourse you've had."

"What? How?" I ask in an uncertain tone.

"It works by scanning the tissues, checking for any

stretched, torn, or irritated areas. It then, shows us if you are intact." He leans over and reaches for my hands. I take a deep breath knowing what's about to come out of his mouth. "My dear, you're a virgin and that's a medical fact."

I squeeze his hands hard as my eyes fill with tears. One of them travels over my cheekbone and drips off onto my collarbone. I meet his calm and caring eyes.

Finally. Finally. "I know," I say.

"I don't understand, why you didn't proclaim your innocence? You shouldn't be here," Sutton says while shaking his head.

"It wouldn't have mattered," I say simply. "No one would've believed me."

"Even, your mother?"

"Especially her. You know she's the one who accused me. Her mind was already made up…just like everyone else's."

Sutton's lips form a thin, white line and I hear him exhale through his nose. "So it's true then." He shakes his head and runs his hands through his hair. "Why in the hell would she do such a thing? To you, to her own daughter?" It's the first time I've seen such hatred come from Sutton and I'm not sure what to make of it.

I close my eyes, bite my lower lip, and release it because there are some things I can't hold in any longer. "Jealousy," I say. "She was jealous of me. She was jealous that my stepfather paid more attention to me than her. That he was always so worried about my whereabouts that he controlled everything I ever said or did. And one day, she just snapped."

He blinks rapidly now. "I can't believe what I'm hearing. Your stepfather, did he ever touch you, molest you?"

"No. It was never like that." I look down as I fiddle with my hands.

"So, what was it? What really happened to you?" Sutton moves even closer, almost leaning in, for my response. His eyes are fixated on my face as I turn away.

"Please, it doesn't matter—"

"Oh, it matters all right!" I look at him and see his jugular veins bulging from his neck.

"Sutton, not now…I can't," I beg. "Please, just let it go."

Before Sutton can say another word, my mouth falls open when I see Cole. He's standing in the doorway with his jaw hanging open. His eyes are practically bulging from his head. I didn't even realize he'd returned. *Did he hear our entire conversation?* I've been sullied and vindicated all at once. Sutton turns and sees Cole's expression.

"Why didn't you tell me?" Cole says, straightening up. "I would've believed you."

Yep. He heard everything. "Would you?" I ask him in a hushed, cracked voice.

His eyes flash at me and I see the muscles in his jaw tighten. My shoulders slump over and I cross my legs under the sheets. I don't care if anyone else on earth knows the truth about my sin—the two people who saved my life know the truth, and for the first time, I feel free. *Not free. I'll never be free from the past.*

I wipe a tear away with my forearm and glance at Cole. He leans against the closed door now with his hands in his pockets. And I'm pretty sure I know what he's thinking. *He wonders what really happened to me before I ended up here.* Despite our differences, I owe my life to him over and over already. I can't imagine what I'll owe him for the lifetime of sacrifices he's made to protect me. There's no way I can ever repay him. *Or is there?* If he asks me for the truth, can I overcome my fears and tell him?

Sutton stands up, breaking the tension. "I'll come by tomorrow to see how you're doing. Right now, I have to get back to the hospital to check on my patients. If anything changes or you have any questions, please call me."

"Is there any way I can shower? I have to get this blood out." I pull a clumpy mass away from my head, showing him what I mean. A shower would cleanse my soul as well as my body.

"If you must, please use Cole's shower. It's big enough for a chair. And I want you sitting down," he says. "Just make sure you don't touch your wound. All it takes is one scratch and you can introduce infection. You'd be disgusted if you knew the germs we can carry under our nails. I'll see you soon." He kisses my forehead and leaves the room.

Under my nails. I inspect my fingernails, holding them up before my face with disgust. The blood from the guard's face is still fresh underneath them so I ball them into fists.

Cole stands with his hands in his pockets as he leans on the wall for support. He walks over to his safe, places his weapons inside, and removes his boots. He lies down on the mattress next to my bed. And we lay there in silence.

I pick between my fingers as they shake and see streaks of blood on my wrists. I rub them furiously. Sobs wrack my body, but no tears come—just anger. I slam my fists down into the bed.

"What can I do? Please tell me what I can do for you." His words implore me. My fury builds into frustration as I raise my hands for him to inspect.

"The blood, I need it off. Now."

His eyes rest on my bloodstained fingers. He climbs up, goes to his bathroom, and starts the water. He returns with a warm, wet cloth and begins to wash my hands. I don't want him to touch me, yet I do. I don't want him close, yet his closeness is the only thing that makes me feel safe. We're quiet again, and when he finishes drying my hands, he takes the cloth back to the bathroom.

He was doing his job when he saved me. He was doing what was expected of him. Yet, in this moment, it feels more intimate than that. He lies down, pulling a blanket over his shoulders. His face looks tired, a thousand years older than it is.

"Thank you," I whisper as I roll away from him. I don't want to hear his response or see his face.

* * *

The smell of frying eggs and bacon wake me up. My mouth is

dry, and my stomach twists with hunger.

"I made breakfast," he says. He stands next to my bed with a plate in one hand and a glass of water in the other. All of my senses perk up.

"Thank you." I rub my eyes, then my pounding head. "Did I sleep, all day and night?"

"Pretty much. I tried to wake you earlier, just to make sure you were okay, but you nearly bit my head off." He smiles unsure.

"Ah. I'm sorry." I look for Zeus and see him lying on the floor gorging on bacon. "I don't remember doing that. Is that a bad sign?"

"No, I'm pretty sure that's normal." He laughs. "Do you think you can eat?"

"I'm a little hungry, I guess." I lie. I'm starving.

He hands me the plate and glass. I inhale the water and scarf the food down like Zeus.

"That was really good. Thank you," I say. My manners were horrid, but who cares.

"Um, that was interesting," Cole says. "I never knew a girl from high society could eat like such an animal." He shakes his head as he picks up the plate and glass and washes it in his sink.

I'm too embarrassed to say anything, so I sit back and gaze out his window. Faint popping sounds echo up to his room from a few blocks away.

"Is that what I think it is?" I ask.

Looking over his shoulder, he answers, "Don't get too close to the window. It sounds like a skirmish, but it's only a few blocks away. There's a lot more fighting going on these last few days. Not sure why."

"Oh." I raise my eyebrows, but don't ask any more questions.

"Are you feeling any better?"

Is he really asking me that? My eyes grow wide and my hands drop to my lap. "Not really, I feel like crap. And sitting around makes me a little stir-crazy."

"Tell me what I can do to help you."

"A shower would do me some good, I think."

"Lexi, I'm not sure—"

"Please, Cole, I'm disgusting!"

Cole hesitates for a seconds before giving in. "All right. But it has to be quick."

I pull my blankets away from my body and let go of a deep sigh.

"What's the matter?" he says, sitting on my bed facing me.

I back away from him a few inches. "I'm a little shaky right now, and obviously I can't see the back of my head."

"Okay? So what are you asking me?"

"Would you mind helping me…helping me—?"

"Wash your hair?"

"Yes, that," I say with a hushed voice.

Cole shrugs his shoulders and stands up. "I can't promise I'll do a great job, but I'll do my best."

"Oh thank you, thank you very much!" I rub my arms. "I'm not taking my clothes off, though."

"I never thought you would," he says in a shrill voice. He's not being perverse. In fact, he's rocking back on his heels while licking his lips and gulping water. *I wonder if he's scared.* Fear is an interesting emotion for him to display when I'm the one who's vulnerable. This is humiliating. It's hard enough to know the condition he found me in, but it's even harder to let him help me with something so personal.

I hesitate before saying, "Okay, well, I'm not exactly sure where to go from here."

"Wait here. I'll go warm the water."

He flicks the light on in the bathroom and starts the shower. I unwrap the bandages around my head, grimacing as I pull them off. Then I push myself up with my arms and swing my legs over the side of the bed. My vision swerves like a car with no brakes and then darkens for a moment. I close my eyes to steady myself. My feet rest on the mattress below. He stands in the doorway, staring at me while rubbing the back of his neck. *Is he afraid he'll hurt me?* "You won't break me…if that's what you're worried about."

He walks over, places one arm around my back, and lifts me from under my legs so they dangle. I feel like a baby. I rest my head on his shoulder and smell his fresh cotton shirt.

"After this, I'm not sure anyone could," he whispers. The sound of his heart soothes me, like it's reminding me he's real and telling mine to beat with his. *Why do I keep thinking these things? Lexi. Stop it. This is his job...nothing more and nothing less.*

The steam from the shower coats the mirror and water droplets drip down the tiles, leaving streaks behind. He gently sets me down on the toilet. Reaching behind his head, he pulls off his shirt. I stare at the strength in his back, shoulders, and arms. I tear my eyes away and shake my head as I stare at the cream-colored linoleum floor. He places a rubber matt in the shower and then the chair.

"Now, don't laugh. I need to make sure the chair will stay put," he says. He steps into the shower. His arms flail as he loses his balance and falls over the chair with a thud.

I burst out with a laugh. "Oh my gosh! Are you okay?" I place my hands over my mouth to muffle my giggles. My ribs ache from the exertion. I lift my shirt slightly to examine my ribs and find three deep purple bruises. The one in the middle of my stomach is slightly bigger than a fist. The other two, sit parallel under my breasts and toward the outside of my body. Maybe where two hands were holding me down? I cringe, wanting to disappear inside myself.

He lifts his head and I let my shirt go, covering my bruises. "Well, you don't want to step in front of the matt. At least we know that." We laugh together, but I stop because the stabbing pain darts from my ribcage all the way up my spine. He reaches for my hands and I hesitate. "Come on, I'm not gonna bite you," he says. "And I promise...I won't let you slip. Just leave that to me to make a complete ass of myself."

He tucks a piece of my hair behind my ear and I look up at him. He gives me a crooked smile. I take a quick breath as his eyes fall back to my hair. When I look at his fingers that just touched my hair, I see dark crusted blood on them.

"Are you cut?

He inspects his fingers for a minute. "No, it's your blood." He pulls the shower curtain back. "Lexi, it doesn't bother me, really."

Again, my mind flashes to how I must've looked to him when he discovered me covered in blood and half-naked in the basement of the hospital. I shake my head to block the thought and take his hand. Then he helps me over the side of the tub and seats me into the chair. He stands in front of me and tilts the showerhead so it barely hits my back.

"Can you tilt it up a little? The warm water feels so good," I say, letting out a whimper.

"All right." His voice shakes. "Tell me when you want me to stop." His words break into my thoughts and startle me. I nod. The heat warms my skin and I take a deep breath as I stretch out my fingers. The water runs down my aching muscles. He touches my shoulder and I jerk backward.

"I'm sorry," he says with concern in his voice. "I should tell you when I'm about to touch you—" He pauses and clears his throat. "I'm such an idiot."

"I just wasn't expecting it. That's all." My breath comes in puffs as I try to calm myself.

"Well, you scare me," he says under his breath. His face lingers inches away as he reaches for the soap. I want to reach out and touch him, wondering what his skin might feel like and yet I'm afraid.

"What do you mean?" I heard him say it and refuse to ignore it. "How do I scare you?" I look at him while lathering my hands and arms.

"You just do," he says without further elaboration. He steps out of the shower and I rinse as much of my body as I can, getting rid of all the ugliness caked in my pores. I rinse it all off until the pink water runs clear.

My shirt, my pants, everything is soaked through. I pull the curtain back. He tries not to invade my privacy, so he stands facing the plain white drywall.

"Now, for the hair. I'm apologizing ahead of time. It's a beast."

"I'm sure I can handle it." He averts his eyes, but his hands begin to pull my hair backward. "Are you able to lean back some?"

"I think so."

Slowly I dip my head backward until he says. "Okay, that's enough." *His hands.* His hands are strong but gentle as they massage the water through my hair. Blood drips off the tips into the tub. He puts shampoo in, carefully scrubbing around my staples. He gently pulls my head side to side as he rinses everything off. I keep my eyes closed and sigh. I've forgotten how nice it feels to have someone wash your hair.

His one hand rests on my forehead, keeping the soap from running down to my eyes. When my hair's finally clean, he begins brushing it with his fingers. I expect his hands to release me but they don't. They just keep caressing my hair. I turn slightly and our eyes meet. His are black with emotion like deep pools. His lips part, his hands caress my hair, and water drenches us both. My body's full of nervous energy and I've never felt so many butterflies in all my life. I'm twitching, not because I'm cold, but because I can't control this battle within myself.

Oh my goodness.

I clear my throat and he rips himself away. Suddenly, I'm blowing out a series of short breaths as quietly as possible. I unconsciously place my hands over my chest.

"Want me to wash…anything else?" he asks quietly but his voice hides some intense emotion and cracks at the end.

"Nope. I'm good." I spit out between breaths.

My eyes dart toward him as he turns the knobs. Beads of water run down his face and back as he reaches for his towel. I can't tear my eyes away as he dries off. He leans over me, and his jaw is so close to my lips that I grit my teeth and tighten my lips into a line.

As he carries me out of the bathroom, I see my reflection in the mirror. Purple bruises mark my face and the stitches on my lip look nasty. My eyes stand out like turquoise stones amidst the damage. A mass of sopping wet curls hang over his shoulder, but he doesn't seem to mind. He puts me on the bed and hands me a clean pair of scrubs. A violent shiver sprints up my spine and he sees my body jerk.

"You, all right?"

"Fine," I say with frustration.

He grabs his towel and hands it to me. That's when I notice the goose bumps running up his arm.

"Sorry, I only have one towel. I'll get more later," he says.

But I wave it off. I dry myself and out of the corner of my eye, I swear I see him looking back at me then quickly snapping his head away again. It's silent except for our breathing. Even Zeus senses the tension in the air. My ears feel like a toaster oven slowly heating up. *Man it's hot in here.*

"Don't turn around. I'm going to change now."

"Oh, right. Here…I'll go back into the bathroom," he mumbles as he walks in.

When the door's closed, I carefully peel off my top layer, dry off again, and pull on the new one. All the while, I'm tensing my muscles, waiting for the next zap of pain. Once my shirts are on, I realize… *Dang. He forgot to give me a bra and I'm not about to ask him for one.* I've given up enough privacy already. It takes me longer to get my wet pants off. I kick them to the floor and pull the new ones up. Every muscle aches and my eyes feel heavy. Who knew a shower would take such a physical and mental toll?

I lie down again, fresh and clean. It's a relief to wipe away the dirt, the blood, and the invisible, violating handprints all over me. *Except his hands left new, soothing ones.* I still feel them tangled in my hair, still see his face. I shake my head. *Enough of those thoughts already!*

"You can come out now," I say.

Cole appears and says nothing as he pulls a new shirt over his broad back and looks my way. I snap my head toward the wall and glue my eyes shut, praying these emotions run dry. I'm screaming at myself for even thinking maybe, just maybe, he might feel this way too. My eyes flick to the photo of the Commander mounted on his bedroom wall and I grimace. *I need to get out of here; I can't stay in his room.* But, I don't move. Because honestly, being alone terrifies me right now, and I wouldn't be able to sleep. Plus, Sutton said rest is a must. So, I make a deal with myself. After tonight…I'll leave his bed and things will go back to the way they were before. He's just my guard, and I'm just his job. Because anything more will get us both killed. And I never want to be the cause of someone else's death. So like a light switch, I flick it off, and swear to never turn that one back on again.

"Not tonight, please not tonight!" I say, pounding my arms into his chest. He grabs my wrists, yanks them behind my back and ties them together, leaving me unable to fend for myself, yet again.

"This wouldn't have to be so difficult if you'd just learn to cooperate with me, Lexi," he says in my ear with a hushed voice. I can smell the whiskey on his lips, which automatically turns my stomach into a frenzy. He drinks on nights like these— the nights where he wants control, the nights where he decides to torture me.

I open my eyes to a room the size of a small walk-in closet. Except nothing's in here but cement. Four cement walls with a cement floor and cement ceiling. To my right sits a small flashlight that's already dimming in and out. I can feel the hair on my neck and arms lifting. I'm digging my nails into my fisted palms that are still tied behind me. Sweat pours down my back and a sudden rush of heat fills my core. I lose control of everything in my body. I vomit for what seems like hours and when I finally stop, I dig my heels into the floor and scoot myself back to rest against the wall. I bring my knees to my chest, before heaving some more. Nothing's left.

My legs and arms twitch furiously and I can't control them. All I hear is the rapid drumming of my heart…reminding me I'm still alive, and it's not over. Not yet.

I look over to the left corner across from me and see a

shoebox. My eyes widen and my breaths quicken. I don't remember seeing it there before, but I see it now. The lid starts to move and a shrilling scream escapes my mouth. Spiders the size of a quarter start climbing out and dropping to the ground. I push my body back into the corner as hard as I possibly can.

I'm screaming. And I'm crying. And I'm watching them, as they climb the walls around me. They cover them like a black blanket. A blanket that steadily creeps closer to me, a blanket that's about to cover me.

I feel them drop on my head just when the flashlight burns out.

My eyes flip open like switches and my heart pounds in my ears. It was just another nightmare. My pillow's soaked with sweat. I look around and it takes me a moment to realize I'm still in Cole's room. I take deep breaths to calm my racing heart and my trembling nerves. My chest aches with the reminder of my injuries. *Inhale. Exhale.* I lie down on my side and grunt as stabbing pains shoot through me.

Zeus takes up a lot of room, so I move toward the wall. I reach for my sheet. *Where is the sheet?* I feel around for it, knowing I'm starting to make too much noise. My fingers find the edge and I pull. It's stuck. *Great.* I roll over and gasp. Cole's body is next to mine, and his face, only a few inches away from me.

I shriek. "What the hell are you doing?"

His eyes jump open. "It's not what you think!" He shoots up to a sitting position. "Please let me explain!"

"I think you better!" I say, glaring at him.

"Look, you were screaming in your sleep." He pivots his body to face me. I hear a click and the room lights up. I groan, wondering what happened in the room that I missed. The sheet looks like confetti thrown all over the floor. Zeus has slivers stuck to his chin.

"Zeus pulled off the sheet and ripped it to shreds. I'm guessing he thought it was attacking you. I tried waking you, but you kept screaming. I thought maybe if I held you it would help. I'm so sorry. I didn't know what else to do." He leans away from me with both hands in the air as if pleading his innocence. "I swear, Lexi. That's all it was." Zeus starts howling. "*Shut up*, you idiot!" He throws my pillow at Zeus, hitting him in the head. Zeus picks it up and whips his head left and right while growling. "Oh, so now it's the pillow's fault," Cole says, throwing his arms in the air.

"Stop!" I sit up. "Don't yell at Zeus."

"All right, I'm done."

"Look, it was just a night terror. I have them now and then." I pat his shoulder. "I'm not upset with you. But waking up to your face only an inch from mine was unexpected. I freaked." *Whew.* His jaw loosens as he flips around to face me. I don't move. He looks at me and hesitates.

"What was it about?" he says.

I knew he'd ask eventually. "I don't want to talk about it, not now," I say. "Can you please respect that?" But he persists.

"No, I can't. I've never heard you scream like that, ever. Not even when you were branded." I push away from him, stunned.

"You were there? Why didn't you tell me?" My face flushes red with the humiliating memory. I want to run out of this room and never look back. He grabs my hands. I shake them away. I feel the Commander's icy blue eyes mocking me from the portrait and I want to tear it to shreds. I grit my teeth.

"Just listen to me for a second," he says.

"No! Please, just leave me alone." I curl my legs to my chest, wrapping my arms around them.

He flinches. Then he starts talking. "I'm a guard. You're my assignment. I had to watch you from the moment you came into the compound. It's an order, and I had to follow it. I didn't know you then. I only knew of your sin and that I was your escort," he says. I don't take my eyes off the wall. "It wasn't my choice. I know you won't believe me, but I'm going to tell you anyway. I saw the pain they inflicted on you and I have no desire to watch anyone go through that. It's sickening. When I joined the guards, I thought things would be different.

I had the impression that what I was ordered to do was for the best. I was ordered to come, ordered to do my job, so I did." He takes a cleansing breath and continues his passionate rant. "I truly believe there was a reason I was placed here. I know there're good people here. Innocent people. They shouldn't be here. Lexi, *you* shouldn't be here." My heart thaws, letting him in. "Acting like I don't care is really hard for me. The other guards, some of them watch, and *he* watches. The Commander has hidden cameras—" I hold up my hand to stop him.

"Wait, he watches us?" I ask. "He records us for his pleasure? Why didn't you tell me before?" I ask. My eyes flick back to the picture hanging on his wall, and I suddenly feel naked. I pull the blanket up over my knees and gnaw on my lip.

"You were a prisoner, so I didn't tell you, but everyone knows. He has cameras hidden in the streets so he can watch. He loves the power and some of the guards get off on it," he says. "Thankfully, he can't bug every room since there are too many people in the Hole." He slides over, taking my chin. He lifts until I look at him. "Promise me you won't say anything. Not only would they kill you, they'd kill everyone you have contact with in here," he says with disgust.

"Including you and Zeus?" I ask.

He nods his head. "Yes, including us."

"Are there cameras in our rooms?" I ask.

"No, he only watches the streets." We hold each other's stare for a few seconds until Zeus barks. We both jump and look at him but he's asleep.

"You should sleep," he says.

"Like that's possible now," I say with sarcasm. My mind runs a marathon. He stands up to move and I grab his shirt. "Please don't leave," I say. "Stay with me."

"I'm not leaving you. I'm just going back to the floor." I don't release his shirt. Instead, I lift the blanket up. He looks at me, and knows what I'm asking him to do. He climbs in, turns the light off, and rolls on his side with his back toward me.

"Cole," I whisper

"Mmm?"

"For some reason, I'm starting to trust you and it's freaking me out."

He reaches back, grabs my hand, and squeezes. "Lexi, you can trust me. I'm one of the good guys." His back rests against my left arm, causing my arm to go tense. "But, thank you... I'm glad you're at least starting."

CHAPTER 10

The piercing siren blares outside Cole's window, reverberating through my temples. He faces me, eyes open, and my right arm lies across his chest. Sometime during the night, I'm guessing I pulled him toward me. *Or he just realized what happened.*

"I better get ready. Can't be late for training," he says as he backs away. He frowns.

I feel like a line was crossed last night, but maybe I'm wrong. "What on earth am I supposed to do while you're gone?" I sit up on one elbow, fearing the thought of being alone.

He laughs shakily. "Well, Sutton arranged for Bruno to stay with you while I'm gone."

"Wait a minute. Who's Bruno?" I sit up and see the mess Zeus made of everything last night. He didn't just shred my blanket—he completely annihilated it. "Holy crap, Zeus, what did you do?" He looks up and I can't help but laugh. Pieces of cloth hang from both sides of his head and he gives me a guilty look. He's busted.

"He's a friend of mine. He and Sutton go way back. I promise you'll be in good hands. We both would trust him with our lives." Cole goes into the bathroom and closes the door. "He'll be here any minute. The guy's never late."

I guess I should change too. I feel like a sweaty mess. At first, my muscles are taut, but as I move around, they loosen. I stretch upward, then touch my toes and arch my back.

The siren coincides with the blatant sound of steady gunfire. *That's twice in two days.* The building rocks violently, and people stampede in the hallway outside the room. I hear the light bulb dangling in the center of my small cell shatter from the jolt. Fear gnaws at my insides as I steady myself against the wall using my hand. *Don't give out. Don't give out.*

My legs start to wobble and threaten to collapse as I press against the cold cement. When the tremors stop, I jump to the window in hopes of seeing what's happening.

A voice shouts loud enough from below I can hear it up here. "Did you see that? That red car that passed by earlier? It was a bomb and it just leveled five buildings!"

"Holy shit!" another says. "What the hell was that about?"

"It's the resistance! It has to be!" I hear a woman's voice this time. Their voices fade as panic ensues.

Cole swings open the bathroom door and he looks furious. Shaving cream covers half his jawline and the tip of his nose.

"What the hell was that?" he asks.

"All I heard was a car bomb took out five buildings." I press my cheekbone against the glass and try to get a better look. "And that it might be the resistance, whatever that means."

People emerge from the curtain of smoke blocking the street from four blocks away, covered in dust and blood. Some of them scream in agony. The heavy smoldering of ashes, dust, and chemicals rises upward like a mushroom. Vehicles, mostly the men in black, clog the street, attempting to cordon off the bombed section of the Hole. Their dark figures form a checkpoint, and woe to anyone who fits the description of who they're looking for.

That easily could've been our building—I shiver just thinking about it.

He squints his eyes and shrugs. "Nothing I can do about it now," he says. "When I leave, I'll go check it out." Cole walks back in the bathroom without closing the door and resumes sliding his razor over his face.

"Much better, you were starting to resemble a caveman." I hear him chuckle and something about his laugh makes me smile.

Should I worry? I guess not. If he's not shaken, then I shouldn't be, but I can't tell that to the delicate nerves in my hands. Needing something to occupy my mind from the gore, I begin to clean up the strips of linen on the floor. Zeus warily follows me around as if he also smells danger. Or maybe I stink. I take a quick whiff of both of my armpits. Nope, still fresh.

"Zeus, it'll be fine." I chat with him while bending over and sweeping things up. I go into my room and attempt to clean up the shattered glass. *Guess I won't have any light at all in here now—and I can't stay in Cole's room forever.* The thought of spending another night in his room sends warmth flooding through me. I feel more secure knowing he's within arm's reach. I smile to myself but stop once I hear more footsteps down the hall.

Cole comes out of the bathroom in his dark-black dress uniform. It's newly pressed and formfitting.

"What's with the uniform?" I eye the formalwear pensively.

"Just playing it safe." He stands in place. "Whenever we're sent on a special assignment, we have to wear this crap. I'm still trying to figure out why. You should try running in these pants. It's ridiculous."

"They are a little on the tight side. You can almost call them tights." I push against the window again and view outside. The thick cloud covers everything with gray soot. Except for the guards, the street's almost shut down.

"Very funny."

A knock on the door makes me shudder and Cole opens it. He lets in a large black man, and they talk as if I'm not here. He stands taller than Cole and almost another body wider with a pronounced brow and high cheekbones. A small glimmer reflects in his pupils as if he's capable of mischief.

"Dude, how'd you get here so fast?" Cole asks.

"Aww, man, it's nuts out there," the guy I assume is Bruno says.

"What the hell happened?"

"A hijacked car was loaded with a bomb. It went off a couple blocks down, took out five buildings. And as if that wasn't bad enough, it took out the buses as well. Bodies, limbs—crap is everywhere. Never seen anything like it…"

"Makes me sick," Cole says. "And so it begins."

I clear my throat, interrupting their conversation.

Bruno's head pivots toward me and evaluates my appearance with a raised eyebrow.

"Oh, my bad. Let me introduce you two," Cole says as he suddenly remembers why Bruno's there in the first place. "Lexi, meet my friend Bruno. Bruno, meet Lexi."

His massive size makes me forget my manners and I don't stretch out my hand to shake his. "He'll be patrolling the hallway. So, if you need anything, anything at all, let him know."

I nod while staring at Bruno with wide eyes. I've never seen a man his size before. He's enormous.

He smiles, showing a set of perfect white teeth. "Nice to meet you," he says to reassure me. He doesn't know about the attack because we kept it a secret, but the way he scrutinizes my injuries tells me it makes him unhappy. "Don't worry. No one's getting past me!"

"I can see why!" I say. "But, thank you. I appreciate what you're doing for me."

Cole grabs a protein bar and darts for the door while coaxing Zeus along with him. "Come on. You can't stay here," he pleads. Zeus follows him with his head down and his tail between his legs. "I'll see you tonight," he says to me. Then Bruno, Cole, and Zeus leave with the slamming of the door.

Sigh. *Alone again.*

The day drags. I lie down, get up, and lie down again. I clean dishes, hand wash my dirty scrubs, and sweep the floor. As I sweep my old room, I trip over the bucket of chalk, scattering it in all directions. Seems like years ago that Cole gave it to me. My landscape remains unfinished, and even though I'm sore, I decide to draw more.

I begin with blues and greens, adding mountains. Then I realize how bland it looks in the dim lighting of my cell. I dip my hand into the bucket and pull out oranges and reds to form a brilliant sunset. I smudge the colors together, biting my lip as I try to capture the raw beauty of the sky at dusk. My hands are stained with chalk but I finally finish the wall. Only one remains blank now. Unsure of what to do, I start with yellow.

The yellow becomes waves of blond hair, blue for eyes that are large with tears of happiness.

Alyssa.

Tears fall silently as I recreate her beautiful, young, determined, and brave face. I didn't intend to draw her, but it happened. When I finish, my arms hurt from reaching so high. I shake them out at my sides.

I sit on the floor to rest and stare at my room. The memories play like music. First, the breeze blows over the bay with its clear, blue water surrounded by majestic mountains. Next, the forest rises up behind my childhood home, and finally, Alyssa's face—my sister and friend. I close my eyes, remembering every detail.

A sharp knock resounds on the door, making me panic. Do I answer? *What if it's Bruno? What if he's not as nice as he seems?* Cole made it sound like Bruno and he were best friends, but my trust has already been shattered more than once, so convincing me of that is hard to do. I swallow hard.

The knock sounds again, followed by Bruno's voice. "Just me. May I bother you to use the restroom?"

I want to be relieved, yet my heart quickens at the thought of being alone with a guard other than Cole. Despite my reservations, I call out, "Of course you can." This guy still petrifies me—he could crush me with his foot.

The door beeps after he swipes his card, and he hops up and down like a young boy in agony, waiting for the teacher to give him a hall pass.

"Sorry, it just hit me all of a sudden."

I nod my head. He's lucky Cole trusts him or I'd make him wet himself in the hallway.

"Thank you," he says. He sprints to the bathroom in Cole's room and closes the door.

After a few minutes, he returns, staring at my artwork. Sweat beads down his forehead from the heaviness of his dress uniform. His jaw drops in awe when his eyes rest on my latest drawing.

"Who's the girl?"

My eyes glaze over, but I answer. "My friend, Alyssa. She passed away last week."

"I'm sorry to hear that. She was a gorgeous little girl." He smiles with kindness. "You've got talent young lady. And you honor her with it."

I feel my shoulders relax and smile in return. He carries himself with confidence, yet he seems cautious in his movements, like he's afraid to startle me.

"Oh wow, thank you."

"Feels real—like it came straight from your heart." He points to Alyssa. "She looks young," he says. "Never easy when they're young."

I open my mouth to say something, but he turns toward the exit.

"Hey..."

He looks over his shoulder and pauses with his hand on the door.

"Do you know why...?" I fidget with my hands and look down at the floor. I can't help shifting my position. When I speak, it's little more than a squeak. "Why Cole's still guarding me?"

Still facing the door, he says, "Because he's been ordered to." He swipes his card and stands halfway in the hall. "Thanks for letting me use the bathroom."

"Sure, anytime."

I turn around, disappointed, and hear the door click shut.

The minutes and hours tick by, but I can't keep track. No clocks hang on the walls and Bruno doesn't come inside again for me to ask. I find myself missing Cole and Zeus—missing the distraction of Cole singing something off-key in the shower when he doesn't know I hear him or when Zeus drinks water out of the sink in Cole's kitchen. It's funny what you miss when you're alone.

And then I miss my father. I miss my mother. *Yes, even her.* I miss the way she was before my dad passed away—her free-spirited smile, bright blue eyes, and sing-song voice that used to read me books before bed. My throat tightens. I miss my brother, wherever he ended up. I feel hollow in my chest as I see their faces in my memory.

I don't even want to think about lying down again, although I should. So I pace my room. My bruises turn a yellowish color. *I don't look so bad, do I?* Heading into Cole's bathroom, I twirl my hair to style it a little, but the bruises on my face and the stitches on my lip make my eyes the only attractive part of me. *Why do I care?* Cole's already seen me at my very worst, but I wish he could see me at my best. I have nothing though—no makeup, no clothes other than scrubs, and no jewelry. *Thinking this way will only bring more trouble—for everyone. Maybe someday...Ahhh, there I go again!* Yet, I want something good, someone who believes in me and will stick around.

The door slams open. I jump back and Zeus sprints inside. I laugh as he jumps up to give me kisses.

"Good Lord, Zeus! Get down! You're such a goof!" I crumple under his weight and reach out for the wall to steady myself. He lathers me with affection. Soon, Cole arrives behind him.

"Hey," I say.

"Hey," he says back.

"How was your day?" I push past Zeus and manage to get out of the bathroom.

"Same old. Same old," he answers as he stops in my room and stares at my new landscapes. "I see you've been busy." He walks through the open doorway and rubs the back of his neck.

"Yeah, I got a little bored, so I worked on my room," I say.

His fingers reach out to touch Alyssa's face. "It's beautiful. She looks happy."

"That's because she's free."

He grasps at the high collar of his uniform and pulls it open as he turns to face me. "Up for some dinner?"

"Yeah, that sounds good."

He pulls off the top layer of his uniform. A simple white T-shirt clings to him underneath. "Let me change first. This freaking uniform is killing me." He walks into his room and begins to change without closing the door.

Okay, I can handle this. Then he drops his shirt. *Then again, maybe not.*

"So where did Bruno go?" I ask. I keep my head down, but watch him through my lashes. It's impossible to rip them away from his form.

"He went home for the night. Don't you worry. He'll be back tomorrow." His head turns up to face me while he tugs off his socks.

"Oh, okay. I wasn't sure. Will he be the only one covering for you?"

"Yeah, he's the only one I trust to be here." His shirt and pants are off, and I see his muscular legs as he stands in his white underwear. "Why?"

I turn my head so I don't look like I'm gawking. I'm completely gawking though. "Just curious, that's all."

He pulls on light-grey sweatpants but stays shirtless.

He's killing me.

The sudden warmth of his skin against mine catches me off guard as he pulls me into a tight embrace. "I'm sorry...You have every right to know who's watching your back." He rests his chin on the top of my head. "I've got a lot on my mind right now. I can't think straight."

The display of affection sends my heart fluttering and I feel conflicted. I long to stand like this forever and that scares me. I unwrap his arms and push him back, shoving down my desire for him. He puts his head in his hands, instantly apologetic. "I'm sorry. I didn't mean to make you uncomfortable." He tears his hands from his head and leans forward, pleading to me with his whole body. "Please, tell me what happened to you."

I meet his eyes, willing myself to be honest with him even though it makes me feel vulnerable. "I can't."

"Why? What are you afraid of?" He swats at the air with his hands.

"I really want to trust you, I do. But there're times I feel like you're lying to me and I just don't know if I can."

"I could say the same for you. You've never said a word about your innocence. Nothing. Don't you think that's a bit hypocritical?"

"And what if I did? Then what?" I fiddle with my hands as they shake. My nerves can't handle the stress of arguing with him. "Nothing, because nothing can come of it." I'm unable to meet his gaze, so I stare at the bag on the floor.

"I risk my life every day. For you." His voice has a serious tone. "And you're telling me, you still don't know if you can trust me?"

"It's not you. It's me. I know it doesn't make sense to you, but I just can't talk about it." A tear falls off my chin. "I'm begging you, please let it go."

He's steel and I'm liquid. He turns away, retreating to his room, and I hear things slamming around. Zeus comes to my side and nudges my hand while whining. I slide down the wall, everything aching, and bow my head, defeated.

Can anything ever go right? I'm *so* tired of being weak. I'm sick of being a victim. *Damn it, I don't have to tell him anything.* He's a guard for goodness sake, not family, not even my boss. The words keep going through my head, but I know they're excuses for how I really feel.

I push my back against the wall and walk myself up. I slide into his room and flop on his bed. I don't care where he sleeps…*but I do.*

He sees me as he munches on something like crackers for dinner. He didn't even bother cooking whatever he brought back.

I lie on my stomach, facing away from him and I feel Zeus hop onto the bed.

"We really need to talk," Cole says. He sits on the bed and places his hand on my lower back. His warm, tender touch makes it hard for me to breathe. I don't want to hold a grudge against the only person who protects me, cares for me, bathes me, and maybe—just maybe—desires to be with me too.

"Please, just please give me some time," I say.

What I don't tell him is that I'm fighting a major battle within myself over him. It's a hopeless war, but it rages on, giving me a headache. *To trust or not to trust?*

Zeus pushes himself between us and Cole removes his hand, beaten. I feel the fireworks on my back where his hand once laid.

"All right, but only till tomorrow," he says in a serious tone.

"So, are we okay for now?" I plead. My entire being feels suspended.

He lies down beside Zeus and reaches his arm over to touch me. "The last thing I want is for you to be afraid of me. But I want you to trust me. I need you to trust me." He sighs and I hear the pain and confusion in his voice.

"Why?"

"I don't know why, and it scares the hell out of me." He swallows hard and then scratches the back of his head while biting his lower lip.

Part of me screams for him to run for his own safety, yet I don't want him to move. My heart begs...*Please stay with me. Forever.*

"I hate when you leave, and that scares me too." I face him and our eyes meet. I see the conflict between his duty and his feelings mirrored in his face. His dark eyes glitter in the light. The hand with the bloody knuckles rubs my shoulder, my arm, and then he touches my chin.

I want more. So much more.

Zeus yawns and rolls toward me, placing his paws in Cole's face and ruining the moment.

"Come on, Zeus!" he yells with aggravation as Zeus's paws scratch him.

I laugh freely, breaking the tension, but Zeus doesn't budge.

"I guess that's how it's going to be, then," Cole says with sarcasm as he flips off the light.

"I hate leaving you," he says into the darkness. "And that petrifies me."

The smell of rotten flesh brings me around. I give my eyes some time to adjust to the dim light of the burning candle that sits in the same corner the spiders were in two weeks ago. My clothes stick to my body, soaked with my vomit.

But the smell, it's not a vomit smell.

I keep telling myself not to look around, and to stare at the wall ahead. Don't think about what's around or open your eyes to the shadows. Just lock your eyes straight. Better yet, close them against the dancing darkness.

I feel something crawling up my leg. I squirm and force my eyes open. Little grains of white rice fall to the floor.

But they move.

It's at that point I see a line of them inching their way back to something.

I'm choking on my own screams when I realize what it is. A cat. Its intestines look like blown-up sausages protruding from its mangled gut, only to be joined with hundreds of maggots weaving in and out. My insides retch.

I lose control of everything, and I scream for help, while soaking in my own vomit, urine, and feces. But no one hears me. No one comes for me. No one ever comes for me. I slam my head again and again into the wall.

Hoping to make it end.

Permanently.

CHAPTER 11

Gunshots don't faze me anymore. Not a second goes by that I'm not reminded where I am, who I am, and what I'm not.

Heavy clouds, pregnant with water, *drip, drip, drip* down the windowsill. Zeus lies on the floor. I guess he was too hot on the bed overnight. Cole wraps around me, his warm breath caressing the back of my neck each time he exhales. We're so close, but at the same time, not close enough. While he's pressed against me, I trace the outline of his arm with my fingertips. His skin feels like silk, but it's firm at the same time. A sigh escapes his lips. I wiggle around some, and eventually he stirs, releasing his grip. He grumbles something like an apology and rolls over. *Dang.*

I shake him. "Hey, I hate to have to wake you, but you better get your butt in gear or you'll be late for roll call." I take the opportunity to touch his hair and run my fingers down his faded haircut.

He moans. "I'll never get up if you keep doing that."

Oops. I pull my hand back, afraid I shouldn't have touched him. Zeus starts howling at a light knock on the door and jumps onto the bed.

"Zeus. Shut up!" Cole says in a grumpy voice. He leaps out of bed, disoriented. "Bruno must be here. Crap! I'm late." He runs to the door in his sweatpants and opens it, expecting to see Bruno.

Sutton stands there with water droplets running down his overcoat.

"Hey, is something wrong?" Cole asks while rubbing his eyes and shaking his head.

"No. I'm here to check on Lexi, remember?" Sutton's brows pull down, inspecting Cole's appearance. "Are you going to let me in, or do I have to stand here forever?"

Cole opens the door wider. "Oh right, sure, come in. I was expecting Bruno, that's all."

Sutton's eyes narrow as he scans the room critically over the rim of his fogged glasses. "Looks like she's cleaned up the place."

"Uh, yeah…she got a tad bored. Can't say I really blame her." Cole doesn't know how to act. He moves his hands to his hips, leans against the wall, and then crosses them.

"Well, your room was rather difficult to maneuver through," Sutton says.

"You're right. It was pretty bad, but I blame Zeus for that."

Sutton tilts his head while mentally weighing the situation. His jaw's set and he's avoiding eye contact with Cole. He carries a black leather bag that clinks as he walks. His face turns into a frown when he looks my way. "What part of 'I want you to rest' did you not understand?" He smoothes his rumpled appearance, takes off his glasses, wipes them with his shirt, and places them back on the ridge of his nose.

I make Zeus jump off the bed as Sutton sits down. He crosses his arms and I watch his eyes as they move over the room. First, he inspects the spot where Cole was sleeping, while biting his lower lip. His eyes move to my bedroom and scan the empty mattress. He raises an eyebrow.

This is not good.

"I know what you're going to say…but laying around was driving me mad. I had to do something—"

"Lexi, you should show him the drawing of Alyssa. It's amazing, really. It looks just like her," Cole interjects.

Sutton gives him an unhappy look and then returns his face to mine. "So, besides disobeying my orders." He pulls a small light out of his bag and examines my eyes. "How do you feel?"

"Pretty good, actually. I can move all my body parts without excruciating pain, which makes me happy. And you know, this may sound funny, but I think I'm more flexible now," I reply. *Maybe that wasn't the best choice of words. Lexi, you're such a moron!*

"Interesting," he says. "Let me take a look at your wound."

He puts on a pair of rubber gloves after washing his hands. He touches the back of my head where the gash was. It's still sore, but not as tender. "It's healed up nicely. The glue's holding up, so let's get rid of those staples." He digs through the bag and shows me a small piece of equipment that looks like a pair of scissors with claws on the end.

"Will this hurt?" I ask.

"I'm not going to lie, it's not pleasant. But trust me, you've been through much worse." He bends my head down, tilting it into the light.

A *click* of the contraption, followed by Sutton's strong pull, leaves me with a sharp burning pain each time he pulls out a staple. I count as I hear each one clink into a metal pan. The pain only lasts a few seconds after the staple is pulled out, so I endure it without biting off my lip. *Twenty-six staples? Are you kidding me?*

"It looks great," Sutton says. "And thank God, no signs of infection."

I place my hand on the back of my head, running my finger down my scar. "Holy crap! You shaved the back of my head for that wimpy scar?" I ask. "That's pathetic!"

He takes my hand, moving it over a little to the left.

"Ahh! It's huge! How didn't I notice before? It's the size of a—"

"Five inches in length and two inches in width," Cole says. "I measured it when I washed your—"

"When can I go back to work?" I blurt out to change the subject. I give Cole the drop-dead look that my mother perfected in her last few years, so he seals his mouth and decides to go get some food.

"Be right back," he says.

Sutton watches Cole leave, his jaw clenched and then he answers me in a grim voice. "As soon as your bruises fade. We can't have anyone questioning why you look like hell." He runs his hands through his hair. "And Lexi, this is never to be talked about again. Ever. Do you understand me?"

His change of manner alarms me and something doesn't

feel right. His shoulders slump and the tightness in his voice seems out of character for him.

"Then tell me," I say. My voice sounds shaky. "What's going on?"

He fixes his glasses and meets my eyes with a drawn-out sigh. "It's horrific. I've never seen it this bad. Just when I think it can't get any worse, the violence escalates. If you walk the wrong way, they blow off your head. Gang fights are constant, sending victims by the dozens to the hospital, and we have limited staff." He avoids my eyes. "I'm not pushing what happened to you under the rug. Please try to understand. They'd have murdered you. And I know you'd agree we need to protect those who saved you."

I nod. Of course, I'd never want anything to happen to them. Cole, Zeus, and Sutton are all I have.

"I completely understand," I say. "Sutton, I know you care about what happened to me. But it's not the primary concern, I get that."

"That's good." He smiles.

"So, back to the violence." I lean back and cross my arms across my chest. "Why now? Something has to be causing it, right?"

He puts his hands on his head and struggles for an explanation. "Lexi, that's classified information. I'm sorry dear."

"Yeah, I figured that much," I say. "But I swear on my father's life…I'd never say a word about it, to anyone."

Sutton's furrowed brows and tense face suddenly melt away and now he wears a wavering smile. "I know you wouldn't. For reasons of my own, I trust you, Lexi." He releases a long deep breath. "Sinners are fighting back. And even a talk of an uprising has surfaced. That's all I can tell you."

I don't know how to respond, and he continues in a whisper. "The Commander suspects something's up, and that brings me to my next point…"

I swing my head up to meet his eyes.

"If there's anything, and I mean *anything*, going on between the two of you, it needs to stop. I will not allow either of you to be tortured and executed over a crush and raging hormones."

His words hang in the air. Suddenly I'm rocking back and forth, holding my breath. I want to deny my feelings outright, but can't, so I squeeze my lips together, only allowing small amounts of air escape at a time. But the silence says it all.

Just then, the door beeps and Cole struts in whistling while holding a brown paper bag. "I got four bagels. Anybody want one?" As he focuses on our faces, he raises an eyebrow. "Oh, looks like I've interrupted an important conversation. You two go ahead and finish...I'll go...clean up." He goes into the bathroom and shuts the door. Next thing, I hear the shower running.

Sutton exhales, leans over the table, and holds his head up with his hands. "He's a good man and an outstanding guard, probably the best one here. But he's got some difficult decisions ahead. So do you." I watch him dig his nails into the top of his head. "If either of you slip, you're dead." Turning his head toward me, he says, "Lexi, it's not worth it. Trust me. In here"—He motions around us—"Love will only bury you." He clears his throat, reaches over, takes my hand, and turns it, palm up. "The last thing you want is Cole's blood on your hands."

My stomach drops to the floor. He's right; I'd never forgive myself if Cole died because of me.

"Nothing's...going on." I swallow the dryness in my throat and clench my teeth. *What am I thinking, allowing myself these feelings when they can't go anywhere?* Sutton brings me back to Earth like my father used to, and just like in the past, I weigh each of his words individually, fighting a battle between heart and mind.

"Keep it that way," he says with a stern tone. "I have to get going," Sutton says, breaking into my inner monologue.

"Thanks for checking on me." I speak loudly so Cole can hear. "See you soon!"

Sutton stands, wraps his coat around his shoulders, and grabs his bag as he turns to leave. He eyes lock onto mine with intensity. "Now remember what I said about the difficult decisions you'll both have to make."

I nod. It requires some effort since a million thoughts run rampant through my brain.

Suddenly, the bathroom door bangs open, and Cole stumbles out while pulling on his tall boots. He clunks to the door and puts his arm out for Sutton. "Thank you. We're indebted to you. Forever." Cole smiles and squeezes his arm as Sutton frowns.

What was that? "We" are indebted? He makes it sound like *we* are together. That's not good. Not good at all. Why doesn't he just ask for Wilson to come and lop off our heads now? *But we're not together. Nothing has happened and nothing can happen. I won't be the reason Cole gets killed.*

"Be safe," Sutton says to me.

"We will." I squeak out. "I mean, I will." *What's wrong with me!*

He raises his eyebrows at me and cocks his head to the right. He turns to Cole, shakes his hand, eyes me with warning again, and closes the door.

"Man, he was in and out fast," Cole says. "I even brought him a bagel."

"He's got lots of patients to tend to. You know, all the shooting victims," I say. I push for a response.

He looks at me like I shouldn't know what's going on out there. His mouth moves like he wants to say something, but nothing comes out. He slowly walks over to his safe, pulls out his pistols, and shoves them into his holsters one at a time. A knock interrupts the awkwardness.

Cole answers, opening the door slowly to find Bruno standing outside, looking droopy from the wet weather. He lifts the hood over his head and smiles.

"Morning, buddy."

"Yeah, yeah, come in," Cole says.

Bruno pushes past him and removes his wet poncho, placing it over a chair at the table. "What's for breakfast? Or more importantly, how's it taste?"

"Bagels. And I don't know. I haven't had time to eat," Cole replies. He pulls on an overcoat and double-checks the room to make sure he doesn't forget anything. In the meantime, Bruno nods his head my direction.

"Hey, I hope you're ready for another titillating day standing outside my door," I say with sarcasm.

He smiles his big, contagious smile. "As always, I'm ready for hours of excitement."

Cole looks at him, at me, and then back at him. He puts his hand on Bruno's shoulder. "I hope your day isn't too exciting. I don't want to have to beat your ass when I get back." He claps his hand jovially on Bruno's shoulder as he speaks, but I sense the threat behind it.

"No fun, just complete boredom." Bruno grins and steals a glance at me.

Cole calls Zeus and they're out the door. He doesn't even bother saying good-bye, which is a good thing because now, I need to find a way to distance myself from him. Not just emotionally, but physically as well.

Before Bruno steps out into the hallway, I stop him. "Hey, I have an idea."

Bruno turns his head toward me, squinting his eyes with suspicion.

"Actually, it's more like a favor."

"Now this should be interesting. What is it?" He tilts his head, his arms folding across his massive chest. "And if it will piss Cole off, you can forget it." His tone indicates I'm Cole's property. That aggravates me, so I take a deep breath and straighten my shoulders.

"It's nothing like that. It's just—I've been in so many bad situations. Wrong place, wrong time type things and wondered if you'd show me the basics of self-defense. I hate not knowing how to protect myself...especially if something happens to one of you." The words fall out, pleading and hopeful as I try to read his expression. "Leaving me helpless is cruel, don't you think?"

He hesitates and, noting my bruises, seems resigned to do

it. "I guess you've got a point. All right, I'll help you."

His eyes rest on the dark bruises that pattern my upper arms. The handprints are obvious from where the guard held me down—they're taking the longest to fade. Looking at them makes me clench my fists and want to punch a hole in the wall, but watching his expression change to one of solemn anger helps assure me he's one of the "good" guards. He pulls his Glocks from their holsters and lays them on the counter after removing the magazines.

I stand and face opposite him, hands hanging at my sides.

He looks around again, unsure.

"All right, I'm ready," I say.

So he begins. "First things first. Always be aware of your surroundings. Don't walk anywhere alone. If you must, carry something sharp between your knuckles if you can find something. Avoid dark places—that's a given. Use common sense and always trust your gut." He circles around me as he speaks. "I'm guessing you're not in the best physical condition, right?" he asks, but it's more of a statement.

"Most definitely not," I say.

"Well, we're going to whip you into shape. You don't stand a chance if you can't run or punch correctly, so let's begin with that."

Next thing I know, I'm doing push-ups. I can barely bang out twenty when he yells at me to go faster. He makes me sprint back and forth between the rooms, throw a mix of punches, and do more push-ups. I was sore before, but now I know I'll be an invalid.

Two hours later, I've had enough. I'm throwing up in the bathroom when he says, "That's enough for today. You're tough. I'll give you that. And I'm willing to bet you'll have this down in no time."

"Thanks, I appreciate that," I mumble before I heave again. *My freaking stomach.*

I can almost hear the smile in his voice. "Don't be ashamed. Believe me, at some point we've all had our heads in the toilet bowl. Although, I prefer to puke in a trashcan myself. There was this one time the water splashed back in my face. Probably one of the nastiest things that's ever happened to me." Then he takes up his post outside our rooms in the hallway.

I stumble to Cole's bed and lie down. Every muscle, including the tiniest ones I didn't know existed, hurt. *Should I keep this from Cole?* The answer is I can't.

I've never been a liar, but I've had plenty of experience around them. My stepfather was the prime example. He lied all the time. He lied to all of us when he married my mother and when we moved to High Society. At first, it was all rose-colored glass and then he smashed it. He showered my mom with flowers and cards. He bought my brother and I ice cream and took us to school. But he did it all just to win her heart, and when he did, everything changed. He began feeding her pills to the point she was barely coherent half of the day, and when she was, she was angry...*angry at me.* His hypocritical behavior and my mother's inability to distinguish the truth drove my brother away. I resigned myself to never, ever be a liar.

The thoughts make me antsy, but when I try to get up, every muscle screams. I sit in a huff, knowing walking off my anxiety won't work right now.

At last, Zeus bounds into the room, making his entrance with lots of wet kisses. Cole speaks in whispers to Bruno in the hallway for a minute before he comes in.

"Hey, heard you had an interesting day." He smirks at me.

"Uh, yeah. I figured it wouldn't hurt if Bruno taught me some basic self-defense. I hope you're not angry with me," I say.

He pauses in the doorway, looking around the room. "I guess I don't have a choice, do I? I'm betting if I said no, you'd do it anyway. And knowing Bruno, he'd teach you," he says.

That's it? That was easy. "So...you're okay with it?" I want to jump up and down, but my body won't allow me to move.

He can't hide his surprise. "Sure, it's a great thing to learn. Self-defense can save your life. Just refrain from using it on me because I don't want to be the one responsible for putting your ass back on bed rest." He laughs, takes my chin in his hand, and tilts up my head, his lips so close. I move my head to the right and he releases my face. He rubs the back of his neck and I avoid eye contact.

"Lexi, please be careful. Just because you know a few things...doesn't make you invincible. Plus, I'll still do everything in my power to protect you," he says. "Which reminds me, we still need to talk," he says. I raise my face to his. "Now don't freak out. I'm going to ask you some basic questions about your past, and if you're uncomfortable we'll stop."

My entire past makes me uncomfortable. "What do you want to know?" I ask, already moving away from him toward the chair.

"Your father. What did he do for a living?"

I cock my head to the left. *That's not the question I expected.* "My father, well, he was a humanitarian. An extremely wealthy one, but you'd never know it. He cared deeply about people, including the sinners. He thought the system was unjust and was fairly vocal about it. While he had some wonderful supporters, he also had a boatload of enemies. He never discussed his actual line of work with me, and I was too young and naive to think much about it," I say. "Why do you care about my father?"

"I'm trying to put all the pieces together." He shrugs as he pulls off his shirt and throws on a black T-shirt. He begins making something for dinner, and the smells are intoxicating. My stomach rumbles.

"Are you hungry?" he asks as he puts something on the plates.

"Starved, actually." *Wow, that's something I haven't said in a while.*

He sets the table and motions for me to sit down. He sits, bows his head, and says grace. It puzzles me.

"Where'd you learn that?" I ask.

"My mother, she taught me when I was young. I always give thanks for what I have because in an instant, it can be gone," he says.

"You're right about that." I pause while chewing and look at him. "Your mother, was she good to you?"

"She was." His eyes never leave his plate.

"Do you have any siblings?" I ask.

"No, but didn't you say you had a brother?" he asks, changing the subject.

The steak and potatoes with cheese rock my world. "Is this a special occasion or something...because I haven't eaten like this in ages...?"

He shrugs and raises his eyebrows while shoveling in another bite.

I take my sweet time answering his question because I'm too busy stuffing my face. Zeus props his head on my shoulder, so I cut off a piece of steak and sneak it to him when Cole looks down at his food.

"Your brother?"

"Oh, Keegan?"

Cole nods. "What happened to him?"

"I'm not exactly sure. All I know is shortly after my mother remarried, he took off." I start tapping my fingers on the table and rock in my chair. "He was my best friend, and he didn't even have the decency to say good-bye...or ask me if I wanted to go with him. It haunts me, still to this day."

Evening brings darkness so Cole flicks on the light. He leans back with his arms behind his head, fully relaxed. It's wild to have a normal conversation. *We should've started this way, getting to know each other, but instead, we do everything backward.*

"Your face is beautiful—"

"What?" I say, scrunching my nose.

"Has healed beautifully. Geez, I can't even get my words to come out right." He slides a sideways grin at me, his eyes sparkling in mischief.

I'm not sure if he's teasing me or not, but his comment makes me blush, and I refuse to look up from my plate.

"Well, that was nice of you to say. I haven't checked, too

afraid to see my reflection," I mumble, placing the last bite into my mouth. I feel his eyes on me. I curl my shoulders around myself and tuck my chin to my chest until I'm done eating. "This definitely hit the spot. Thank you."

I put my fork on my plate and sit back for a minute, soaking in his face. He's not smiling anymore like I thought he would be. Instead, he looks pained. His eyes are distant, his lips pursed, as if seeing a mirage in the desert.

"Something wrong?" A familiar feeling grips me. I feel the hair on the back of my neck rising. It consumes me at times, creeps up my throat, and constricts my airway. "Cole…"

He snaps to attention. He looks everywhere but at me, avoiding my stare.

The walls start collapsing. "There's something I need to tell you."

I have to remind myself to breathe. *Inhale. Exhale.*

"What? Tell me." I wrap my arms around my stomach and wait.

"I'm leaving tomorrow." He pauses, making eye contact with me. "I've been summoned on another mission." My stomach drops. I'm about to interrupt when he lifts his hand to stop me. "Don't worry. Bruno will be with you while I'm gone but, it's what I'm about to show you that will change everything." He pulls a crinkled piece of paper out of his pocket. Despite the folds, I see a stamp embedded into it and a photograph. He slides it across the table.

I crinkle my forehead and squint my eyes, trying hard to focus. The photograph's small with torn edges and faded in places, but warmth saturates my heart when I look into the eyes of…Keegan.

"Oh my God! That's Keegan!" I'm tripping over words. "Where did you get this? Is he alive? Do you know where he is?"

"Lexi," Cole says with a tone that deadens my excitement.

"Oh no, please don't tell me he's dead," I plead. "I can't—"

"He's alive. But he's in some serious trouble. I don't know exactly what he did, but it's bad. Real bad." Cole leans forward, pulling the order back. "Do you have any idea what he could've done?"

My mouth falls open and I manage to say, "No, of course not. How could I possibly know anything? I haven't seen Keegan since he left." I interlace my fingers and put my hands behind my neck. "Cole, please, whatever you do...don't bring him here!"

Cole drops the hand with the orders in it and looks me in the eyes. "Lexi, he's already here." I can hear the conflict in his voice, like he didn't want to break this news to me.

I gasp and my fingers fly to my lips. "How? Why? No. No. It's not true. It's just not...It can't be true." *Keegan's been here all along?* The weight of the situation dawns on me like an anvil attached to my beating heart. "I don't care what's he's done. He's still my brother! Where is he? I have to see him." I'm shaking and biting the inside of my cheek until the metallic taste wets my tongue and I force more words out. "Does he know I'm here?" I stand up, nearly pushing the table over. A million thoughts trample through my brain.

He shrugs his shoulders. "I have no idea." He stands and takes a step toward me. "Lexi, I don't know what to do."

"What do you mean?"

Cole's calm voice can't conceal the panic within his eyes. "We've been ordered to capture Keegan and take him to the Commander."

I step back. Searing emotional pain darts from my throat to my chest and into my soul. Everything blurs. I put my hand against the wall to hold myself up.

"Don't you dare," I say. I stand and push Cole into the wall, throwing my hands in the air. "I'll hate you—if you do that...I'll never forgive..." My insides scream as his eyes plead with me to give him a solution.

"Then please, tell me what the hell I'm supposed to do... because I don't have a damn clue! Orders are orders! They're not my choice." Cole steps toward me and puts his hands on my shoulders. "If I follow them, I'll lose you. If I don't, I'll be executed and then you'll lose me. Either way, we're screwed.

Damn it, you've complicated everything." His voice sounds anguished.

"*I've* complicated things? How's this my fault?" I shrug off his hands.

He collapses into the chair. "I'm not allowed to fall for you, but I did." His eyes don't leave mine; I stare at him blinking rapidly. "You're my assignment. You're my job. But somewhere during all this, you broke me, and my feelings got in the way. And because of my weakness... Well now look at me. Stuck between two walls that won't budge either way. I'm trapped by you and my obligations as a guard."

"Wait a minute. When you say...you've fallen for me... Do you mean—?"

"You're all I think about. My mind is constantly consumed by you, and it scares the hell out of me."

"No! No you can't! It's forbidden. They'll kill you! They'll kill me!"

"Don't you think I know that? I didn't choose to feel this way. I didn't mean for this to happen—it just did." He blows out a hard breath and seems to steady himself before continuing. "Everything about you sucks me in. No matter how hard I try to hate you or be disgusted, the opposite happens. You're like my magnet. You pull me in. No matter how hard I pull away...your force is stronger. And when I get too close, it takes everything I have to remain at a safe distance."

"You can't. We have to smother our feelings somehow. Nothing can happen!"

He rises from his seat, his eyes boring into mine. A softness overtakes his face. "So you feel something for me?" He pulls me into his chest, wrapping his arms around me.

"Of course I do. But it doesn't matter."

"How would they find out? If we keep it between these four walls, we'll be safe."

"No! Absolutely not!"

"Lexi, we can hide this." I feel his head resting on top of mine as his arms smother me in their warmth.

"Do you even hear what you're saying? You know what

we'd be risking? No, Cole! I refuse to be the cause of your death!"

"You already are!" he says.

"What?"

"I need you," he says.

"You don't need me." I breathe him in and my heart starts to flutter. "You can't have me...I'm branded. And you're a guard...my guard." I bite my lower lip. "We can't cross that line...because if we do, there's no going back."

"You think your brand bothers me? You think I can't see past the person they've labeled you to be?" He brushes my cheek with his thumb. "You're amazing just the way you are. There's not a single thing I would change about you. When you smile...my entire world stops. And all I see is you. I need you, Lexi."

My head shakes back and forth, willing his words away. If he keeps this up, I don't know if my promise to Sutton will stick. "No you don't. You have to stop."

"I can't. I've already tried." His arms break away from me, and he steps back. "You're the last person I ever wanted to fall for." His arms hang at his sides, his fists clenched.

His words ignite a switch I never knew existed. The words sting. A minute before, he said he needed me. Now, he tells me how I was the last person he would ever choose for himself. He's ashamed of his feelings for me. Before I can stop myself, my emotions take control.

"Well, why don't you say how you really feel? Huh? That being assigned to me was the worst thing that ever happened to you. I've ruined your life. But you know what? It's not my fault. You can't blame me because you can't be like all the other mindless guards that have no attachments beyond themselves." I spit at him as I feel my face heating up. "Why can't you be numb?" My mind wanders back to the thought of Cole hunting my brother and it's too much for me to bear. I fall to my knees, banging my fists on the floor, my breath coming in rasps as the pain crushes my chest.

"Enough! That's enough." He pleads as he kneels down to

put his arm around me.

Sutton's words come back to haunt me, and now I know exactly what he meant. *Difficult decision—choosing sides. Now I understand.* It's as if he knew this was coming.

"Why would you do this? Cook me dinner and then spring this on me? How'd you think I'd react?" I stand back, pushing his arms off me, and face him with my arms folded across my chest. Zeus comes to my side, sensing the tension.

"I was scared to tell you. It's been tearing me up inside, believe me." He steps toward me, but I move back and Zeus growls. Cole raises his hands in innocence. "Look, you need to trust me."

"Trust you? Seriously? After what just happened, you want me to trust you?"

"Then we can't be together. Without trust it would never work." His lips seal into a thin, pale line.

"Trust or no trust...it's never going to happen. It can't!" I throw my hands in the air. "And you're going after my brother!"

"Come on, now you're being unfair. I mean, you're getting upset with me for being, what, honest? Yet you can't be honest with me."

"Oh, no. Don't go there!"

"I would never judge you. What happened to you obviously wasn't your fault." He leans over and kisses the top of my head. "All I want is to help you heal. To hold you when you cry. To glue you back together when you break apart. I want to reach out my hand and help you back up." He kisses my forehead this time and I sigh a heavy sigh. "But trust goes both ways. If there's no trust, there's no us. I can't do this without you."

Us. His words freeze me in place. He steps away and starts shoving his clothes into his duffle bag. I watch in silence while Zeus whines. "Cole, I'm not sure what you want me to say. I trust you to keep me safe...isn't that enough?"

"No. That's different," He clears his throat and puts his hands on his hips. "See here's the thing, I care about you, and

I know you feel something for me too. But damn it, I risk my life every day for you and I never once second-guess it. But I need you to open up to me. I need to know everything there is to know about you. No secrets. Trust is the backbone of a relationship, you know." He's finished.

"What on Earth are you talking about? We're not allowed to be together even if we both want it." Tears leak from my eyes and my lips form a tight straight line as I stand watching him pack his things. Did he say he wanted to be together? Did he say *relationship*? Does he think I'm his girlfriend? *I can't.*

Everyone's keeping secrets from me, breaking me into pieces.

He doesn't even bother folding his stuff, just throws it in. He proceeds to kick things around his room on the floor and Zeus scurries to my side. I flinch when he wrenches the Commander's portrait from his wall and smashes it on the floor. Glass shatters everywhere as he picks it up and throws it again.

"I won't let him ruin this!" he shouts. I wrap my arms around myself, attempting to hold myself together. I can taste my salty tears as they slide over my lips. "Is this what I have to do to prove I can be trusted?" Sweat rolls down his red face, and I can see his defeat when his shoulders finally slump.

I swallow, but can't find the words to answer. He grabs his head with both hands and closes his eyes. Then he begins picking up the shards of glass, making a plinking sound. I kneel down, attempting to help pick up the pieces, but he pushes my hands away.

"Just…let me do this." His voice sounds empty and tired. He stands up, retrieving the picture and shoves it, half torn, under his bed. When he's finished, he drags my old mattress into the other room and stays there.

I want to climb into his arms and plead with him to lie next to me. But I can't. I won't let him die because of my own selfish desires. Then my thoughts wander back to Keegan and I cringe.

Zeus puts his paw on the bed and I allow him to be my

comfort for now. I lie on Cole's bed, my face buried in the pillow, as he jumps up beside me. I rub his ears and cry. Nightmares easily overtake me.

Wilson and my stepfather, wearing twin, sadistic expressions, stand on the podium in front of the hospital.

"Come on up. We won't hurt you. We swear."

Like a lamb to the slaughter, my legs lead me up the rough, wooden stairs onto the stage. The whole world watches, and a spotlight rests upon my face, burning my eyes with its excruciating white light.

Cole stands with his hands tied behind him, and on the other side stands Keegan, also bound. Except Keegan looks like the boy I knew as a child. He's ten again, with wavy brown hair and a knack for getting into trouble.

"Choose," Wilson says, shoving me forward.

I fall onto my knees, prostrate before them. "I can't. I don't understand..."

A hand smashes across my face, sprawling me out and sending pain throughout my body. My vision blurs and I see double of my stepfather standing over me.

A chilling smile precedes his words. "Choose who dies. Or we kill them both."

My eyes wander to Cole, standing with bound hands and pleading eyes. And then they hold the image of ten-year-old Keegan close. The past or the future...what to do when I love both?

Wilson moves toward Keegan and whips back his head, forcing a scream from his throat.

"You always were a weakling." My stepfather nods at Wilson, who promptly slices Keegan's neck. His head falls forward in an awkward motion as the scarlet blood soaks through his dirty blue T-shirt.

I scream.

The siren mixes with my silent scream as I wake in a sweaty panic. My shirt and pants stick to my body as I gasp for air. The dream was so real.

Checking my old room, I see Cole's asleep. I very slowly grab a pen and a piece of paper. Then I sit at the table and write. When I'm finished, I fold the paper in half and tuck it down into his bag. I climb back into bed quietly just as the sun starts to rise.

I think I hear the scuffling of boots on concrete, but the crust forming on my eyelids makes it hard to open them. My hand comes up, rubs the yellow flecks away and I peek between narrow slits into the other room. Cole's standing in his dress uniform looking handsome and crisp. His face tells another story though. He looks pained, his eyes anguished with the decision he has to make. I quickly shut my eyes, pretending to be asleep as he crosses the room. The next moment, he kisses my forehead, pulling wisps of hair away from my face, and he's gone.

CHAPTER 12

I chew on a protein bar from Cole's stash in the kitchen, but it tastes like cardboard. I keep munching, but I struggle swallowing it. His absence leaves a strange, eerie silence over the rooms. I sit on a chair at the small, square table in his room and put my head in my hands. It should make me feel better that he was honest, but instead, it confuses me more. He really doesn't want me hurt. Well, this hurt. It hurts like hell, and I can't smother the fire. He was trying to do the right thing, right? Then why am I more angry and confused than I've ever been in my eighteen years? I need him but I need my brother more. I miss Cole. I miss Zeus. I don't know what's wrong with me. I miss us. I slam my cup of water on the table and liquid splashes over my hands. *Serves me right for losing my temper.* He changed everything. Alyssa changed everything. *What is right in this situation?* I put the glass in the sink and stand there for a moment with my hands against the counter.

The door clicks open, but I don't even notice because I'm immersed in my own thoughts. His footsteps alert me to his presence and I swing around, expecting Cole to be there.

"Ready for training?" Bruno asks, holding up his wraps. After scrutinizing my face, he steps forward. "You okay? You look like hell." He glances around the room. "And it looks like someone tore up the place."

"It's nothing." But I feel the tightness in my face reflected in my voice.

He shrugs and raises an eyebrow. "We can skip today, you know. I'll be here tomorrow too."

I'm already wrapping my hands though and I give him a hard look. "No, I need this today."

After two hours of relentless training, Bruno stops to grab a drink. Sweat soaks through my shirt, my fists are bruised, and some knuckles bleed. My hair sticks to my neck and face, and I feel like the fire has gone out a little.

"I think it's time we call it quits," he says while unwrapping his hands. "Unless you want to go on."

"Whatever you think." Yet I know I've got nothing left in me.

He puts his guns back in their holsters and clears his throat while evaluating my appearance. "We'll attack it some more tomorrow."

I pick myself off the floor and grumble while heading to the bathroom to shower. I barely have the strength to stand but I let the water wash over me. Training gives me clarity, but not enough. It's a small reprieve, but not what I need. *What I need are answers.* All I can think about is our argument and Cole's words—his words that stung like flaming darts aimed directly at my heart. I close my eyes, hold onto the wall, and let the water run down my battered body. All I see is him smashing the portrait of the Commander and glass flying everywhere on his floor. I can only imagine what he'll think or how he'll react when he reads my letter, if he reads it all. I didn't go into great detail, but I laid out the basics. The torture's humiliating enough and makes me feel dirty and worthless. But, I swallowed my pride and laid it all out before his eyes. I came to the conclusion if there was anything I could say or do to possibly save Keegan, I will gladly suffer the consequences. After all, it's about Keegan…not me.

I step out of the shower, towel off, and put on the same beat-up pair of scrubs. They smell of body odor, salt, and sweat. *But there's no reason to be self-conscious now that he's gone.* And to make matters worse, I might lose my brother before I even get to see him again. I clench my fists. If anything happens to him on account of Cole, I'll hurt him. *Could I really hurt him though?*

Just as I slide my feet into my tattered slippers, the siren blares like an evil witch waiting to ambush me. The thought of going back to work makes me want to hurl.

Bruno bursts into my room, panting and shoving his guns

into his holsters. "We've gotta run. Now!" He slides his key and opens my door into the hallway. I shuffle backward. "Come on!" he yells.

After a moment of confusion, I follow him.

"There's no time to explain...I've been called out and the building's being evacuated," he says.

As if proving his point, a group of people push past me, shoving me into the cement wall. I slam into it, feeling stunned. Bruno wraps his thick hand around my bicep and drags me along behind him. My feet barely touch the floor as he rips me through the crowd, weaving this way and that. My pulse races. The people around me wear panicked, bulging eyes. They don't care who's in the way, they just shove past. I can barely breathe amongst the tightly packed bodies and my nose crinkles at the stench. When we reach the last floor, I feel the building shudder violently.

"Another car bombing," someone says while holding their shirt over their mouth.

"Outta my way," another yells gruffly. His elbow catches me in the stomach but I shove him back. He doesn't bother turning around in his rush to get outside.

They spill into the courtyard, coughing and covering their mouths. A layer of dirt and dust covers everything, almost like a snowy day, except more gruesome. That's when I see the bodies lying in the street. The dark-red blood streams like ribbons through the grayness.

Another blast sends people ducking for cover. I jump. I feel prickles up my spine as I try to breathe. The mass sways to its knees in search of anything or anyone to hide under. Silence. Another layer of blown particles gives us a mummy-like appearance. Gray hair, gray skin, gray clothing, and the constant hacking up of whatever we've just ingested. I cover my ears and then my eyes and then realize I lost Bruno. I cough from the dust, but inhale more in the process.

The sound of heavy machinery grinding down the street brings me to my senses. The clanking of heavy metal stops across from the courtyard. I search for Bruno, shoving through the shocked crowd, but only see dusty silhouettes of tanks and guards.

"Bruno!" I scream.

"Watch it. What's your problem?" A man tries to pull me back, but I slip free of his grip.

"Get off me," I say as I move forward. "Bruno!" I'm pushing people aside just as they did to me. I need to find him. But he's nowhere in sight.

Panic climbs up my throat. I cough violently. I can't breathe and don't know where to turn. The people push to escape the confines of the courtyard and suddenly it becomes suffocating. I'm shoved against the chain-link fence and squeezed. I feel my nostrils flaring as I try to catch my breath. The rusty metal embeds in my cheek as I turn my head sideways, scraping my face. I grimace against the pain. The screams of compacted people reach my ears, but I fight for my own survival. I claw at the fence. *I'm going to die if I don't move.*

Feeling desperate, I pull myself up and begin to climb. The fence jerks toward the street as the crowd forces its way. I don't dare close my eyes for fear of crashing to my death. My bruised hands hurt from clinging to it. Without thinking about it, my lips begin whispering a prayer. *Please don't let this collapse beneath me.* A deep voice penetrates my ears and immediately I know it's Bruno.

"Lexi!" he shouts.

"I'm here…" I cough uncontrollably from the particles in the air. "Help me!" I scream. I can't see him but hope he hears me.

"Don't let go!" he commands. "I'll get to you!"

His strong voice steels my nerves, and I clench my hands tighter around the links, determined to hang on. I can just barely see my scabbing knuckles breaking open and bleeding from the stress of hanging on. My toes begin to ache from being cramped in their footholds, but I still cling to hope. So many faces hang in my mind—they wouldn't give up, and neither will I. I'm determined to survive…for myself and for them.

Minutes feel like hours before the guards calm the people enough to organize an exit. As they disperse, I start to slide down. My fingers feel stiff and ache. My muscles burn with slow fire as I meet the hard, cement pavement.

"However are you surviving with Cole being gone?" A sharp, high-pitched voice shakes me from my stupor.

Please not now. I look up and meet the sadistic eyes of the head guard, Wilson. Instant fear seizes me as he pulls me closer to him. He smiles, smelling of tobacco and cologne.

"I was a little concerned. Haven't seen you around lately," he says. "Guess if I was in your shoes I'd try to stay under the radar as well." He kicks the dirt. "Rumor has it your brother's been found. But again, it's just a rumor, so I guess we shall all wait and see what Cole brings home."

I remain silent—part preservation, but mostly terror. I can feel the tremor in my hands, so I clasp them together.

He backs away, still smiling, and motions for Bruno. "You should really keep a closer eye on this one—I don't like her."

Bruno salutes and replies, "Yes, sir."

"Carry on." Wilson steps aside, waving us off, and instructs the others to block off the street.

My feet feel stuck in the cement as the sudden urge to cry washes over me. I bite my lip as Bruno pulls me away with a stoic face. My heartbeat echoes in my ears. We step over broken bodies, yet all I hear is *thump-thump, thump-thump.*

Bruno leads me in silence as we witness the full impact of the destruction. More tanks roll in and hoards of guards pop out, eager to investigate. They line suspects up against the wall of the building across the street with their hands behind their heads. A guard holds a pistol up behind them and pulls the trigger.

Oh my God, no! The harsh exhale of the gun makes me jump. I fall on my hands and knees, feeling dizzy as the thumping in my head grows louder.

"Get up," Bruno says.

"I'm trying." I sound unconvincing, even to myself.

"Get up! Before they make you the next target." He picks

me up and puts me on my feet, wary of others watching. "Just move, even if it's slow."

So we plod along to the hospital. The pent-up tears finally drop down my face, racing through the grime. The fear of suffocation consumes me as well as Wilson's words. He knows my brother's here and Cole's hunting him down. I clench my teeth in anger and refusal to break, although my world shrinks by the minute.

Once inside the hospital, I attempt to clean my face in the bathroom. It smells like urine and feces mixed with other bodily fluids. My feet make a sucking sound as they lift. But nothing compares to what I see in the broken shards of the mirror—the turquoise of my eyes amidst the wreckage of everything else. Again, I'm reminded of my father and hear his voice telling me, "Be strong, Lexi. You can overcome anything short of death." His words bring me strength, and I resolve to hold it together.

* * *

Day Two of Cole's absence. Nothing makes me loathe work more than seeing Amber's sly smile when Bruno drops me off and picks me up. I try to ignore the stares, but it's pointless. They're all speculating about my absence, about Cole, and the reason I'm miserable. Being here brings back so many memories of Cole, Alyssa, and the assault that it's like a slow death of the soul. My body works while my mind wanders. My arms function, but my shredded heart roams elsewhere. I imagine Cole strapped down with equipment, sweating in his uniform while tracking my brother. Could he really pull the trigger, knowing he'd destroy me in the process? My stomach flips, so I run to the bathroom and heave.

"Everything all right?" Sutton says.

"Sure," I say out of habit. Since it's fairly obvious that I'm not okay.

"What can I do to help you?"

I don't answer because I'm pretty sure he knows the answer.

"I know Cole's gone, so if there's anything I can do to help, let me know," he says.

I sit back and wipe my face with a towel. *Yes, he definitely knows I'm a mess.* "Okay. I will." I wave him off, then stand up and compose myself. He's already gone by the time I look back. There are too many patients rolling in each minute for him to worry about my issues.

In the back of my head, Cole's words keep replaying. *"You won't open up to me. How can I ever trust you if you won't tell me the truth?"* I try to convince myself things are better this way, but my mind swings back and forth like a pendulum.

I know he cares, and I know the danger we'd be facing, but I'm not going to give up yet. Not now that I know he has some good in his heart. He wouldn't have professed his feelings or damaged that portrait if he wasn't sincere. He didn't even have to tell me about Keegan, but he cared enough to be honest. I bite my cheek. I want to believe he's real. I want something, anything to be real. I can't function knowing he and Zeus won't be there when I get home tonight. I can't function thinking about my brother in the Hole, unprotected.

*   *   *

Day Three. Bruno and I train early in the morning. I wake up anxious and can't sleep, so I might as well fill my time hitting something since I can't punch the Commander or Wilson. Bruno punches; I block. He kicks; I counter. My mind sees Keegan as the little boy I knew him to be. I try not to imagine Cole scouting him out, but I can't stop the nightmares from coming. I grunt as I throw a straight punch. Bruno takes me down, and I try to free myself. But nothing, *nothing*, fills in the hole in my heart.

Cole's worth being vulnerable, but it took his departure for me to realize it. I promised myself I'd never speak about my past—not ever. He might be disgusted and never at look me again—the stigma attached to people like me isn't positive. My eyes turn to slits as I do pushups. Some days, I can barely look at myself. I begin doing squats and then kicks. Salty tears mingled with sweat burn my eyes. *Either way, I can't lose much more than I already have.*

* * *

Day Four. I go about my duties as if having an out-of-body experience. I'm here physically, but my mind climbs the walls in hopes of news about Cole and my brother. I never agonized so much over anything this way. The anxiety forces me to bite my fingernails, and makes me experience mood swings like I'm constantly pms-ing. One minute, I'm raging mad at Cole for going on the mission. The next, I'm worried about him. Lastly, I'm crying over the fear of losing my brother when I just realized he's alive. My stomach roils. My body is rebelling against me. All the while, victims of street violence pile into the hospital. The business of cleaning rooms and aiding nurses should distract me, but it doesn't. I'm helpless to do anything about my situation and I hate it. Hate it. Hate it. Ben takes another body to the morgue and I have to clean the room. I sit behind the curtain and agonize.

"Lexi," Bruno says, leaning in through the door.

My head snaps up. "What?" I say with a sharp tone.

"I'm going to stand out here and wait for you, all right? Unless you want me to come in and help you. It's been three hours and you're still cleaning the same room. I think they're getting pretty backed up," he says gently. He must know why I'm secretly agonizing.

"Three hours is a bit of an exaggeration, don't you think?" I can't keep my sarcasm from getting the best of me.

"Maybe a little, but you know what I mean. If you need help, I don't mind," he says.

"No, it's no problem. I'll pick up the pace. Thanks for the offer though." I grab the sheets off the bed and throw them on the floor. I pick up the pillow, throw it back down, and start punching the daylights out of it.

Bruno runs to me, grabs my waist, and hangs me in the air.

"Chill out," he says. He holds me there.

I keep kicking, though, because I'm breaking down.

"You can't do this. If they suspect you know anything, they'll kill you. And with the way you've been acting the last few days, it's not hard to put two and two together. So you better snap out of it or I'll lose my buddy and you'll lose your brother. That's a no-win for both of us. There are more important things going on in this hell hole besides your breaking heart." His scolding voice makes me feel guilty. "Feelings you're forbidden to have. And honestly, what do you think could ever come from it? Nothing... You need to grow up, girl, and think about what you're doing."

He's right. I try to calm myself down by exhaling. The violence in the Hole has escalated, sending more people to the hospital than ever. Even children arrive with injuries, but I've reached my mental threshold. I can only think about two people...and one silly dog. I go about my duties oblivious to the news that citizens bring in. My mind plummets in a downward spiral interrupted by one sane voice.

"Put her down, Bruno." He sets me down. Sutton stands behind me, and I turn around one inch at a time. "Come with me. There's a matter we need to discuss." He sounds stern. I hesitate. "Now, young lady." He walks out the door and waits for me in the hallway.

What have I done now? This is never good. I already know what's coming. I'm going to get in trouble for my behavior, slacking at work, and letting my small situation get the better of me. *I've let him down in so many ways.* I fidget and take a few quick breaths.

"Close the door and take a seat," he commands.

I slump into my seat and wait for him to rip into me. I can't handle Sutton being mad at me, not right now. But that doesn't stop the anger from flashing through his green eyes. He pushes his papers aside as he sits on his desk.

I can't keep eye contact while he talks. My head spins.

"You're playing with fire and it needs to end right here, right now. You're careless and the reason is way too obvious. I won't tolerate it," he says.

My eyes flip to his face and my mouth opens to reply, but he shushes me.

"Do you think I'm blind? Do you think I'm stupid?"

"No, not at all." My arms are limp in my lap, and I don't have the heart to make up an excuse.

"The feelings you have for him must die, or both of you, without a doubt, will be executed." I seal my lips, waiting for him to continue. "If you don't get your head together and fast, and use your brain to make sound decisions, I'll make Bruno your permanent assignment, which will only escalate their suspicions."

"How could they—?"

"They take this kinda thing very seriously. In their eyes, loving a sinner is by far the worst offense."

My eyes well up, but I blink back the tears in defiance. They aren't tears of sadness, but of anger—anger over life, over Cole leaving and my brother disappearing all those years ago, and being in this damn place. My mind is imploding. I bite my lip in an attempt to keep from screaming.

"You think your situation is the center of the world. But it's not. I am demanding your affair to end, got it?" His question is more like a statement. "I warned you this was going to happen. You said you understood. So, please, stop being angry at everyone and start doing something about it." His sharp tone hurts my ears and then he folds his hands. "I've got a lot of patients in this hospital sick with the same virus Alyssa had and I don't want to see you, for one minute, feeling sorry for yourself."

I nod my head once, swallowing hard. "Is that all?" I struggle to keep my voice from breaking.

"And take this extra pair of scrubs. You smell worse than the hospital." He tosses a folded pair of scrubs into my arms and pushes me out the door.

Heading down the hall and into the bathroom to change, I think about what I wrote to Cole. But regardless of what he thinks about me after he reads it, I just wrote it all for nothing.

I replay the ending of my letter in my head and it makes me quiver.

My stepfather murdered the girl I once was, and he was so damn proud of it. All I wanted to do was die and I was too pathetic and weak to even accomplish such an easy goal.

I hate the skin I live in. I cringe at my reflection and vomit at every sight and smell that reminds me of those days.

And now I'm here with you and all of a sudden my life makes sense again. The way you look at me makes me feel human—not a lifeless soul trapped in my own skin. So I thank you from the bottom of my heart for saving me, reviving me, caring for me, but most of all, for being my friend. I'm a train wreck—I know this—but with you by my side, I'm starting to mend.

So please, don't give up on me. I need you to remind me every day who I really am and what I can become. If you can't find it in your heart to love me, I understand why, but please don't run away from me, at least be my friend. Cole, even though we can't ever be together, promise me you'll stay.

All my heart,
Lexi
P.S. Deep down I know you'd never choose to hurt me, so if you see Keegan, please tell him I love him.

Just thinking about his response makes my hands shake as I pull on my new clothes. I can only hope and pray he doesn't hate me. *And that Sutton forgives me.* However, I can't stop being angry. I won't let anyone quench the fire inside because that's something I have to do for myself. I have some choices to make and they won't be pretty.

* * *

Day Five. Victims of street violence, both branded and guards, line the dim hallways of the hospital. The air is choked with blood, vomit, and humidity. Nurses struggle to pull bodies out of the hall and into a pile while guards patrol each room, looking for instigators. Their dark presence makes me feel as if there's an anchor in my stomach, weighting me to the floor. I keep my eyes downcast and stay busy with my hands.

Patients die so fast we can't keep up, so the nurses develop a method of deciding who's most likely to live and then mark them with a pen. The marked patients are sent to the eighth floor and the others are left to die. Nightmares of their ragged, desperate faces envelop me at night. All it does is stoke the flames inside of me.

* * *

Day Six. I'm pretty sure I'm losing my mind. He said he'd be gone a full week, which means he should be home tomorrow. I want to know what's going on with Keegan. Is he alive and well? Or is he one of the ones unmarked with a pen, left dying in the violent streets? I pull my hair out of my face and put another sheet on the pile of laundry. I don't think I can wait any longer even though my insides shake with the anxiety. I wonder if Cole read my letter and how he'll respond. *Does he think I'm disgusting? Weak? I wish I could read his mind.*

"I've been calling you. They needed you in room three about twenty minutes ago," Bertha commands. She stands in the doorway with sweat dribbling down her face.

I drop the basket of sheets on the floor with a thump and sprint to the room. My feet slip on the floor. Five people with gruesome injuries are shoved into the small candlelit space. I gasp. Only one of them lies in a bed and the others rest, moaning, on the floor.

"You need to clean up this putrid mess!" Amber points to the body lying closest to the wall, a man who obviously wet himself. A putrid yellow puddle forms around his body, but since he's unconscious, he doesn't know.

But without fail, my stomach lurches, and I swallow it back. "It'd be my pleasure," I say.

She laughs at me in the snide manner that suits her so well.

"And don't you worry. He doesn't miss you one bit. He never could keep his pants on." She tosses me a napkin and leaves.

A passionate, angry retort bubbles up within me, but I refuse to give in to her rude behavior. I hold my tongue while heat crawls up my face. Instead, I unfold the napkin and throw it on the urine, watching it soak up. Then I grab a sheet and start scrubbing while holding my breath so I don't puke on this poor man. I try to push his body aside to clean under him, but he's too heavy and he just moans.

Three guards slam through the door and swarm the man I'm cleaning. They shove me out of the way as Bruno enters behind them. I fall back onto my behind, clamoring away from them. Their eyes narrow into slits and their mouths pull down at the corners.

"Leave," Bruno whispers in my ear.

"What?" I ask.

One of the guards pulls out his pistol, pushes it against the man's temple, and executes him—right there on the floor. A scream catches in my throat as Bruno shields me. My hands fly to my face. They stomp heavily out and leave his body lying there in a mix of crimson blood and urine.

As soon as they pass, I crumble on the floor, gasping for air. My ears ring with the explosive sound of the gun. The image of the patient's body, the bodies in the street, and Claire, the gorgeous girl in love with a guard, on the platform bleeding her life away, grasp at every thread of sanity I own. My clammy hands cover my eyes.

"It'll be okay. It'll be okay," Bruno says. He kneels down next to me.

It'll never be okay as long as I'm here. I want to scream at him.

"It's seven. Let's go…but first you need to snap out of it so we can walk out of here. If I carried you, it wouldn't look right," Bruno says. He pulls me up and brushes me off, worry etched on his face. His large eyes give nothing away, but I sense his anger in the way his shoulders tense. I wonder if he's as bothered as I am over the deaths of innocent people.

Straightening my back and wiping my face, I enter the hallway. Amber stands at the nurse's station, flirting with Zane. She didn't need me to clean the room; she just wanted to humiliate me. The way she smiles and flips her hair makes me want to go psycho and overturn the huge desk in front of her. I seethe under my skin and give her the nastiest look I can muster.

Bruno walks beside me and we ride silently in the elevator.

I stumble through the parking lot, unaware of my surroundings while deep in thought.

"Someone's back early," Bruno says.

CHAPTER 13

Our eyes meet and it feels like time freezes. The ball cap Cole's wearing doesn't hide his bloodshot, pained eyes as he motions for us to get in. My stomach drops. *He's leaving me. I know it now.* My heart shatters within me and it takes all my strength to climb in and secure myself. I'll never survive this…never breathe again without him.

As soon as we clear the guard checkpoint, he peels out into the streets. The sun's falling behind the walls and the moon begins to show its full white face. The heavy moisture in the air is as thick here as in the hospital.

We travel in silence. Only Zeus's subdued kisses distract me from my inner turmoil. I feel like a rope that's being pulled from both sides and one end eventually will weaken first, but which one? I gave him my heart when I wrote that letter. *I was such a fool to imagine we could've had anything…such an idiot for thinking he'd accept me for the battered girl I am.* I care about him, but I don't know how I feel at the same time. Maybe he should ignore me. Maybe I need to let it go. After all, Keegan's survival depends partly on him. I dig my fingernails into my seat.

Not once does he glance in his rearview to look or even speak to me. But I stare at him. His jaw clenches and his knuckles are white on the steering wheel. *Oh God, he probably doesn't want to tell me he caught Keegan.* My hands ball into fists. *Don't punch him, don't cry, don't punch him, and don't cry…ugh!*

Cole parks the Jeep in the garage and Bruno gives him a sympathetic look before leaving.

I dread the silence as he leads me to our building. The kind of silence that hangs over your head like a stretching water balloon. And once it pops, all your emotions just spill out at once, which usually is never a good thing.

The fence still leans into the street, looking warped from the pressure of the crowd this morning. I can smell the spilled blood mixed with sulfur, and it burns my nose. The heavy metal tanks park along the curb, and the makeshift checkpoint is thriving as people go back to their quarters. They pass through quietly as angry-faced guards inspect them. A crude area has been set up to load bodies from the explosion and some of the citizens add more to the pile. A large lantern grossly lights them. I can see the exhaustion in their faces from the black bags beneath their eyes. How many bodies must lie there? I don't count. The sun disappears, leaving darkness except for the lights the guards carry and the red burning of cigarettes.

Zeus nudges the back of my knee, pushing me along. The little energy I have left drags my corpse up the stairs and into his room, ready for Cole to say he's done with me.

But he doesn't.

Instead, he runs his hand down my face, wiping the tears as they pour down my cheeks. Looking into his face, I sense his anger, yet I see compassion in his eyes. The way he cradles my face with his hands and kisses the top of my head only confuses me.

"Did—did you find Keegan?" I ask. I can't stand here until I know the truth.

"Yes…"

"Oh God!" I say, pulling his hand away from my face and looking down. "Don't tell me. Oh God, please don't say it."

"I couldn't do it." His husky voice belies his feelings, and I glance up with a slight smile forming on my face.

"What did you say?" I have to hear him say it again. I can't let it go until I know Keegan's safe, regardless of his offense.

He sighs and throws his arms in the air. "Oh, hell! I wasn't strong enough, all right?" Cole kicks over the trashcan and pushes a chair out of his way. Zeus attacks the trashcan, pulling out all of the trash and tossing it all over the room.

I slowly back up into the corner to steady my swaying body. "So…"

"So yeah, I found him. He was right there, and all I had to do was reach out and grab him. And just like that, it would've been over," he says while talking with his hands. "But no! All I could think about was the pain I'd cause you. All I could see was the heartbreak painted on your face. And just like that, I turned around, letting Keegan walk away."

Suddenly, I'm struggling to speak and everything in the room starts to spin. I hold on to the counter before I can take a head-dive to the floor.

When three knocks on the door cause us both to jump, I shake my head and rub my eyes as Cole opens the door.

"Seriously, what the hell do you want?" Cole says.

I peek around Cole and see Crazy Bill drunk as a skunk, leaning on the doorframe and staring at Cole.

"You're definitely not Melinda," Crazy Bill says. "I thought this place looked different." He sways against the doorframe.

Cole shakes his head and grunts. "You're something else, you know that? Drunk as a skunk. Let me show you to the exit." He looks back at me and rolls his eyes. "Be right back."

"Okay," I say.

The suspense is killing me. I try to find my bearings as I wait for him to return and continue our conversation. I need to know what happened to Keegan. *Did my stepfather make him leave or did he leave of his own accord?* I need Cole to reassure me that everything will be okay, but I'm afraid he'll reject me…even though he should. *Even though I should.* I shuffle backward until my back finds the wall for support, glancing at the ceiling as tears overflow my eyes.

Cole returns, opening the door carefully, as if he's afraid to disturb me.

"Cole, I don't know what to say. But thank you!" My voice is so shaky I'm not sure if it made any sense. "You have no idea how much this means to me."

Cole doesn't acknowledge me; instead, he continues to stare at the floor and says, "Lexi, I need you to tell me… How I can help you get through this?"

"But, I did get through it. I survived," I say. "I'm alive and

I'm not some junkie on the street, trying to numb my pain. You know what's sad about all of this... I almost let him win. I was seconds away from ending my life because I thought I wasn't strong enough to keep going, and turns out, I was wrong." I let out a huge breath. "Just be my friend, that's all I want, that's all I need."

"A friend?" Cole looks like he's struggling to speak. He moves his mouth to say something more, but nothing comes out.

"Cole, I need you to try and understand something. Because of my stepfather—"

"I swear to God, Lexi. If I ever see him, I'm going to kill him." Cole locks the door behind him and slams his fists into the door, once, twice, and a third time. He turns, his nostrils are flaring and there's tightness in his eyes.

Seeing how pained he is over my past shatters my wall. My lungs gasp for air as the room seems to strangle me. My eyes release pools of tears as my chin starts to quiver uncontrollably.

Cole opens his arms. "Come here," he says. My legs won't move because if I move, I'm not sure I have enough left to push him away again. So instead, he rushes over and pulls me into his chest, securing me with his arms. "I'm so sorry. I'll never let him hurt you again. Ever."

My knees give way and he swoops me into his arms, carrying me to his bed and holding me tight. His smell, oh my God, his smell is enough to make my head spin. He didn't kill my brother and he's here... here with me. My skin burns with the need for him to just hold me. My entire body aches just being this close and not giving in to the desires I know we both have. It's exhausting.

He wipes away my tears with his calloused hand and kisses my forehead. "Here, I have something for you." He pulls something small out of his pocket, takes my right hand, and slides a gold band down my index finger. Instantly, I recognize it and my heart collapses as I grab onto his arm. I thought the Hole would strip the humanity from everyone who was forced to endure this purgatory, but I'm reminded, once again, that love can exist anywhere regardless of the circumstances.

"How...? How—?"

He stands and crosses his arms across his chest. "During your transformation, during your branding, you were stoic the entire time. Never screamed, never flinched. But when you were ordered to surrender your ring, your face was pained. And knew I had to get it for you."

"But, you didn't even know me then," I say. "Why would you care?"

"That I can't answer."

"What if they would've caught you?"

"I wasn't worried about that. They just pawn all the stuff. So, when they weren't looking, I took it."

"You stole it?" I say sarcastically. "Sinner!"

"Well, not exactly...I just gave it back to you, didn't I?"

"Why now? Why are you just now giving it to me?"

He takes my face between his hands and stares into my eyes. "With everything that's happened, I totally forgot I even had it. But when I read your letter, I remembered. You're only alive, and here with me, because of that ring."

He's right. It was the only reason I hesitated the night the guards came to get me.

And suddenly I can't feel my heart beat and my ears ring so loud I can't think. Then my voice comes out, breaking the static in my head. "That's the nicest thing anyone has ever done for me. And you didn't even know me," I say. "Cole, you saved my brother and my ring, yet I have nothing to give you in return."

"You already did, by trusting me and letting me in."

My gaze lowers to the floor and I take a cleansing breath. "I had to. The night before you left, I couldn't sleep knowing I could lose you forever, and that's when I knew." I meet his gaze.

He curls his lip and tilts my face up. He pulls me in with his eyes. "You knew what? That I would never leave you?" He kisses the top of my head, then my forehead, and my head again.

My head explodes like a bomb. I look up and he holds my gaze. I know he can see my pain. I pull away slightly, but he locks his arms and I'm unable to move.

"Knew what?" His lips are only inches away and he's pulling me into him. I'm biting my lower lip and blinking rapidly. "Tell me."

"Even if it was only for a day, an hour, or a minute—I would risk everything just so I could be with you." I tremble just saying the words out loud.

"Do you know what you're saying?" His concerned face morphs into one of determination. He kisses the tip of my nose, then my cheek, and I'm melting into him.

My body shakes, not because I'm scared, or maybe I am. It feels so wrong to want his arms around me, and I'm furious with myself for allowing it to get to this point. My brain and my heart are at war—one feels and one thinks. It's a deadly war that no matter who wins, both of them will die.

"Do you really mean that? Because if we get caught—"

"I know. I do."

"Lexi, we only live once, and I have no doubt we're going to make it." His lips part slightly and he's so close to kissing me. I want him close, but at the same time I want him far away from me because his life is too precious to be in my hands. The hands of a sinner, guilty or not, could get him killed. He's too good for me, too good for anyone in the Hole. Cole deserves a relationship, a family we can never have...but here we are, here he stands in front of me, giving me his heart.

"I'm scared out of my mind. I could never live with myself if anything would happen to you." I search his eyes for any sign of hesitance or dishonesty and find none.

"Nothing's going to happen. I'm capable of performing my role as a guard, but I'm also capable of being what you need me to be. I'm right here and I'm not going anywhere."

"What if...?"

"Shhh..." He grips me gently and pulls me closer to his chest. I can feel my body heating up. Cole tilts my chin up and softly whispers in my ear, "I'm about to kiss you, and once I start I won't be able to stop. Just thought I should warn you."

"And if you do, I won't be able to stop."

That's when I feel his lips on my jawline, and a chill shakes my entire being. He lightly kisses my chin, and then he kisses the corners of my mouth with such tenderness a moan escapes my throat. He exhales and I breathe him in. My pulse races to an unseen finish line.

Slowly, he leans in and presses his lips against my neck, and with every breath, he kisses me. I wrap my arms around his head and tilt my head back as his kisses make their way to my collarbone. I feel his hands move up my back and our breaths become heavy between each kiss. My body shakes.

He takes my face in his hands, rubbing my cheekbones with his thumbs. He kisses my forehead, my nose, and my eyelids. I open my eyes and smile. The room starts to spin when his eyes lock on mine, and I'm losing my fight. He leans his face closer and closer, but not close enough.

"Please. Kiss me," I say.

He smiles his crooked smile, pauses a minute, and then brings his lips to mine. They're warm, gentle, and soft. My heart flutters as he runs his finger over my lips and kisses me again. Then he pulls back, leaving my mouth yearning for more.

"What are you doing?"

"Teasing."

"Oh no you don't!"

I grab his head and press my lips to his. His kisses grow hungrier and more passionate by the minute. I open my mouth slightly, allowing his tongue to gently caress mine, and a quiet moan escapes him as I scrape my nails across his back. His mouth tastes minty and I want more, so much more.

"Don't stop." I'm left breathless and even my toes start tingling.

He drops his hands from my face and slides them under my shirt, grabbing me around the waist. He lifts me up and pushes me back onto the bed. My lips never leave his as he lowers himself on top of me. I'm losing all control. I wrap my arms around his neck, holding him closer, tighter so he can never leave.

His hands wrap around my hips and pull me into him as he kisses me with more intensity than before. He's killing me.

I need to feel his flesh, so I grab the bottom of his shirt, pull it over his head, and throw it on the floor. I look down and my mouth drops open. *Holy muscles.* He laughs at me and shakes his head.

"That bad, huh?"

"Disgusting actually. Mind if I grab your shirt? You looked much better when you had it on."

"Is that so? Well, in that case, I'll keep it off so I can continue to gross you out… Just don't puke, all right?" He pushes up on his hands and winks at me. "It's kind of a turn off, you know."

"I'm trying my hardest to keep it down."

"Are you really?" A flicker of concern darkens his face.

"No, silly. Lay on your back." I can't help but laugh as I try to pull him down.

"Why?"

I don't answer. Instead, I roll him over, straddle him, and kiss him. Then I run my tongue down his neck to his chest and kiss every inch in between as my fingers glide over his biceps.

I can't believe how amazing it feels to touch him and nothing could make me stop. I want all of him…all of him on me. I take his hands and place them on my shirt. He looks at me and shakes his head.

"No, I just want to kiss you," he says. I run my hands up and down his chest, feeling him tremble underneath my palms. My hands are clammy but I can still feel his skin and a slow smile grows on my face.

He growls. At least I think it's a growl. "Your turn. On your back you go!"

This time he straddles me. He interlaces his fingers through mine, guiding my arms above my head, and holds me there while he kisses my wrists, elbows, and back to my lips. I will kiss this man until the day I die.

We stare at each other, more vulnerable than ever. Desire dances in his black eyes and the green of my eyes light up his darkness.

He runs his mouth from my collarbone to my lips, kissing every delicate area on the way. I'm on fire. I wrap my legs around his hips and force him closer. Unleashed.

"I won't," he says between kisses. "We can't." He gradually tries to pull away from me, but I use my legs to lock him in. He stops arguing and gives in, only to try again. "Not here, not like this." His voice is rugged with desire as he unwraps my legs from his hips.

I pull away, breathing hard, confused. *I was just getting started.* I turn my head to the side, trying to hide the tears in my eyes.

"No, Lexi. It's not what you think."

"And how could you possibly know what I'm thinking?"

"You're pretty easy to read. Would you at least look at me?" He turns my head until it's facing his. "Think about it. I'm your guard. We can't risk getting you pregnant… They'd automatically suspect me. If they found out, they'd kill me, wait for you to deliver, and then force you to kill our child before finishing you off," he says as he stares down at me from above. "I won't put you through that."

I bite my lip while reading his face. I still don't see any sign of regret. My past has conditioned me to look for the deceit in others. He wipes a tear from my eye with his thumb and flashes a weak smile. My mind was so wrapped up in him, I totally forgot where we lived, and he's right. We can't risk getting pregnant no matter how much we want *it*. I sigh in frustration and try to think over the pounding of my heart.

"This really, really sucks."

"Yet you look relieved," he says. He rolls off to my side and props himself up on his elbow while using his free hand to play with my hair.

"Just relieved you still want me. I was so scared while you were gone, scared you'd hate me or think I'm weak and disgusting." I choke on the lump in my throat and roll to face him. "And now, we're stuck hiding what we are. Now I know how Claire felt and it scares me even more."

"Not once, ever, did I think you were any of those things." His eyes widen with intensity as he places his hand on my cheek. "To tell you the truth, I think you're incredible. Seriously, look what you've been through—the fact that you're still sane and functioning…"

"Okay, that's enough. I don't want to think about that right now… Let me soak up this moment with you." I roll onto my back and play with the gold band on my finger. My ring doesn't weigh much, yet it brings a burden of responsibility with it. My father must've known the road ahead wouldn't be easy when he gave it to me. He wouldn't want me to flippantly give up or give in. The inscription, as always, gives me strength for the moment.

"So…how are we going to be able to hide this? Sutton and Bruno already suspect. And it's going to be really freaking hard to look at you without smiling or fainting," I say as I turn my head toward Cole. "No one can know about us…I can't lose you. There's no way I can overcome that. And what about the ring?"

His smile fades into a solemn expression. "If anyone asks, just tell them Alyssa gave it to you."

"All right."

Banging on the door makes Cole fall off the bed. Zeus, who was lying at the foot of the bed, begins howling. Cole's feet get caught on Zeus as he tries to answer the knock, and I stumble to the chairs at the table. We must look ridiculous, scrambling to look normal, but our survival depends on it. My fear wins over my sense of humor.

Cole swings open the door, looking slightly flustered. "What is it?"

"This building's on lockdown until further notice," a man says.

"Whose orders?" Cole asks.

"Wilson's."

"Great," Cole says. Then he closes the door while shaking

his head. "Looks like we're stuck here...damn, that really blows." He runs back to me with a hungry expression.

Another knock interrupts him and I roll my eyes. "Really! Hurry up and answer it." He throws on his shirt and swings open the door again. Wilson stands there looking formidable in his uniform and polished black boots. Two other guards stand off his shoulders in the hallway, loaded down with ammunition and large guns. My heart pounds so hard I'm sure everyone can hear it. I can scarcely breathe for fear of him sensing my weakness.

Cole immediately salutes and steps aside. Wilson motions the two guards into Cole's kitchen and their hard eyes inspect me.

"This building's been placed on lockdown. Two suspects came through here. One's dark, about five-foot-nine and the other is light skinned, about six foot. They're carrying stolen weapons. Have you seen them or anyone suspicious come through here?" Wilson's commandeering voice cuts me to the core. His gaze settles on me, sitting at the table, trying to look inconspicuous. Then it flicks to the walls of Cole's room, to the holes where the portrait once hung on the wall. Something flashes in his eyes before he refocuses on Cole.

"No, sir," Cole says. "I'll be sure to keep a sharp eye."

"Shoot to kill. The last thing I need are more prisoners. We're over crowded as it is." Wilson replies while keeping his steel eyes locked on me.

They unnerve me, so I cast mine down to my feet, hoping he doesn't inspect my room and see the drawings on the wall.

"All night we'll be performing random searches, so don't expect to get much sleep," Wilson says. This time he turns toward Cole. "You're still expected to report on time to training tomorrow." Wilson looks over Cole's shoulder. "What the hell is she doing in your room?"

"I was going over the rules with her, sir. She seems to have forgotten some... Just keeping her in line, sir." Cole sounds confident. If I didn't know him better, I'd never assume he was going against their laws either.

"Write them down. Make her read them... There's no reason you should be having a one-on-one. Now get her ass back to her room."

"Yes, sir," Cole says.

"Now," Wilson commands.

The other two guards stare, lusty-eyed, as I stand and move toward the door. My hands tremble at my sides as fear rushes through my veins. His narrow eyes and icy demeanor instantly terrorize me and I'm tempted to run. My palms sweat as I turn the knob and go to my room, praying they don't follow.

CHAPTER 14

Time *tick, tick, ticks* past. I know it's going slow because I stopped counting how many times I can pace the room when I hit fifty-six. Anxiety claws at my insides, ripping holes into my sanity. It feels like I've been trapped in here forever. All I hear are doors slamming and people cursing in the hall, along with the heavy footfalls of guards outside my door. My eyes feel stuck wide open as I sit on my mattress, wrapping my arms around my knees.

I lie down, attempting to fall asleep, but Cole's words keep playing through my head. *This is our secret and no one else can know about it.* But what about Sutton and Bruno who already seem well-informed? I put a hand over my eyes. And now I completely understand how Claire and Mac were caught—everyone always watches you. It makes me worry for Keegan too. I doubt he'd be pleased about my relationship, if you want to call it that. Would he even know who I am anymore? Maybe Alyssa was right about life in the Hole. Maybe she did have it easier knowing she'd never have to grow up in this forsaken place.

I roll onto my side and huff. But I can't deny how I feel toward Cole. Nothing and no one could ever compare to him. All I can think about are his honest brown eyes, the scar on his lip, and the intense expression when he kisses me that sucks me in like a vacuum. I feel drunk on him—just crazy about his face, his hands, and his body. Too crazy.

"Lexi, you awake?"

I push up on my elbows and see the door cracked open with light pouring in from behind. Cole stands there squinting his eyes into my cave-like room.

"Yeah, can't sleep," I say. "Is the lockdown over?"

"Nah, I can't sleep either. Figured if you couldn't be in my room, then I can at least sneak into yours." He slowly walks over and plops himself next to me with his head leaning back against the wall.

"You know, he really freaks me out...makes my stomach uneasy and I really don't want him to come back." I motion toward the door and he knows exactly to whom I'm referring.

"I hate to break it to you, but everything makes your stomach uneasy."

"No. This unease is different. There's nothing I can do about the uncontrolled puking. It just happens. But now it's more like a sickening nervousness."

"Right. Whatever that means."

"If he's second in command, then where's the Commander?"

"Well, Wilson usually oversees the transformation center and lab while the Commander controls the Hole itself...but rumors of the revolt have changed that, I guess."

"Hmm, well, they're both disgusting." I lean my head against his shoulder, staring into the shadows. "Do you think he noticed the Commander's picture wasn't on your wall?"

"What makes you think it was him?" Cole shifts toward me.

"I've seen the same photo a few times. First at the transformation center, and now here." I shrug. "I don't get it."

"What's not to get?" He raises an eyebrow.

"I thought his identity was to be kept a secret?" I picture his regal face in my mind—black hair, deep blue eyes, strong jaw, and plastic smile.

"Lexi, think about it. It's not that hard to figure out," he says. I scrunch my face at him. "Once you're in the Hole, it doesn't matter if you know or not. We...they...assume you aren't getting out."

"So you plaster his picture...just anywhere?" I cross my arms.

"It's used as a reminder that he's always watching us." He sighs. "It shows our loyalty."

"But aren't they worried that sinners who work outside the

hole will recognize him?"

Cole's head shakes. "That photo is older than you, I bet. Plus, I'm pretty sure the Commander uses a double for security reasons. Like I said, he's paranoid." He runs his hand over his head. "Paranoia and power are never a good combination."

"Well, in that case, I'm glad you took it down." I tip my head back for a moment and close my eyes.

"It's no secret, they both abuse their power. It's sickening, really." He wraps his arm around me and pulls me close. "But you're safe with me."

I savor the heat rolling off his body and fall silent for a moment.

"You okay?" he asks.

"Fine…just a lot on my mind," I whisper back.

"Mmmm... I know what that's like."

"What are we going to do about Sutton and Bruno?"

"Not much we can do." Cole reaches back and rubs the back of his neck. "But I do know for a fact they'd never turn us in. Of course neither of them are fond of the idea of 'us' for good reason. The last thing they want is for us to be executed. And believe it or not, I'm not the only one who cares about you." He takes my face in his hand and reassures me. "So outside of these walls, we can't stand each other."

"It shouldn't have to be this way." I sigh. "I don't know, maybe I'm wrong. But I think everyone deserves the chance to fall in love, you know?"

"Yeah, actually I do," he says. His eyes soften. They remind me of a warm cup of coffee.

"All right. When we're out in public, I need a distraction. Give me something to think about that would repulse me. So when I look at you, I can be totally disgusted."

"Like what?" He contorts his face in confusion.

"I don't know, anything. Want me to give you one?"

"Oh no, I have one in mind already." A smile plays on his lips.

"That's so not right…It can't be anything from my—"

"Lexi, come on, you should know I would never do that."

He narrows his eyes and gives me his half smile "Okay, are you ready for this?

"Now, I'm not so sure…"

"Well, too bad. Here it goes. All I have to do is picture you taking a dump, and I'll be fine." He throws his head back and laughs hysterically toward the ceiling.

I playfully smack his arm. "Ew, seriously! Now that's just wrong."

"It works… Try it."

"*No*. Come on, think of something else. There's no way I can be around you if I know you're thinking about me—"

"See, there you go." The moonlight glints off his teeth as he smiles wide.

"What?"

"Now you're disgusted that I'm thinking about you pooping. So it works."

"Oh my God, you're impossible." I scoot away with a huff. "And sick."

"Ha. Good, because we have to go back to the important stuff."

I lift my head up and meet his serious stare. "As in, why would Sutton know some of your inside stuff?" I give him a questionable look.

"What are you talking about?"

"He sort of warned me about the order to hunt down Keegan—well, not specifically, but he knew. I know he did."

"Lexi, he's a doctor. He sees and hears a lot of things. And who knows, maybe he carries some weight with the Commander. But of course, I don't really know…just all speculation really." He reaches up and plays with a lock of my hair, twisting it around his finger. "If he wanted to hurt us, he could've by now…so I'm not worried about him."

"True," I say. "But still it's kind of strange." I lean against him and let him cuddle me. My thoughts are muddled from lack of sleep and being on constant overdrive. Zeus lies on my other side and pushes my hand with his nose so I pat his head between yawns.

* * *

The siren blares us awake, startling Cole. He jumps up and sprints back to his room, willing everything to be normal. Next thing, he's dressed in his uniform, guns strapped into his holsters, and he's shoving me out the door.

"Let's go! We have to run today."

"Why?"

"Bruno needed the Jeep."

I follow behind him, past the tanks hogging the road and the guards at the checkpoint. The humidity chokes me as I struggle to keep up with his stride. I glance back over my shoulder and notice most of the bodies have been hauled away. None of the sinners linger outside like they used to in the courtyard. The dilapidated, rusty fence has been ripped out of the ground and shoved into the back of a truck. I turn my eyes forward, willing myself to focus on what's ahead. Once in the alleyway, Cole's shoulders relax a little and he turns to speak to me.

"That was edgy…"

"What?"

"The checkpoint. They've made it permanent. Didn't you notice the barricade they set up overnight?" he asks.

"I only saw the tanks. And I noticed they took the fence down." What I don't say is that I never make eye contact with the guards when we pass through checkpoints.

He shakes his head and motions me forward. We cross the crowded street to the hospital and squeeze our way up to the eighth floor since the elevators are broken again.

Nurses breathe hard while lugging stretchers with marked patients up and down the staircase. I duck out of the way when a stretcher tips and an older man with a blue brand tumbles onto the cement stairs. His groaning, coupled with the cursing of those around him, grabs my attention. My heart goes out to him.

I attempt to help, only for Cole to rip me away. His eyes give warning as a troop of guards march up the stairs.

"Move!" he orders under his breath. "Get out of their way!" I let the nurses struggle to roll the man's body back on the stretcher without me. The eighth floor isn't any better. The halls teem with bodies, nurses, and supplies. I stick to hugging the walls to avoid getting in the way. Cole signs me in and immediately the nurses beg me to help. Their eyebrows draw together and I can smell their unwashed scrubs. By the end of the day, my hair is matted to my forehead from sweat. My slippers smell like upchuck from stepping in puddles of human waste. My knuckles bleed from washing my hands, and my lower back aches. Cole raises an eyebrow when he sees me ambling toward him in the hallway.

As we push through the exit, Wilson waits with his men. Cole stiffens by my side with his fingers steeled around my bicep.

"There you are!" Wilson says with a smirk. "Just who I was hoping to see."

Cole salutes. The hair on my neck stands up with fear.

"She's coming with me," Wilson says to him.

Instantly, my body responds to his words and I start shaking uncontrollably. Cole releases his grip on my arm and steps in between Wilson and me.

"Sir?" Cole says. "My orders are—"

"To go back to your quarters and wait."

"Wait for what, sir?"

"Now, Cole, that's something I can't answer for you. Simply because that all depends on Lexi. And her cooperation." Wilson shoves Cole aside. Zeus bares his teeth and Cole's nostrils flare as his right hand moves toward his pistol. Zeus won't budge. Instead, he sits on my feet so I'm unable to move.

I have to get Cole out of here before he gets himself killed.

"Let's go," I say to Wilson. "Zeus get up."

The other two men grab my arms and haul me toward the black SUV parked on the curb. The tinted windows make it impossible to see anything inside.

I don't even have a chance to glance back at Cole as they shove me inside the vehicle, but I hear Zeus barking ferociously as they slam the door shut. Wilson slides in next to me, and the guards sit in front. They watch the road as they drive and leave the talking to him.

Immediately, he reaches over to pat my hands and thoughtfully traces the ring on my left finger. My back goes taut and my muscles constrict in terror. *Tell me this is a nightmare. Please wake me up.*

"That damn dog, he should be shot." I don't acknowledge his comment. "And Keegan seems to have a knack for eluding my men."

Already, I don't like the way this conversation is heading. I pull my hand away from his and bite my lower lip to keep from saying anything that will give away my terror.

"All right, let's make this plain and simple. I have questions, and you're going to give me the answers I need." He slides closer to me, invading my space.

I blink frantically, afraid to meet his gaze. I'm afraid his hardened eyes will see right through me and see how vulnerable I really am. My heart feels like it's in my throat and I'm about to gag on it.

"Where is he?" Wilson grabs my chin and makes me lock eyes with him. His sickening, sweet façade fades with the violence of his movements. "Talk! And don't you dare lie to me. Because I'll know…and if you think your life is miserable now—trust me, I will make it worse. Much worse."

"I—I have no idea where he is," I stutter. I flinch away from him while making eye contact so he can see I'm not lying. "I swear to you I had no idea he was even here until a few days ago." I'm practically pressed against the door handle. I wish I could just pull it open and jump out.

His hand releases my face as he weighs my words. "Hmmm." Then, sighing, he goes on. "It's such a shame. First your father, who you have a remarkable resemblance to, and now your brother…Seems your family's determined to piss off the Commander." He doesn't wait for me to speak. "I don't like chasing squirrels, if you know what I mean. I'd much rather spend my time on more important things. So you can see how this is a great inconvenience to me."

I shift uncomfortably in my seat. Sweat pours down my back and sticks to the black leather.

"I can, however, make your life very, VERY easy if you cooperate with me."

I drop my eyes and fiddle nervously with my fingers. "How?"

"You find out where your brother is, inform me, and I'll reward you. Then you get a nice little place in the Commander's residence and I go back to my lab experiments."

I can't even entertain the thought of betraying my brother or anyone for that matter, but I try to act like it. I've never been a good liar, but lives are at stake. "All right, I'll do it. I'll try my best," I say as I dig my fingernails into my palms.

"Thought so. Wouldn't want you to end up like your dear Alyssa..." his voice drips acid.

"What do you mean by that?" The door flings open in front of my building and a guard pulls me out."

And here's your stop. It was nice chatting with you, Ms. Hamilton." Wilson waves me away, and they disappear down the block.

I feel like I just made a deal with Satan himself, although I have no intention of following through. My legs shake beneath me, but I straighten my shoulders and look around.

Cole appears from the courtyard and nods his head discreetly in my direction. I swallow hard, knowing he's going to ask what happened. My body feels numb as I follow him into the familiar dark of the hallway. Our entire trip to our rooms is a blur as my mind digests what just happened.

He turns to face me and places his hands on my cheeks. "When you're ready to tell me, I'm here."

I nod back him, unready to do so. The first thing I do is take a shower in his bathroom. I kick off my nasty slippers and peel off the scrubs while standing in the tub. Afterward, I scrub my clothes down and watch the dirt flow in circles down the drain. I cry while remembering the faces of the people dying in their indignity and releasing the fear I pent up while riding with Wilson.

When I step out of the shower, I wrap Cole's towel around myself and gaze at my reflection, inspecting the blue brand on my neck. I pull away my hair, remembering what I looked like without it. Instead, I place my hands over it as Cole walks in.

"I hate that whenever I look, it's there," I say. Tears stream down my face and I don't bother wiping them away. "Those poor people at the hospital today…dying from some unknown virus we have no medicine for…and then Wilson—I feel like a target everywhere I go."

He wraps his arms around me, and I turn into him, burying my face in his chest.

"I know. I know. I'm so sorry. You don't deserve this," he says. "I'll find a way to get you out of here, I promise…I just need—"

My back goes rigid. "No. You won't. You're already risking too much just being near me."

"I'm ready to do whatever it takes if it means I can have you."

I push him away for a minute and rest my hands on his chest. "We shouldn't even be here in the first place… I just don't understand how—"

He wraps his hands around my wrists and leads me into the kitchen. "Get dressed. Then we'll talk. That towel's calling my name and making my head spin. If it falls off we won't be talking—trust me."

"I'm okay with that." I steady my voice.

"After we talk, I promise I'll kiss every inch of your skin until you're on your knees begging me to stop."

And with that, I hurry and put on the one other pair of scrubs I own and place the slippers on the windowsill to dry. Then I sit at the table, tapping my fingers, and stare at him, waiting. He tosses me a granola bar from his bag and leans against the wall.

"The Hole exists because people were stupid," he says. He takes a large bite out of his granola bar, leaving only half.

"That's a little vague, don't you think?"

"You saw it in the video. It's too late to stop *him* now."

"More like propaganda, really. Tell me. What really happened?" I take a bite out of my snack and chew slowly while waiting for his response.

He pauses for a minute. "Well, society was all up in arms about the crime rate and unemployment that they failed to see the first Commander rising through the ranks. He had a way about him—all charming and sly at the same time. Of course, he used it as an advantage—brainwashing people left and right. He seemed so non-threatening I've been told. A true master manipulator. That alone should make you puke."

"I just swallowed it."

"Perfect. Thanks for the visual," he says with sarcasm.

"Don't mention it."

"All right let me finish before I—"

I lean back in my chair, put my feet on the table, and lick my lips.

He raises an eyebrow. "You're evil."

"Okay, sorry…go on. I'll behave."

"Thank you. Here's the most disturbing part—he killed whoever questioned his reasoning or opposed him. He had no morals or values. He worshipped the power of control. Supposedly, he grew up in a household where he was severely punished for bad behavior. But either way, his predecessor is no different. Rumor has it that he's sick, Lexi—mentally sick." He takes another bite and wipes his hands on his pants. "I'm betting that's what happened to your dad. Anyone who gets as vocal as you say your dad did is put away. Sad part is…this Commander is probably already training a successor."

"Do you think it's Wilson?"

"I'm not sure. It's always a state-held secret." Cole finishes his last piece and scratches his head while thinking.

I put the granola bar down on the table after only nibbling on it. I suddenly lost my appetite. My father's face, while always smiling at me, carried the weight of the world in his wrinkles. Sadness lurked behind his turquoise eyes and now I understand why. It was only inevitable that he'd be taken away—inevitable that he'd become a martyr for what he believed.

Cole kneels down beside me and takes my hands into his warm grip. "I take my duties seriously, but I can't ignore all this hatred I have tucked inside any longer. You showed me what it's like to really care about a person for the first time in my life, and now that I have you, I'm not going to let you go."

Zeus pushes Cole's hands away from mine and swipes Cole's cheek with his tongue. I laugh, although my heart's in my throat, overwhelmed with emotion. I have no idea where it came from and never realized I felt this way until my lips move.

"I love you," I say. *Holy crap, I said it.*

Before I can say it again, I'm caught between the wall and Cole. His hands trace my silhouette, stopping at my hips, and he pulls them into him.

I'm trembling. I'm trembling from wanting him so desperately it's taken over my body.

He's breathing faster, leaning into me, kissing my forehead, my temples, and my cheeks. He runs his lips down to my ear and whispers. "I love you too." *Oh my God, he feels it too.*

For a second I'm frozen, my heart skips a beat, and I'm swimming in ecstasy. "Kiss me—please—kiss me," I say.

He takes my face between his hands, gently tracing my lips with his thumb.

"Please," I beg.

His hungry eyes search me like he's trying to read my mind—wanting to know exactly what I need from him. He leans his head down and I part my lips. His warm tongue lightly strokes mine. He moves his right arm to my waist and holds the back of my head with his left hand. Grabbing my hair, he pulls my head toward my shoulder, giving me kisses along my neck, shoulder, and across my collarbone. His touch is intoxicating.

I reach over, guiding his face back to mine. He sucks in my lower lip, caressing it with his tongue while staring into my eyes.

He's so gentle. So gentle it drives me crazy.

I'm struggling for oxygen as his hands run down my arms. I don't want to move an inch, afraid of breaking apart. I never want to break apart. His hands linger, his touch like feathers as he makes his way to the hem of my shirt. I lift up my arms and he pulls my shirt up over my head and tosses it. Zeus growls and that's when I feel my straps slide off my shoulders.

He wraps his arms around me, pulling me away from the wall and turning my back toward the bed. He unhooks my bra and I let it drop.

"Take off your shirt." My voice comes out in a whisper.

He lifts his T-shirt up over his head and chucks it behind him. He swallows hard and his words are soft and shaky. "Lexi," he says, "I want you…all of you. I want nothing but you. It's making me insane."

Smiling, I say, "You already have me."

"Are you okay…with me touching you like this? If not, I can just hold you and kiss you." His fingers stroke the side of my face as he looks into my eyes for approval.

"I'm more than okay—trust me."

He kisses me again, this time harder, longer, without coming up for air. I don't want him to stop—I never want it to stop. He pulls me into his arms, picks me up, and carries me to the bed. He gently lays me down and straddles my hips. I shove his pillow onto the floor.

"I want to kiss your brand…if that's all right?" He pushes my hair off my face. "Maybe, this way it can have another meaning for you."

"I love that idea," I say.

And that's exactly what he does. He gently kisses every millimeter of my brand. He rolls me onto my left side, my right side, and my stomach trying to heal my emotional wounds with the touch of his lips.

"Come here!" I wrap my arms around his waist and bring his body down on the bed so he's lying on top of me. He moves his right arm down to my thigh and grabs on, pulling my leg over his. I lean into him and he moans. One hand strokes my hip while the other grabs my thigh. I guide his hand from my thigh and rest it on my lower back. I feel his heart racing as he breathes heavily into my ear.

"Oh God," he says. He sits up and pulls me into the center of the bed. I yank him back down on top of me, kissing him. And we kiss each other as if we'll never be satisfied. Again and again.

He pulls away. "Can you handle this?" I nod even though I never want to stop. He takes my face in his warm, large hands. "Should I stop?"

"You better not."

"Whew, thank God, because I definitely don't want to." His lips press mine with such intensity I'm losing control.

"You feel amazing," I whisper in his ear. He groans loud. I push him off. His eyes are unfocused and eager. I place both my hands on his chest.

"Lay on your back. I need to feel you," I say. He lies down, unsure. I swing my leg over and straddle him, running my fingertips over his perfect muscles. *Is this really happening? Is he really mine?* He places his hands on my lower back and pulls me down to him.

Caught in his heat, I breathe him in as he runs his hands down my spine and pulls my hips into him. I lean back and feel the bed quake causing my nerves to jolt through my body. It creaks. My eyes widen, and then I feel it give way from under us with a crash, and my stomach drops to the floor along with the bedframe. Zeus darts away, howling at the bed. I jump and Cole bounces out from under me, reaching for his gun.

Standing next to the bed, I realize the mattress is now on the floor. Splintered remnants from one of the legs lies at the end. Laughter escapes before I can stop it.

"I'm pretty sure we just busted the bed. How on earth did we manage to do that?" But Cole can't hear me because Zeus is still howling and attacking the mattress with his teeth. Of course the mattress is too heavy for him to swing back and forth with his neck, but he does his best to cause the mattress pain. And to show it who's boss. I fall on the floor, laughing so hard tears leak from my eyes. Cole's bulging eyes and crinkled forehead give way to a massive smile as he too understands what happened.

"That's a shame, really. We barely broke it in." He scratches his head while laughing. He gets on his knees and inspects it. Zeus growls at him and he pushes Zeus's head away. "Shut up, Zeus! Way to ruin a perfect moment." He sits up on his knees and looks at me. His eyes sparkle.

"Cole, I'm pretty sure the bed was the killer of the moment. Not Zeus."

"Yea, yea, whatever." That couldn't have been worse timing." I pull my clothing back on, feeling self-conscious. He stands and puts his hands on my arms, forcing me to be still. His smile stops and he becomes serious.

"Okay, serious now... I need to tell you something. And I need you to believe me. No matter what...you have to believe me."

"Okay, I promise—I'll believe you." I still can't make my smile disappear. It's stretched across my face.

"I love you."

I clasp my hands to my chest while I tip my head back and laugh.

"You have no idea how much I love you," he says. "Despite the fact my bed is now ruined."

"Might as well leave it on the floor." I stretch onto my tiptoes and kiss him, full on the lips. His smile fades, and he wraps his arms around me.

"No one can make me smile like you. I don't ever want you to question it. I love you. I'd give my life to save yours. I'd die without you. I know it now."

I pull back. "If you die, I die—right?" I take his hands in mine. "No matter what comes."

"No matter what comes." Cole wraps his arms around me tightly. And holds me.

CHAPTER 15

A knock on the door makes us jump and we bump heads, hard. Cole yanks the sheets off and pulls his shirt on. "Well...that felt great," he says. "You have a hard head."

"So I've heard." I smirk at him.

I call Zeus onto the mattress. He smells the sheets and makes that awful sound he makes when he eats too fast. I rush into my room, bracing myself for the visitor, and peek around the doorjamb.

Cole opens the door and Bruno stands there with his arms crossed, holding a small, paper-bagged lunch. He looks ridiculous.

"Don't you have somewhere you need to be, or did you forget already?" Bruno asks. He frowns at Cole. "What happened to your bed?" His eyes open wide with surprise. "Don't tell me. Zeus broke the bed, didn't he?"

"What are you doing here?" Cole asks. He rubs his eyes.

"Your building's on lockdown, so I've got Lexi duty. But unfortunately for you—you're still mandated to show up, sucker!" Bruno waves hello and I wave back as I cross back into Cole's room. *Please don't notice my rumpled clothes or frazzled expression.*

"Fine. Just give me five minutes, and I'm outta here." Cole throws on his uniform, straps on his guns, and all but sprints out the door with Zeus scampering behind him. With Cole gone, Bruno and I have some business to take care of.

"Morning," Bruno says. "What do you say to us getting your ass in gear?"

"Sounds perfect," I say as I pull my hair back into a ponytail.

"Okay, let's start with a warm-up and then we can get down to business." He drops his bag in the doorway and pulls out two long wraps. He opens his large hands and begins to weave them intricately through his fingers. When he finishes, he pulls out two more. I remove my ring and place it on the counter, away from the sink. I hope he didn't notice.

"Let me show you something. First of all, if you want to protect your hands and wrists from an injury, you'll have to wrap them a certain way. When we're done with that, we're going at it full force—no holding back. If you can't hang with us big boys, we have a serious problem," he says.

I hold out my hands, spreading my fingers as he loops the cloth through. When he's done, both hands are tightly wrapped. I turn them over and admire them.

"You mean I'm as good as dead?"

"Yeah, pretty much."

"That's very reassuring." I rub the back of my neck and frown. "I hope I remember how to do this."

"What's that old quote they used to say?" He snaps his fingers and cracks his knuckles. "Oh right, 'practice makes perfect.' And we'll practice over and over until it's ingrained into your brain, and then it'll become second nature to you."

And so we begin doing push-ups, jumping jacks, and sprints across the room. Next, he shows me how to punch. He drills me like a soldier. "Jab, cross, upper cut," he says over and over.

My arms feel like Jell-O, so he decides to show me some kicks. I learn front kicks and back kicks. I feel like an anchor has been attached to each of my limbs by the end, and I'm dragging them along with each move.

"Well, you aren't yacking today, so that's a start," he says with a smile.

"This is true," I say. I pull back from him a little bit, so I can see his face. "I'm most worried about my strength." *Or lack thereof.*

"Then you're in good hands. I've been training since I was sixteen. I live and breathe this stuff." He starts to unravel his hands. "In our training, we don't use wraps anymore—too unrealistic. But for you, it's wise to start with them until you get used to the grind."

"At least I don't have a chest big enough to get in my way."

Bruno laughs so hard he has to lean against the wall for support. "You said it, not me."

I smile and shake my head. "Yeah, it is what it is…and honestly, it never bothered me before. I hate bras and the whole underwire thing…forget that."

"Alrighty then," he says uncomfortably. "At least you know how to wrap properly now." He laughs.

"Works for me. The last thing I need are broken wrists," I say. I follow his cue and begin to unroll my wraps as well. They fall to the floor, snakelike, in a pile.

"I think you're doing just fine. Give yourself some credit." He looks around for something in his bag.

"I can't. Not yet."

He takes a drink of water and offers me some. It's quiet long enough to hear the *pop, pop, popping* echoing through the streets outside. I run to the window and look but can't see anything but heavily armored tanks parked out front and guards directing limited personnel through the checkpoint. It's been a few days since the bombing and the riot and they're still there. Cole was right about the checkpoint becoming permanent. It makes me want to talk to Sutton about the resistance and find out more about it. Were they really behind the bombs? Was that their way of making the Commander take notice? I push away from the window. I wonder where Keegan is and what he's doing right now.

When I get out of the shower, I feel refreshed. I brush my hair and place my ring back on my left hand where it belongs. Training makes me feel capable. It gives me what little confidence I need to survive, to feel good about myself, and grow stronger. *And I need to grow stronger if I ever want to break free.*

But just when I feel content, a loud banging on Cole's door reverberates through my being. I flip my head around, wondering who's out there. Bruno jumps up, startled, and cracks it open. I hear the terrifying, high pitch of a familiar voice and panic rises in my throat. *Could it be? Why would he come here after we made a deal?*

I sit on my mattress and hug my legs while waiting for the inevitable appearance of Wilson. And he doesn't disappoint.

He struts in like a king, looking immaculate in his fresh-pressed, stiff uniform. His knee-high boots shine with a new coat of polish. He scans the room, resting his callous eyes on me.

I blink away the smell of his heavy cologne and stand. "Wilson, what a pleasure."

"Don't patronize me, girl. I have news for you. Bad news," he says. He narrows his eyes and places his hand on the hilt of his gun. "It must be genetic, you know. The fact that you can complicate things when they're already complicated."

"I'm not sure what you're talking about." My mouth turns down in a puzzled expression. I feel so vulnerable without Cole here.

"You've been accused—again," he says in a flat tone. "Tell me something. Do you honestly find pleasure in being a whore?" Wilson whips out his gun and presses it to my forehead in one quick motion. "Are you trying to make me look like a fool in front of my men—in front of everyone? If you think for one minute I won't pull this trigger because you think I need you, you're wrong. I'm quite capable of finding another way to get to Keegan." As he holds the gun to my head, he scans the room, taking in the drawings and finally resting on my ring.

I want to scream and beg but can barely breathe with the cold metal digging into my brow. How is it possible to be accused, not once, but twice? I've been so careful not to flaunt my love for Cole. I just don't understand. I hold my breath and wait for him to pull the trigger. I wait some more. It doesn't come.

He lowers his pistol and then suddenly hits me across the face with it.

I crumple to the floor, holding my cheek and crying. "I don't know what you're talking about! I've done nothing wrong!" I'm lying. But there's no way he could possibly know about us—right?

"You know exactly what I'm talking about. You're a slut!" Wilson screams into my face.

Bruno walks in the door after hearing the commotion, his face a mask of confusion and horror. But he can do nothing but stand by and watch.

Blood trickles down my face from a cut in my cheekbone. I can already feel it swelling through my agony. My hands shake. My body tremors with fear.

"Any other sinner would be executed for what you've done!" Wilson pulls me up by my hair and pushes me against the wall. "But I can't do that. The Commander ordered me to give you one more chance. He seems to believe you're the only one who can bring us Keegan." His hot breath and heavy cologne coupled with my injury make my head pound with a ferocious headache. His eyes search mine with an evil glint and a wicked smile. Then his opposite hand puts away his gun and touches me. He kisses my neck and slobbers on my collarbone. He moans with delight as he runs his hands over my shirt and I close my eyes. My insides crawl with disgust and humiliation.

"If you fail, you're all mine...and trust me—I will take it slow. Really slow." His eyes undress me. Then he pulls back sharply and lets go. "Oh, and don't forget. If you die, Cole dies. If it happens again, you'll all die...Keegan included. Together—on stage!"

I slide down the wall, shock overtaking me. My heart thunders with adrenaline, and my brain feels like it's bleeding from the inside. I put my hands on my face, feeling the swelling where the gun connected with my skull. Worst of all, he knows about Cole...but how? And I just want to disappear into a tiny million pieces. My worst fear, of all fears, has come to fruition.

"Okay." As I reply, my eyes meet Bruno's. He stands still as a statue in the doorway. His face is frozen. He just witnessed the deal being made and my humiliation with it. I bow my head into my arms in defeat.

"See, Bruno, that's how you get things done." Wilson turns on his heel and smacks Bruno on the back, pulling him into Cole's room.

I've got to get out of here. I've got to protect Keegan and warn Cole that Wilson knows. I've got to make Bruno promise he won't tell a soul about what just happened. My brain feels overloaded and I sit, pressed against the wall, for what feels like hours. All I want is for Cole to wrap his arms around me and tell me it's going to be okay. *This is so confusing.* My head swirls, feeling foggy from the impact of his gun. I hear a loud banging. It matches the thundering of my blood through my ears.

Bruno storms into my room, practically sending me into cardiac arrest. "He's gone. You're coming with me."

"Wh-what?" I blink, feeling the pain shoot across my jaw from where Wilson pistol-whipped me. My hand runs over my cheek, feeling the swelling get worse by the minute.

"Screw the lockdown. We're going to Sutton—now!" Bruno starts throwing his stuff into his bag and pulling on his boots.

"No! He could kill you." I stand up, teetering against the wall.

"Lexi, stand up and start walking—now!" He opens my door to the dark hallway and gestures me to follow him.

"What about the checkpoint?" I ask.

"Shh." He whispers, "We're not going out that way. Try to keep up."

I stumble along behind him as he leads me in another direction, past an empty guard station and down a pitch-black staircase. At the bottom, he checks both ways before leading me along the back of the building.

I'm blinded by the bright sun at first and cover my face with my hand. As soon as my eyes adjust, I feel my jaw drop open. I never noticed the shantytown behind my building before. Thousands of tarps hang in a subdued array of colors, along with hundreds of tin shacks, forming a poverty-ridden community. *It's no wonder the car bombings have been staged out of here.* It's too hard to pinpoint from whom or where they came when surveying the possible hiding places.

Bruno whistles, low and slow, to get my attention. My head snaps forward, creeping behind him through some of the flimsy houses with corrugated metal roofs. It brings back memories of learning about third-world countries in school, except even they had it good compared to the desecration in the Hole.

The thick smell of fetid garbage and hollow, angry glares greet me as we pass through four to five huts. I can't breathe. Their skeletal appearances shock me into silence and I put my right hand on Bruno for support.

After we pass through, we make our way back into the streets. My head injury begins to weigh on me, making me feel dizzy in the blistering heat. The sun beats down overhead and the slight breeze kicks dirt into our eyes.

Bruno slows for a moment and glances back at me. "You never saw those people before, have you?"

I shake my head. "No."

"That's where sinners go when they don't have a job. All of them are starving to death."

"I-I thought everyone had a job."

"Nope. Once you outlive your usefulness, they find another body to take your place," he whispers over his shoulder, keeping an eye out for danger.

The image of their emaciated bodies infuriates me. *How can anyone be so cruel?* It just becomes one more thing to fuel my anger. With each step, I feel more and more determined to survive and maybe even conquer. The reminder of Wilson's hands, his words, his cocky behavior…*I won't let him get the best of me.* Then I stumble and fall to my hands and knees.

Bruno gently picks me up and throws me over his shoulder. He jogs to the hospital, doing his best to stay out of sight. When we arrive, he takes me in along the side of the building, forcing me to walk on my own two heavy feet. Little black spots fill my vision like polka dots. His hand on my elbow is the only thing keeping me steady and reassures me that I'll make it. He props me against the wall, and I put my hands over my face to shield my eyes from the sun. I feel the urge to throw up coming on, so I concentrate on breathing. *Three seconds inhale, three seconds exhale.* I hear the jingling of keys and am vaguely aware of him pulling some out of his uniform.

After scouting for prying eyes, he opens a window along the base of the building. He picks me up by my waist and I climb inside, dropping to the floor and almost crashing into an old rickety chair below. It hurts, but not as bad as my head. Bruno climbs in right after me. When the darkness gives way, I realize where I am. The basement.

I can't move. "Bruno...I—can't."

"It's the only way we can get in without being noticed. Don't worry. I'll be with you the whole time. I'm not leaving you."

I feel goose bumps pop up on my arms as I force myself to swallow the lump in my throat. *Breathe, just breathe.* I step into the darkness. I freeze in panic.

With a grunt, he picks me up and carries me through the crowded basement and up eight floors while I keep my eyes closed. His sweat soaks through my clothes as he steadies himself on the concrete steps. I feel myself drifting out of consciousness. At the final door, he uses his key and unlocks it. I hear the door click open. *I made it.*

The light blinds us as the door swings open, and I squint at the massacre that's become Sutton's usually well-organized floor. Bodies lay everywhere, some alive and some dead. Nurses sprint from room to room with bloodied scrubs. I don't think anyone even notices us as we wait outside Sutton's door.

"What happened to her? Are you all right?" Sutton's voice sounds concerned, yet frightened.

"She's fine—needs some care, but overall okay. We need to talk," Bruno says.

"Hurry, come in." Sutton opens the door to his office and locks it behind him. He doesn't even bother sitting as he smears his gory hands on his jacket and attempts to clean his glasses.

As Bruno explains what happened, Sutton doesn't react.

His face remains stoic. As he listens, I notice how exhausted he looks. His hair looks a shade whiter than it used to and his hands shake while holding his glasses. He examines the cut on my cheek, swabs it, and hands me a bottle of water to hold against it.

"I knew it'd come to this," he says. He steps away from me, looking pensive and edgy. Then he picks up the phone and next thing I know, Cole stands outside the door.

I brace myself for his reaction.

When Sutton lets him in, I can see pure rage on his face. He immediately wraps me into his arms as Bruno and Sutton watch. My lungs feel crushed and my heart rips apart with fear for him.

"Did he touch you?" Cole demands.

I can't bear to look him in the eyes as he grimaces. He puts his hands on my shoulders and insists. "I swear to God if he hurt you—I'll kill him!"

When I look into his face, he knows immediately that Wilson didn't just hit me. He launches his fist into the wall, forcing a hole through it, and starts yelling.

I begin to cry. "Cole, I'm okay, really."

"No, you're not okay! Don't lie to me! I know you—you're not okay!" Cole's face looks like it's going to explode with fury. The vein in his forehead pulses and his fiery eyes look possessed. He paces around when Sutton stops him.

"That's it. I've had enough," Sutton says. All traces of compassion leave his expression. "It's apparent you two have failed to listen to me. Now, I have no choice." He motions to me. "Too many people's lives are at stake here and the two of you are going to get us all killed. I have no other choice until things settle down. Lexi, you're going to your brother."

"The hell she is!" Cole says.

"This isn't your call and you know it! I'm doing what needs to be done here. You couldn't stop whatever it is you two have going on—so I am! It's over and she's going to Keegan. I don't want to hear another word about it."

I give him a questioning look. "You know where he is?"

"Yes."

"I don't understand. Why would you know where—?"

"There's no time to explain. I'm calling for transport now." Sutton mashes a button on his phone. "Cole, Bruno, please make sure she gets there safely." He squints as he reads something on his phone. "Oh, good. There's a black van waiting for you outside the side entrance." He pulls a drawer open and reaches out his hand toward me. I take the book. "I saved this for you. Thought you might like to have it."

"Thank you," I say.

I press it against my chest. *The Last Silk Dress*, the book that Alyssa loved so dearly and wanted me to read to her every night. My heart crumbles thinking about her. "See you soon…I hope."

Sutton nods as he opens his door and sends us away without a good-bye. "Hurry!" At that, he briskly walks away and I meet the eyes of Amber, standing, staring at all of us in the hall.

Her murderous glare gives me goose bumps, and immediately I know we need to move or she'll be the one to report us.

Bruno, Cole, Zeus, and I hop into the rusted black van idling outside the side entrance. There's no joking around as we drive, just anxious glances through the filthy tinted windows. Zeus whines so I pull his head into my lap.

I rub my watering eyes and see a dead body lying alongside a building. It's a younger man. Even through the heavily tinted windows, I can make out the vivid colors of death. His long blond hair partially covers his face, and his clothes are a dusty, faded blue color. Blood pools around his midsection, seeping from gunshot wounds. I turn away, feeling sick.

I feel suffocated. The world is crashing around me, taking everything away that I ever cared about. Now I'm going to lose the only person I want more than anything—the man I love.

My chest tightens with fear of the unknown. I twist my ring around on my left finger while waiting. It's a turbulent ride. The lack of a seatbelt makes it hard to sit in one spot, and I keep sliding into Cole. He finally wraps his arm around me to console me, but I can see in his eyes that he's afraid too.

Suddenly, the sound of bullets tinging off metal rings my ears. Cole pulls me onto the floor as the van swerves left and right. I smash my elbow onto the floor and wince as someone else bangs into me. All of our bodies lie jumbled in the middle, and we cover our heads with our arms as if that'll help.

"Stay down. Stay down!" The driver shouts from the front seat.

Cole puts his arm over me and I begin screaming. Yet, I can barely hear myself against the background of shooting, grunting, and howling. I stop to catch my breath. One second, inhale. Two seconds, exhale. *Got to hold it together.* I peek over and Bruno lies against Cole. His eyes meet mine for a second and he smiles. Zeus huddles against me, barking and whining.

The van hits a ditch and it feels like we're catapulting through the air. I hear the driver cussing furiously. Cole crawls to the front and checks on him as blood pours from his arm.

"Let me drive," Cole yells.

We hit another pothole and lurch into the air, slamming back down. My brain collides with my skull, rattling my senses, and darkening my vision momentarily.

"It's just my one arm. I can still drive," the driver yells.

Cole hunkers back down, startling each time the bullets pierce the body of the van.

I check Alyssa's book under my stomach to make sure I didn't damage it and groan with each bump. The shooting gradually fades into the distance and Bruno sits up with Cole. They count fifty bullet holes, which miraculously didn't kill any of us.

Finally, some freaking luck in this forsaken place.

Cole grabs my arm and gently pulls me against him. He brushes my matted hair away from my eyes and grips my arm tightly. I don't know what I'd do if I lost him. Or Zeus. Or Bruno. *Even he's become part of our inner circle.*

But there's no rest, even for the very, very weary.

The driver hits the brakes and I slam into Cole with enough force that he stumbles onto the floor. Tires squeal, smelling of burned rubber, while male voices scream all sorts of profanity outside. Cole's arm wraps around my waist, pulling me back to my seat, and Zeus starts barking wildly.

"Your stop's here. Keep low to the ground. Head five blocks east and they'll find you."

I want to ask what he means, but next thing I know, the sunlight rips into me and we step into the unfamiliar street.

CHAPTER 16

The landscape looks like a concrete jungle with tin shacks shoved between large buildings. The contrast of the gray dust and the faded red of a nearby tarp draw my attention. It captivates me for no other reason than the fact that it looks like art. We had all kinds of paintings and photos hanging on the walls in our High Society condo. They were all names of famous artists I can't recollect, but I know beauty when I see it, even if it is in the slums.

Overhead, clouds roll in like waves and cover the sun's brilliant rays. I lower my hand from my face and blink. I don't see a soul on the streets. I fall into place behind Bruno with Cole and Zeus behind me. Bruno leads slowly, carefully scanning the slums. I suspect he's attempting to avoid the cameras the Commander had mounted. My shoulders tense up just imagining where they could be.

I spy a bouncy ball and know somewhere there's a child missing it. The thought makes me ache inside. *Another child whose life is riddled with violence.* I can't change what happened to me at my stepfather's hands, but maybe—just maybe—if I ever escape from the Hole, I can make a positive difference for the sake of another child.

The intensity on Cole's face keeps me from speaking. I can tell the surrounding area has him and Bruno on eggshells as they check each corner, alley, and street we pass. Their hands tightly wind around their weapons and their eyes widen, surveying the area for any suspicious movements. First Bruno moves and then motions us with his hands to follow. The dull thud of our footsteps echoes through an otherwise ominously quiet block.

One block down. We follow Bruno into a narrow alley and stop to gather our thoughts for a minute before moving on.

"Hey." Bruno motions from the front and Cole comes around me with his gun cocked and ready. "We've got four blocks to go. You want me to stay point?"

"Yeah, Zeus and I will bring up the rear," Cole whispers. "Keep her in the middle."

Bruno nods, then squats down as a troop of guards runs past the entrance to the alley. We all hold our breath and pray. Cole pulls Zeus close to his body to keep him from sounding the alarm. I squeeze my eyes closed and hear the blood rushing through my ears. My heart pounds with adrenaline.

The guards seem too involved in whatever they're doing to notice us hiding between the buildings. *Thank God,* I think. *That counts as two strokes of luck today.* But as soon as we leave the alley, I hear the sound of boots following us. First slow and then quicker, as if they're sharks catching the scent of blood.

"Halt!" A voice cuts through the air.

But of course we don't. Bruno sprints, looking for cover, as we tag along behind him. My breath comes in short, ragged bursts and I feel like my lungs will explode before we find somewhere to go.

"By order of the Commander, stop!" the voice yells again. "Or we'll shoot!"

I know it's only a matter of seconds before they open fire because we have no intention of stopping—for anyone. *Come on, Bruno. Come on!* My insides scream in desperation thinking about Cole behind me and our lives hanging in the balance. I lick my cracked lips, imagining how good water would taste as I puff along with them. Zeus's tongue hangs out as he runs without effort. I know he could out-sprint us all if he wanted, but he's loyal and slows to keep up with our pace.

Seeing nowhere else to go, Bruno kicks in the door of a small house and weaves through it. Just as Cole enters, I hear the automatic *rat, tat, tatting* of guns open up outside. Dirt spits off the ground where bullets hit. A lone man sits at his table about to eat when we startle him. His bread flies through the air. He dives under the table with wide eyes.

"Get out! Go!" he yells.

"Sorry, sir!" Cole apologizes as he runs through the kitchen, stumbling over a small wooden chair. "Just passing through. Oh Lord, Zeus, put that down!" Cole yells.

We crash through the only other room of the house and barge through the back door into another shanty. *Where are we going?* The muscles in my legs burn from trying to keep up with Bruno, who's a physical machine. Sweat drips down my face and stings my eyes, forcing me to wipe them with my dirty hands.

"Lexi, move faster. You have to pick up your pace," Cole says behind me.

I can't stop to check him, but as long as he talks, I know he's there. I don't want to lose him. I don't want to die yet... I'm not ready. Not when I'm this close to being safe and seeing my brother for the first time in years. I don't want this all to be for nothing.

We stumble through three, four, five more shanty houses before spilling into another street adjacent to the one before. It looks exactly the same as the last one.

"Oh, this is great! Now where the hell are we?" Cole says under his breath.

My heart's in my throat and I gasp for air as my chest heaves up and down. I look down and one of my slippers is missing. No time to stop though.

Bruno hooks a left and moves along the buildings. As I follow, my fingers touch the buildings for support, feeling the difference in texture between the brick and cement, hoping against all odds we survive or at least find a place to hide.

Cole's hands grip his pistol, following along and checking to make sure the guards didn't catch up. I can hear his steady breathing behind me.

Only two more blocks to go. But two blocks seem like an eternity when fighting for your life. Every breath, every stride, and every sound is magnified in my mind. The colors are more vivid, the feeling of suffocation more powerful than ever.

A loud crash lets us know we haven't escaped them. I

automatically lower my head, but feel Cole push me forward. They come thundering after us, firing nonstop. I don't have time to scream, just sprint with all my might after Bruno, hoping Cole follows with Zeus. I glance back. The guards outnumber us as they pin us in another alley.

There's nowhere left to go. We don't have the manpower or firepower to take them head-on. Bruno and Cole take turns shooting back at them, but we know it's only a matter of time before the guards figure out we're at their mercy. I bite my lower lip and grab Cole's shoulder roughly.

"Give me a gun," I say.

Cole glances at me. "Have you ever shot one?"

I shake my head. "No. But it's not hard to figure out."

He thinks for a second. "Keep your finger off the trigger until you're ready to shoot. And keep shooting till your target falls." He places his other black pistol in my right hand. "It's loaded. Just aim and pull the trigger."

Bruno empties a full magazine, hits the slide, and then slams in his spare. Then I shoot Cole's other gun and empty it. It's the first time I've ever touched one, and it feels good to fight back, although I'm sure my shots are nothing more than a deterrent.

The spray of bullets answering us forces us to shoot blind. Zeus barks ferociously while standing in front and Cole reins him in by pulling his collar. Dirt, dust, and pieces of debris shower us, leaving flakes of blood behind, but we rotate shooting for as long as the ammunition holds out. I look down at the gun in my dirty hands. It smells of sulfur and a thin trail of smoke wisps from the barrel. I glance up at Cole and shake my head. It's empty. After their last shots, Bruno and Cole lock eyes knowingly. We're all out. They toss their empty magazines on the ground. They press against the wall and communicate with hand motions. I squeeze my eyes closed, trying to block out the sounds of hell being unleashed around us. But I can't block out Zeus's barking, the crashing noises, whizzing bullets, and the thunderous sound of tanks approaching no matter how hard I try. It makes me clench my jaws. Then we wait for the inevitable onslaught of violence from the guards. Cole pushes me behind him to protect me, and Zeus growls low and deep in his belly in front of us.

By now, we've sweated through every layer of clothing possible. The acrid smell of hot lead bores through my senses. I swear I feel a raindrop on my cheek as we wait and wait for the guards to kill us. I look up and see the dark clouds gathering as I press my head against the wall. *Is this the last thing I'll see before it all ends?*

The gunfire continues but fades, confusing all of us. I turn my head toward the entrance. I feel my eyebrows scrunch together. Male voices, some yelling and some moaning, creep across the street like ghosts. I want to look around the corner and find out what's happening, but I know Cole would never allow it.

Bruno shrugs his shoulders and Cole furrows his brow and shakes his head in response. Nothing happens. "Where the hell are they? Damn it, they should be here by now," Bruno says to Cole as he swipes his forehead with his large hand.

"Stay here—I'll take a look around." Cole ducks his head around the corner slowly to get a better look. He turns back toward Bruno. "I see nothing. No eyes."

Bruno's jaw tightens as he thinks. "I don't know, dude. Could be a trap."

"Why would they trap us if we're already cornered?" I ask in a whisper.

"Damn if I know… These guys are sick." Cole's intense eyes rest on me for a moment. Despite his glistening face with dirt smeared across the side, he still looks amazing. *If Alyssa could see us now… Maybe she can.*

The building I lean against is full of pockmarks as if it's seen decades of battles. My fingers touch the grout and it crumbles in my palms, skittering to the ground. I scan it more and notice barely any of the glass remains in the windows. Another raindrop lands on my arm, and this time, I know I'm not imagining it.

"Well, what're you thinking?" Bruno asks Cole.

Zeus sounds the alarm with a sharp bark, snapping us to attention. Just then, a figure looms in the entrance. I feel my breath catch. But it's not a guard. He's skinny but muscular and short with a long beard. Slung over his shoulder is a large strap with long, slender bullets lining the outside. He carries the largest gun I've ever seen a civilian carry and he points it at us. The dark black brand around his neck is unmistakable.

"Come with me," he says with an authoritative voice. He motions for us to move with the tip of his gun, swinging it with ease.

I frown and look to Cole, who stares at Bruno. I can see Bruno tilting his head, weighing our choices. Zeus growls again, baring his sharp canines and poised to attack.

"What about the guards?" I ask.

"They're dead, so I suggest you follow me now unless you'd like to sit here and wait for more to show up." He rounds the corner and disappears.

"What other choice do we have?" Bruno says. I see him grimace. "Let's see where he goes."

Cole shrugs his shoulders. "After you." Cole and Zeus follow so close behind me I can hear their breathing over the footsteps.

With edgy nerves, we follow the anonymous man. He takes us two more blocks while avoiding unseen cameras and around a tall building. Then the sky opens up with a thunderous clap as the rain pours down in waves. I feel my hair cascade down my back like a giant, dripping mop. My scrubs soak through completely, and I try to pull them away from my clammy skin. I kick off my last slipper in the mud, hoping I can snag a pair of shoes soon. When I wipe the water away from my eyes, I can see Bruno and Cole's clothes plastered to their bodies too. We parade around like a funeral procession—shoulders slumped and feet dragging.

"Hold up. Don't move," the man commands.

We pause, frozen in place, trying to figure out what he's talking about. The scenery here looks much the same as where the driver dropped us off. The small shacks with their corrugated roofs pile onto each other like an overcrowded bookshelf. The rain pounds the metal, making it almost impossible to hear his voice.

"Now!" The man motions us past him, through a heavy metal door, and into the building. "We have to wait for the camera to pan away before entering. We finally know where they're hidden so we avoid them at all costs." He fiddles with his sopping beard while examining us with vigilant eyes. "Sutton sent you—that I know. But why so early in the day and who, exactly, are you?"

Bruno sits on the hard floor, rests his head against the wall, and catches his breath. He pulls off his drenched, sweaty shirt and wipes his face with it.

"Nothing happened," Cole says. "We're here to see Keegan. We brought his sister with us." He also pulls off his shirt and rings it out. Water spatters onto the floor.

The man raises his eyebrow and moves closer to me. "You're his sister?"

"Yes," I reply. My whole body wants to collapse from exhaustion. My hands shake and the pain from my cheekbone resurfaces after the adrenaline stops flowing. All of a sudden, I want to sleep for days. *No, months.* A feeling of weariness seeps through my muscles and down to the tiniest veins.

Cole wraps his arm around my side to steady me. "We were told we could come here…"

"I'll see what I can do." The man makes up his mind and motions for us to follow…again.

"Dang, man, how much longer till we get there?" Bruno asks with sarcasm as he stands up, stretching.

"If we didn't have all this security, we would've been blown away by now. Don't like it, then leave," the man quips back. I can hear his boots squeaking as he stomps away.

Cole drags my weight along with his own down a narrow corridor and says, "He's not complaining—just being sarcastic."

Bruno chuckles under his breath.

The man steps into a room, removes a board from the base

of a closet, and a dark opening appears. He steps in and crawls down. "Hope you're not claustrophobic. Last person needs to place the board back on." *I can never win…Breathe, breathe, just keep breathing.*

First, Bruno squeezes down the creaking ladder into the dark tunnel. Then me. And then Cole carries Zeus on his shoulders. Zeus's goofy face slobbers all over Cole's head and he descends with a look of disgust. I feel either free or delusional enough to laugh at them. Zeus is over half Cole's size. After Zeus paws Cole's back, Cole crawls back up the ladder to slide the board back in place. It's a miracle none of us slipped coming down the tiny ladder.

Then everything is dark. I press my eyelids together, trying to make out my surroundings, but they haven't adjusted yet. I feel something sharp jab me in the back.

"Ouch."

"Keep moving," the man says.

"Hey, do you have a name or should we call you bearded dude?" Cole asks.

"Steven. My name's Steven."

"Thanks for helping us, Steven," I say as I fumble around.

"Don't thank me, at least not yet…If you're lying about who you are, Keegan will put a bullet through your skull. Not once have I heard Keegan talk about a sister—or a family."

I do a double-take, stopping in the darkness for a moment. Then I begin feeling sick in my stomach. What if Sutton made the wrong decision sending me here? What if Keegan isn't happy to see me at all? I don't want to be resentful, but if Steven's words are true, then maybe Keegan doesn't want me here at all. I hate the constant unknown. It eats at the pit of my soul.

"Keep moving." Steven's impatient voice reaches my thoughts and breaks through.

"We know, chill out," Cole says. He gently tugs on my arm, and I find my bearings.

In the distance, I can see a faint glow from a flame. The walls open into underground tunnels. I raise my eyebrows and feel my lips open with awe. They're wide, laid with metal bars, and tile runs up the sides. The mildew shows through the cracks, and the tiles are tinged red in places. Body odor mixed with the humidity makes my stomach churn. Something wet keeps dripping on my head. *If it's anything other than water, I'm going to vomit.*

Cole rests his hand on my shoulder as if reassuring me. I'm so glad he's here to help me through this. The warmth of his touch keeps me sane when darkness and fear envelop my mind.

It feels like hours before we reach the light. The warmth of the small fire heats my face.

"Stop here." Steven swings his gun around in warning, so we come to a halt. I swallow the lump in my throat when I feel the eyes of others staring at us. Water drips off my clothes into puddles on the floor. I glance up. I see heads lowered while evaluating us. Some whisper, some have set jaws, but I notice some of them also smile. I try to stop biting the inside of my cheek and give a weak smile back.

"Who the hell's that?" a familiar voice shouts from an adjoining tunnel. I try to move toward it, but Steven steps in my path, blocking me. The dark silhouette approaches. Then it stops abruptly.

"No *way*! Oh my God. Lexi—is that you?"

My stomach flips hearing him call my name. "Keegan! It's me!"

"Get your ass out of her way!" he commands Steven, pointing his finger. Keegan pushes his way through the crowd and around the others.

When he reaches me, he grabs my legs and scoops me into his arms. I wrap my arms around his neck, hugging him so tight I think my arms might break.

I shout, unable to contain my joy. "You're here! I can't believe it! I never thought I'd see you again. I've missed you so much!"

His arms tighten around me as he laughs. "I know! I missed the hell out of you. What happened to you? You look like crap."

His comment makes me laugh out loud. He always was honest. "Thanks."

"We've gotta talk!" Keegan says. His eyes light up and his smile reaches from ear to ear.

"Yes, please can we?"

He puts me down and I look up at him. He's much bigger than I remember. I reach up and touch the top of his head.

"Damn, you're like three feet taller than me now!" He laughs and slams me into another hug. "And you're much stronger than you used to be." My voice comes out muffled so he releases me. *My brother's buff! When did that happen? And where is his brand?*

I reach up, pulling his bald head to my level. If it weren't for his voice, I would've never picked him out of the crowd. His curls have been replaced with a bold, dark tattoo wrapping around his entire head.

"Um, what on earth did you do to your head?" I smack his chest.

"It's a cobra," he says. "It suits my personality." He winks.

I nod my head, unsure of what to say. *Looks pretty freaking intimidating to me.*

His cobalt-colored eyes fix on my crew. "Who are these guys? And why are you all soaking wet?"

"Oh, that's Bruno, Cole, and Cole's guard dog, Zeus." I motion to them behind me.

Keegan shakes their hands and gives a tight smile. "You need to put some clothes on if you're around her." He lets go after what seems like minutes. "Lexi's coming with me. We need to talk. You guys can rest up and dry by the fire. We'll be back so don't go wandering around." He squints his eyes at them.

Cole locks eyes with me and shakes his head, not wanting to let me out of his sight. I shrug. I guess it's safe. I mean, it *is* my brother. So I follow Keegan down a narrow tunnel and through a small opening. He opens a second door and I shuffle in, ducking under a five-foot walkway and into a room that resembles a cave more than a bedroom. I shiver from the cold. "You okay? I'll see if I can get you another set of clothes." Keegan carefully lights a lantern and the room comes alive. "This is where I sleep." He smiles and his teeth gleam. It's almost bare except for the cot covered with a quilt and a pile of books lying in the corner. The quilt forces me to pause. I pull it between my fingers and examine the stitching. "Is this?"

"Yeah. It's one of the things I took when I left... It reminds me of our good times," Keegan says sadly. He sits on the cot and gestures me to sit as well. "I have more I need to show you but right now, I just want to talk."

"Oh. All right."

He takes my hand and reads my mind as I examine the plain space. His room reminds me of a burrow with dirt-caked walls, dim lighting, and a musty smell. "It's not as bad as it looks. I only sleep here."

"I guess. I don't do well in small, closed spaces—that's all." I face him, but can't think of what I want to say. Or I know everything I want to say and don't know how to verbalize it for fear it'll all come out wrong.

Thankfully, he senses my hesitance. "Lexi, you need to know how much I regret leaving you the way I did." He clasps his hands in his lap. "But...I had no choice. There was only a small window of opportunity to get in here. And I had to take it."

My mouth twists. "The Hole? Really, Keegan? What the hell were you thinking? Well, it's pretty apparent you weren't thinking of me...that's for damn sure. Not once did you bother to check on me, not once did you write me, not once did you leave any clues that you were alive... I thought you were dead, and it killed me." I'm spitting through my teeth and clenching my fists. "Do you have any idea what that did to me? You were my best friend and you abandoned me like a dog in an alley. Like trash you wanted to throw away. Not only did I lose Dad, I lost you and our mother. I had nothing! Nothing, Keegan. My family who should've always been there for me...left me to fend for myself." I inch away from him. I don't want to be resentful, but part of me just can't fathom leaving him behind if our places had been switched. I feel my joy slowly fading, as my feelings from the last few years spill out between my lips. "With Dad gone, you were free to be on your own and you didn't want your little sister tagging along. Isn't that right? You knew I was here! You knew I was branded and fighting to stay alive every day since I got here. But you never came to see me." I take a deep breath and narrow my eyes at him. "You know what's different about you and I? If the roles were reversed, I would've done everything in my power to find you. To get to you, to be with you again. You're my brother and I never stopped loving you. I needed you! And even after all the pain and heartbreak you put me through...I'm standing here saying I still need you." Tears stream down my face. "Didn't you love me?"

He puts his face in his hands. "Of course I did—I still do. Lexi, you don't understand. It's very complicated. This was never about me, and what I wanted. It's about what dad wanted."

"What do you mean by that?"

"Because it's the truth."

"I don't believe you, not even for a second. How could you be so cruel?"

"Trust me, at the right time, I'll tell you everything and you'll understand."

"I hope so, Keegan. I really hope so."

Keegan takes a step toward me and I take a step back. "Just give me a chance."

"All right. I'm sorry."

"I will tell you everything, but not right now. Not when you're upset with me. You need to have a clear mind and a calm heart to see what I'll show you. Now, please let me at least explain something to you. Can you do that? Keep your mouth shut and listen just for a minute?"

"Okay, I'll try my hardest."

"It wasn't my choice to make. Dad gave me strict

instructions and I had to obey him."

"What are you talking about?"

"He never told you?"

I throw my hands in the air. "Tell me what?"

"Dad hated everything about this place. He hated the Commander. He hated his lack of morals and how the Commander snuck up on everyone just to gain control. He hated that he took away the 'innocent until proven guilty.' He hated watching all these innocent people getting torn away from their families simply because someone didn't like them. It's sick. I mean, look at you. We both know you did nothing wrong. You shouldn't be here and there's thousands more who are innocent." Keegan breathes deeply and exhales while looking up at the ceiling. "Dad's goal was to destroy the Hole and revive the old judicial system. No, it wasn't perfect. The system failed some innocent people as well as freed some who should've been found guilty—but it was better than this. Dad fought day in and day out, trying to find ways of making it better." As Keegan's words register, it hits me.

My father believed in the revolt.

One time, he told me that he wanted to change the world for the better. He wanted justice for all citizens, the way it should be. Honestly, I never understood what he was referring to, but now, I have no doubt he wanted to destroy this hellhole. He wanted the stories of countless faces unjustly accused heard. *People just like me.*

"Why didn't you tell me? I would've come with you." My voice softens as I lean into him and feel his warmth wrap around my shoulders. "I miss Dad. I miss him so much it hurts. When he died, a part of me died right along with him, but I realized I still had my brother—he'd love and protect me. Then you disappeared and my entire world shattered into a million pieces. Every person I ever loved and trusted vanished out of my life and I was left in the hands of a—" I stop.

His arms squeeze the air out of my lungs. "Lexi, I can't tell you how sorry I am but I couldn't tell you. It wasn't the right time. Look, I can't take back what I did to you, but you have to believe me when I tell you I had no idea what kind of man our stepfather was, what he was like. If I did, I never, ever, would've left you. Ever.

"Wait...What? How—how do you know about that?" I ask, sitting up ramrod straight.

"Sutton," he says. "He said he was a controlling bastard and he treated you like shit."

"Wait, what? Sutton told you?" I stand up as anger shoots through me. "What the hell's going on? How would he know? I never told him a damn thing!"

Keegan grabs my hands and swings me around. "He didn't tell you, did he?"

"Tell me what?" I cross my arms over my chest.

He doesn't answer.

"Tell me what, Keegan?" I notice a twitch above his eye. He sits back down and pats next to him. I remain standing.

He inhales. "Sutton was Dad's best friend."

CHAPTER 17

My heart stops for a moment and I gaze at him in shock. "What are you talking about?"

"They'd been best friends since childhood. They were practically brothers."

"Then why don't I remember him?" I shake my head. "How come I never meet him?"

"After Sutton became a doctor, he traveled a lot. His residency wasn't anywhere near where we lived so Dad didn't see him much when we were growing up. They kept in close contact, of course. Sutton volunteered to come here and work at the hospital. He wanted to take care of people, but at the same time, he wanted to have contact with the inside. Think about it. How else would Dad have gotten all the information about the Hole?"

His words confirm my suspicions. "So Sutton was his informant?"

"From the beginning. Sutton knows way more about the revolt than I ever did, but Dad never told me in great detail. He didn't want us to know anything that would end up putting our lives in danger. Lexi, Dad truly was an amazing man. He loved humanity and saw potential in everyone. All he wanted was to get the judicial system up and running again and let the accused have their day in court—like it was before. Because of Sutton, he knew everything that was going on in the Hole— the living conditions, the violence, the torture. All of it. Every day he internalized his anger, his disgust, his hatred for the Commander, and did it well." He leans back, resting his head against the wall. I sit down beside him and rest my head on his shoulder as he continues. "I snuck in the back of a guard's truck before he entered the Hole, and I managed to hide under his supplies. Luckily for me, he had a ton of crap. When he finally stopped, I jumped out and made a break for it. By some miracle, I ran into Sutton, and right away, I recognized him. I'm not sure how or why, but the second I saw his face, I knew who he was. It sorta freaked me out."

"I'm actually pretty pissed off right now. Why wouldn't Sutton tell me? He didn't think I had the right to know—that I couldn't handle it?"

"No, it's nothing like that. Look, we both agreed it'd be best for you to hear all this from me. Sutton didn't want to overstep his boundaries. He's loyal, honest, and has a damn good heart. When this is all over, we'll control this place together, making it right again." Keegan's head tilts back and he smiles as he turns toward me.

"I'm well aware he's a good guy. It's just all the damn secrets I despise." I purse my lips.

"Some things, Lexi, you're better off not knowing." Keegan lowers his voice in a stern manner.

I sigh and let Keegan take my hand in his. "Would you please stop trying to protect me? I'm well aware of the horrific things that go on here. I'm living it every day."

He stays silent for a moment and then examines my other hand. "Is that the ring Dad gave you?"

I hold my body as still as I can. "Yeah, why?"

He pulls my opposite hand closer to his face, turning it around and watching the light reflect off the gold. "How the hell did you get it back? They would've taken it from you." He glares at me. "Did that guard give it to you?" He squints, and I notice small wrinkles webbing out from his eyes. "You seem to trust him." I pull my hand away, and rub it with my opposite hand.

"They did take it, but I got it back and that's all that matters. Just don't ask me where I hide it sometimes, all right?" I give him a half-smile.

He winces in disgust. "Oh, no you didn't. Wow, that's—" He shakes his head with disgust.

"Eww, enough. Please, can we talk about something else— anything," I say. I hear him laugh under his breath before he speaks.

"I must say, you have great critical thinking skills."

"Keegan!"

"All right. I'm sorry."

"Here...I'll change the subject. Life in the Hole, it's glamorous, isn't it? I especially love the food." I roll my eyes and he laughs at me.

"Crap, that reminds me. You're probably starving, right?" A mischievous glint sparks in his eyes.

I sigh, relieved I don't have to explain that Cole gave me the ring back. *That Cole's amazing, loyal, and I'm in love with him.*

"Hey, did you hear me?" Keegan asks again.

"Uh, yeah sure, food sounds great."

"Okay, and while we're at it, I'm going to see if I can find you a pair of boots. No offense, but your feet reek!" He stands and pulls me up after him.

Keegan leads me down one dank hallway after another. I feel my shoulders release their tension after confronting him with my anger, even though I still don't have the answers I seek. *It's enough, for now.* I shiver, my clothes still damp. The maze that makes up his hideout must've taken years to build. Each passage looks and feels the same with metal bars climbing up the walls, the musty smell, and the constant dripping of water from pipes above.

My feet sting with cold, but knowing I'm safe brings comfort I haven't experienced in years. Keegan stops, slides open a black gate, and continues down the hall. Then he swings a left and opens a large, heavy door. *I wonder what Bruno, Cole, and Zeus are doing while we traipse around?*

Just then, the door creaks open and I'm blinded by lights and noise. He holds it and motions for me to go in first.

The room opens up into a large area where people sit, eating from trays at their tables. Dirt doesn't cover these walls. They're all cement with white paint slapped over top. The fluorescent lights hang in rows over each table, making the room the lightest I've seen. Around the right side is an area where the people fill their trays with meat, potatoes, and vegetables. The smell wafts to my nose, making my stomach grumble with desire. I haven't eaten a decent meal in ages. I have to restrain myself from sprinting to the line and filling my plate until it spills over in heaps, but then my eyes catch the black, bold words painted along the back wall of the cafeteria.

HUMANS WILL NOT BE A FORM OF ENTERTAINMENT. AND REMEMBER, MY BRAVE FRIENDS, YOU CAN OVERCOME ANYTHING SHORT OF DEATH—SO FREE THEM.
—C. HAMILTON

I feel my mouth drop open and my eyes begin to water. My heart wells with pride. The words are those of my father. I twist my ring around my finger, drawing strength from the inscription and feeling his presence with me.

"Sutton had someone paint it years ago. It's our daily inspiration."

"It's incredible. I love it. Just wish Dad were here to see it," I say quietly. I wipe a tear away, but although I'm crying, I feel hope spring up within me. Everything makes sense now— the personal guard attached to me from the beginning, Sutton's hiring me at the hospital when I had no experience at all, and Wilson's harassment. *My family's been involved with the revolt for much longer than I ever knew.*

"I know. Me too. Come on. We'll talk more later, but for now, you need to eat." Keegan loops his arm through mine and gently pulls me in the direction of the line. He yells greetings to several people as he parades me through the room. People seem generally happy to see him and they even smile at me too.

Most of them have brands. They're many colors and sizes, but they eat together like family. They even joke around as if they have no cares. Children weave their way through the lines and dodge trays as they play tag. I jump back, letting them scramble around me and I feel a smile play at the corners of my mouth.

I spot Cole and Bruno sitting at a table, gorging themselves. The sight of Zeus hovering over Cole's plate makes me laugh out loud. His slobber drips onto Cole's forearm, and I can see Cole's face wrinkle with disgust.

"Come on, Zeus!" Cole complains. He pushes Zeus's head away, but not before Zeus grabs a pork chop off his plate and drags it onto the floor.

"Dude, the dog's gotta eat too," Bruno says with a huge smile.

They wave at me and I smile. They haven't showered and are still covered in filth, but they look happy. I notice they have new shirts on at least. Cole's perfect white teeth take my breath away. Keegan sits down to talk to them and I think about how perfectly Cole fits into my family. I think my father would approve of my choice.

I go through the line, picking up extra for Zeus, and then sit next to Cole. I enjoy the bantering around me, breathe in the relaxed atmosphere, and relish the thought of new shoes and a shower.

I shovel the food into my mouth and before I know it, I have to untie my pants to loosen them a bit. "You can have my fruit if you want. I think I ate way too fast. My stomach feels like a balloon that's about to explode," I say to Cole.

He smiles at me while he scoops my fruit onto his plate with his fork. "It's because your stomach shrank from not eating right. But I'm proud of you. You almost finished your plate and refrained from feeding Zeus," Cole says.

"Ha, I'm just sneaky that's all." I wink as I reach under the table, and Zeus's warm tongue runs up my hand. We laugh as Zeus swallows a piece of pork chop whole. He never seems to enjoy his meals.

Keegan examines us with a raised eyebrow and I clear my throat, trying to distract him. "So, when did you decide to shave your head and cover yourself with all those tattoos?" I say.

The bright lights make his multiple tattoos more visible. They interlace the whole way down both his arms, and of course, I can't miss the cobra wrapped around his head. I almost want to reach out and touch them.

He laughs. "The first thing I did when I got here was shave my head. My curls would've given me away, don't you think?"

"Yes. I can relate," I say.

"Anyway, they didn't hurt much. You should think about getting one," he says. "I know a fantastic tattoo artist. He's actually sitting right over there." He points three tables away, but I don't bother looking.

"No way." I rub my neck self-consciously. "I'll never get a tattoo. I hate them."

"So you hate mine?" Keegan says, drooping his eyes in mock disappointment.

"No, not exactly. Since they're on you and not me, they're fine." I wave my fork at him before stabbing another piece of food for Zeus.

"Believe it or not, the girls dig it."

"I'm sure they do," I say. "A cobra on a guy's head is completely irresistible."

"Tell me about it." Keegan stands and stretches for a minute. "I have a meeting I gotta run to. It's probably best if you come with me. Then afterward, I'll walk you to your room and the showers so you can clean off your nastiness."

I glance at Cole, who shrugs, and then back at Keegan. "What about them?" I ask, referring to Cole, Bruno, and Zeus. "Shouldn't they come with us?"

Keegan's eyes narrow, but he nods. "I guess."

After another long series of tunnels and some creepy stairs down, Keegan leads us into a dark room. "Welcome to the nerve center of the revolt. Here we keep track of the guards' operations and our planned attacks. It's really genius of Sutton, if you ask me. He procured the whole map himself." Keegan presses a button and a table in the middle lights up. "The red markers represent the guard bases we're aware of, and the red lines are the routes they patrol and the training in our sector. The green represent the rebel bases and their routes. At this point in the game, we're ready for a fight!" He turns it off before I can look twice. His face is proud, like my father.

"What do you mean by our sector?" I ask.

"Since the Hole's so large, we have to divide it in to sectors. A single leader runs each sector. The one we're in now is mine to maintain."

"Now we're in trouble." I laugh.

"Very funny." Keegan punches my arm. "But I take my duties seriously, and I'm damn good at what I do."

"So there's an entire network?" Bruno asks, shifting on his feet.

"Let's just say we're a lot stronger, larger, and more prepared than the Commander thinks." Keegan holds his head high and even sounds a little cocky.

"So does the Commander ever leave his headquarters?" I ask.

Keegan squints his eyes and clenches his fists while glancing at Bruno and Cole. "I'm sure your guard could tell you that one," he says with his eyes pinpointed on Cole.

His response renders me speechless. *Why the hatred?*

"So you know the guards' routes?" Bruno asks.

"We do. We've been watching them for years now. Of all people, I'd think you'd know that," Keegan says. He looks around the room, his eyes settling on my ring again.

I have to redirect him. "Wow, that's impressive, Keegan. So…who built these tunnels?" My hands fidget as Keegan's stare makes me uncomfortable.

"They were here before I came—we just needed to finish them off. And we added some others." He holds his hands loosely behind his back and smiles. "And we're almost completely self-reliant when it comes to food."

"How's that?" Cole asks.

Keegan stares him up and down. "We grow our own down here. It's taken years, and we don't have a ton of variety but it works…and we're all healthy."

"Sounds like a lot of work," I say.

"And a lot of lives lost," Keegan replies. "Anyway, we're out of time and I'm sure you want to shower and sleep. Give me a minute to find someone to accompany you to your rooms."

His words catch me by surprise since he originally said he'd take me to his meeting, but I nod in agreement and hug him one last time before he abruptly stands to leave through another door.

"That was strange," I say.

"I thought so too. Something's not right." Cole pulls me to him and hugs me. "But at least you're safe—that's all I care about."

"I hope our rooms are close." I kiss his lips once, then twice. My hormones race and all I want to do is be with him.

"Yeah, um, I'm still here—standing right next to you," Bruno says.

I laugh as Cole loosens his hands around my waist and then I see seriousness in his eyes. "I'm not sure we can trust Keegan yet...I think we should hold off on telling him."

"It's not hard to guess. I'd be willing to bet he already knows," Bruno says with a chuckle.

I step away from Cole, feeling hesitant. Just in time too, because the door opens and Steven beckons us to follow him to the showers and our rooms.

My room is small and plain like Keegan's. A lamp hangs on a hook in the wall and a cot protrudes from the right side of the room with a large wool blanket folded on the end. On the left side, I notice a tall chest where I can put my clothes, which I don't have.

I find the showers at the end of the hall. One entrance is for the men and one for the women. We're limited to five minutes, but it's the best five minutes I've had in days. The warm water running down my skin melts away the goose bumps. I breathe in the steam and relax.

Someone sets rugged clothes for me to wear on the sink for afterward. I pull on olive-colored cargo pants, thick wool socks, and a tight cotton T-shirt. I fluff my curls and put my ring back on. I peek out the door.

"Wow. You look incredible," Cole says.

I jump back, hitting the back of my head on the tiles.

"You all right?" He laughs as he leans against the wall in the dimly lit hallway. His plain T-shirt matches mine, but he has black cargo pants. It doesn't take much for him to drive me insane.

"Yes." I rub the back of my head furiously. "And thanks. You're not looking too shabby yourself."

He pinches my cheek and gives me a smile that melts my insides. I love how he looks dressed, but wish I had time to undress him too.

"A pair of shoes would be nice, although I've been wearing those worthless slippers for so long I think my feet are permanently flat." I bring my foot up for his inspection and he wrinkles his nose.

"I'm pretty sure these might help." Keegan interrupts, giving Cole a dirty look. "Here, these are the best I could do." He hands me a sturdy pair of black leather lace-up boots. "Hand me your scrubs. We can rip them and use them as rags."

"Oh, by all means! Please take them." I slide my feet into the boots and lace them up. "They're perfect! My feet thank you."

"You're still weird, you know that?" He grins while shaking his head.

"Yup," I say. "That hasn't changed."

"They're pretty durable and they have steel toes, which you'll find useful," Keegan says.

I look at my new boots with pride and then glance up at him. His face fluctuates between anger and fear.

"Really—how?" I ask.

He turns away from me and clears his throat. "Just go lie down and get some sleep. We've got a strict schedule to keep and you'll start training in the morning."

"Training?" I say.

"If you're living here, then you adhere to the rules. Make yourself useful. Train with us, eat with us, and so on."

"Should we train while we're here?" Cole asks. "Maybe I can even help teach you guys a few things."

"No need. I'd expect you've had enough." Keegan's stiff

posture and authoritative voice give me the impression that he doesn't want us to ask any more questions. "Why don't you get some rest? You'll need it." Keegan steers me toward my door, signaling the end of the conversation. And truthfully, I am tired. I haven't slept in almost forty-eight hours. I just wish I could have Cole's arms wrapped around me while I sleep. But the Sandman comes and my eyelids drop with ease.

* * *

I startle awake, feeling the sweat pour off my forehead and stick to the blanket wrapped around me. *Cole was murdered in my dream.* I breathe like I just ran a fifty-yard dash. My hands shake and I roll onto my back, staring into the shadows above me. I can't get my mind off the image of his neck being sliced open by another guard. *He died right in front of me and there was nothing I could do to stop it.* I flinch at the *drip drops* of water from pipes in the hallway and wipe the beads of sweat from my forehead. I scan the room. I have no idea what time it is or how long I've slept, but there's no way I can go back to sleep after that.

Sitting up, I pull on my new boots and stand. My legs feel a little shaky as I squint outside my room. I stretch my hand out to find the wall when Cole practically smacks into me. I let out a shrill noise.

"It's okay. You're okay, Lexi... It's just me," he whispers as he puts his hands on my shoulders to calm me.

"God, you scared me. I had a bad dream and—" My hands fly to my chest and I slide down the wall.

"I know. I could hear you screaming from my room. I knew it was you. I'd recognize your scream anywhere." He pulls me into his arms and I relish the warmth of his chest, his arms, and his body against mine.

"I screamed? That loud?"

"Scared the crap out of me. I thought—I thought something was happening to you. I was terrified."

"I'm sorry."

"Don't apologize." He kisses my forehead and I melt. There's something about his lips touching my forehead that sends me over the deep end.

"What were you dreaming about?"

"I don't even remember." I lie. I look up into his face, admiring his strong jawline and his glittering dark eyes. *When was the last time we were alone?* I run my hands over his chest and then pull his head down to meet mine. "Please, I need you right now."

His lips touch mine and electricity surges through every vein in my body. I need him to erase all the bad images from my dream. My hormones take over and next thing I know, we're stumbling to my cot and kissing passionately as he lays me down and positions himself on top. His hands grab at me, desiring more and more. They wander up my shirt and rip it over my head so my bare skin rubs against his. Then he unhooks my bra and I let him ravish me with his mouth.

He moans when I kiss his neck and run my fingernails down his back, pulling his hips into mine. His closeness intoxicates me to the point of irrationality. It's a race to the finish and neither of us wants to slow down. His hands fumble with the button on my pants.

"I've missed you," he whispers in my ear. "I want you—I want you so bad."

"I've missed you more."

"I doubt that." He kisses my lips and goes back to my ear. "Please, come here."

Just then, the lights in the hallway brighten and Cole jumps off my cot with alarm. We scramble to pull our shirts back on, and I button my pants, feeling frustrated.

"Damn it! You've got to be kidding me! Do they have a sex radar or something? I mean, seriously, are we ever going to have time alone?"

Just as I put my hair into a ponytail, Keegan storms in. His red face and narrowed eyes tells me he's not happy to see Cole in my room. "What the hell are you doing here?" he asks.

"She was screaming. I came to make sure she was all

right," Cole says. I can already see the vein beginning to pop out of his forehead.

Keegan squints his eyes and clenches his jaw while deciding whether to believe Cole. Then his eyes turn to me as he draws in a slow, steady breath.

"It was nothing, just a stupid nightmare. And apparently, I was screaming." I put my hand on his chest and force him to look into my face. "Seriously, he's being honest, Keegan."

He scrutinizes me and turns back to Cole. "From now on, I'll be the one looking after my sister, not you. Stay out of her room."

Cole's eyebrows form deep crevices and he curls his lips. I can feel a fight coming on. *He hasn't been around for years and now he thinks he can just waltz back into my life and tell me who I can talk to?* It makes me want to punch him myself. But then I see the anger flashing through Cole's eyes and know I have to deflate the situation.

"Please, don't be angry, okay? He was just doing his job." I keep my voice level.

"Yeah, I'll bet he was," Keegan sneers. "I'm sure he's quite convincing."

I shoot Cole a look, pleading with my eyes for him to calm down. "It's not like that, I swear."

"Look, man, I'm not trying to cause any problems here… but I'm still her guard." Cole relaxes his fists and tries to placate me. He knows I wouldn't want them to fight.

"Yeah, her guard up there. Not here. She doesn't need your protection when she's with me, and I can assure you no one down here will lay a finger on her." He takes a step toward me.

"Okay, that's enough, you guys. Keegan, you were coming here for me—what for?" I ask to distract Keegan from blowing a fuse.

His stiff jaw loosens and he breathes deep, trying to calm down. He reminds me of a caged cat, wild and unpredictable with his moods. "It's six a.m., training time."

"Oh right, then we better get going." I gently tug at his arm to break his trance.

"Can I ask why she's training? She won't be fighting," Cole says. I give Cole a dirty look. *Seriously? Does he have to push the issue?*

The expression on Keegan's face turns livid. His mouth twitches a little and I know that's never a good sign. I just got him somewhat calmed down and then Cole had to stick his foot in his mouth.

"Of course she'll fight. We all are." Keegan steps closer to Cole, and the air thickens with hate. I come between them, sensing the tension rising twofold.

"Please, guys, calm down, we can figure this out—"

"Oh no, she's not! Sending her into war isn't exactly what I call protecting her. I've worked my ass off to keep her safe—alive and in one piece. And you're going to throw her into combat? Something she knows absolutely nothing about! You're going to kill her!" Cole's voice sounds hardened and he glares at Keegan.

"You better watch what you say." Keegan pushes me to the right, but I step back between them.

"Both of you, stop," I beg. I don't want to see them come to blows. I just know it won't end well.

"If you really care about her, you'll protect her. Not send her out to fight," Cole says as spit flies out of his mouth. His fists clench at his sides and his eyes darken.

Keegan moves in closer and raises his voice. "Protect her? Like you have? By doing what—trying to get in her pants? Try to schmooze your way into her heart just to tear it to shreds? Don't think for one second that I haven't noticed what's going on between you two. You're the one treating her like a branded slut!"

Then Keegan shoves me onto the cot and fists begin swinging. I start screaming for them to stop, but no one listens. Cole knocks him to the floor, straddles him, grabs his collar, and sends his fist straight into Keegan's jaw. Keegan returns the punch, forcing Cole backward onto his side. Cole moves to hit him a second time, so I throw myself between them just as he swings a punch that lands in the middle of my back.

I land on Keegan. I try to inhale when a sharp pain shoots down my back, making me arch. I can't get words to come out of my mouth.

"Lexi," Cole says, rolling me over onto my side. I curl into a ball. "Damn it. I didn't mean to hit you."

"Get the hell off of her, you idiot." Keegan shoves him into the wall with a burst of speed.

I'm immobile on the ground just trying to catch my breath. I look up just as Keegan moves toward Cole and delivers a head-swerving hook. *Oh my God, make them stop.* Blood spurts from Cole's nose and drips off his face. I close my eyes and open them again just to make sure I'm seeing it right. I blink hard, and see the look of fury on Coles face. I shake my head and say, "Would you two please knock it off before someone gets killed?"

CHAPTER 18

The noises of grunting and barking hurt my head. It makes me want to put my hands against my ears and hum something soothing. But I can't and I won't. Instead, I close my eyes, take a deep breath, and open them in time to see Bruno charge into the room, closing the door before Zeus can enter. He pulls Cole away, and they both fall down. He curses under his breath. Blood trickles from Cole's nose as he covers it and his eyes hold hatred I've never seen before. Keegan bolts to my side and lifts me up.

I groan while digging my fingers into his arm. The pain on my right side cripples me.

He puts his strong arms around my waist and pulls me upright. "You're out of control," Keegan says to Cole. He sets me on my cot. "Who the hell do you think you are?" he yells.

Cole turns to him, wiping his nose with his shirt. "Who the hell do I think I am? Who the hell do you think you are? What, her brother? The one who walked out on his sister when she needed him the most? Face it, Keegan, you don't have the slightest clue who she is now. The woman she's become. But I do. I know everything about her." I cringe with every word, knowing that it's true, but trying to put it behind us.

"You prick," Keegan says. "You've got no idea why I left, and it's none of your damn business. That's between Lexi and me."

"Stop it! Calm down, both of you!" Bruno commands.

Bruno plants himself between them before another fight breaks out. He takes Cole's arm and drags him away.

By now, other men have filed into the room and they point their guns at Cole and Bruno. I feel my eyes widen at the amount of people who can fit into such a small room. Then I tense up even more as Bruno pulls out his gun and points it at Keegan. Zeus bolts in and plants himself in front of me. He growls low in his belly as the tension dams at my throat. I don't even know where to begin.

"Are you all right?" Keegan asks, ignoring the insanity that's about to erupt.

Part of me doesn't want to speak to him at all. He can't seem to find a way to be respectful toward Cole, and it feels like a slap in the face to me. Yet he also believes I should fight. *And I want to.*

"No. You idiot. You're being absolutely ridiculous. He didn't mean to hit me. He would never hit me," I shout at Keegan. I try to pull myself up, but feel weak.

"Lower your guns! And someone find her a medic." Keegan stands tall like there isn't a gun pointed at his face. Reluctantly, the men lower their pistols and place them back in their holsters. Bruno follows suit.

Keegan turns back to me. "Now, seriously, how are you?"

I feel my eyebrows form deep crinkles in my head. "Well, let's see…the two people I care about the most are ready to tear each other's heads off. How do you think I am?" I say. The pain forces me to clench my teeth.

Cole butts in. "Keegan, there's no way in hell she's fighting."

Please shut up! I want to say it, but Keegan cuts me off.

"How about you back off? She's quite capable of making that decision for herself." I can see Keegan's jaw twitching.

Cole pushes from behind Bruno and meets Keegan's eyes with his own death glare. "You just got her back and you're willing to lose her that easily? Throwing her into combat? No way can anyone train her in such a short amount of time! For God's sake, the revolt's about to begin. She's not going out there. Use your brain, Keegan! These are trained guards we're talking about. She won't last a minute out there and you know it!"

"Yeah, and you'd know all about how well-trained the guards are! But you don't know shit about me," Keegan retorts. "She'll be ready and you can just sit and watch!" He cracks his knuckles. "We'll see how prepared they are."

I feel sick to my stomach hearing their words. I need time to think things through, but everything's happening too fast. I put up my hand to get their attention.

"That's enough. You two are acting childish." Bruno puts his arm around me, leaning in close and looking me in the eyes. "What do you want to do?"

All eyes rest on me—Keegan's angry deep blues, Cole's pleading obsidian, and Bruno's logical glare. I don't know what to say. My answer won't make Cole happy or make things easier for myself. But if I ever want to be treated like an independent woman then I have to make my choice known to both Keegan and Cole. I swallow and clear my throat. This is something I have to do, and no one else can decide for me.

"I want to fight," I say while reaching my hand toward Cole. "I'm not about to sit back and let all of you fight without me. I want to be a part of this." I push myself into a sitting position and grit my teeth as my back throbs.

Cole's jaw clenches and his knuckles turn white. I can tell he feels like I'm betraying him. "Don't you dare, Lexi. You have no idea what you're talking about or what you're getting yourself into." His jaw relaxes. "If you fight, I'm not leaving your side and I can't guarantee that'll be enough to keep you alive. Do you see where that leaves me? I'm not fighting—I'm protecting you. Please...I'm begging you. I love you. I can't lose you. Not like this."

I grasp his hand with all my strength and feel myself start sobbing. The loud, uncontrolled, obnoxious kind. "I love you too, but it's what I need to do—for me. My father would want me to stand up for what he believed in—what I believe in."

"He wouldn't want you dead."

Keegan's head jerks up. "Oh, and you know our father how?"

Cole ignores him completely. "What are you trying to prove? Losing you isn't an option. You're staying put and not fighting!"

"Damn!" Bruno says. "I mean, I knew you were getting

weak around her, but holy balls! You love her...Wow!" He raises his eyebrows and steps back.

"He doesn't love her, and she doesn't love him," Keegan says. "This is all just immature stuff. Not love."

"Yes I do," I say forcefully. I push aside my pain, swing my legs over the side of the bed, and take a step toward Keegan. "Don't you dare tell me how I feel. You might be my brother, but Cole's a part of my life now and you're going to have to accept that whether you want to or not."

"You're kidding me, right?" Keegan throws his hands in the air. "You can't be serious."

I gasp for air between sobs, trying to calm myself down enough to make sense of the situation. Instead, I get hiccups, which make me feel even more humiliated. "I do love him and it's real. He never used me for anything and you should respect him. He protected me when you couldn't."

Keegan glares at Cole, at me, and back at Cole. "Wow, you really pulled one over on her, didn't you?" he asks with a skeptical voice.

Cole stands up, his entire body shaking. "No, it's never been like that—ever."

"Now, that's just bullshit." Keegan punches the wall in explosive anger.

Zeus bares his teeth, growling deep in his chest. "Zeus, back off," Cole says. Zeus stays in position, not heeding Cole's command. His fur makes a dark, raised tuft on his back.

Keegan practically spits in my face. "What were you thinking, Lexi? A guard? You can't trust him, even if he is one of the 'nice' guys. Where's your head?" He throws his hands up in the air in frustration. "It takes a long time to trust any guard, and here you are, jumping into bed with one."

"You don't know anything about him," I say. "How dare you judge me." I chuck my pillow as I clench my teeth and shake with anger. Keegan chucks it back at me, and Zeus snags it, ripping it into pieces.

"Don't stand up for me, Lexi. I have nothing to hide." Cole narrows his eyes at Keegan. "From the minute she became my assignment, my job was to keep her alive. I never knew why. But I was ordered to do so and that's exactly what I did. I was professional from day one, and with every bone in my body, I fought my feelings for her—believe me, I did. But each day I was falling for this girl who loves life but doesn't know how to show it because she doesn't think she deserves to be happy. I watched her befriend a dying child. I watched her give that little girl the best days of her life before she passed away. Please tell me how the hell was I not going to fall in love with her? Without a doubt, she's the most amazing person I've ever known. So you know what? Yeah, she broke me. She weakened me. But it's the best thing that's ever happened to me...because I have her. And that's one thing I wouldn't change. Not once did I ever take advantage of her. Not once did I ever consider her a whore. Even deep down before I knew the truth, I knew she was innocent. Keegan, you can think what you want of me, but the truth is I'd take a bullet and sacrifice my life if it meant I would save hers."

Before I can say anything, Keegan says, "It will only end badly and you know it." Keegan glares at Cole. "The safest place for her to be is with me. Not you."

"What makes you think that?"

"Because she'll make you a weak fighter. You'll be more worried about protecting her. She already made her choice. And since I don't trust you," Keegan says, "she's fighting with me."

"Over my dead body!" Cole raises his voice.

"Man, Cole. You're freaking whipped," Bruno says under his breath, but loud enough that I hear him.

"Get the hell out of here. That was a lovely speech, but I'm telling you to leave!" Keegan steps toward Cole.

I feel my insides jump. "No! He's not leaving. He's staying here with me. I need him. Keegan, you know he can't go back yet! Wilson knows I'm gone, and he knows Cole's my guard. He'll torture him to find me, or even kill him." I plead with Keegan, placing both hands on his chest.

"I don't give a damn what happens to him. That's none of

my concern, but he can't stay here. He won't let you train if he's here. He's got to go!"

I pull Keegan aside to talk in private and say in a whisper, "Keegan, I'll talk to him...I'll convince him to let me fight. I just need some time."

"No. There's no time for that. He's leaving."

I pound on his chest now, and he rips my wrists away. His blue eyes bore holes into mine.

"In case you forgot, Sutton sent you here to be with me. I'm your blood and I'm in charge." He forces my wrists away and I stumble back onto my cot. "I have your best interests in mind. You'll see." With pillow stuffing plastered on his face, Zeus barks a warning. Keegan's men drag him out of the room while trying to avoid his sharp teeth.

Cole jumps in Keegan's face. "Who left her?"

"Stop it!" I yell, but they ignore me.

"Here we go again," Bruno says. His hand slips down to the gun at his waist.

Several of Keegan's men inch their hands toward their holsters, sensing the rising tension.

"If you really care about me like you claim, then you'll let him stay." I stand back up and slap Keegan across the face before Cole can pull me away. The sound bounces off the walls like a thunderclap. I see Keegan's eyes turn murderous. My emotions overwhelm me. *Why can't I just make my own choices without someone dictating them to me?* It reminds me of how my stepfather treated me. Always picking out my clothes, telling me whom I couldn't associate with or forcing me into the darkness of the closet. I can't breathe remembering his obsessive need for control.

Keegan's voice pulls me back. "Lexi, you're all I have left. You're all I care about and you have to trust me. There's a reason for my madness, and I'll prove it." He turns to Cole. "Now get the hell out of here before I kill someone," Keegan commands. He extends his arm from across his chest and points toward the hall.

I step in front of Keegan, but he pushes me aside and

restrains me against the wall as his men force Cole out of the room. "No, Keegan. No! I swear to God, I'll—"

"You'll do nothing," he threatens in a low voice. His hands lock around my wrists and squeeze until they go numb. "Remove them!" Keegan demands to his men.

"Fine! We'll go. But it's not because I'm afraid of you, Keegan. I just don't want to kill you in front of her. But I'll be back, make no mistake about that!" Cole shouts. The men drag him through the doorway. I feel the resentment and anger building up like a geyser inside of me.

"Damn it! Keegan! Let me go!" I lunge forward, trying to break free from Keegan's grip, but he's like steel and I can't move.

"I can't, Lexi. I'm sorry." His voice sounds solid and strong. "And soon you'll understand why."

Cole's gone and I hear him yelling the entire way down the hall before silence settles. My heart shatters into a million little pieces. I want to beat in Keegan's face.

"It's better this way. You'll see." Keegan pats me on the shoulder but lacks pity. I feel dead inside and I'm afraid if I look at Keegan I'll strangle him.

I stand up, brush the dirt off my pants and lock eyes with Keegan. "The only reason I'm standing here is because I want to fight. That's it. Nothing more. Nothing less. You can't and won't control me, Keegan. I'm not a little girl anymore and I don't need you telling me what to do. When this is all over and you get to know him, you'll see what a good guy he truly is."

"Are you done now?" He raises his eyebrows, and I see the steel in his gaze.

"No. I'm not." I spit back. "Cole loves me. So you can either suck it up and get over it or you can continue on your way without me. Either way, I don't give a damn what you say about him. I know the real Cole. You don't."

He shakes his head, giving me a look of pity. "Lexi, he doesn't love yo—"

"Shut the hell up." I push him away from me with both hands. He narrows his eyes again, shakes his head, and slams my door. My adrenaline seeps out and I begin to feel the pain of Cole's absence.

My world feels like it's collapsing. *He's gone, really gone. And it's my fault.* He might get killed going back out there. I have no idea where he'll hide from the Commander or Wilson. *What did I just do?*

My body hurts so much, yet I burn with anger toward Keegan. How is it possible to love someone, yet feel so conflicted about them? Tears pour down, soaking my blanket, my clothes, and my pillow. The nightmare feels like it just came true. I cover my head under the pillow to drown out this hated place.

A few hours later, Keegan stomps into my room. "Get up!" He yanks off my blanket and tosses it to the floor. "We're running out of time. If you want to fight, like you said you did, then get your ass out of bed and get to the training center." He throws my clothes at me with a look of annoyance.

I sit up slowly and inspect the shirt. The last time I wore it, Cole was here, in my room, in my bed with me. I catch a faint whiff of his cologne and pull myself up straight. I won't allow Keegan to see me crumble. *Ugh.* I look up in time to catch my boots in midair.

"We don't have time for you to lick your wounds." He stands over me, a dark, shadowy figure.

"I'm not licking my wounds. Let's go." The only way I can keep Cole alive is if I learn how to be a good fighter. I need to set aside my hurt and use it as fuel…to kick some serious ass.

"Believe it or not, I know what's best for you."

"Will you please just shut up about that already? Teach me how to fight." I cut him off with a sharp voice.

"Now *that* I can do. Let's go." A real smile seems to appear at the corner of his mouth.

I've lost almost everything. I'm done losing people without fighting back.

"Lexi, I might not show it, but I'm hurting too." Keegan puts a hand on my shoulder.

"I know you are. You never were good at expressing your

feelings. But I know losing Dad killed you too." A tear trickles down, but I wipe it away. My father loved me deeply. He never yelled and always treated me with dignity and quiet respect. I never went to bed without a hug and kiss from him. Every night the last thing he would tell me was, "Remember, you can overcome anything short of death. I love you."

"That's true, but I lost you too," he says. His voice softens. "I never wanted to hurt you."

I wipe my tear away and shrug off his arm. "I know that, but it still stings."

He looks into my face. "How can I make it better between us? I want our relationship back. I want my sister back."

I take a deep, painful breath. "Keegan, you have me back, and in time, our wounds will mend. But right now, let's just focus on getting the hell out of here."

He reaches out his hands. I take them, and he gives me a strained smile. "I can live with that. Let's do this!" His words make me cringe. I close my eyes and remember Cole's face when I told him Bruno was teaching me. He was so accepting of it, so understanding about why I wanted to learn. *Yet he didn't want me to fight for the one thing I hold most dear.*

"I was recently taught some of the basics, so at least I have that going for me," I say while pulling on my boots.

"Who taught you?" he asks.

"Bruno," I say.

"*He* allowed that?"

I can tell whom Keegan means by the way he says *his* name.

"Yes, *Cole* did." My fingers pull the laces tight as I say his name.

"Interesting. All right, what did you learn?"

"Not much, just some basic self-defense moves."

"Well, that might come in handy, but now it's time you learn the hard stuff," he says.

I scrunch my eyebrows in confusion. "The hard stuff? Meaning?"

"Pulling the trigger and ending lives," he says in a

nonchalant manner.

I raise my eyebrow with skepticism.

"I know what you're thinking, but guards aren't people," he says. I give him an indignant look. "Well, most of them anyway. They're animals. They're trained not to give a shit about anything or anyone except their orders. Just like damn robots."

"But they're easier to kill than robots."

"Ha. This is very true." Keegan smirks at me. "Here this might help. Channel all your anger into your training. It gets easier as you do it. Believe me. After you kill a few, you'll become desensitized and it'll be like shooting a tree. You won't feel a damn thing."

His words reflect his cocky ignorance, but I refuse to get into an argument with him. After all, he's had to survive here a lot longer than I have and has probably seen worse things. *Maybe.*

"Now, time to focus on the task at hand. And put these on." Keegan throws worn wraps on my bed. "We train for two hours in the morning and three in the evening. If you're going to fight, these sessions are mandatory." His tone demands obedience and I get the feeling he's used to having orders followed.

"Wait," I say.

"You changed your mind?" he asks while raising an eyebrow.

"No, not about that, but I wanted to ask you if you have any paint down here? And if you do, could you possibly get me some?"

"What are you talking about? You want paint?" He does a double-take. "What the hell for?"

"Yes, I know it sounds crazy, but painting…well, it's like my therapy."

He gives me a funny look and sighs. "Whatever, if it helps you get over what's-his-face. I'll get you paint."

I exhale and pull myself upright. I feel numb, detached from the world. I don't care if the whole place caves in at this rate. I just can't shake the disparity of my situation. *Cole is gone.* Why couldn't Keegan let him stay in another part of the compound? *Or trust* me.

I stand in front of the mirror and pull my greasy hair into a bun. Then I wrap my hands the same way Bruno taught me. They're so tight the blood flow is partially cut off to my fingers. I shake my arms and legs out to relax myself. *I can do this. It's just a couple of hours.*

* * *

A blow to my cheekbone rouses me.

"Come on, Lexi. You're getting your ass kicked," Keegan shouts across the room.

I rub my face in surprise. A girl dances across from me with her fists raised. She's taller with straight black hair and a nasty glare. She hits me with a hook on the side of my head.

I groan.

"Protect yourself!" he yells at me again.

I won't be humiliated anymore. *Focus. Just focus.* I jab and then hit her with an upper cut right in the sweet spot, and she stumbles backward.

"Better!" Keegan claps.

We do push-ups every ten minutes. We run sprints to warm up and run sprints to cool down. In the mornings, I learn hand-to-hand combat, and in the evenings, we go through weapons training in an indoor range. I can feel myself getting stronger and want to push myself harder. The fire inside burns bright, never waning. I don't want to be helpless anymore. I want to fight.

When Keegan hands me a gun, my hand shakes so much that I don't hit anything near the target. Last time I attempted shooting, it was to save Cole and Bruno. It's not as easy when I have to think about it.

Keegan stands behind me as I try again and seems agitated by my lack of focus. He hands me a smaller pistol. "Here, use this one. It's more your size."

"What kind is it?" I ask. I turn it over in my hand while keeping the barrel safely aimed at the target. I like the smooth feel of it.

"It's a .40 caliber Glock. It's a subcompact so it'll fit perfectly in your hands. Just try it," he says.

I stand with my feet shoulder width apart, using both hands to steady myself. I shoot and miss the red circle around the target. *Crap.* "That sucked," I say as I glance at others as they shoot, feeling self-conscious because they all seem comfortable with what they're doing. Even the younger citizens seem at ease.

"It's okay. You'll get better with practice—lots of practice." Keegan encourages me. "Just don't put your finger on the trigger until you're absolutely ready to fire."

I exhale. I've got to improve. I fill my magazine again and try from a closer standpoint. The gun kicks as I squeeze the trigger, but a small hole appears in the target. Excitement over this small accomplishment gives me some satisfaction. A small smile creeps its way across my face. I try again and hit it again. It's not close to the first hole, but I hit it twice in a row.

* * *

I wake up and see two tin cans sitting in the corner of my room with two paintbrushes lying on top. I jump out of bed and touch them to make sure they're real. Black paint fills the first one and the second one contains red. I inhale and the fumes make me light-headed, but I don't care. It's here. It's real, and I get to paint. *Thank you, Keegan.*

After grabbing a small breakfast at the cafeteria, I shuffle back to my room. I keep my head low, making sure to avoid eye contact with everyone. I have no desire for small talk. The only goal I have right now is to get back to my room without an incident.

I balance my body just right to ensure I don't fall over when painting. This is different from anything I've ever painted before. It's the future. I arrange the tins perfectly in order to access both colors. I brush up and down, left and right, red and black, black and red. My arms go numb from painting so long. When I'm not eating, sleeping, or training, I paint. The tension melts away as I do it. I draw the silhouettes of my father and Alyssa sitting on Lexington bay, watching the waves roll in and out.

"What's that?" Keegan asks as he points to the Monet-style paintings.

I jump, almost falling off the stool.

"Sorry, didn't mean to startle you. I was just watching," he says. He leans against the doorframe.

I begin putting the brushes away and placing the lids back on the cans. "Squint your eyes and look left to right."

His eyes widen as he inspects my work. "Holy cow. It's the Hole getting blown to pieces," he says while shaking his head. "Damn, that's amazing. I didn't know you could paint. It's kinda Gothic. I like it." He smiles with satisfaction until his eyes come to rest on part of the painting.

"Is that…?" He stares at the figure of our father.

"Yes, and my friend Alyssa who died of some kind of virus."

"Was she from the outside?" He sits down on my bed, taking in the bay. It's breathtaking even when painted in black and red.

"Yes, when she was very young…but she was exiled to the Hole a few years ago," I say with sadness.

"As if she deserved to spend her life here…so how'd you meet her?" he asks.

"She was just my patient at first, but we became friends, and she ended up becoming more like a sister to me. God, Keegan, whatever virus she had was nasty, and poor Sutton tried everything he could to save her."

He looks at me with questioning eyes.

"Maybe she would've survived if she was treated outside of the Hole," I say. It feels like years ago now but hurts all the same. "But I think Sutton said something about there being no cure, so I guess it wouldn't have mattered. Still, it pisses me off."

Keegan shakes his head in loathing. "That's disgusting. How can they deny a life?"

"You're a hypocrite," I say.

He jumps back. "What? How?"

"You're going to deny lots of lives with this revolt," I say. "Whether you consider them worthy or not."

"That doesn't count," he says in a flat voice. "Alyssa was young and shouldn't have been here in the first place. Which is exactly the reason why this revolt's happening, and why I won't feel anything while killing the guards."

I don't respond.

"Who's that laying in a puddle of blood?" he asks, changing the subject. His eyes squint as he peers at a small figure in the corner of the painting.

"Me," I whisper.

He shakes his head in confusion. An uncomfortable silence lingers, so he stands and leaves.

I turn off my lights and lie in darkness. I smell like sweat, but getting in the shower requires energy, and right now, I don't have any reserves. I kick off my boots but can't kick this feeling of abandonment. I thought we both wanted the same thing—to be together. Isn't this the only way?

I squeeze my eyes closed, but Cole's face, his beautiful face, is etched perfectly in my mind—his long, dark lashes over his charcoal eyes, his dimples when he smiles, his full lips kissing me.

* * *

"Come with me. I want to show you something." Keegan takes my hand but I pull away from him.

"Not now, Keegan, I want some time alone." He stops mid-step and turns to face me.

"I know you're not happy with me right now, and I understand, but there are reasons for my actions and why I'm acting this way." His eyes beg me to listen. "Lexi, I don't have a good feeling about Cole. Something's not right," he says with a sincere tone.

He's my brother and he's being protective of me and I get that, but I think Keegan's forgotten that I've grown up and I'm not the young girl he left behind years ago.

"You don't even know him!" I say with my hands on my hips.

"Know him? I don't have to know him." He leans against the wall. "Please, come with me. I don't want to have this conversation here."

"Why?"

"Because it's time you know the truth."

Keegan starts down the narrow hallway, and I follow close behind because I don't like the feel of this place. The lighting is dim and I'm afraid the walls will collapse around me. I feel the familiar tightening of my throat just being reminded of the closet where my stepfather locked me. Thankfully, I haven't seen any creepy insects yet.

We enter Keegan's bedroom and he gestures me to his bed. "Sit down." I push the hair out of my face and do as he says.

Keegan walks over to his closet, pulls out a key, and unlocks the door. He bends down, picking up a box before setting it next to me. It's slightly warped and about the size of a large shoe box.

"Remember when I told you I brought more things from home?"

"Yes." I fiddle with the buckle on my pants for a second before folding my hands in my lap.

Keegan tightens his jaw, slowly opens the lid, and places it beside him. He reaches in and pulls out a picture frame and says, "Here, I thought you'd want to see this."

I take the picture out of his hands and feel my eyes widen when I see it. Immediately tears fill my vision when I see my father's turquoise eyes and kind smile staring up at me. He's wearing his favorite light blue polo shirt, the one he always wore on Saturdays. I run my fingers up and down the glass of the picture while tracing his face—almost like I'm painting the picture in my mind. My tears fall onto the glass and I use my sleeve to wipe it dry. The edges of the frame are made of wood and it fits perfectly in my lap.

"It's nice to see him again, isn't it?" Keegan says as he puts his arm around my shoulder. "I miss him too, Lexi. I miss him more every day." His voice cracks.

I'm struggling for words, I'm struggling to take my eyes off my father, and I'm struggling to let go. "I know you do." I tilt my head and smile slightly. "You know, I still hear his voice, I still smell his aftershave and I can still feel his soft skin on my face when he would hold me in his arms. I used to tuck my face into his neck, and those were the moments...I felt safe and loved." My hands are trembling now, so I lock my fingers around the frame and squeeze. "God, Keegan. I would do anything if we could just see him one more time."

"Me too." He takes his arm off my shoulder and takes out another photo. I recognize it almost immediately. This one is of the three of us. I was four years old in this picture and I remember it like it was yesterday. Keegan's on my father's back with his arms wrapped around his neck. I'm standing to the right of my father, holding onto his leg and all three of us are laughing. It makes me laugh out loud.

"You remember this?" Keegan says.

"Of course, this was taken the day before we went on our first camping trip." I smile.

"You have a great memory."

"When it comes to moments like this, how could I possibly forget?" I peek over at Keegan, who's staring at the photo. "He really did love us, Keegan. We were so lucky to have had a father like him, who would do anything for his children. That man was the best man I've ever known."

Keegan nods in agreement. "Do you remember that night in the tent when he told us he'd always be there for the two of us?" Keegan's now staring at the floor rubbing his hands together. "For the longest time, I was angry at him because he lied—he's not here for us now. But after a while, I realized he's still with us, just not physically." He puts his hands over his head and says, "I can feel him sometimes. I can hear him telling me to be a man, to stand my ground and fight for what I believe in. So I do. I fight for Dad."

"He would be so proud of you, Keegan. I'm proud of you."

"Thank you." He uncovers his face and exhales. "Oh, do you want to see the last picture I have?"

"That's a stupid question."

Keegan hands me the last picture, and instantly, I scream and glue my eyes shut.

It's her.

"Get it away from me!" I demand. It's the last family photo we had together. The photo that was taken a week before my father died, and my mother has her arms wrapped around me kissing my cheek. "Seriously, take it."

"I'm sorry. I didn't mean to upset you!" Keegan takes the picture out of my shaking hands and puts it back into the box.

"Don't ever show that to me again! You hear me! Ever!" My voice trembles.

"I just thought…"

"Well, you thought wrong. I don't want to see our mother. I never want to see that witch again."

"Lexi, she loved you too."

"Loved me? Are you serious? Keegan, she accused me. She sent me here. She betrayed her only daughter because she was jealous and she only cared about herself." I can feel heat crawling up my neck and across my face.

"I don't believe it."

"How… How can you say that?" I give him a dirty look. "What? You think I'm lying?

"No, I don't think she accused you for the reason you think she did."

"What the hell are you talking about?" I jerk my head his direction.

He cocks his head to the side. "Think about it. You were sent to the Hole, you were given a guard to protect you, and you're working with Sutton, Dad's best friend. I don't know… it seems all too coincidental to me, that's all."

I'm shaking my head even before he finishes. "No way!"

I want to stand up and walk away, but he catches my elbow.

"All right, you know what, let's not make this about mom. What I'm about to give you has everything to do with our father." Keegan hands me an envelope with my name on it. The handwriting is our father's, and I gasp, afraid to open it. My hands are covering my mouth and I swallow hard.

"Keegan, I don't know if I can..."

"You can, and you'll be glad you did. Here let me open it for you." Keegan gently opens up the white envelope and pulls out a sheet of paper. When he gives it back, I hold it in-between my hands and I tap my foot on the floor.

Dear Lexi,

My daughter. My heart. By now, you've probably figured out what happened to me. I apologize for keeping it hidden from you, but hoped that in doing so, I'd protect you against those with evil intentions. If there were any other way, I would've moved heaven and earth to do it for you.

There's so much I want to say to you. I'll have missed the best part of you growing up. Please know I want to be there, but sometimes being a parent means making sacrifices for the greater good. Would you want to marry, have children, and raise them in this kind of world? I don't believe so, but I want you to have that chance.

I hope you took care of your mother. She's depended on me for so long. Despite your differences, you're so much alike. And I want you to forgive her for any decisions she may make in her grief.

I'm sorry for the pain I've caused you and I under-stand the anger you must have toward Keegan as well. But, my sweetheart, forgive him, for he's only doing what I asked of him in my personal letter to him. I know he's a fighter and won't rest until he accomplishes what I've begun. Even if that means he has to leave everything behind to do so.

There are so many things I want to tell you about life, but I know that you're an intelligent, brave, and compassionate young lady who will always find her way. I hope that you love deeply as I have loved your mother. I hope that you strive for justice and integrity in everything you do. I hope you know that I always, ALWAYS loved you, regardless of the path I chose for myself.

And here's what I've been trying to prove to both of you kids since that night in the tent. When I told you I would always be here for you. It's true. I might not be where you can see me, but I can promise you I'm fighting right beside you. This letter is living proof of the strong bond our family shares, in good times and in bad.

Be strong for the times ahead. Stand up for those who cannot. And remember, you can overcome anything short of death.

Your loving Daddy.

I pull the letter to my chest as my tears pour out. Keegan wraps his arms around me and I bury my head into him. This is what matters now. This is what my father wants. And fight we will. I won't ever question Keegan's motivations because now I fully understand.

"I love you," Keegan whispers in my ear.

"I love you, and I'm sorry I was angry with you."

"Don't be. We're together again, and that's all that matters."

"You're so right." I pull away for a moment. "He said he gave you a letter too?"

Keegan nods and wipes a tear away with his fist. He reaches into his jacket, and pulls out another plain white envelope. "They were both in my bedroom at home, hidden by Dad. He knew I'd find them. He had to know someday we'd see each other again." He swallows hard as he hands the letter to me. I feel my hand quiver as I pull it open.

Dear Keegan,

My favorite hide-and-seek player. I knew you'd find this letter and that you'd keep it. I'm blessed to have you as a son, and now you're becoming a young man. I hope I taught you enough to survive in a world that's unforgiving and harsh at times. Don't ever give up. Don't ever let anyone take your strength from you. I look at you, and you remind me so much of myself as a young man. I didn't always make the right decisions, but this time, I know I am. I trust that you'll do the same.

I'm asking you to carry on my legacy as a man, and as a Hamilton. You're the last man in my line, the one who carries our name for eternity. Carry it with pride. Fight for those who seek justice. Lead the ones who have no leader.

You'll have to leave home. You can't take your mom or Lexi with you, as they need each other and Lexi is too young to understand it all yet. You'll have to get into the Hole, make contact with Sutton, and do things you'd never imagine possible. You'll put yourself in some scary situations. Don't doubt yourself or your abilities to lead. You know the evil that exists, and you possess the maturity it takes to fight it. Go. Don't falter or let anything stop you from doing the right thing. I wouldn't ask it of you, if I didn't believe it. One day, if we're all lucky, we'll be together again. I'm hoping you can forgive me for leaving and that we can all forgive each other for doing what was necessary even though painful at times.

I love you my son. You can overcome anything short of death...so free them!

Love,
Your Dad.

My tears leak down my cheeks in small rivers. "He loved us. He knew this would happen." Keegan stuffs the letters back into their envelopes and sniffs.

"Keep yours." He rises, puts his envelope in a top drawer, underneath a short stack of clothing, and says, "It'll help you be strong, even when everything seems hopeless." I nod and stand up to hug him.

"I'm not angry anymore. Not with you." I swallow and my lower lip trembles. I step back from Keegan and meet his glassy gaze. "Dad is right. We've got to forgive each other for our choices, even when it's painful, because we all want the same thing." Keegan rests his head on top of mine.

"We sure do."

CHAPTER 19

Tuesday. Target shooting.

Wednesday. Obstacles. Climbing ropes, scaling walls, running through a course, and crawling through another. My hands burn and my knuckles are scabbed over. Every time I make a fist, one of them cracks back open and they start to bleed all over again. *But hey, it's a sign of toughness...right?*

Thursday. Shooting moving targets, shooting while lying down, falling, running, jumping, shooting everything. It's a lot harder than it looks. At first, I missed them every time, but after a few hours, I'm hitting them with each shot. My confidence is building and I'm starting to truly believe in myself. For the first time in my life, I feel in control.

Friday. Scenario training.

Saturday. Knife training. Bomb training. Training in everything. It feels great to occupy my brain with something useful for once.

Sunday. I run my finger up my calves and thighs, feeling the bumps and rigid muscles forming. I flex, my biceps pop up, and I smile at myself.

I unintentionally paint Cole's eyes on the third wall of my room. I begin with an oval, and next thing I know, it's his eyes. Always watching me wherever I go. I can train all day, every day, but he'll never be far from my mind. *I wonder if he's okay, if he's still alive and if he is...I hope he's safe from Wilson and his mad men.*

Monday. I jump out of bed, put my boots on, and already I feel my heart starting to race and I get that itch to fight. I feel the strength in my legs as I walk to the bathroom and I hold my head up high. My father was right. I can feel him living through me. I can feel him pushing me, preparing me, and leading me to a better life. After taking a hot shower, I pull on fresh clothes. I bind my hair tightly while inspecting myself in the mirror. My face has regained its color, which I'm sure is from eating better and exercising, but it's still lean like the rest of me. My form-fitting shirt flatters my athletic frame. I smirk, pleased with my transformation. *I wish Cole were here to see it. No...I can't think like that today.* I squash the argument in my brain and bounce into the cafeteria. Keegan looks up from his crowded table and stares at me, dumbfounded.

"Would it be all right if I joined you?" I say as I put my tray of food down beside him.

"Of course, why wouldn't it be?" Keegan says. "And if you ask me that again, I'll smack you."

"So, when do I actually get to shoot a guard?" I smirk at him and he turns to me giving me a hug.

"*Finally!* Thank God! I've been waiting for you to say that." He smacks me on my back. "Watch out, fellas, my little sister here is going to do some serious ass kicking."

"I don't know about all that," I whisper.

"You will. I have no doubt about that."

"Oh really? What makes you so sure?"

"Because I've been watching you. Lexi, you have so much potential. You're just blind to it. Have some confidence in yourself. You've earned it," Keegan says. "But to build more muscle, you need to eat." He shoves more food in my direction, and I laugh out loud.

"I'm going to barf if I eat any more." I push his tray away. "So how do you get all this food anyway? Everyone up top has to scrounge for it."

"We grow what we can and barter for the rest." He shovels in a mouthful of potatoes and keeps talking. "Told you we have connections."

"Eww, well your manners suck. You're spitting food all over me." I pick up a napkin and wipe my shirt.

He laughs and more falls out of his mouth onto the table. "Like seafood?" He opens his mouth and a chunk of potato falls onto the table.

"You're gross!" I swat him and we laugh. *Some things*

never change.

The others at the table look at him and then at me. It's the first time I really see them. They smile politely and laugh along with us. We're an athletic group, a multicultural quilt of people. I feel at home here and it's the safest place I've been since I came to the Hole.

This time in training I run faster, hit harder, and Keegan matches me up against some of his guys. We wrestle, and I get pinned a few times. I feel the sweat pouring over my forehead as my face gets shoved into the mat. A grunt escapes from between my teeth, but I keep fighting.

"Damn it. Push yourself!" Keegan shouts. He circles the room, keeping his eyes on everyone. He stops at my mat, evaluating me as I roll around. "Wow, I'm impressed! You held your own out there. It's nice to see you've finally got that idiot off your mind."

I clench my teeth and ball my hands into fists. *Don't do it. Don't do it. Oh, but I would give anything to deck him right now.*

"All right, let's do this again," Keegan says.

My partners rotate, so I stand in front of a new one. Immediately, we go to the ground. In a real street fight, we'd use whatever we could to get free, but in this particular session, we're just learning how to get out of a bad position. In a quick move, I reverse my competitor's guard and end up in a full mount. I can't help it. I feel my smile stretch across my entire face. I stand up and shake hands with my opponent. He's a little taller than me, slim, but I still beat him.

The training is rough. In the beginning, my body hurt everywhere, but I feel it adjusting to the grind. The daily torture dampens my mental anguish because I'm too busy to think about Cole.

"That's it for the morning, guys. Go rest up," Keegan says. He puts his arm around me. "When the revolt breaks out, you're on my team." He turns to walk toward the showers.

I chase him, tugging at his shirt. "What do you mean, your team?"

He continues walking, so I match his stride. "For the main operation, we divided everyone into teams. I'm assigning you to mine. One, because I love you, and two, because you're that damn good." He cracks his neck and stops with his hand on the light switch. People pass, but we don't move.

"Who leads the other teams?"

"Sutton, Bruno, and a lot of others…people you haven't met. Why?" His eyes search mine with a cool stare.

"Just wondered," I mumble. *Obviously Bruno's alive if he's going to lead a team,* I think with satisfaction. If he's still kicking, then chances are so is Cole.

"For God's sake, please tell me it's not because of Cole." His cobalt eyes see right through me. "He can't be trusted, and for that reason alone, he's not allowed anywhere near my group." He takes a deep breath. "But enough about him. Go shower. I'll catch up with you later."

I start to speak again, but he's not in the mood. He slams the switch down and the lights flicker off. The room feels lonely and smells like body odor.

I shuffle to the women's showers and tiptoe past the stalls before anyone can talk to me.

"I love you, Lexi, more than you'll ever know," Cole says as he kisses along my jawline, my ear, and my neck. Bright light frames his perfect face, and warmth from his body radiates against mine.

I wrap my arms around him, pulling him closer. "And you have no idea how much I love you."

His eyes light up, and he pulls my left hand to his chest, fingering my ring. "I'll never let you down," he says.

Even though I haven't seen him in weeks, his face appears in my dreams regularly. It haunts me to remember the hurt in his eyes, his face when I chose to fight with Keegan over him. *But I didn't choose it over him. I chose to fight for us, for my father.* My mind twists, desiring to see him, yet nervous he'll hate me for everything.

The longing always seeps back in despite my attempts to keep busy. The longing for his face, his voice, and his body against mine. I retch in pain while remembering how he touched me. His hands caressed me here, and I touch my cheek. And here. I touch my lips.

I take the ring off my left finger and read the inscription again. "Dad, if you hear me, please, please watch over Cole. I don't want to lose him," I whisper.

"Morning!" Keegan says, causing me to jump out of my own skin. "Hope you're ready. We have a busy day. First, training, second, a meeting, and we have to fit lunch in somehow," Keegan says as he walks into my room unannounced.

"Would it kill you to knock?" I ask, sitting up in my bed. "Or is that too much to ask?"

"What's it matter? Are you trying to hide something from me?" he asks with his arms folded across his chest.

"No, but scaring the hell out of me isn't really necessary," I say in frustration.

He arches his eyebrow and evaluates me for a minute. "Whatever, it's not like you sleep naked. Come on, get up. We gotta go." He nudges me with his hand.

"Fine." I stand up, pull on my boots, and draw my hair away from my face. When I finish, he rolls his eyes and exhales deeply, as if searching for an ounce of patience. Then I follow him down the hall as he enters a few other rooms to rouse people.

He leaves halfway through training and we continue on like good pupils.

Two hours race by. My brain spins from experimenting with pressure points. I see stars when they practice on me and I even get dizzy a few times. One person passes out, and the medical personnel take him away. *I'm glad it wasn't me.*

Everyone rushes to shower and meet at the main conference room. I have no idea where to go, so I follow the crowd. They stand outside the heavy doors, waiting to go in. They all form their cliques, but I stand alone against the wall. The light above me keeps flickering, but no one seems to notice. It's quiet except for the murmuring within their closed circles.

Keegan arrives, and everyone parts like the Red Sea. Several large, armed men follow him. I glance at his entourage and my mouth falls open when I see Sutton, Bruno, Zeus, and Cole following along. His face is hard and his jaw clenched. My stomach drops and I blink hard, making sure I'm not imagining them. Nope, they're still there. I smile when Sutton nods his head in my direction, but says nothing. Zeus lunges, jumps up on his hind legs, and wastes no time before licking my face.

I stumble backward into the wall, laughing. "Zeus! Man, I've missed you, even your slobber!" I wrap my hands around his big ears and kiss the top of his head. The joy is short-lived when I notice everyone staring at me.

Keegan looks mortified. "Would someone remove that dog?"

Cole and Keegan's men move toward Zeus, but he refuses to move. He plants himself in front of me and bares his canine teeth with ferocity. They try to grab his collar, but he growls and snaps at them.

"It's fine. Just let him stay with me, unless you want someone to get bit," I say. I put my hand through his collar and he doesn't mind. When I look up, Cole's eyes meet mine for the first time in weeks. I gasp for air. His hair is newly faded, the way I like it, and his short-sleeved T-shirt gives a glimpse of his well-muscled arms. Something like regret passes behind those familiar, dark eyes as he approaches me, and I want to dive into his skin.

"He needs to spend time with you. He's really been hurting," Cole says. His voice comes out flat, lacking the touch of tenderness that usually dances at the edges. He winces when he speaks and his eyes look almost cold and distant.

I'm unable to respond. My heart deflates, and I want to drop to my knees and beg him to forgive my brother for coming off as a jerk. But his tall, masculine figure passes me as Keegan shouts for everyone to go in.

"What the hell? Are you trying to start a riot?" Keegan

grabs my arm and shoves me through the doors. Zeus growls at him but stays closely by my side. "Can you keep that dog under control?"

"Yes. Don't worry about him. He'll be fine," I say. Keegan gives me a skeptical look and cocks his head to the side. "I promise."

I recognize this room as the control room where Keegan first took Bruno, Cole, and me. I walk to a spot around the large table in the center and take a seat. People file in until the space is packed with bodies.

Zeus huffs and lies on top of my feet, practically cutting off my circulation until I force him to move a little. "Zeus, seriously…" He refuses to move more than three inches away from me, so I end up sitting cross-legged in my seat, feeling a bit childish. Oh well, I miss him too much to make him get up.

Someone dims the lights as the screens mounted on the walls light up, showing hundreds of people, also underground in other areas of the Hole, anticipating the meeting.

Keegan paces around the center table. "Greetings, fellow warriors! You're probably wondering why we're having a meeting this early." He stands with his fingers steepled in confidence. "It's time we finalize our plans. Many of you know Dr. Sutton, or Sutton, as we call him. He's a doctor in the hospital, and most importantly, a leader of our great rebellion. He has high connections. With his leadership and knowledge, we'll take down the Hole, and the Commander."

Everyone cheers and claps. The person next to me whistles, and Zeus's ears perk up. I arch my back a little to scan the crowd and see Sutton sitting in the front row along with Bruno and Cole. They look uptight, but they still clap at all the appropriate times.

"Without further ado, Sutton is here to speak to us today. He doesn't have a lot of time, so we ask for your complete attention." Keegan sits down, and the people clap again as Sutton stands.

I catch Cole's eye. I don't want to look, but I do. I don't want to stare, but I can't stop myself. I pry my eyes away somehow. But I still feel the weight of his eyes on my face as a deep flush crawls up my cheeks. *He doesn't hate me. He can't.*

Keegan hands Sutton a remote. Sutton turns on a hologram that seemingly floats over the center table. The picture is fuzzy at first, but as it clears, a 3D diagram of the Hole becomes defined—the large walls encircling the Hole, the Commander's residence, and the streets with their buildings and shantytowns. I'm confounded by the size, the thickness of the walls with the pathway on top, and the distance we'll need to travel on foot. My eyes settle on the tallest building—the hospital. It sits central to all the activity. It sickens me to think there's only one hospital for everyone. It's no wonder it was always packed, always busy, and disgustingly dirty. *Well, except for the basement where the guards train.* Yet, how lucky was I to receive a job there, working under Sutton, of all people? The thought brings back the conversation I had with Keegan earlier. *Maybe it's not all a coincidence.* I blink my eyes, and attempt to refocus myself.

A smaller picture also pops up of the remote transformation center and the lab where everyone is branded before entering the Hole. *So this is where Wilson prefers to work.* It strikes me as interesting that the transformation center is separate from the Hole. *Not that it matters. It's all for the purpose of torturing people.*

Sutton's voice cuts through my inner thoughts, bringing my attention directly to him.

"This is the only map of the Hole that's ever been made. Not much has changed since it was constructed. A lot of people died for this, so please take me serious when I say this is top secret. I became a doctor because I love the human body and it gives me joy to help others. My mission started decades ago when I saw the injustices created by a system that accuses, brands, and tortures its citizens. My best friend growing up was an activist. He openly spoke with disgust of the Hole—"

Sutton's eyes focus on me in the crowd as he refers to my father. *Please don't let my courage fail me now.* I nod at him, acknowledging and respecting his words as a torrent of emotions wells up in my chest. Pride. Pain. Memories.

"My friend, my brother, was murdered for speaking openly in defense of those who couldn't do it for themselves. Since then, I've dedicated myself to helping your people. I've given up so much for the cause and I know you've sacrificed the same. The time of watching is over. It is time to act." He pauses as everyone stands and cheers.

I find myself standing and clapping along with the crowd. The people connected by satellite also stand and clap, their faces ranging from joy to fear. Keegan motions for us to sit, so we do.

"Over the years, we've compiled an arsenal of weapons. We've constructed all the tunnels reaching our target areas for the battle. We've carefully misled the guards to think we're just aimless terrorists with no real agenda. We've made a plan that will overthrow the current leader and install a new, more fair, justice system for all," he says.

Everyone stands to clap again. The thunderous applause echoes so loud I look up at the ceiling, hoping the Commander can't hear us. As I drop my eyes, I catch Cole staring at me, and my heart rate increases.

"We've broken everyone into teams with leaders. Each team has a specific goal to accomplish. After this meeting, the list of teams and their leaders will be hung in the hallway for you to see. You'll meet with your team and leader to begin your specific training this week." He motions to the large screens. "Those of you who aren't present but are connected by remote satellite will be notified of your teams by your local team leaders."

Some of the faces on screen smile, while others look solemn. We all know what's at stake. *Relationships. Lives. The future.*

"Next week we begin the full offensive." A hush moves across the room, all eyes glued on Sutton.

"I bear the full weight of my responsibility as a leader. I know some of you won't survive, but take hope in the knowledge that you're giving the younger generation a chance you never had. A chance to live freely without terror, without want, without injustice. You give them the hope that they can overcome anything—short of death."

The crowd roars as they stand and applaud him once again. The last sentence of his speech resonates with all, and I finger the ring on my hand, feeling my father's presence. Wishing he were here. Wishing Alyssa could witness this.

People start moving around, talking in loud voices, and crowding out into the hallway to see their groups. The lights come back on slowly, and the remote satellite links are disabled one by one. Men stand with Sutton and Keegan around the hologram in the center, discussing tactics. Zeus waits with me.

"Of course you're in Keegan's group," a familiar voice breaks into my thoughts.

I take a deep breath and spin around. Cole stands before me with his hands on his hips. I drop my eyes, looking anywhere but at him. I can't control my hands, so I twist them together. He eyes my ring, squeezes his lids shut and shakes his head.

"Does that surprise you?" I say.

"No, but it pisses me off. You deserve the right to choose who you want to fight with."

"Why? No one else gets to choose. Why should I be any different?"

"So now you're defending him?"

"Cole, please…I don't want to argue with you."

"Of course you don't. You've made your choice and so have I."

"What do you mean?"

Cole stands there grinding his teeth and I see sweat dripping from his forehead. I find that strange since it's not exactly warm down here. "Nothing, just forget it," he says with a sharp tone.

I swallow the lump in my throat and push it down to my stomach. "Are you all right?"

His eyes dart to mine. "I've missed you, that's all." His voice sounds pained. "I'm seriously going crazy. I can't stop thinking about you. I'm constantly worried that you're hurt, worried that you need me, and worried that you'll—"

I put my hand on his chest to stop him but his body tenses with my touch, and I let my hands fall to my side.

"I know how you feel...You're always on my mind, and I don't know how to make it stop," I lie. I haven't been thinking about him constantly. Of course, I've missed him, and I would've rather him be with me. But I can't help but wonder if I would be the fighter I've become if he were here. "But our feelings are exactly the reason why Keegan doesn't want us fighting together."

"Like that's going to stop me. I'm still going to protect you," he says. He shifts his weight, dropping my hands, unsure of himself. "You're my priority." He lets out a sigh and takes my hands in his. "Not matter what. We're going to make it and we'll be together." He squeezes my hands and I smile. "Now, more than ever I need to get you out of here."

My soul screams for him, longing for him to touch me, kiss me, and desiring to rewind time. "I hope you know I never thought he'd force you to leave..." I stumble over my own words and he stops me.

"It doesn't matter now. What's done is done," he says. "It's in the past, so let's leave it there. Plus, if we could rewind time and fix our mistakes, we'd never learn from them. Right?"

My insides crumble and I have to swallow my desire to jump into his arms. Instead, I kneel down and put my arms around Zeus, who promptly licks me from my chin up my nose.

"Eww, Zeus!" I laugh out loud, breaking the physical tension between Cole and me for a quick moment.

"Well, it's pretty apparent you didn't break his heart," Cole says. He kneels down, patting Zeus's head too. *Does he mean I broke his?*

He takes my face in between his hands. His lips meet mine with a desperation I don't recall. He kisses me with hard lips and he wraps his fingers in my hair so tight my head starts to hurt.

Someone clears his throat, forcing me back to reality. Then

I notice people are outright staring at us as we hold hands.

I stand up stiffly, pulling my hands away, and shake my head. "I better go. If Keegan sees us, he'll never let you come back."

"Last time I checked, Sutton's in charge—not him." Cole steps closer. "If I want to kiss you, I will and he can go screw himself!"

"Cole, please don't make a scene. Things are already complicated enough."

"He can kiss my ass!"

"Stop it!"

"You know what? You're leaving with me—"

"No!" I take a step back. "Please just try and respect the decision I've made…even if you don't agree with it!" I dart out so fast that I can't remember which door I entered. I wish I could turn around and look at him one last time, but talking to him was enough torture for one day. I won't choose between him and my brother. *I need them both in my life.*

I push through people and find the lists in the hallway. Scanning the paper, I see my name under Keegan's, as expected. I check and find Cole's name under Sutton.

This is killing me. I bang my forehead on the wall in frustration and leave. I rush back to my room and climb into my bed as the dam breaks and my tears flow freely.

This is all moving at a pace so fast I can't keep up. I feel weak, even though I'm strong. I feel incapable, even though I can do it. I know I'm doing the right thing for so many reasons. It's not just about Cole. It's for my father, Alyssa, and so many others I've seen die grisly deaths in the last few months. Now, more than ever, I want the Commander to pay for all I've lost. And mostly, I want to fight for those people like me, who were branded sinners when innocent. Whatever the cost, I'll fight. I'm as ready as I'll ever be.

CHAPTER 20

Air rushes from my lungs as his fist slams into my stomach. I double over and take a jarring knee to my forehead. Swirling flashes of white pierce my vision as I fall backward, covering my head to avoid the inevitable onslaught of punches. A voice cuts through my fogginess.

"All right! That's enough." Keegan's voice sounds satisfied.

I blink my eyes, seeing a shadowy outline slowly come into focus. My opponent, a stocky young man who looks to be in his twenties, reaches down to me. I'm holding my head with one hand while he pulls me up with the other. I just got my rear end handed to me for the first time in a while. I didn't even stand a chance.

"Lexi, he's not gonna kill you," Keegan says. "He's the best fighter we have and therefore, he's the best practice for you." Keegan pats my adversary on the back. "This is Sheldon."

I nod my head and smile weakly. "Nice to meet you, I think."

He smiles in return. He has a wide gap between his two front teeth and a large bruise covers his cheekbone. "Nice to meet you, too…I think." He smiles and I see the sparkle in his eye. I snort at his lame joke.

"How about a warning next time?" I playfully punch his arm but then I feel the wooziness coming on and I put my hand against the wall to steady myself.

"The guards won't warn you, so neither will I," Keegan says. I feel my smile fade away and a thin line replaces it. His words are light, but his face gives away his seriousness. Keegan wraps his arm around Sheldon's back. They look like two tough characters with their shaved heads, tattooed arms, and bulky muscles. I straighten up my back and let my hands drop to my sides.

"I'm assuming you've all met. If not, do so. As you know, I'm the leader of this group, and since we'll be fighting as a team, you'll be doing everything together," Keegan says. "We'll train together, eat together, and yes, even sleep together. We must become one."

I count thirty of us there. I see a few familiar faces, but no one I've spent time with outside of training.

"We'll continue weapons training, but our concentration will be mostly close-quarters combat. We get to do *all* the fun stuff." He stops to smile. I pan their faces for a reaction and see most of them smirk back. I'm not sure why that's considered exciting. In fact, a chill goes up my spine. I know as well as any sinner how the guards fight. *It's never fair.*

"Every group here has an objective," Keegan says. I watch him, waiting for his words and fidgeting with my fingers behind my back. "And ours will be to penetrate the Commander's main residence."

I flinch. I hear a hush over our group. I struggle to maintain my thin curtain of composure. Fear creeps up my throat and tightens like a vice around my vocal chords. I survey the group of people around me. I don't know their names other than Keegan's and Sheldon's although we've all fought each other in rotation, but all of them look physically ready. If they're fearful or uncertain, they do a good job of masking it.

"As you already know, Sheldon's the best combat trainer here, and trust me, you'll hate him when he's finished with you. But remember, it's his job to put you through hell—to make you the best fighter you can be. I also want to take this opportunity to introduce you to Isaac, our bomb specialist." Isaac raises his hand and we all nod. "We'll be fighting in close quarters the majority of the time, but we'll still need his expertise to conquer some aspects of the residence. We'll go over all of this after dinner. In the meantime, pack up your crap and move it to wing C of the compound. You'll all bunk together during this last part of training."

Keegan dismisses us, and I walk back to my room. I don't

join in the cries of excitement the others partake in. I hear them down the halls as they run to their rooms to begin packing. I feel completely sober. I feel ready, but not overjoyed to fight. My father taught me that making great sacrifices always comes with a great price.

I breathe deep when I enter my room and gaze around. I don't own much—some clothing, my ring, Alyssa's book, and Zeus. Zeus's ears perk up as he lies sprawled over my tiny cot. I can't help but laugh at his dangling legs. He may not be mine, but I'm thankful he showed up in my room late last night and comforted me while I reread my father's letter. He lies his head back down, leaving me little space to work around him.

I sigh. I hate losing my privacy and my only outlet— painting. I only have one wall left, but it seems like such a waste. *All that hard work for nothing.*

I begin tossing things together for the move to the new wing of the complex. As I'm packing, I look down at my hands. I stop for a moment and turn them over. They're covered in callouses, hardened from training, and tested repeatedly. I look at my knuckles now. I can see where they used to bleed out in those first few weeks of training. But now, they're just white scars. I hold my hands in front of my face and inspect my filed-down nails. I drop them down, push Zeus over, and sit on my bed as I put Alyssa's book on top of my pile.

My hands remind me of myself. I was a blister. I was rubbed constantly raw by life. I broke open and oozed with pain when my mother accused me, when Alyssa died, and when I read the letter written by my father before his death. I laugh, startling myself.

But now, I'm a callous. I'm not desensitized to the pain, just conditioned to withstand it.

"What's on your mind?" Keegan stands in my doorway, his eyes intent on my face. I startle and my hands fly to my gun before I realize who it is.

"Sheesh, when will you learn not to do that crap? It scares me to death every time."

"Never, I guess." He grins. "How'd you like my

announcement today? Pretty sweet stuff, right?"

I turn away from him. "Yeah sure."

"Out of all those groups, we get the Commander." He stops and realizes I'm not smiling. "You should be happy, Lexi. It's finally payback time."

I exhale. "I am."

"Lexi, you don't fool me." He puts his hand on my shoulder. His eyes radiate excitement. I compose my face and control my voice in order to keep from making him mad. "What are you worried about?"

"Do you honestly believe we're capable of getting in? I mean…do we have the weapons and skills to even stand a chance?"

He flinches. "Damn, you're gloomy." He shakes his head at me. "Of course I do. I wouldn't risk all our lives if I had any doubt, any doubt at all, which obviously I don't. And in all seriousness, don't you believe it's worth the cost?" He juts out his chest as he speaks.

"Yes, you know how I feel."

"Then think about it, if this works and we win, then we'll have the power to do things the way we want. We'll be able to take back everything we lost and make *them* pay." He lifts my head with his hand. "Imagine that. Imagine the sweet revenge you'll have for your branding. For taking our father—for taking everything away from us." The change in his tone gives me goose bumps. His words are hard like steel and just as cold. "Giving society the chance to live like they once did."

"It's not so much the revenge for me. I just want things to be right. That's all I want." I shrug his arm off my shoulders. The hunger for violence in his eyes makes me uncomfortable. The brother I just recognized is again lost to the warrior he has become.

"If you're having second thoughts about fighting—"

"I'm not," I say sharply. "I'm in this till the end." I soften my voice then. "Only because you make it seem possible, you make it feel real…and that's all the hope I need."

He gives me a hug and steps back with his hands on my

shoulders. "Good." He moves to leave and stops. "Oh, I almost forgot, in two days we're throwing a shindig. Well, more like a celebration of the revolt. Make sure you keep Cole and that idiotic dog under control. Neither of us need more trouble."

"There won't be any trouble, I promise."

My head feels scrambled after he walks out. I tuck my precious letter inside Alyssa's book and slide it into my small duffel bag. I may not have much, but what I own is priceless. I motion to Zeus, and he follows me out into the dim hallway one last time. I glance back and take one last look at my drawling. *Here goes nothing.*

A complex maze of tunnels link together, forming a vast underground that I didn't know existed when I first arrived. I stumble my way to our barracks by following Zeus and watching for familiar faces. I hear them before I see them. Wing C is small, though, and darker. Light bulbs dangle intermittently along the narrow tunnels. Water drips down and mud forms, immediately coating my boots with a thick crust. I feel goose bumps push up on my arms when I imagine all the creepy crawly things that could be hiding in the dark. But I straighten my shoulders and keep moving, knowing I have a much bigger enemy to face in a few days' time.

When we finish dinner, our group chooses bunks in a damp room. The doorway opens into a narrow hall between crude wooden bunks that line each side of the room. Metal dressers sit in between each bunk, but they're barely big enough for three days' worth of clothing. I notice that all of us—male and female—share the crowded space. Keegan takes the bed closest to the doorway. Sheldon bunks directly across from him and winks as I pass. I mumble a hello and take an empty bunk at the back of the room because I don't want to be too close to everyone. I fight with the drawers on the metal dresser next to my bed. They screech as I pull them out and place my meager belongings inside. Zeus lies down uneasily and whines.

After settling in, we meet with Keegan in the control room. He pulls up a hologram of the Commander's residence. I feel my eyes widen at the size of the place but I quickly focus. It's large, concrete, and attached to the main outer wall of the Hole. It looks familiar, and my memory of it is validated when I realize it's located next to the entrance of the Hole. I saw it when Cole escorted me in.

Keegan's rubbing the back of his neck, and I can see the beads of sweat rolling off his tattooed head. "Next question. Anyone?"

A hand raises and he acknowledges the person with his eyes. "Yeah, how exactly are we getting in? The doors look like they're made of—" the man says with his hand still in the air.

"Thick metal, I know." Keegan zooms in on the picture with his remote. "The only way to open them is by using the keypad or blowing them." He smiles but it fades quickly. "The entrance to the main compound is at the top of the wall, so we'll get there by using a back staircase. The stairs are loaded with guards, so be prepared for that. Sheldon you'll go first and clear the way for the others." My eyes flick to where Sheldon sits and his head nods enthusiastically.

"We'll wait for his signal and then proceed. When we get to the doors, Isaac will detonate them." Keegan steeples his fingers. "More?" He raises his eyebrows as someone else's pops up.

"All right, say we get inside. Then what?" a man asks.

Keegan exhales. "Unfortunately, we can't predict what we'll encounter once we're inside. But luckily Sutton was able to get a rough map of the residence, but the copy is a few years old, so things could've changed. I want every single one of you to memorize it anyway. There're enough copies for everyone. Look, I know it's a lot to absorb, but we're running out of time." Keegan hands out maps to each person, and I watch as their heads lower to inspect their maps simultaneously.

I open my map and follow the lines. The specs for the residence are palatial. I see everything from normal bedrooms, dining rooms, and bathrooms to the observatory room, where supposedly the Commander watches the sinners.

"What about the other groups' objectives? Will any of them be joining forces with us?" I look up at a girl with purple hair. Keegan nods.

"Good question, Veronica. A few groups will be attacking the head training center that's located on the hospital's ground floor. Others are leaders of safe groups that'll blow holes in the outer wall to free innocents who can't fight, and some will build roadblocks to try to prevent the guards from interfering with the whole operation. And so on." He continues. "One other group is supposed to assist us, but it's only for backup. Otherwise, we're on our own. That's why I selected the best of the best for my group." I freeze as he says those last words.

"If there's nothing else, go back to your bunks, and breathe this map. Sutton will go over the main details at a later time." Keegan turns off the hologram and dismisses us.

We return to our bunks, exhausted, and I curl up with Zeus and open my map. The Commander's residence looks huge. Dread permeates my soul as I trace the hallways with my fingers like I'm painting. Late at night, someone turns off the lights. I fall into a fitful sleep while twirling the ring around my finger.

"Lexi," a soft, familiar voice says. I struggle to clear the fog from my brain as the face comes into focus. "Don't be afraid. It's just me." I rub my eyes.

"Who?"

"It's Mommy, Lexi," she says. I feel her hair brush over my face and then I see her blue eyes. I jump away from her touch.

"What're you doing?" I feel groggy. My arm burns, and I can't seem to move my body where I want it to go. "Go away! Leave me alone, and don't ever come back." I try to muster more strength in my voice but my words come out limp and weak.

"You'll understand some day, I promise," she says. She kisses my forehead and I roll over. I feel confused, but the darkness is so heavy that I don't care.

When I wake, I lie on my back for a few minutes, digesting my dream. I feel my fists clench and I have to control my breathing. I don't want to think of my mother as anything but evil, but I can't square that with whom she was when my father was alive. It makes no sense. *Nothing makes sense.* I pull myself out of bed and shake my head. Sometimes I wonder what dreams were real and what dreams weren't. I remember one dream; she was crying and holding me as her body shook uncontrollably. She whispered in my ear over and over that she was sorry I had to go through all of this. That it would all be over soon. "Only a few more left, Lexi," she told me. *But what did she mean? Did she know about the torture? Only a few of what was left?* I shake it off. It's not worth it to dwell on that part of the past. I only want to look ahead. I tie my hair back and loosen up my limbs. At least I have Keegan, Sutton, and hopefully, Cole. That's all I need. *Oh, and of course Zeus.*

Two days pass, full of training and tactics. I feel like I live on a mat, practicing ground fighting techniques. And I sleep with my gun under my pillow and a knife strapped to my pants. I feel as prepared as possible. If Cole hasn't been caught, he'd certainly be proud of my progress. Most of the time, I try not to think about what he's doing, only because I don't want to give myself a panic attack. Before I know it, I'm chewing on my bottom lip and it's bleeding. *He's alive, he'll fight with us.*

Electricity flows through the atmosphere due to the party directly after the evening training session. I can tell everyone's ready to blow off steam by the lack of focus at the end of our session. Keegan throws his hands up in the air a half an hour early.

"I'm letting you go a little early today. You deserve a break. Have a good time, get smashed for all I care. Just make sure you're ready for when the time comes." Everyone whoops loud and runs out of the training area, including me.

All the late nights, concentrations on maps, and combat has worn me down. Looking into the mirror, the reflection staring back at me is ghastly. I let my hair down over my shoulders. I feel someone nudge my arm, and when I glance right, Veronica is putting deep, dark lipstick on. She smiles and then smacks her lips together.

"Try this," she says. She tosses me her mascara. "It'll make your eyes pop even more."

Nervously, I apply the mascara. "I have no clue what I'm doing," I say. I shake my head, looking at my reflection. "But these bags under my eyes are really attractive."

"Girl, you know you're sexy. The guys won't be able to stop staring at your eyes," Veronica says as she pins up her hair. "You'll have first pick, that's for sure."

"Oh no, that's all you." I hand her back her mascara and make a face.

"Oh really? Then why are you so worried about your eye bags?" She laughs and it echoes off the walls of the bathroom.

"I'm not, really."

"So why are you staring at yourself, making that weird face?"

"Because it doesn't look like me… I've never worn makeup before. My mother wouldn't allow it." I lean against the wall and watch her as she lines her eyes and curls her lashes.

"Well, makeup or not, you're beautiful," she says.

"Thanks," I say with a shy smile. I'm not the best when it comes to compliments.

She stops and looks at me directly. "Look, tonight, try to loosen up a little. Have fun!"

I shrug. Maybe I should let go for a little. Maybe I should try to have fun. *After all, this could be my last opportunity.*

We enter the main training room, which has been decorated. I laugh out loud when I see the training ammunition from the machine guns strung across the ceiling. A good-looking, red-branded sinner offers free tattoos in the well-lit back corner of the room. People mingle with tiny plastic cups in their hands. Two long tables sit with a banquet of food laid out and drinks for all.

"Drink for Keegan's sister?" I turn and a man offers me a clear cup with something sparkling inside. My eyes meet Veronica's, and I nod my head. She smiles, and Keegan joins us.

"Cheers, ladies! To insurrection and our last party!" He

laughs and downs an entire cup. Some of it trickles down his chin.

"Cheers!" I find myself saying. My shoulders relax and warmth fills my body as I sip from my cup. I feel so good I soon grab another.

"Keegan, are you getting drunk?" I say.

"No, just relaxing a bit." He winks at me. "Don't worry I can handle myself."

Pretty soon, people fill up the room. The music blasts from an old-school, beat-up piece of crap boom box that Keegan somehow managed to rebuild. Everyone dances even as their drinks spill. I laugh out loud as Keegan pulls me around, introducing me to others and giving me more to drink.

"Hey, Ryder, my man," Keegan shouts to a guy standing with his back toward us. "Wanna give Lexi a tattoo?" Keegan grabs my hand and I shake it loose.

My face heats up. I smack Keegan's chest and spin around before Ryder gets a glimpse of me. "I told you I don't want one, you idiot!" I can't stop smiling. Even Zeus gives up following me and takes a post by the door.

I pan the room, watching as Veronica's hair falls out of her pins and flings around in wild circles while she dances. Sheldon relaxes at a table with a girl I don't know. I raise an eyebrow when I spot Keegan kissing a woman with long, dark hair. I see a guy I don't recognize fill Keenan's cup that sits on the table behind him. The music slows, and people partner up. My inhibitions are dulled, but I still refuse to dance with anyone. I sit next to Zeus and lean on him.

"Dance with me." I'd recognize that voice anywhere.

I look up and Cole stands there, hand outstretched. He wears different clothes, and smells like he just hopped out of the shower. I blink to make sure I'm not imagining him.

"You're here!" I jump into his arms a little too enthusiastically, and he laughs. I feel tears of joy trickle down my face. "I'm so relieved you're okay!" He puts me down and I step back. "How'd you get in here?" His eyes bulge out of his head as he puts his arms back around me.

"You're all muscle and brick now, Lexi. I can't believe it." His eyes look troubled and I don't miss that he ignores my question. "Come, dance with me...please?"

He begs with his eyes, and I can't refuse him.

I take his hand, forgetting everything around me, and follow him onto the floor. He holds me close as we dance. I press my head against his chest, breathing in his familiar scent. Just being this close is enough. His hands rest on my lower back, and my skin burns at his touch.

"When we get out of here, I'm not leaving you, even if you think it's what's best for me," Cole whispers in my ear.

"And what about Keegan?" I say.

"I'm assuming he'll be joining us?"

"Yes, he will."

"Go figure." Cole lets out a long sigh.

I close my eyes and say. "He just needs the chance to get to know you, then he'll come around.

"We'll see." Cole kisses the top of my head.

"Cole, I don't want to discuss this. Please, just dance with me. Don't ruin this." The lights around us glow and blur as tears fill my eyes.

He remains silent as if agreeing with me. I glance up at his sharp jawline and his full lips. How I want to kiss the scar that runs through his lip. I reach up and touch his face, and he leans down. I begin to pull him in, my heart beating faster, and the music stops.

"I hope everyone's enjoying the party. This could possibly be our last night together. So, I wanted to take this opportunity to thank all of you, who have joined the revolt... Do you remember the first party we had? Our force was so small and smelly...and Sutton helped me to—"

The loudspeaker cuts off, and no one dances anymore.

"I do believe Keegan's wasted," I hear someone say.

"That's because some dude keeps filling his drink," another man says.

"What?" I say to the man. He turns to me and shrugs his shoulders.

"Don't worry about it," Cole says. "Your brother's going to be just fine."

My eyes widen and I say to Cole. "How do you know that?"

"Lexi, chill out!" Cole says.

"Did you have something to do with it?"

"Stop it. He's coming over to us."

I see Keegan pushing his way through the crowd with a different girl on his arm. I push Cole away, shaking my head. He looks confused and hurt, but I can't think about that. Keegan stumbles up and grabs my shoulder.

"What are you doing?" Keegan says. His eyes dart to Cole and back to me. "Are you purposely trying to piss me off?"

Sensing danger, I step between them and put my hand on Keegan's chest. "No, not at all. Just calm down! We were only talking. And he was just about to leave." I feel instantly sober, like someone threw a glass of cold water into my face.

His eyes squint, and he leans left into the girl, who laughs. We stand opposite, and I wait for a fight to break out, but Keegan abruptly turns away. After I'm sure he's gone, I turn back to Cole.

"You should probably go," I say while glancing at the floor. I don't want him to go, but the last thing we need is another fight to break out between them. Plus, alcohol makes Keegan even less predictable than before.

"Look at me, I'm just as much a part of this group as he is, and I'm risking my life as well," he says while grabbing my hand.

The very thought makes me sick. "That's not what I meant. Of course you can be here. I just think it's best for both of us… if you don't hang around *me*."

"You can still back out. You don't have to do this. Nobody will judge you."

"Absolutely not! I need to do this for myself, for my father, and for us. Not once, in my life was I given the opportunity to fight for anything I believed in. Now here I stand, and I have the chance to make a difference, to at least try. And I'm ready to break free." I pull away my hand, regardless of how much I want him to hold it. "Just promise me you won't die, because losing you would—"

"Lexi, I'm not going anywhere. You and I, we're going to get out of here, make no mistake about that."

My heart breaks into tiny pieces. It's hard to even imagine what life would be like without him. "Cole, you know I love you, right?"

"Of course I do." His lips touch mine and I lean into him, breathing in the moment.

"Dude, we've gotta bounce. I'm freaking tired," Bruno says placing a hand on Cole's shoulder, interrupting our moment. "Sorry, man, I'll give you two a minute." Bruno winks at me and I smile.

Before I know it, Cole's lips press against mine again. He pulls my body against his and holds me securely in his arms, like it's our last time. *And it might be.*

I put my hands on each side of his face and pull his head down until his forehead rests on mine.

Bruno taps Cole's shoulder. "Come on, lover boy. Time's up."

Cole releases me without taking his eyes off mine. "Till then." Then he turns and follows Bruno out.

Instantly, I feel my heart leap out of my chest and I want to run after him. But I tell myself no. I feel all twisted inside, like someone's wringing out my soul. My head throbs and I suddenly feel alone and out of place.

Everyone's drunk and I've had enough, so I don't feel bad leaving. I whistle for Zeus and he follows me back the long winding way to wing C. As I sit on my bed and pull off my boots, I realize I'm the only person in the room. It's eerily quiet, but I'm comforted with Zeus by my side. He climbs into bed with me. I turn on my side, inching back as far as I possibly can without falling off. He lays his head on my pillow next to mine, with his back against my chest and I wrap my one arm around him. I might not have Cole, but I've got Zeus, and because of him, I somehow manage to fall asleep.

Early morning, someone pukes on the floor. I hear a groan and watch a shadow crawl to the bathroom. Lifting my head slowly, I wait for the nausea to pass. Maybe I shouldn't have drunk so much. I feel like a hammer pounds away at the back of my skull. *Ugh.* My muscles creak as I sit up. I must've slept through everyone coming back last night, and I'm strangely okay with that. Zeus hops off my bed as I stand. I hold the wall for a minute and focus my eyes. I slept in my makeup and didn't change my clothes because they smell of Cole. It wafts to my nose and brings a smile to my face. *At least that was worth it.*

"Everyone up. Training's in fifteen minutes," a voice shouts into the room.

I hear a collection of groans in reply. After removing the oily stuff from my face, I'm first to arrive in the training room. I start running to warm up and gradually others appear. I might not feel one hundred percent, but at least I look nothing like the others.

Veronica shuffles in first and gives me a weak smile as she munches on crackers. Her eyes are rimmed with red and I wonder what time she went to bed. I smell Sheldon before I see him. He enters by throwing up in a trashcan on the edge of the room. When he's done, he wipes his face with his sleeve. What a bunch.

"Where's Keegan?" I say.

"I'm sure he's waiting for us in the training center," Veronica says. "He's always on time."

Of course Veronica is right. Keegan stands in the training room with his arms folded across his chest, leaning against the wall. We begin running sprints to warm up and then sit down to stretch. His eyes are blood red and sunken. His face is pale, and he carries a bottle of water.

Sheldon heaves again, making a god-awful retching sound. It almost makes me puke just listening to him.

"Seriously, if you're that sick, you should probably go lie down and rest," I say.

"No. If you party like an animal, then you train like one,"

Keegan says. "Now, everyone line up."

Sheldon stands at attention, but looks miserable, along with everyone else. Okay, so maybe last night wasn't such a good idea. If the revolt were to start now, we wouldn't make it fifty feet.

"Let's go! Start with a 'knees to the core' work out," Keegan shouts.

We all choose partners and begin kneeing each other across the room. My poor partner looks green. I'm scared if I knee him one more time, he's going to barf all over me. In fact, the session ends with most of the group puking in the trashcan. It smells deplorable so I hold my nose before I get sick.

We train for what feels like hours when finally Keegan holds up his hand for us to stop. "All right, everyone head back. Grab something to eat and rest up. Tonight's the night we finalize the plan. Come tomorrow, the revolt will show its ugly head."

I might be the only person who isn't barfing, but I'm tired. I can't shake Cole's face from my memory, how troubled his dark eyes seemed last night.

"Hey, wait up. Who was the amazingly handsome guy you were dancing with last night?" I turn around and see Veronica, shuffling behind me.

"Just a friend," I say. *The only reason I've survived the last few months.* My head rewinds the night. I didn't think anyone noticed Cole and me dancing together since most of them were pretty sloshed.

"Wasn't he a guard?" She tilts her head while looking at me.

I exhale. "He was."

She doesn't say anything else, and I don't elaborate. Lying in my bunk with Zeus after training, I relive the night over and over in my head.

Training in the evening is light, but I feel the heaviness in the air at the meeting afterward. All the groups from Keegan's sector meet in the command center again and details of the operation are laid out for all to inspect. I watch as Sutton points to areas of strategic importance while the leaders ask him questions. Then he moves to speak to all of us.

"Timing is everything. If even one group is late, the whole operation could collapse. Coordination is imperative. It's risky, but it has to be done in order to disarm the guards. If not done properly, the guards could rearm or reinforce themselves for a stronger assault. We have to take control before that happens," he says. "Keegan's group will assault the main compound and take the Commander into custody. My group will assist in blowing the main gate open and backing up Keegan's group. Bruno's group will lead the main assault on the headquarters." Sutton continues speaking, but I look around for Cole and Bruno.

They sit in front with maps sprawled out before them. I can see Cole marking his map using a red pen while Bruno compares their routes.

I wish I could hear what they're saying. By chance, Cole glances up at me and then back down at his map. His lips form a frown, his face heavy with concentration. Sutton's voice becomes background noise as I watch him.

Keegan rubs the snake tattoo that wraps around his head and cracks his neck. He's antsy, his hands constantly busy. In fact, his posture mirrors that of all the citizens. They shift their positions and whisper questions to their neighbors as Sutton pulls up another hologram of the Hole. At the conclusion, we break into our small groups. Spying on Cole, I see him rendezvous with his squad.

"We'll begin at 0300. Now I know sleeping will be difficult, but try your best," Keegan says as we huddle. As I look around, his words fall upon solemn faces. The joy experienced by all at the party fades as we contemplate tomorrow.

Trying to snatch a glimpse of Sutton and Cole as I leave is impossible. Too many people embrace and say their good-byes in the control room. I'm not tempted to cry. I just want to do the one thing I was meant for, the one thing my father wanted me to accomplish—for him and for all of us. In the end, that's the most important thing.

No one sleeps. Whispers of prayers echo throughout the room. I swear I hear someone sniffling, but I can't tell where it comes from. I'm pretty sure no one will close their eyes tonight.

I lie under my blanket, peering at the map of the Commander's quarters. It looks impossible to breach. I sigh and fold it up while rolling onto my back. I wonder what Cole is thinking right now. I didn't get to say good-bye, but maybe that's better for both of us. I just wish I could tell him I'll be waiting for him afterward. I wish I had the opportunity to hug Sutton and to let him know I'm not mad at him. But that never happened.

Most of all, I wish for peace. If I survive this, all I want is to live with Cole and Keegan and to live in peace for the rest of my life, knowing I made the right choice.

CHAPTER 21

The blaring alarm wakes us up, or in my case, gets me out of bed. I barely slept a wink. I hear Keegan's voice shouting through a megaphone.

"This is it!" Keegan's voice carries throughout our room. "Let's do this!"

Bodies jump up and wrestle with their clothes in the dark. I can hear them bumping around between the furniture. I lace up my boots, check to make sure my knife's tightly tucked into my side, and pull my gun from beneath my pillow. I feel like a robot, too tired to think, and too wired to want to. In my haste to get out of the room, I trip over Zeus in the dark, and let out a curse word. Not the way I want things to begin.

We're lined up in the dim hall as Keegan evaluates us. He moves up and down, his boots making thumping sounds as he inspects our equipment. I watch as he stops next to Isaac and helps him pull his harness over his shoulders. His eyes move back and forth over each item, like he's checking off each item in his head.

"All right, my man, you're good to go." He slaps Isaac on the shoulder and moves on. He joins Sheldon handing out supplies like helmets, jackets, and extra ammunition. He makes eye contact with each person who stands before him. I admire him—his calm demeanor, relaxed posture, and solid blue eyes that drip with confidence.

I step forward. Keegan stops. He looks straight into my eyes. I don't notice anything else, just him. Here we are, after so much time, going into battle together. I see the little boy with curly hair who used to put gum in mine. I remember the boy who always found the best places to hide when we'd play hide and seek, and it took me hours to find him. I see so much of my father in him. It makes me proud. From the intensity of his gaze, I can tell he's proud of me too. He snaps out of it, hands me a helmet, and some ammunition.

"Thank you," I say in a low voice. "Wherever you go, I'll follow."

He clears his throat, and I see his eyes glaze over just a little. "We can overcome anything, Lexi." He gives me a tight smile and moves on to the next person. "We're going to succeed."

Next thing I know, we're standing in a tunnel that heads out into the Hole. All I can hear is the shallow breathing of those around me. And prayers. Some people whisper prayers while we wait for the command to go. *Say one for me too.* I feel the strap from my helmet digging into my chin, and I loosen it. I figure if I've survived this much already, one overly tight strap won't keep me alive.

I watch as an arm, bent at the elbow, motions for us to hold. I hate rushing to get ready and then being forced to wait in full gear, sweating like a pig on a roast. Then a few minutes later, it pumps, telling us to move out. I grit my teeth and shake my body loose. *Here it goes...I can and will do this!*

In a silent parade, we step out into the empty streets. It takes me a few minutes to gather where we are. The moonlight glints off our equipment, and I can see another squad move away from us toward the hospital. Their figures fade into the early hours of morning. *Good luck, my friends.* I hope this is all over soon.

Sweat trickles down my nose within minutes. I can taste the familiar dust in my mouth and smell the trash lying out in the open. Every second feels like hours. My shirt's already sticking to my back and I wipe the sweat from my brow. I glance around at my squad. An array of assault rifles stolen or bribed from the guards mingles within our group. Some people, like Keegan, have M16s while others, like myself, carry handguns with knives as a secondary weapon. I like what I have. It's lighter and gives me the ability to move faster.

I look left, right, and then left again. We need to get to our destination before the rest of the groups proceed. I breathe hard and fast as I sprint across a road behind Keegan. I turn around and wave on the next person, who crosses behind me. I'm wide-awake from the adrenaline running through my veins. My eyes take in everything around us—every piece of trash, broken fencing, mud-caked and sunburned roofs of the tin shack houses that line the thin street. My mind contemplates the plan while staying fully alert for enemies.

Sutton set it up so each team would assault various points of strategic importance at the same time with the hope of causing mass confusion within the guard structure. I hope with all that's in me that it works. We've all witnessed the havoc the guards can wreak when prepared. Now, we'll find out how they act when assaulted. *For a change.*

I allow my mind to drift to Cole—where he is, how he feels, if he's thinking of me too. *Of course he is.* I carefully wrap the memory of his face inside my heart and close it for later. I need to focus on each step and thinking of him only draws my attention away from my mission. I turn off that switch and bring myself back to the present.

Sheldon slinks away and I follow him with my eyes, amazed at his agility. For all his bulk, he moves with finesse and motions us to advance forward. I can barely hear the sound of his footsteps on the cement, even with all of his equipment strapped on. Even Zeus can't make movements that subtle.

Keegan follows Sheldon across the street and then turns to wave me on. I can tell he's tense by his rigid movements. For a brief moment our eyes meet, he's stoic and he gives nothing away about his feelings. But my eyes are wide, my teeth are clenched and I'm blinking fast. His finger rests next to the trigger of his gun, ready for the slightest change of plans.

Sheldon holds his fist up, halting our progression. Keegan immediately squats down, and I can see his knuckles turning white from how hard he's gripping his M16. I kneel on one knee and listen. Someone's crying. I can tell by its shrill pitch that whoever it is, is terrified.

"Mommy! I want my mommy!" And then I know it's a child. I look to Keegan, whose lips press together in a grimace.

Sheldon back steps, reaches around Keegan, and grips my shirt. I flick my gaze to his face. His sweat seeps down over the creases in his forehead. He motions me forward.

"Get her to shut up," he whispers roughly. I give him a blank look.

"Me?"

"Yes, you, damn it. You're a woman. Help her."

I bite my lip, inching ahead of him. I know we need to make her stop. If we can hear her loud and clear, then so can the guards if they're around. I come to the edge of a small, concrete shack and peek around the corner, into an alley.

She looks at me with wide, wet eyes. "Where's my mommy?" she whimpers. Her eyes bulge when Zeus steps into the alley beside me.

"Shhh, shhh. It'll be okay." I gently scoop her into my arms. She's light as a bird and reminds me of Alyssa. I push her hair from her face and see she's not branded. "He won't hurt you, I promise. He only eats bad guys." She smiles. "I'll try to find your mommy, but if I can't, do you think you can find a really good hiding spot…until she comes for you?" I whisper. The little girl stares at me with frightened eyes. "Do you think you can do that?" Again she says nothing. "Don't you worry, your mommy's looking for you, and she'll come." I'm not convinced that's true, but I'm not sure what else to say. She's burning up our time. "Is this your house, here?" I look into the window. She nods.

When I come back around front holding her, Sheldon and Keegan's eyes widen. I shake my head. "I know she can't come with us, but we can't just leave her here. Please, Keegan, just help me get her inside," I whisper before they can protest.

Sheldon pushes open the door, while Keegan steps inside, sweeping the room with his gun. He jumps back as a woman stands up, holding her hands in the air. "I'm sorry, I'm just looking for my baby girl, I can't find her anywhere," she says. "I swear…I've done nothing wrong, I didn't leave her alone in the streets!" she stutters. "She sleepwalks sometimes, and I'm worried sick something's happened to her." She swallows.

"Please, I promise I won't get in your way…I just need to find her." I step inside the small one-room house with the little girl, shaking in my arms. Keegan stands down.

"Calm down. We're not guards," Keegan says in a low voice. "We're not going to hurt you."

"Ma'am, is this your daughter?" I stop and the woman rushes to me, plucking her from my arms.

"Oh my God, Kelsey…you scared me half to death!" Tears burst from her eyes. I watch as Kelsey clings to her mom the way I used to do to my mother when I was younger. I put my hand on her shoulder, and her mom looks up at me, her eyes glazed over.

"I don't want to scare you, but stay inside. Hide under your table or find friends who'll protect you." I back pedal into the doorway.

"How can I repay you?" the woman says.

"We were never here. You never saw us. Do you understand?" She nods and pulls her daughter even closer. "Thank you," she whispers. I nod back to her and shut the door. I'm not sure if she's thanking me for finding her daughter or if she's thanking me for something else. I sense more to it though.

Once outside, Sheldon gives a deliberately quiet exhale and begins moving forward. Keegan looks up at the sky, exhales, and seems to refocus himself.

"You did well," he whispers to me. Then without another word, he takes off behind Sheldon. We trek a few more blocks this way. I've already put the little girl and her mommy into the back of my mind. My breathing evens out, and I make every move with a precise sharpness.

That's when I see it. In front of us, in the distance, looms the stark outline of the main wall surrounding the Hole. I suck in my breath and release it. *Almost there.*

With every block navigated, we get closer and closer. Pretty soon, my neck hurts from staring up at it. I blink as my sweat burns my eyes and it stings, forcing me to squint. The thick cement blocks grow larger and more intimidating as we converge on them. They tease us with their steadfast reputation and their unwillingness to allow our freedom. No one has ever escaped the Hole. Either the guards caught them, shot them as they attempted to slip away, or they weren't strong enough to climb out.

But we've come to change that.

Sheldon creeps into a shanty butted up against the barrier in order to avoid the cameras. Keegan follows, then me, and the others. Once inside, I see a metal bowl on the table with some kind of mush left inside. Steam rises off it, so the owner hasn't been gone long. Zeus puts his face in it and slurps it up, knocking it to the floor and making a loud clanging noise. I snatch it away. My insides freeze and I tighten my stomach muscles with anticipation. Sheldon tosses me a nasty glare and Keegan's eyes slant.

"Watch that dog, will you?" he whispers. I pull Zeus to my side and hold my breath. The rest of our group piles into the small shack, forcing us all against each other. I hear the elbows smacking and equipment banging into the sparse furniture. I bite the inside of my cheek. Any trained person within hearing distance had to have heard that.

So far, too good. The lack of surveillance has me unnerved. *Wouldn't the guards have noticed by now?* The silence screams the obvious, for nothing is ever quiet around here. The hair rises on the back of my neck and I wipe the sweat off my hand on my pants before I grip my Glock again. I feel all jumpy inside. *What is that old saying? If something can go wrong, it probably will.*

Just then, I feel a deep rumble and hear the metallic clanking of a tank slowly ambling down the street outside. My eyes lock onto Keegan's, fearing the worst. He quickly motions for all of us to lower ourselves, so we immediately duck below the window and wait for it to pass. I press my back against the wall, holding Zeus's head to my chest. I can feel him growling in his belly. The faded, red, torn curtains blow lightly from the window and I can see the tank. Its large figure and painted camouflage do nothing to hide its formidable appearance. My blood curdles and adrenaline pumps through my limbs. I can feel my heart pounding away. *Get us out of here.*

When the tank finally passes by I hear boots. Lots of them. Beads of sweat form over my lips but I do nothing to wipe them away. I push myself as far back into the wall as I can. It reminds me of when they came for me, the first time. I feel dread crawling through my insides.

Keegan pushes against the wall the same way I do. His eyes look up and his lips move silently. *Is he praying?*

"Halt!" One of them shouts. I clench my gun, ready for them to discover us. Keegan's hand moves to mine. I look at him, and he shakes his head, no.

"Where's Hoyt?" the voice asks. I hear a mumbled answer. "Well, he better catch his ass back up to us." I hear the boots of a single person tromping around. "Since we're here and everyone's being lazy, drop and give me twenty!" I hear the groaning response of several male soldiers.

Just then, Zeus makes a snuffing sound. I suck in my breath and feel Keegan go rigid next to me.

"Did you hear that?" the voice asks.

"No, sir," another answers.

"Well I did. Hurry, go look around," the male, I'm guessing the leader, orders.

"What about Hoyt?"

"Who gives a shit about Hoyt? When he catches up, I'll give him latrine duty."

I open my eyes wider. I can almost feel them breathing down my neck. The atmosphere inside the shack is tense with trigger-ready fingers and copious sweating. I swear the guard's standing at the window, staring at us.

One, two, three seconds pass.

I wait for shouting or shooting, I'm not sure which. I just know they'll discover us. Zeus begins to squirm next to me and my body goes rigid. But thankfully, the sound of feet approaching covers up any sounds he makes.

"Hoyt, you're a douchebag and a lousy guard. Tonight's your night for latrine duty." I can hear the other guards laughing, presumably after doing their pushups. "All right men, move out."

Finally, the squad of guards passes by the window. I can hear them moving in unison, thumping into the distance. I shut my eyelids, willing them to go without seeing us. I bite down with my teeth, flexing my jaw. Zeus whimpers. I realize I'm squeezing him too tight and relax my grip. But just a little.

Then it's quiet like death.

"Holy crap that was close," I whisper to myself.

Keegan turns his head and nods while exhaling. "Too close."

Sheldon's the first to stand and peek outside. I watch as he twists his body around the corner, his gun ready. He waits a moment and then motions us forward using hand signals. I stop to listen intently. Nothing.

He disappears into the darkness; next is Keegan, and then I follow with Zeus. I step out of the door, crouch down, and look for Keegan's signal to head for the stairwell that leads to the top of the wall. It's a small, unnoticeable opening to those who don't know it's there. My eyes strain as I focus on his silent movements. Clenching my jaw, I sprint to him. I turn, look around, and seeing nothing, I motion Isaac forward.

Just as Isaac is about to follow suit, shots split the air, tinging off the metal roofing of the shacks. *So much for surprise.* I crouch down and watch as he dives for cover near the wall, grimacing under the weight of his load-bearing harness. He belly crawls, cringing every time dust spits up around him. I lean forward, making myself a target. But I can barely reach him.

"Come on!" I scream at him. The volume of the guns deafens me until all I can do is watch Isaac's mouth move. He's yelling back, but I can't tell what he's saying. My insides jump with each shot. The tracers light up the dark sky, giving off an eerie red glow. Isaac's eyes bulge and dirt is smeared across his forehead.

"Move, damn it!" I'm screaming while reaching out. His sweaty fingertips meet mine, and I yank him inside the small mouth of the stairwell, knowing the worst is yet to come. My heart thumps rapidly in my chest as I slam back into the cement.

I watch as Keegan motions frantically for the rest of the group. After watching Isaac cross and seeing the amount of tracers zipping through the darkness, they hesitate. I can see the whites of their eyes widen as if the Grim Reaper himself beckons them to hell. In their moment of indecision, an explosion rocks us to our knees, and confusion abounds.

When I look again, all that's left of them are bits and pieces of flesh, combined with the pungent smell of smoke. My helmet disappears in the concussion and searing pain hits me like a jackhammer. It feels like my head is on fire, and I grasp at an object stuck in my hair. Some sort of flaming ember burns my fingertips as I rip it out of my hair and toss it.

Our cover has been blown.

I turn left and see Keegan shouting at me, but I can't hear what he's saying. My left ear rings from the damage and my eyes water from the smoke. I put my hand to my ear, but it does nothing to dull the pounding. The *blam, blam, blamming* of the guard's guns opening up on the wall makes my head throb. I blink my eyes. A few citizens of the Hole spring from their houses with terrified expressions. They glance at me, and I know they can't hear what I'm saying from the bewildered expressions on their faces, so I do the unthinkable.

I step out from the shelter of the wall.

"Take cover, go!" I scream and wave my arms at them to take cover, but not before the guards mow them down with a serenade of bullets. The bullets kick up clouds of dust, heading in my direction, and I squint my eyes.

"Oh shi—"

A hand latches onto my arm and yanks me back into the stairwell. Bullets smash into the place where I was just standing. Focusing on his mouth, his lips form a tight line and I can tell Keegan isn't too happy with me. I can't even process what happened and what I just witnessed.

He saved my life.

Before I can say anything, Keegan runs back outside, directing traffic in chaos while bullets rain down. In the stairwell, Sheldon holds on to Zeus. I gulp air and nod at him, *thank you.* Zeus's teeth are bared and his fur stands straight up as he barks. I put my arms around his neck and wait for the others. One at a time, people crush into the narrow opening.

When I glance back up, I can see Sheldon's eyes tallying up bodies. I know at least one man's down from the constant gunfire, but judging Sheldon's dull eyes, there could be many more. *Or all.*

Bang! Bang! Bang!

I feel flecks of concrete hit me in the face. I duck down, unsure of where to go because I don't know where the shots are coming from. My heart races as the bullets ricochet around me, bouncing around the walls like rubber balls. *We've got to move!*

Keegan slams past me and I lift my head. He fires up the staircase, back at the guards. They have us trapped at the bottom. Another few people cover their heads and dash into the entrance. One gets cut down immediately. He lands on my right foot and I have to step on his body to get away. The heavy gunfire forces us to step back. We're almost out of the staircase and into the street when someone comes in screaming to warn us. I can barely make out the words over the melee.

"What!" I'm screaming back, but it's useless until I read their lips.

"Tank! Tank!"

Oh shit. As the words register, fear envelopes me like a black hole. I can only imagine the horrific power a tank possesses. One shot alone would blow us all away. A chill forces the hairs on my arms to stand on end. The wall of gunfire from up top becomes so intense I feel like I'm living an outer body experience. There's nowhere to hide as the unionized force of the guards rain down bullets that disfigure the walls around us and cut people down. If we don't get out of here, we'll be pinned between the tank and the guards on top of the wall.

I glance at Isaac and his eyes meet mine. His nostrils flare.

In desperation, he pulls a grenade from his harness and lobs it up the steps along with a primal scream.

KABOOM!

I drop down, half covering my head, and half covering Zeus. Then I look up with hesitance after rocks shower us from above. Isaac's chest moves up and down and his eyes look wild. He gives me a brief smile. Then he lobs another one.

KABOOM!

Cement chips hit us like hail in a winter storm. Ash, smoke, and dust cloud the air. But I can't hear the guards answer back.

He just bought us the precious time we needed to get out before it's too late. I jump to my feet and watch as Keegan gives the signal for us to go up the steps. Sheldon starts up first, taking two at a time, gun ready, and begins rapid firing at the guards waiting at the top. I see him take out three of them, but it's such a blur that I feel like I'm not even watching. Keegan follows him with all that's left of us trailing behind. Sweat burns my eyes and I can barely focus as I fire off a slew of rounds.

I attempt squeezing the trigger again and nothing happens. Just a *click, click.*

Damn it, I'm empty. My hands shake as I pull out the spent magazine and slam another one in. Just in time too.

The narrow staircase opens into a wide path on top of the wall edged by barbed wire and manned by more guards. I start shooting again, but stumble over Zeus, who faithfully followed me into the fray. I can feel the bullets zipping past my head when I shove him behind me. I don't want him to get shot.

Sheldon reaches the top and immediately engages two guards. Keegan stabs one from behind, and Sheldon shoots the other one in the stomach. Blood spurts out like a fountain and Sheldon shoves him into the barbed wire wrapped around the outside of the path.

As I clear the last step, a guard grabs me from behind. I gasp as panic surges through me like fire. Remembering the knife stored in my cargo pants, I relax momentarily to reach it, and then I plunge it into my assailant's leg. He grunts with the shock of pain, and as his hands loosen, I spin and stick him again and again in the chest. Watching him fall backward is surreal, but I don't have time to think about it. I glance around me, and everyone is firing off rounds while pushing forward. The guards swarm us like piranhas, taking chunks out of our team bit by bit and shot by shot.

I hear a shrill, penetrating scream and scan the wall. One of the girls from my group has been disemboweled. In her hands, she holds her intestines. A young guard stands in front of her, but hesitates finishing her off with his bloody knife. I fight the urge to puke. I leap over a body, and just as I get there, Zeus jumps in. He snarls as he slams into the guard's body. I watch as the guard and Zeus go tumbling to the cement ground. Zeus hops off after biting the guard's hand. He bares his teeth and foam sticks to his gums. Then the guard whips out his gun and aims it at Zeus.

"No!" I yell. I aim my gun toward the guard and pull the trigger.

He falls to the ground, holding his abdomen. With his unfocused eyes looking at me, I pull the trigger again, finishing him off.

Zeus stands in front of the girl as if protecting her. I see tears tracking down her face, but she's no longer screaming. Her eyes look into the distance. I'm pretty sure she'll be dead in a few minutes without medical attention. I feel torn leaving her, but know I can't stop.

Our situation looks dire. We've lost almost half our team already and we haven't even penetrated the Commander's residence. Then I remember Keegan. *Where is Keegan?* I lock onto him about ten feet away from me.

He's shouting something, his eyes wide and darting around. I can't hear him over the hammering of guns and screaming, so I focus on his mouth. *"Radio for back up!"* He fends off another opponent, slicing his knife through the air and twisting it into the guard. His shirt is covered with sweat and blood splatters. The artist in me thinks it looks like red paint, splashed all over him. I snap back to reality. *It's not paint.* Sheldon moves to find the radio but gets tied up with two guards who resemble beasts. I look around for Isaac, but he's already moved forward to set up the explosives in the main doorway. Despair seeps into my bones like venom as I search for the radio. And then I spot her.

Veronica lies on her side, her face ashen as she holds out the radio. She opens her mouth to speak, but blood trickles out. I duck under a punch and take it from her. My opponent slashes with his knife. I jump back as he barely misses my torso, and Zeus takes him down. He digs his teeth into his wrist with a vicious bite and frees the knife. I pick it up in a flash, and stick the guard in the neck with it.

The screaming and blasts of gunfire unnerve me, and my hands shake under the duress of combat. I fiddle with the buttons, hitting them all while yelling for back up. Everything sounds muffled. I can't hear myself think let alone what I say or what the person on the other side replies.

I drop the radio when another explosion blows out half the wall with a loud *boom*. People stumble over the side, and I leap to grab Keegan's arm as he begins to slip over the edge. He pulls himself upright just in time to see Sheldon plummet over the wall with his adversary.

Oh God, no.

I can see the tank facing the wall from down below, its long barrel pointing up at us. I glance around. There's nowhere else to go. The cement barrier lining the walkway is gutted with twisted pieces of barbed wire dangling over the side. I see the barrel move up and stop.

"Oh sh—" I begin.

It fires again, sending us airborne. Debris collides into me mid-air. I land on my side and cough. I already know I've got bruises all over. I groan and crawl to where I see my brother lying in the rubble. Gray dust poofs over the wall, and now I can't see outside ten feet.

"Keegan!" I'm screaming. My voice echoes in my head, muffled and strange. He blinks his eyes and shakes the particles out of his hair. His face is coated with soot and sweat and dust. I grab his chin.

"We've gotta go!" I scream. He waves me off. So I try again. "Keegan, get up!" He looks around, and blinks. "Now!" Zeus must sense my desperation because he pushes between us and licks Keegan's face. It's like a light goes off in Keegan's head. He jumps to his feet and shoves me aside. I can see his eyes surveying the wall.

This isn't good. I yank Keegan's jacket before he can fixate on the spot where Sheldon used to be. His eyes snap to my face with unbridled fury. The dust settles after a few minutes, and somehow, five people from our team show up. Keegan grabs my arm and the rest of our small group advances under a hailstorm of bullets. With three hundred yards to go, I begin hoping we can pull this off. My eyes can't help but take in our surroundings as we run.

The walkway is littered with rubble, half the width it was when we started. Pieces of barbed wire lie strewn across the middle, the sides, and over the edge. Bodies litter the top of the stairwell. I look out over the Hole. The sun breaches the horizon, reflecting off the metal roofs of the houses and bringing a clear view with it. Smoke billows over the buildings like dark fingers reaching toward the sky to escape the carnage. I grimace at the smell of charred flesh and my eyes burn fiercely. I wipe them with my sleeve. Through the haze, I view the stark outline of the hospital and wonder how the assault on the training center is going.

I trip over a body riddled with holes and keep going. *Come on, Isaac. Come on. Don't fail us now.*

The large main doors of the Commander's residence blow open with a deafening blast that makes the wall beneath us quiver. I feel my knees wobble but don't stop running. Rocks and cement rain down on us and strike our bodies with force. I trip over chunks of cement but Keegan grabs my arm and yanks me forward. Dust mixed with smoke makes sight impossible.

I pull my jacket over my face to breathe. Minutes pass, but they might as well be days. We continue sprinting toward the entrance as bullets zip over our heads. No doubt, the guards will reinforce their lines soon.

I glance back and see more of the rebels have arrived to support us, and relief sweeps through me. *They got my call.*

As we storm the entrance, I notice Sutton off to my right. The hope within me continues to build. I'm breathless from carrying guns and inhaling mouthfuls of thick dust. If Sutton made it, then maybe Cole did.

We slam inside the doorway of the residence. Only eight of us, including me, arrive mostly unscathed. I open my mouth and then close it. I can't believe we've lost so many. We push ourselves as close to the sides as possible to allow the other team to reinforce us. Sutton's team files in, lines the opposite side, and I scan their dirty faces for Cole. I don't see him. I wrinkle my brow and feel my neck muscles tense. *Where could he be?*

"What the hell took you so long!" Keegan shouts.

Sutton's forehead crunches up. "We ran into…" He fires a few shots from his gun. "Some trouble!"

"They knew we were coming," Keegan shouts to Sutton over the war waging behind us. "But how?"

Sutton shrugs his shoulders, lets his gun sling slide to the side, and makes another team member take his place near the door so he can talk to Keegan. "It's possible someone tipped them off," Sutton says. "But, part of the assault wasn't timed properly! Didn't happen fast enough—gave them time to figure it out!" Sutton's voice is raw and his words scratch out. I can barely understand him.

"Where's everybody?" I try yelling to make myself heard.

"All communication was cut off." Sutton's face is covered with a mask of dirt, but I can still see his worried eyes and thinned lips. The gun strapped to him doesn't look natural after being used to seeing him in scrubs. He pulls it back up and holds it in place. He nods to Keegan.

"Let's finish this!" Keegan shouts. With those words, he motions for our team to break off from Sutton's and search the compound for the Commander. We head left down a wide path toward the Commander's personal quarters and Sutton's group heads right toward the main control room. I watch them fade into the darkness, still wondering where Cole is, but too afraid to ask. Knowing we'll rendezvous in the middle doesn't give me confidence.

I bite my lip, and push another magazine into my gun. *Last one.* Keegan leads us since Sheldon disappeared over the wall. I focus on his broad shoulders as we move down the main hallway. It's wide, about five feet across, but the lights flicker. I imagined it'd be nicer inside the main doors, but it's still just cement and incandescent lighting. It reminds me of the transformation center. I swat sweat from my forehead with my free hand and get goose bumps from the cooler temperature inside. Something doesn't feel right. I put my hand on Keegan's shoulder and he stops. He swivels his head to look at me and raises an eyebrow.

The lights buzz. They flicker. Then they burn out.

CHAPTER 22

My first reaction is to squeeze Keegan's shoulder. I turn my eyes toward the ceiling, but can't see anything. I hear him say something, but my ears haven't stopped ringing yet.

He advances, going small steps at a time. My left shoulder rubs against the wall, giving me some point of reference. I grip my gun and keep my finger poised next to the trigger. It reminds me of playing hide and seek in the woods with him. *But this is for keeps.* I focus on breathing and strain my eyes, seeing dark shapes in the hall. I shut my eyes and open them. It's still dark. It plays with my mind, but we press on because this is what we trained for.

Keegan abruptly stops, and I smack into him as Zeus almost bowls me over. He taps my shoulder. I can't even see him. I feel his sweaty hands on my face, trying to push my head down.

"What the hell are you do—?" Then I see it. A thin red line beams horizontally across the hallway. "It's rigged."

He pats me on the shoulder as if saying, *'Way to go, genius.'*

Nausea and fear climb up my insides, but I push them back down. I turn behind me and fumble around, trying to find the next person. I accidentally grab Zeus and he barks, breaking the chilling quiet. I clench my jaw. This is proving much more difficult than I imagined.

I feel a hand come out of nowhere, and I force them to see the beam. Then I step over it cautiously, balancing on the balls of my feet. I swallow hard, search for Keegan, and whisper a prayer.

After a few more feet, I feel Keegan and how the wall turns left. He goes around the corner first. I'm biting my lip as the muscles in my legs twitch. I try to remember where we are from the maps we studied, but it's hard when you can't see anything or know if you missed a turn before.

I count one step, two steps, three steps, four...before I see little glowing red dots light up the wall in front of Keegan. I grab his shoulder, yanking him back. And then a barrage of gunfire blitzes us.

I drop into a squat and fire back. After three shots, I stop shooting back. My gun's nothing compared to the short bursts of gunfire coming down the hall. I don't want to waste all my ammunition either. I put my hand on Keegan. I can feel his arm flexing as he returns fire.

"We're pinned!" he screams. I glance behind me, thinking maybe I can see something, but I don't. I want to cover my ears, but know it won't help. *Where are the others?*

BOOSH!!!

I feel it before I hear it. My body tumbles forward and sideways across the hall, smashing into objects in the dark. For a moment, I'm completely disoriented. I think I'm breathing. I quickly pat myself down, making sure I'm still in one piece. I am.

Something wet slaps across my face. Tentatively, I bring my shaky hand up to see. I feel his warm tongue on my cheek again.

"Zeus?" I whisper. I know no one can hear me but him. Mass chaos ensues around us, but I can't see anything, so I pull his body close. Everything echoes around in my head, bouncing off the insides of my skull. I'm moaning and roll onto my stomach. Despite the constant chattering of guns, screaming, and moaning, I feel around with my hands and army crawl toward where I believe the wall is. *Or was.* Though my adrenaline is juiced up, I feel nagging pain.

I reach down and feel that my pant legs from the knee down were torn away in the blast. My fingers feel slick and bloody from cuts I know I have. I don't know where my gun landed. It was ripped from my hands in the blast.

The only thing I can think about is my brother. *God, I hope he's alive.* I hug the wall, while lying flat. Bullets chip the cement above my head and I curse.

"Keegan! Keegan!" I shout through the darkness and deafening shots. I need to find him and make sure he's okay. "Damn you, Keegan, answer me!"

A hand grabs mine from out of nowhere. It's sweaty and rough and squeezes mine tight. When it lets go, I feel confused. Should I stay along the wall or grab it again? Then it roughly pulls me through a doorway and my shoulder smacks the right side of the frame. Clenching my teeth, I scramble against the wall and cover my head with my arms. I'm trying to lick my lips but dirt and dust coat the inside of my mouth, making my saliva thick as paste. Then a small light, like a book reading light, flips on and I see Keegan crouching across from me. He looks awful. His face bleeds with multiple cuts, and he's covered in a mix of dust and residue. He reaches across to me, checks my face, and then eyes the cuts on my legs. I sigh with relief. He's okay.

"You all right?" His eyebrows draw together.

I shake my head and shout. "What'd you say?" I point to my ears. "I can't hear very well."

I think he shouts, "Are you all right?" while using his hands, like I can read sign language or something. Next he tries giving me a thumbs-up.

I nod. "Still kicking." My eyes roam the room.

It's a storage room of some sort with collapsed racks of cleaning solvents and towels. I don't remember this being on our maps at all.

"Your gun?" Keegan holds his up. "Where's your gun?"

I shrug. *Gone during the explosion somewhere.*

He hands me a .9mm Glock but keeps his M16. I have no idea how he held onto it.

"Where's everyone else?" I draw in as many slow, deep breaths in as I can in an attempt to clear my head of the dizziness. I rest with my hands on my knees and look at him as he stands. I'm starting to hear a little, the ringing's fading and the noises are faint, but they're there.

Now it's his turn to shrug. "Are you ready to go?" He pulls a towel from one of the racks, causing a clatter of noise, and then wipes his face with it. His hand holds out another for me. The salt and grime from the Hole ooze off my face.

"You bet I am!" Even though I'm terrified, I won't be a coward. "Let's end this."

Keegan gives me a wink. "Works for me." His face beams with pride, and I can't help but feel that he views me differently now. Like I'm no longer just his baby sister.

He pulls out a wadded up, wrinkled map and stretches it out. I can see his sooty finger moving across the lines, checking for something. He exhales and wraps it back up.

"Unfortunately, our only option's to hunker down for a while. Rest for now. Okay?" He's lips are touching my ear as he speaks. And his hand encloses my face for a moment.

I nod my head and rest it on the wall behind me. "Keegan, it's muffled but I can kinda hear you now."

"Well, that's a plus!"

"What?" I say. "Did you just say something?"

He nods yes and I shrug my shoulders. "Okay, maybe not that great, yet."

The walls around us vibrate and I feel a chill rush up my spine. I focus on the task at hand: taking down the Commander. I exhale. I can think about the losses after it's all over.

Keegan slides down the narrow wall between the closed door and the shelves.

The room vibrates from the battle outside, and occasionally another explosion makes the walls groan. The shelves rattle. Bottles fall off, and Keegan raises his arms to block himself. He kicks them away with his feet.

It's impossible for me to rest with these demons loose in my head. I try to close my eyes, but all I can see is Veronica's mouth full of blood, Sheldon slipping over the edge, Alyssa's last breaths, and Cole. My nightmares don't compare to this. That's when it hits me. I jump forward and gasp for air.

Zeus didn't follow me out.

"Zeus! Oh no! Where's Zeus? I—I thought he was right behind me," I say with a panicked voice. "Keegan, he never leaves my side. Where could he possibly be?" I jerk around and put my hand on the door, but Keegan's fist closes around mine.

"Lexi, you can't worry about him right now. You need to stay focused," Keegan says. "Or you'll get yourself killed out there." *Not worry about Zeus? Yeah, that's not going to happen.*

I stand for a moment and narrow my eyes. Keegan shakes his head. I can feel the building shake under my feet, and hear the *takka takka takka* of a new kind of weapon.

I feel my shoulders slump. He's right. I clench my jaws instead. I feel empty, disturbed, and afraid. Zeus was the only constant source of comfort I had—the only piece of happiness I clung to. He's the only one who's always been there for me. I'd never forgive myself if something happened to him. I melt back down the wall and wrap my arms around myself.

With each explosion, I jerk, then close my eyes and pray. The walls feel like they're crumbling around me. I try to make myself invisible by pressing harder into the wall, making myself less of a target. Debris smashes to the floor from the ceiling. I stare up at it, wondering how long it'll hold. A steady thrumming buzzes in my ears. I catch eyes with Keegan. His are stony and flat, his body rigid as he flings through his meager supplies. I hear the tamping of feet go by and Keegan whips around, facing the door with his gun at the ready. I hold my breath, waiting for it to pass. I wonder if anything will be left for us in an hour. Remembering my ring, I twist it around nervously. But the words inscribed on it don't bring me peace like they usually do. In fact, I think about the odds. The Hole's filled with thousands of people—weak, starving, beaten-down sinners. Is it even possible to dream we can liberate it? But then I shake the doubts away. I have to believe the best. I have to trust in the plan Sutton put forth, *even if parts of it fail.*

Time ticks by. It feels like months before Keegan rises to put his hand on the knob.

He listens with his ear to the hall and his gun tightly gripped in his hands. As I watch him, his eyes become more focused. His breaths become steadier. He slides the door open and checks again. Nothing. Then Keegan motions and we creep forward into the hallway. Or what's left of it.

My mouth feels unhinged. A steady light streams in from large holes punched into the walls from explosions. Bodies sprawl in awkward positions on the floor. I carefully step over one. There aren't as many as I would've thought, though I don't know how anyone could've survived. Ironically, I feel lucky. But the revelation also makes me feel slightly guilty for surviving. As I'm stepping over another body, I can see their blood trickling into puddles, pooling around them. I smell death, its heavy lead fingers encircling all of us.

Keegan kneels down, searching for more ammunition and scowls when he finds nothing that matches his weapon. I avert my eyes to keep from recognizing anyone I might've known. I've already got enough gory images imprinted in my memory.

I decide to move around Keegan and glance into a room. The ceiling has crumbled and rubble forms small mountains. Not a soul is in sight. I look around the room, scanning it, and then step inside. I listen intently. Still nothing. I see a portrait of the Commander mounted on the wall with two bullet holes through it. Even with the holes, I can still feel his icy blue eyes boring holes into my head. I step back. I feel naked holding on to my small handgun.

"Psst!" I jump backward into Keegan. He shakes his head and motions me forward. He turns right down another hallway, staying close to the wall.

Another large doorway was blasted through, so I know Isaac made it this far. I pull my jacket up over my nose to prevent myself from breathing more particles and drop it once I realize it's impossible to avoid. An open doorway on the left snatches my attention.

Holding my gun ready, I peek in.

It's a bedroom. It would be beautiful if not for the holes blown through it. In the corner, on a platform, sits a large, king-sized bed draped with a cream and silver embroidered comforter. A crystal chandelier hangs by electrical wires from the ceiling. Again, the photo of the Commander appears, except it lies at the foot of the baseboard with the glass shattered in the frame. I think that's where it belongs. *Although burning it might be better.*

I hear a crashing noise, and feel my muscles tense up. I quickly aim my gun at the first figure I see running through the room. He looks at me, eyes bulging. And I stare down the barrel at his face.

It's a sinner.

I slowly lower the gun as he drops the objects in his hands. He raises his palms facing out and says, "I'm on your team."

"What team is that?" I feel my eyes furrow in concentration.

"Yours!" His jaw twitches. "I'm on your side. I swear it!" I relax and I can see his shoulders loosen up too. He squats down and picks up the things he was running with. They're pieces of crystal dining ware like the kind I had at home. He gathers them into his shirt and begins scouring the room for more.

"How the hell did you get in here?" Keegan asks in a voice of steel. The man straightens up, still holding the loot.

"From the outside," the man says. "Look, the gate's been blown open. And I don't have a single dollar, so I figured I'd at least try to steal shit, you know, to trade for money?" He locks eyes with Keegan. "If you don't shoot me first."

"I'm not gonna shoot you," Keegan says. "But you need to get the hell out of here! And now would be a good time!" I watch the man, branded black, pause to think. He shrugs and leaves the room the way he came in, crystal intact. I shake my head and look at Keegan, waiting for him to give me some direction.

If sinners are already coming into the residence, then the Commander must be losing, right? He tilts his head. I can tell he's wondering the same thing.

"Let's move forward," he commands. "Our priority now is to figure out the situation. Before we're too late."

I continue following Keegan, going room by room, scouting for the Commander. He goes in first. I follow and sweep the room. My hair keeps sticking to my face, so I'm constantly pushing it away. Sweat trickles down my neck. We have to be close to his personal quarters according to the maps. But I wasn't prepared for the way it'd look during battle. Hallways I thought existed are collapsed. Sinners are already in the building looting it. I open a door, only to find another closet. I slowly close it and hold my breath as it creaks.

We see more and more rooms, each one becoming more opulent than the last. Precious artwork dangles from the walls if not blown to pieces completely. I recognize some of the paintings with regret. I mutter to myself. I can't imagine the Commander entertaining wealthy people here while sinners die of starvation just outside. It disgusts me.

Keegan taps my shoulder and I jump, turning and slamming my back flat against the wall behind me. He motions for me to go first this time.

I hold my gun close to my face and hug the walls as I tiptoe over pieces of broken glass, contorted bodies, and cement blocks. My eyes are stretched wide open. I can feel my heart pounding in my chest. A guard lays to my left, his body resting against the wall. He looks peaceful like he's taking a nap on a Sunday afternoon.

Keegan squats, roughly lifts the guard's torso, and takes his extra ammunition. Slamming a new magazine into place, we move forward. I hold my fist up, and we stop. I meet Keegan's eyes and can tell he hears it too. Popping sounds echo from farther in the residence.

I motion to go forward. As I clear rooms, I can't help wondering what happened to the rest of our team. But mostly my mind lingers on Cole and Zeus. I stop to roll my shoulders and neck. They feel so tight I'm starting to cramp.

Crunch.

I freeze. My hearing isn't completely clear, but I'm sure I heard someone step on glass. Keegan taps my shoulder and points to a place where our hallway intersects with another one. I don't think it looks familiar, but I nod my head.

I creep around the corner. It opens into another hallway like an unending labyrinth. I see shattered glass all over the floor, and my hands are shaking. Keegan taps my shoulder. In the distance is a small staircase leading to another floor. He gives me one finger for one person. I turn to look and that's when I see him.

A guard peeks out from the entrance. *Bang! Bang! Bang!* I can barely see the tip of his gun before Keegan yanks me into a room off the hall and fires back. More bullets reverberate off the walls. I clamp down on my fear. I fire back while reaching around the door with my small handgun until the magazine is empty. Keegan shakes his head, leans out again, and lets his gun loose, spraying everything in front of us. Bullets riddle the passage, atomizing anything within the hall, from bodies to splinters of furniture. Next time I glance, the guard's body splays at the foot of the stairs, punctured from head to foot.

I want to throw up, but intuition pulls me to the staircase. Keegan puts his hand on my shoulder, and I nod my head, motioning to move forward. I step over the corpse, and lead Keegan up the dark, steep stairs.

An unnatural light filters out of the room at the top. I motion for Keegan to halt, and we stand on the top step, outside the doorway. He wraps his hand around the handle and slowly cracks it open. His eyes lock with mine, and I nod, allowing him to go in first. My nerves dance as I follow him closely. The dark marble flooring is covered with chunks of drywall and leads into another room. Carefully planting my feet around more bodies, we stop at the next closed door. I take a deep breath. Keegan pushes it open, and I crawl in first, hearing others. On his elbows, Keegan follows.

A heated conversation takes place between two men, both voices I recognize. Chills run down my spine as I lean in to get a better view.

"Brother, what a pleasant surprise!" a man says. "I'm delighted you could join me."

"Oh, cut the crap!" another man says. "You know exactly why I'm here."

I move forward, going in slow motion. I flashback to a conversation I had with Keegan about how snipers can move so slow they can avoid detection even if someone's staring at them. That's how I'm trying to be.

"You know, I must admit I haven't given you enough credit. Not once did it ever occur to me that my own blood could betray me." The man clears his throat and says. "You're such a disgrace. It's disgusting actually. I should've known you'd side with that idiot."

I push forward, sliding slowly on my belly. My heart feels like it's lodged in my throat. I'm glancing around warily when it hits me. I know where we are.

The Commander's control room. We actually made it, and now…we have to end it. A rush of adrenaline speeds up my heart rate and it takes all I have not to dart in.

It's exactly as I imagined it'd be. Four large screens, various computers, and maps decorate the room. The screens cast a fuzzy light, but there's no image, just white noise. *One of the squads must've disabled the cameras.* I guess that means the rebels have managed some small victories. I swallow my anxiety and set my jaw. *We can and will do this.*

A large, formidable character stands against the brightness. I see his silhouette, but can't make out his features. His voice rattles me to the core, the familiar taste of bile rising in the back of my throat. *Do I know this person?* He waves a gun through the air as he yells.

Keegan and I make eye contact. His face looks bluish and pale in the lighting. In that glance, we both understand we're witnessing something important—something the others obviously missed.

"You've abused the system long enough. You're consumed by the power of your position. You're not the brother I grew up with. And you're definitely not the person I once knew," the man with the calmer voice says.

"Ahhh, but people change, don't they?" the first man says.

"That they do," the other man says. "And so here I stand… kicking myself over and over again. Because there once was a time that I truly believed in you. I actually thought you were a good person. I thought maybe you would undo all the wrong in this world, but shame on me for not believing the only honest man I've ever known. Shame on me for not seeing it when Hamilton did."

I find myself staring at the ground, instead of trying to view the people having the conversation.

"Hamilton was a joke, just like you," the voice retorts with a familiar sharpness. I can almost feel a suffocating tightness come over my chest. I look over to Keegan. His chest is heaving, his face tenses, and his nostrils are flaring.

I finally slide forward enough that I can get a better picture of the persons speaking. I peek through the legs of a table and see Sutton standing before the dark silhouette. I feel my legs starting to jerk before all my muscles tighten. *What's he doing here? Who could he possibly be talking to?* I take a cleansing breath and my muscles loosen. I begin to crawl farther in under the cover of large desks and computers. The blank, blaring noise is just enough to cover my movements but not loud enough to hinder the exchange of words. I duck my head down and struggle to keep my composure. My eyebrows squish together as I pull myself forward. If Sutton is speaking, then...

Sutton has a brother?

"So enlighten me...how exactly do you plan on taking over?" the silhouette says to Sutton in a condescending manner. "I'm suddenly curious how you think your little so-called army could manage to take mine out?" He clears his throat.

His army? Is that us? I feel my gaze clouding. If Sutton has a brother, then what's he doing here? No one should be here but the Commander. It's not Wilson. His voice is shriller when angry. I'm narrowing my eyes into slits. But the voice, the voice makes my hair stand on end. I duck my head and cover it with my arms, fighting my reaction. *It can't be. It's not possible.*

"Well, don't just stand there. Answer me," the man half shouts. "Do you honestly believe by killing me—you'll be saving this country?" He laughs at Sutton. "You're pathetic."

Holy shit that must mean... I lock eyes with Keegan a few feet away and see his mouth drop open. He must know what I just figured out because he did too. My cheeks are flushing and my eyes widen with rage.

"You do realize there's another man in line? One who will lead where I've left off? You see, you can't win this battle, brother," the man says in a sharp, confident voice. "I'm not the end...I'm just the beginning!"

The Commander is Sutton's brother.

"I'm aware of that, yes. But in the meantime, I also figured out that behind every genius mind, somewhere hides a fault. And yours just happens to be pride." Sutton pauses. "Even when you were a child, you seemed to overlook even the smallest of details because all you could focus on was the big picture. And you're right, getting rid of you might not solve the problem, but it's a step in the right direction."

I'm clenching every muscle in my body and gritting my teeth. My father wasn't just murdered—he was betrayed and murdered by Sutton's own brother.

I glance over my shoulder to see Keegan ten feet behind me, already in motion. The bloodlust in his eyes give away his intentions.

He and I move in an arc, closing in on them as they speak. I can't seem to focus. My breaths come uneven. I want Keegan to slow down, but he's moving too far away from me. I bite my lip. I don't have a gun but I can use my body. I bang my elbow into a chair, but no one notices because of the noise.

"Why? Why are you protecting Lexi?" Sutton says.

In an abrupt movement, the Commander levels the gun at Sutton's head. I snap to attention. "You're a damn fool. Think of everything you could've had, all the power that could've been yours. If only you would've been smart enough to have chosen the right side, but unfortunately, for you. You failed miserably," he says with a spiteful voice. "I stopped trusting you the second I noticed your friendship with Hamilton getting stronger." His finger tightens on the trigger. "Now, since you decided to follow a dead man's dream, your precious life is about to end! And what a shame it is, that I have to be the one to pull the trigger. Truly, this isn't how I wanted to end things. But you've left me with no other choice." He laughs. "Goodbye!"

Oh no you don't!

Without thinking, I leap over a desk and pounce on him, knocking the gun sideways as he pulls the trigger. It goes off with a resounding *bang* and Sutton falls. I want to check on him, but I feel arms collapsing around me.

The Commander wrenches me to the ground, each of us fighting for the gun that skidded a foot away. He elbows me in the face, and I blink with teary eyes while hitting him. I can feel his sweat dripping onto me as he fights to control my fists. I manage to roll him with my hips, then I punch him in the throat. My breaths come ragged and my vision is blurred.

His hands slacken, so I jump for the gun. But he wraps his arms around my waist, dragging me back. I fold my fingers around the stock, but soon his large hands wrench it from my sweaty palms.

"Keegan!" I scream. The Commander grunts as he smashes me into a desk. I don't let go of the gun even as air bursts from my lungs.

Keegan springs in to help, but as we tussle, the gun goes off again. I can feel it almost immediately. His fingers go limp from around the gun. Out of the corner of my eye, I see Keegan crumple, holding his abdomen—his eyes shocked. Blood seeps through his fingers, flowing over his hands like the trickle of a stream, and I know it's bad.

My pulse speeds up and my heart is pounding. I'm screaming as I shove the gun aside and use my free hand to gouge out the eye of the Commander. He howls with agony, dropping the gun as his hands cover the gaping hole. I pull away from him, focusing on his face for the first time.

No! This can't be happening.

And I'm staring into the eyes of my stepfather.

I'm struggling to breathe, my breath hitching in my throat. Dark memories resurface as I stand, grabbing the gun and slowly pointing it at him. My hands are shaking and I fight with them to hold steady. His expression, smirking and arrogant, hasn't changed. Even as he stares death in the face, he smiles. He raises his hands in front of him.

"Now, this—just got very interesting."

I glare at him, tightly clenching the gun. I'm shaking my head involuntarily. A battle wages in my mind—kill him or let someone else take care of him. Every muscle in my body wants to be the one to punish him, to end his ruthless life. Thoughts of the revolution flee as I focus on the pain he inflicted upon me and my family.

"You sick son of a bitch!" My hands and voice quiver with rage as I stare down the monster. "I get it. I get all of it." I spit at him. "The Hole is just your life-sized closet you *think* you can control." I swallow hard. I never once, in my wildest nightmares, believed my stepfather and the Commander were the same person. What happened to my father? Where's my mother? But I don't ask. I'm struggling to find the right words, but nothing comes out. In the moment of decision, I teeter on uncertainty for a second too long.

He turns, hopping over a desk and toppling some equipment. He almost makes it out, but slams into Cole in the doorway. Both of them recoil into heaps on the floor.

"Get him!" I'm screaming. "Stop him!"

Cole, unfazed, punches him several times. My stepfather returns the favor, and I run, tripping to where they wrestle.

Holding the gun, I aim for my stepfather, but they roll back and forth, trading positions of dominance. I don't want to hurt Cole, but as they exchange punches, a flicker of light catches my eye. My stepfather pulls a knife out of his boot, giving me no other option.

I pull the stiff trigger, hitting him in the shoulder, and his blade clatters across the floor. Cole grabs it, stands, and kicks him in the stomach.

"Lexi, shoot him!" he shouts. "What the hell are you waiting for? Shoot him!"

Still holding my gun, I shake my head.

"What's wrong with you! Shoot him!" Cole yells at the top of his lungs.

The Commander backs himself into the wall, his chin lowering to his chest and holding his gushing shoulder.

I've waited years to see him like this. He took everything away from me. He's taken so much away from so many others. *But I won't sink to his level. Killing him would be easy, but what good is death if he can't fear it?*

I glare into his eyes. "Your time will come. When the entire world can sit back and watch you pay for what you've done." I take a step closer to him with my gun aimed at his head. "There's enough of your filth on me, and the last thing I want is your damn blood on my hands," I say. "My father was twice the man you'll ever be, and one day justice will be served. I want to watch the fear in your eyes as the lethal liquid runs through your veins. But do you know what the best part is? You won't see my father…because he's not in hell."

His breaths are raspy, his hands stained crimson.

I see fear in his eyes for the first time. And it satisfies me.

Just then, Bruno and his team bound into the room. Their faces are clouded with dust, smelling like sweat and lead. Half of them attend to Sutton and Keegan, promptly evacuating Sutton, and the rest surround my stepfather, the Commander.

"Lexi, get out of here," Bruno says. "We'll take it from here."

But I stayed glued in place as Cole lowers my gun for me. "Lexi, I promised you something." He pries the gun from my fingers and holds it steady, aiming it directly at my stepfather's head. Cole's corded neck and fevered stare alarm even me.

What? What did he promise me?

My stepfather arches his eyebrow, giving Cole a look of disgust and scorn. "I know who you sold your soul to. It seems as if you've forgotten where your duty lies. "

"Oh I know my duty all right." Cole's eyes flash with dark fury.

"No Cole! Don't!" I say shaking my head.

My stepfather's face blanches with the loss of blood. He

cackles at Cole as he leans against the wall and holds his shoulder where the red liquid flows from his wound down to his forearm and *drip, drip, drips* onto the floor.

"Go ahead. Shoot me. But be sure you watch your back. My men will avenge me. You'll never be safe—that's a promise." His breaths sound ragged between words and yet he still manages to scoff at Cole. *At me.*

"Don't," I say, putting my hand on Cole's tensed arm. "He's not worth it. He can't hurt me anymore."

"That's where you're wrong," my stepfather smiles his wicked smile. "I'll always be in your nightmares."

With those words, Cole fires the gun.

My stepfather's body jerks with the dull thud of the bullet entering his forehead. Blood and brain spatter the wall behind him, immediately making me feel nauseous. His heavy body crumples to the floor, lifeless at our feet. Everyone stares in shock, unable to tear their eyes away from the once-great Commander who now lies in a pitiful lump, bleeding out like an animal.

Cole hands the gun to Bruno and holds out his wrists for him. "Want to arrest me?"

"Dude," Bruno shakes his head, looking amused. "You should've shot him in the balls first."

The others break from their trance, and tiptoe around the body. The blood pools around his head in a puddle. Even in his death, they're afraid to touch him. Afraid he'll pop up and execute them on the spot for their insurrection.

Cole's eyes meet mine and I crumble inside. When we embrace, I feel his body shaking.

"How'd you know it was him?" I ask in a quieter voice.

"Lexi, all it took was one look at your face and I knew."

"Thank you!"

He squeezes me tightly, almost crushing my ribcage with his strength. I stand with my arms limp, so overwhelmed that nothing comes out—just relishing the comfort of his arms. My legs ache from the bruises and cuts. My hands shake.

I can't cry, but can't rejoice either. I've lost so much. Too much.

The man who haunted my every dream lies dead on a filthy floor. I'll never see his face again but in my dreams. Never have to fear the sound of his voice or the way his eyes could throw daggers into my heart. I can breathe again without fear of him shutting me in a closet or terrorizing everyone I love. But the high price paid for his death reminds me of Keegan.

"Oh my God, Keegan!" I look around frantically, trying to find him. My heart's pounding like a drum. "Where is he?" I'm shouting and spinning around, looking left and right. And that's when, out of the corner of my eye, I see Bruno, motioning me to come. Cole stands in my way and I don't bother to ask him to move, I push him aside and sprint to Bruno.

At first I don't see Keegan because Bruno's men surround him, but then I shove my way through. Two of them are applying pressure to his wound but blood's spilling over their fingers. His ashen face is drawn tight and his lips are almost white, yet his eyes are wide and he's looking around. He smiles when he sees me standing there. I cover my mouth with my hand as I start to cry. My legs go weak and I drop to my knees beside his head.

"Lexi," he says between gasps of air. "You all right?"

I'm shaking my head no and my lips are quivering so fast I can barely talk. "No, I'm not all right because you're not all right!"

"Don't worry about me. I'm not in any pain." He lifts his arm, takes my hand, and locks his fingers around mine. "But I'm all right! I'm going home," he says. I lose it completely.

"No! No! Keegan, you're not going anywhere." I'm choking on my breath. I release his hand and hold his head between my hands. "Stay with me! Please don't leave me!"

"I love you, and you can do this." He manages to say before blood fills his mouth. He gurgles and turns his head so the blood can drip out. He begins coughing uncontrollably and gasps again. I wipe his mouth for him and can see his blood-stained teeth.

"Keegan, please, I can't do this without you," I say.

"Yes…you can, and you will." Now he's gagging and

more blood spurts out of his mouth. I continue to sob and wipe it away. I don't want him to stop talking to me, I don't want his voice to leave. I need to hear him.

I glance up. All the guys are just standing there with strained faces. "Why're you all just standing there?" I'm screaming at the top of my lungs. I'm losing all composure; my entire body's shaking, my brother's dying and no one's trying to save him. "Somebody, do something! Help him!"

Cole comes to my side, sits next to me and says with a calm, even voice. "There's nothing we can do." I turn and my hands fly to Cole's chest. I'm pounding on him even though he's not the one I'm mad at.

"Damn you, Cole. Help him!"

Cole yanks my arms away and spins me back to Keegan. "Lexi, he needs you right now. You need to be strong for him."

Strong? How can I possibly be strong now? He's dying and I'm not willing to let him go. I just got him back. We were going to have a new start, a new life together and now it's being taken away from me. I'm groaning without realizing it, but there's no other way to express my agony.

Keegan's eyes start to roll into the back of his head. I grab his shoulders and shake him vigorously. "Keegan, don't you dare leave me, you can't leave me here…please!" I'm begging and I'm desperate even though I know it's not Keegan's choice. He'd never leave me on his own terms. But I don't know what else to do.

I lift Keegan's head off the floor and place it gently on my lap. I stroke his cheek and the coolness of his skin sends chills up my spine. Leaning over, I kiss his forehead and my tears spill onto his face.

"Lexi," he says in a whisper. "Dad says he loves you." I squeeze my eyes shut and my chest is crushing—my father's here and he's taking Keegan with him.

"Oh, Keegan," I choke out. "Tell him…I love him, too."

"I'm sorry," he says. "I don't want to leave you again." He takes a long, deep breath between coughs. "This wasn't part of the plan."

"I know that." I press my forehead to his. "Keegan, I forgive you…for everything."

"Oh, thank God."

He's blinking and his eyes are starting to glass over. I'm running out of time, but I know there's nothing left I can do. I somehow find the courage to tell him.

"It's all right, Keegan. Go with Dad…I'm sure he can't wait to hug you, and get his son back."

Keegan takes one last look at me and says. "Lexi, you have to finish this. It's up to you now. But please remember, Dad's always with you…and now, so will I." These are his last words he says to me before his chest falls for the last time and his final breath fills my ears. I crumble inside, holding my brother as he dies; he's left this world just like everyone else I loved. I slump over him in my arms and kiss his forehead, feeling his cold-as-marble skin against my lips. And I'm broken. I'm numb and wishing he would have taken me along.

Cole's arms are wrapped around me and he's saying over and over. "I'm so sorry." But I don't respond. He doesn't know my pain or my broken heart and I just want him to leave me alone so I can be with Keegan.

"Lexi, we can't stay here… We need to go, now," he says. "The revolt failed, but we still have a chance to make it out."

"I'm not leaving him here!" I say between cries.

"Yes, you are, and you're coming with me."

"No, I'm not!"

"Yes, you are!" Cole demands "I'm sorry, Lexi, but it's not him anymore."

"You don't think I know that!" I yell at him. "I need to bury him. He deserves at least that!"

"We can't take him with us. It's going to slow us down! Now get up or I'll carry your ass out of here myself." He yanks me up and throws me over his shoulder. I kick and hit his back, but he doesn't put me down.

"Cole, let me go!"

"Not a chance, I'm not about to let you die, too." He locks his arms tight around my waist to keep me from falling off his shoulders. "And you told Keegan you'd finish this. I won't have you break that promise on my account." I give up the fight, he's stronger than me...and he's not letting go.

Bruno and the others heft Keegan's body up and I watch them carry him out. Now I'm praying this is all just a nightmare and soon, I'll wake up.

CHAPTER 23

My hopes crash violently to the floor. *We failed.* I feel my body go completely limp. Cole puts me down, only to pick me back up…one arm under my legs and his other arm's wrapped around my back. He holds me like a wounded child and carries me out of the control room.

My last view is of my stepfather's lifeless form, bleeding out next to the doorway. His head's turned to the side with his mouth wide open and his eyes fixed on the wall. I'm waiting for him to start breathing again, and I'm watching for any signs of movement. Nothing. I don't even smile. I can't. I'm relieved he's dead, but at the same time because of him, now Keegan is dead too. My nostrils flare, and all I want to do is take my knife and slash him into pieces. Tear him apart like he did my family.

"You son of a BITCH!" I scream instead and Cole stops immediately. He turns his head to see whom I'm yelling at. "I hate you! I hate you!"

"Lexi, he can't hurt you anymore," Cole says to me. "He's dead."

"You're wrong," I tell him. "Keegan just died because of him. My father died because of him. That man…alive or dead is always going to hurt me. He took away my family, one by one. And now, it's just me."

"I'm still here, you've got me." He's right, I do…but it's not the same.

Cole breathes hard as he carries me down the steep staircase and back into the hall where Keegan and I walked only minutes ago. I see bodies stretched out everywhere, lying in unnatural positions. Heat rushes up my back and straight to my head, making me woozy. I press my face to his chest and close my eyes. I feel him lifting his legs as he steps over the bodies, and I hear his boots squeal on the floor, slick from blood.

"We're almost out. Just a little farther," he says. "Are you all right?"

I can't bring myself to respond.

"Never mind. That was a stupid question." Cole clears his throat and picks up the pace.

I'm trying to concentrate on my breathing to stay calm; my hands cling to him like a life preserver. All strength has been sapped from my body. I'm leaving without Keegan. But at least I didn't let my stepfather break me. *At least I wasn't the one who pulled the trigger.*

"Oh hell, here they come!" Cole runs with me in his arms like he has so many times before. I peek at his face. His jaw clenches and unclenches, but his grip on me never fails. We move farther down with each staircase and hallway that we take. Cole slams us through the last doorway into the blinding sun. I squint.

The evidence of war is all over—chunks of walls missing, bodies and parts strewn across our path, damaged valuables, and the mass exodus of people the closer we get to the gate. Their hurried strides and panicked voices alert me to the danger that's still ahead. I look around. Everyone runs in one direction.

Out.

The heavy gate of the Hole appears to the right. To my astonishment, it's blown open. Crowds run, shove, and trip their way into freedom. But no one rejoices. Families with children and branded sinners shove their way through into the blast of sunlight and hot, thick air. Most of them take nothing with them, but I do see some looters carrying furniture, paintings, and bedding from the Commander's residence. Yet, I feel empty. I don't have Keegan here with me to witness it. I can only imagine his face seeing the chaos we've created within the country, yet I don't want to imagine it at all. I'm whimpering without knowing it.

"It'll be okay," Cole says.

But it's not. *Keegan can't be dead.*

The constant exchange of gunfire in the distance reminds me that some teams are still fighting. My heart aches for them. Thick, black smoke forms a mushroom cloud that hovers somewhere near the hospital.

Cole turns left and starts heading farther away from the gate. He fights against the tide of traffic, his head on a swivel like he's looking for something. He steps over the high-speed railroad tracks. *No one is going to work today.*

A black SUV halts with a screech in front of us and I grab onto Cole even harder.

"Shit!" Cole says under his breath. "Dammit!"

I'm afraid to look and see the face of the person who has caught us. But I'm caught off guard when the door swings open and Bruno sits in the driver's seat screaming at us.

"Quick! Get in! Get in!"

Cole grunts, opens the back door, shoves me inside and then jumps in the front. Zeus meets me in the back seat, licking my face with delight and whipping me with his tail. I hug him close and begin to sob and I'm curling my toes in my boots.

"Where the hell were you going, man?" Bruno says to Cole. "I had to slam the car in reverse to get to you."

"I... I..." Cole stutters. "I must've gotten confused and mixed up the rendezvous point. My bad."

"Oh," Bruno says. I see him check his rearview.

I feel a tongue run up the side of my face and I'm thankful for the distraction. "I'm happy to see you too, Zeus."

Our reunion isn't sweet for long though as people try to jump onto the vehicle. Their fists pound on the windows, their faces laced with fear and anger. I'm gripping Zeus's neck with clammy hands. They beg for a ride, but Bruno doesn't stop.

"Sutton—what about Sutton?" I say. "Where is he? Please tell me he got out in time!"

"He's fine," Bruno says. "He's in another vehicle."

"What the hell happened out there?" Cole asks Bruno.

"I don't know, man. I've never seen so much blood. Hundreds were killed, and hundreds injured. Only a few of us got out," Bruno says.

"I know," Cole says. "It's a damn blood bath out there."

"Wilson was slaughtering people left and right, and when we got within shooting range, all of a sudden—he vanished. Just completely disappeared!"

"How could he just disappear?" Cole's face hardens and his knuckles turn white.

"We're thinking somehow he managed to get to his lab at the Transformation Center. It's bomb proof. And we didn't have the man power to go after him," Bruno says as he makes another turn. His hands grip the wheel and his knuckles bleed from combat.

Cole slams his head back against the headrest. "Damn it, you're right."

"Man, I was hoping we'd at least get the safe groups out," Bruno says.

"What safe groups?" I say in a shaky voice. I wrap my arms around my waist, trying to hold myself together. But I'm still trembling and I can't make it stop. I want my brother and I can't stomach that he's truly gone. Cole shifts his head to glance at me, but I turn my eyes away from him.

"The safe groups were pre-selected sinners. Sutton picked the ones he trusted, and rounded them up," Bruno says. "Could you imagine the danger if the entire Hole got out?"

"No," Cole says. "Bruno, just get us the hell out of here."

Bruno continues. "If we manage to stay alive long enough, our next mission is trying to figure out a way to free—"

"Bruno!" Cole raises his voice in a demanding manner. "Get a move on it!"

"Roger that!" My back slams into the backseat as Bruno accelerates.

"Where…where are we going?" I say.

"Far away from here," Bruno says. "Don't worry, Miss Lexi, we'll get you somewhere safe."

I lean my head against the window and exhale. I chew on the inside of my cheek and pick at my pants. I'm nauseous and having difficulty swallowing. A part of me wishes I were with

Keegan and my father, at least I'd be safe there. But the other part of me is relieved we've made it out, and the ones with me now are all people I deeply care about. And of course Zeus and Sutton. The fact that Keegan was the only one killed is really a miracle, but he's the one I wanted to share this with the most. He'd be so proud we got out, that we actually managed to escape at all. He'd want our dad to know that we did it.

I'm weeping and I don't care. I feel like an orphan, but then I look at Cole. And I see his face, covered with dirt, smeared with sweat and blood, and I remind myself to be thankful that he's still here with me. This burden. These memories. The rest of the world might be upside down and inside out, but Cole's mine forever.

Cole's eyes don't leave my face; his eyes look pained, and I know he's worried about me, but I'm glad he won't ask me to talk about it. I don't want to. But I'm sure he's hoping in time—I will.

I regret not being able to bring Alyssa's book with me. And I'm beating myself up over leaving Keegan's body behind. He should be here with me. He deserved better. Everyone deserves better than this. Because in all truth, who are we all without dignity? I'm gasping for air and then hiccupping next.

I know I can't change the outcome of the operation. I can't save my father's last letter to me, but at least I have his words written on my heart. At least, I know I made the right decision to fight. And I still believe in justice for all because I'm my father's daughter, and he lives only through me now. He's the last person I ever want to let down.

The scenery passes outside the window, ticking away like time. My eyelids feel heavy with the absence of the adrenaline rush. Cole climbs into the backseat. He's stroking my hair and somehow it calms me. I close my burning eyes and drift off to sleep.

When I wake, the smell on the breeze perks me up. The ocean spray and the piercing call of seagulls make me smile and I know exactly where we are…and it's as if my father and brother are here with me.

Lexington Bay.

Bruno parks the vehicle outside a small cottage in a remote part of the bay after driving ten hours south. It's almost dark, which tells me that I slept the entire ride, not even waking when they stopped for fuel or food.

Cole steps out of the vehicle and opens my door, and I inhale the fresh, salty sea air. My legs feel stiff, and dirt cakes in my pores, but I don't care. *I'm free.*

Bruno opens the front door and light spills out revealing a beautiful, dark-skinned woman. She embraces him with tears pouring from her face and then leads him inside.

I give Cole a weird look.

He smiles. "That's Grace, Bruno's wife."

"He's married?"

"Apparently." He smiles his crooked smile.

Before my eyes, Sutton appears. His right arm is in a sling, but he's clean, and his green eyes shine with fresh emotion. He walks toward me with a sympathetic look. With his good arm, he pulls me in for a hug. He kisses the top of my head.

"Thank God you're alive," he says and my tears begin seeping out. "Lexi, my dear, I'm so sorry about Keegan." A sharp knife stabs my heart when I hear his name. "I loved him like a son…and my heart's breaking, too." I kiss him on each cheek and hug him carefully, beginning to choke on my sadness. For him. For what we've lost.

"Sutton, it hurts so much…and it's a constant pain, one that'll never go away."

"I know, sweetheart. But remember, you'll see him again someday."

I swallow hard and lean into him, afraid I'm going to fall over. He sighs.

"Thank you, sweet girl," he says. "For saving my life."

"No, I should be the one thanking you. Thank you for loving me the way my father would, for doing everything humanly possible to protect me, to keep me alive." I step back, but keep my hands on his shoulders. "But most of all. Thank you for believing in me and giving me a chance to—"

"My dear, I would've loved you either way simply because you're his daughter, and I promised your father I'd watch over you for as long as I was alive. And I will do just that." He spins on his heel then, hiding his tears. "I have something to give you. Something I'm praying will bring you some peace of mind."

I follow him into the cottage, taking in the soft, willowy curtains that waft with the breeze and the lightly flowered wicker furniture lit up by a small table lamp. He picks up something from the counter and hands it to me.

"Do you remember the promise you made to Alyssa before she died?"

"Yes, of course I do."

"Well now you can set her free." My knees buckle and I fall to the floor, unsure of what he could possibly mean. Sutton bends down and hands me a small box.

I run my shaking hands over the gift. The wood is smooth and has ornate carvings of roses alongside. It smells slightly cedar. I've never seen anything like it before.

Cole pulls me close to him, resting his arm around my shoulders. He takes my hand and places it over the latch.

I take it between my fingers, opening it with care and ease. My eyes focus on a bag of coarse, white sand secured inside.

"Do you know what that is?"

Tears streak down my face unhindered. "Oh my gosh, are these Alyssa's ashes?" I hold them close to my heart.

"Yes, my dear, they are," Sutton says.

"I never dreamed it would be possible. But I hoped...I prayed I could do this for her. How did you...?" I can't say another word before Sutton smiles and walks away.

Cole takes my hand. "Walk with me." He leads me out onto the beach, his gentle touch reassuring me.

I'm holding someone who changed my life. Alyssa taught me about holding on even when everything looks bleak. She helped me gain strength when I had none. She was my friend when everyone else judged me. She brought laughter in an otherwise depressing place. When we reach the edge of the clear turquoise water, I let go of Cole's hand. I walk in until the lukewarm water's up to my knees.

I hold her ashes up to my mouth and whisper. "Thank you for being my friend. I love you."

I carefully open the bag and lift my arms into the air. I open my hands as the wind carries her into the ocean…the water the same color as my eyes. The waves, peaceful and unending, bury her for us.

Cole comes up behind me, and I rest my body back into him. He wraps his arms around me as we both cry tears of mourning, of joy, and of peace.

"You know, even though we failed to free the Hole, we didn't completely fail." I take a deep breath and sigh with relief. "Not only did we fulfill Alyssa's wish, now, finally we can be together."

"I know," Cole says as he kisses my cheek. "But, Lexi, we're still not out of the woods," he says. "They'll come after us."

I turn to face him, and he wipes a tear from my cheek with his thumb. "So we'll take one day at a time, because each day is one day we didn't have before."

Acknowledgements

Thank you, God, for sending your son who saved us from our sins, and for blessing us with the ability to write.

Thanks also to: Stacey Donaghy, our amazing agent who had a sixth sense about Branded, read it, and loved it. Your kindness, enthusiasm, and generosity go above and beyond. We wouldn't be where we are today without you, and we can never thank you enough. Georgia Mcbride, our publisher, for falling in love with our story, believing in us and giving us an opportunity we never dreamed possible. We are so fortunate to have people like you by our side.

Michelle Auricht, who was the first person to read the first chapter of Branded and gave us the confidence we so desperately needed. BAM, we are forever grateful for your encouraging words, and even though you live so far away, we will always be close. Your friendship has meant the world to us. Angela Pratt, our assistant and friend. You have been the glue when we wanted to fall apart. Thank you, for your constant support and for taking so much of your personal time, to spend it with us. Lindsay Cummings, you're such a talented writer and storyteller. We are beyond grateful God brought us together.

Amy Eye, our editor from the very start, who helped us beyond belief to make Branded what it is today. Your insight and guidance was untouchable. Regina Wamba, who designed our breath-taking cover. You are truly a shining light.

Sasha Alsberg, our publicist, promoter, and cheerleader. Without you, we'd be lost. Ben Alderson, our UK promoter and friend. Thanks to the both of you, for taking Branded head on and falling in love with it. Your hard work and dedication are untouchable.

To all the bloggers, who have read and reviewed Branded for us. Just to name a few because there are so many. Aestas bookblogger, Amy Austin Reale, Stephenie Risner Thomas,

Kendall McCubbin, Zoe Scott, Jack Brennan, Bella Colella, Sharon De Haas, Bookinity, Bookautopia, Booksfoever19, Chelsea Powis, Damaris Cardinali, Trisha Rai, Andrea Dupree Cunningham, and all the booktubers, Instagram fans and Fandoms. Thank you for the ship name, CoLexi. Before that we didn't know what a ship name was.

To our author friends who helped us alone the way, Cameo Renae, Jake Bonsignore, KL Ruse, and Kim Derting. Your support means the world to us.

To our husbands and children who sacrificed a lot so we could follow our dream. To our families, our rocks, thank you for your unconditional love and constant encouragement. This would never have happened without any of you.

Abi- To my parents, thank you for always supporting my dreams and never doubting my capability of getting there. Dad, you're my real life hero and my true inspiration from the start. Since you always told me during hard times. "Aber, you can overcome anything short of death." I am who I am, because of you guys.

Missy- To my parents, and especially my Dad. Thank you for instilling confidence in me, sharing your love of History with me, and encouraging my creativity to grow throughout the years. I'd be lost without you.

About the Authors

Abi and Missy met in the summer of 1999 at college orientation and have been best friends ever since. After college, they added jobs, husbands and kids to their lives, but they still found time for their friendship. Instead of hanging out on weekends, they went to dinner once a month and reviewed books. What started out as an enjoyable hobby has now become an incredible adventure.

Web: www.abiandmissy.com

Twitter: @abiandmissy

Facebook: https://www.facebook.com/AbiandMissy

Goodreads:
http://www.goodreads.com/book/show/17402117-branded

Melissa Kalicicki

Melissa Kalicicki received her bachelor's degree from Millersville University in 2003. She married, had two boys and currently lives in Lancaster, Pennsylvania. Aside from reading and writing, her interests include running and mixed martial arts. She also remains an avid Cleveland sports fan.

Abi Ketner

Abi Ketner is a registered nurse with a passion for novels, the beaches of St. John, and her Philadelphia Phillies. A talented singer, Abi loves to go running and spend lots of time with her family. She currently resides in Lancaster, Pennsylvania with her husband, triplet daughters and two very spoiled dogs.

Preview More Books from Month9Books!

www.month9books.com

Speculative fiction for teens and tweens...where nothing as it seems!

www.facebook.com/month9books
www.twitter.com/month9books

www.georgiamcbride.com

SARAH BROMLEY

One for sorrow,
two for joy.
A destructive girl,
a damaged boy.

a murder of
magpies

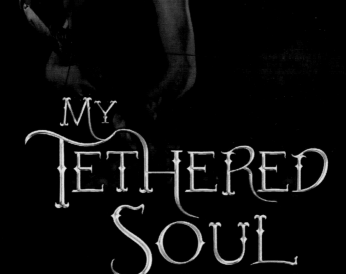

DOROTHY DREYER

MY TETHERED SOUL

REAPER'S RITE - BOOK TWO

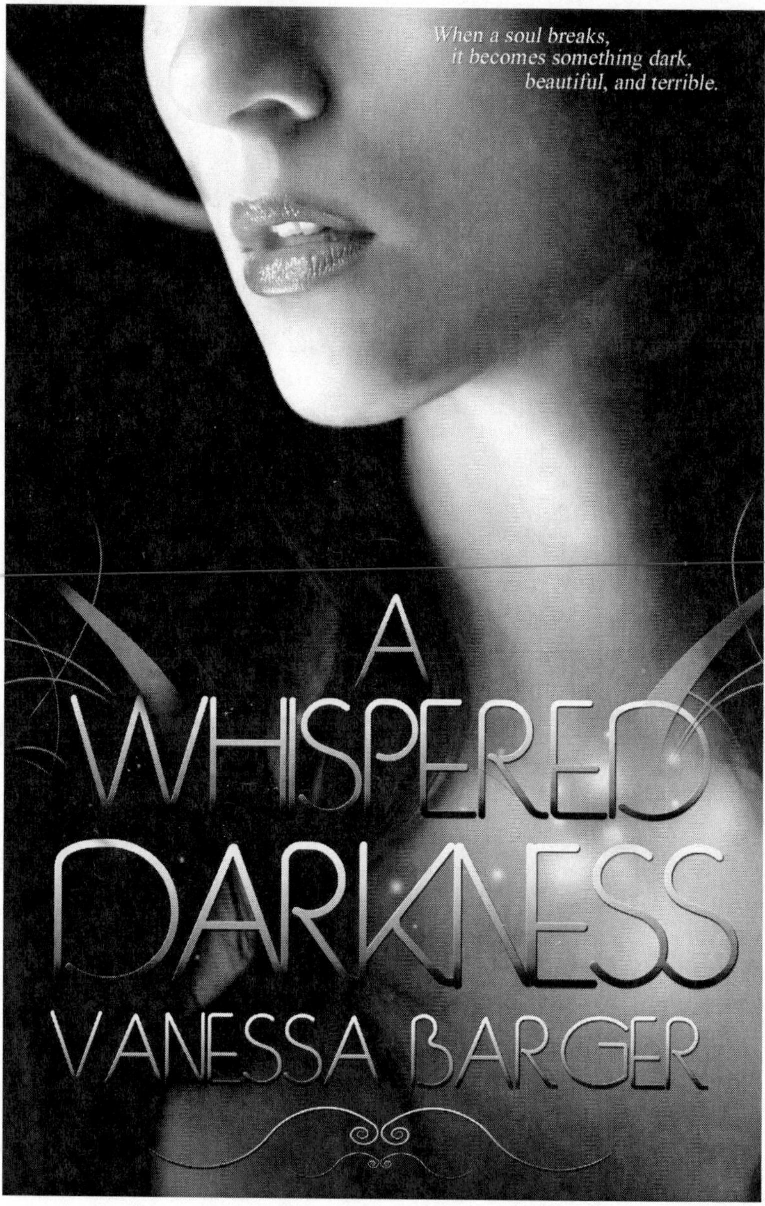
When a soul breaks,
it becomes something dark,
beautiful, and terrible.
A WHISPERED DARKNESS
VANESSA BARGER

ELIZABETH HOLLOWAY

CALL ME GRIM